Praise fo

'Astonishingly assured crim k
noir, set against a vivid and atmospheric . .
The book's explosive finale will linger with you for days.'
Weekend Australian

'This smart, affecting tale owes more to Scandi noir fiction with its sinister twists and aching characters . . . a tour de force.'
Australian Women's Weekly

'A tightly woven and utterly unpredictable plot that will keep you guessing and gasping. A stunning debut.'
Lyn Yeowart, author of *The Silent Listener*

'A vividly described and engaging mystery.' *Canberra Weekly*

'A scintillating thriller.' *Good Reading*

'Past and present collide to create a gripping tale of murder and intrigue.'
Chris Hammer, author of *Scrublands*

'*Cutters End* is one hell of a ride . . . Hickey is a brilliant writer.'
Helen FitzGerald, author of *The Cry*

'The roadhouse novel has been well traversed by male writers – here it is through female eyes. A pacy, atmospheric thriller.'
Jock Serong, author of *The Rules of Backyard Cricket*

'Margaret Hickey has hit the ground running with her debut, *Cutters End*, an engaging, well-written murder mystery.'
R. M. Williams Outback Magazine

Margaret Hickey is an award-winning author and playwright from North East Victoria. She has a PhD in Creative Writing and is deeply interested in rural lives and communities. She is the author of *Cutters End* and *Stone Town*.

CUTTERS END

MARGARET HICKEY

PENGUIN BOOKS

Author's note: This book was written on the lands of the Waywurru and Dhudhuroa peoples, who I would like to acknowledge as the Traditional Custodians and storytellers of their Country. I pay my respects to their Elders past and present, and celebrate all the histories, traditions and living cultures of Aboriginal and Torres Strait Islander people.

PENGUIN BOOKS

UK | USA | Canada | Ireland | Australia
India | New Zealand | South Africa | China

Penguin Books is part of the Penguin Random House group of companies whose addresses can be found at global.penguinrandomhouse.com

First published by Bantam in 2021
This edition published by Penguin Books in 2022

Cover photography by bmphotographer/Shutterstock.com (tree) and Stefan Mokrzecki/Getty Images (background)
Cover design by Christabella Designs
Author photograph by Benjamin Dowsley
Typeset in Adobe Garamond by Midland Typesetters, Australia

Printed and bound in Australia by Griffin Press, part of Ovato, an accredited ISO AS/NZS 14001 Environmental Management Systems printer

A catalogue record for this book is available from the National Library of Australia

ISBN 978 0 14377 834 9

penguin.com.au

We at Penguin Random House Australia acknowledge that Aboriginal and Torres Strait Islander peoples are the Traditional Custodians and the first storytellers of the lands on which we live and work. We honour Aboriginal and Torres Strait Islander peoples' continuous connection to Country, waters, skies and communities. We celebrate Aboriginal and Torres Strait Islander stories, traditions and living cultures; and we pay our respects to Elders past and present.

For Bernie

PROLOGUE

He wasn't coming back. The finality of it hit and hot tears welled, the blindfold growing soggy once more. Her head thumped and now that the blood had dried, the side of her face felt pinched and hard. She couldn't feel her legs.

In the beginning she could kick away the ants that swarmed, but now she imagined them converging, all those creatures crawling over helpless limbs. From somewhere in the scrub, a bird gave a long, drawn-out cry. She knew at that moment she would die, and she waited for the bird to cry again. *If only it would cry*, she thought. Then she would not feel so lonely, it would not be so bad. *Please cry again, bird*, she whispered, aloud or in her head. It was hard to raise any moisture in her mouth and she couldn't have shouted if she'd tried. Her breathing slowed. The time for screams was over and the world became quiet and still.

She thought of her family and her home, so far away. With a deep sadness, she felt a yearning to tell the world that once she had existed. She wanted to write her name in the sky so that everyone could see it. She wanted someone to *read* her name. The urge to do so became overwhelming and the pounding in her head thumped with the words: *My name, my name.*

The splinter of wood she'd concealed for hours in a vague thought of attacking him took on a new and final purpose. Gripping it between the base of her two thumbs, she summoned all her remaining energy to carve her first initial into the tree. Her arms, wrapped around the trunk behind her, felt almost numb. It was hard to balance the piece of wood; her pen. She traced the second letter, tried to push in hard when the bark would not yield. She took a short rest before raising her head and gritting her teeth. The third letter was more difficult and, after pressing the splinter in, she felt it break. A dry sob escaped her. But with one final reserve of energy, she used her ragged thumbnail to finish carving out the last letter of her name, barely feeling her skin tear and bleed as she did so.

It was done. Her head dropped.

In the deep darkness, she listened for the bird. But the bleak and desolate world was still.

CHAPTER 1

New Year's Eve, 1989

Ingrid sat on the side of the road and unbuckled her backpack, buckled it again, unbuckled. She was like a cowboy from one of those Westerns. What was the word to describe the gunslinging action? Quick-draw. She did it again, imagining herself walking into a saloon, drawing the gun and shooting some bad guy before they got the chance to do her in. Split-seconds, that's what counted. She did it again: buckle, unbuckle. Bang!

God, it was hot.

The air was thick with flies and she waved them off her leg, watching the black mass descend just as quickly again. She wiped her forehead and felt about in her pack for a drink. A small ant climbed onto her bag and up her arm. She let it travel for a while as she drank water from her bottle before flicking it off. *Jesus, don't the insects in this place ever rest?*

She lay down, resting her head on the pack and reached her hand out to the side of the road, where the heat made the asphalt soft. She pressed a forefinger deep into it. It gave her a warm sleepy feeling. She did it with her other fingers and then, using a stone, made an imprint of her initials – I.A.M. Head to the side, she inspected it, wondered vaguely if it would stay that way when the road firmed again.

She closed her eyes. An insect flew into her mouth and she coughed it up, spat it out. She took a sip of water. Tired and bored. Tired. And. Bored. She let out a scream of frustration in her closed mouth. Where was Joanne?

The little rocks underneath her back grew hard and she stood, wiping herself, looking up and down the road. Its dark surface shimmered in the heat. To the left, it went right up to the horizon: no bends, no hills, low trees spaced apart. The Stuart Highway, Alice Springs almost 1000 kilometres away. To the right, a yellow roadhouse and the sign 'Hot food, cold beer' banged hard against a metal pole. Not a car in sight.

This was a shitty day. Sunday afternoons would have to be the worst time to catch a lift. Trucks usually made the journey on Fridays for their Darwin run and the oldies would already be settling by their vans in some free spot, party hats on and drinking their moselle. *Happy bloody New Year's Eve,* she told herself.

She opened and shut her mouth, feeling the dryness in the air. She could do with a moselle right now. Probably make the time go faster in this hellhole. All that drinking after Year 12 must have given her a taste. It might help to dull this bloody ache in her chest anyway. When would that ever go away?

She took a bite of the sausage roll she'd bought a few minutes before. Bits of hard gristle stuck to her lip and she spat it out, the dry flakes falling on her top. It was disgusting. Probably been pickling in the bain-marie for days. She threw the rest of it over her shoulder and onto the red dirt. Ants converged. *Gross.*

She was hungry and she needed a drink, but there was no way she was going back to that roadhouse. Bloody old sleazebag; in the store mirror she could see him ogling her through his Coke bottle glasses. Probably a paedophile. She needed to go to the toilet too, but apart from the roadhouse there was nothing, not even a tree nearby to squat behind. She hummed a Roxette song to try to forget her hunger and her bladder. It worked a little, but not really.

A sound to her right and she turned to see a white Commodore pull out of the petrol station in front of the roadhouse. She hadn't even seen it drive up there! Straightening, she took a few steps and held her right arm out, thumb extended. As the car moved towards her, gathering speed, she caught a glimpse of a man at the wheel and a blonde woman leaning into the passenger window, looking at her.

'Hey!' She gave a wave before reaching out her thumb again. 'Hey!'

But the car sped up, the driver gazing straight ahead and the woman giving her a half-smile as they drove past. Ingrid kicked the stones about her. *Bloody couples,* she thought. *They rule the world.* She sang the Roxette song again and pulled her cap lower on her face, looking as she did at the sun, sinking fast.

Now she *really* needed to go to the toilet, and where the hell was Joanne? The whole day had been a failure. Waking up in Yorkies, the dingy Port York backpackers, to a note from the manager telling her Jo had rung and would meet her at the Mendamo Roadhouse at 2 pm.

Was it definitely this roadhouse? Yes, it was; she'd written it down and Mendamo was the last one before the road headed north up the Stuart, through the desert for nearly three hours to Cutters End. She should have just caught the early bus the whole way through from Port York to Cutters End, even if it did cost a mint. She could have slept off her hangover for six hours in a comfy seat instead of all this waiting-around business. What had she saved in bus fares? Twenty bucks? Pathetic. And now she was here.

Ingrid thought back again over the evening before, trying to recall the details of the night. Drinks at the backpackers and then at the pub where they'd met two Swedes. The one called Nils had bought her a drink and she'd been in hysterical laughter with him about something. What was it? Her hungover brain struggled to remember. The painting of dogs playing pool, perhaps? The barman who looked like MacGyver? They'd danced in the beer garden to 'Summer of '69' over a scratchy sound system and kissed briefly before she decided she wanted to go home.

She tried to get Joanne to come with her, but her friend was stuck to the other Swede and said she'd be back later. Ingrid watched them dance. After a while, she left, giving Nils a wave on the way out. He was already talking close with some other girl, but she didn't mind. Outside the pub a group of older men leered and she walked past quickly, arms covered, listening to the usual jeers about tits or arse.

Back in the hostel, she fell into a deep sleep, only to be awakened at 4 am by some couple shagging in the bunk opposite, and then later by the manager who told her Joanne had rung and said to meet her at the roadhouse. *Yorkies, what a dump.*

Where was Joanne? In any case, she wasn't here, and it was now past 4 pm. She'd have to go back to the roadhouse and work out how best to get into town again. Fat chance of that on a Sunday. Failing that, there were little cabins here you could rent for the night, though she'd probably have to barricade herself in the room in case the old creep tried to come in.

Bloody hell! So much for sleeping in the Underground Hotel at Cutters End, and the New Year's Eve party there that was meant to be legendary. It was even mentioned in the *Lonely Planet*. Their original idea, way back when they'd been planning the trip at home, had been to be in Alice Springs for New Year's Eve, but the Swedes and the night in Port York put an end to that idea. Ingrid lugged her pack over her shoulders and started to walk back to the roadhouse, feeling in her pocket the fifty-cent coin she'd need to ring Yorkies to find out if they'd heard anything more from her friend.

She wasn't too worried. No doubt there'd been some mix-up and Joanne had missed her after she'd left. *Oh God!* Ingrid stood stock-still on the side of the road. What if Joanne brought the Swede with her when they met up? That would be the worst. All she needed right now was to be around a loved-up couple.

At the side of the roadhouse she looked left and right to see if anyone was coming, then quickly squatted behind a water tank. Finding a tap on the side, she gave her hands a rinse before patting her face and neck. Pulling her pack by the side-strap now, she walked over to the phone box, opened the door and squeezed in, pack beside her feet. With one hand she dug out the coin and with the other she fished for the phone number of the hostel. There, in the front page of her diary, were the numbers scrawled in red pen.

She put the money in the slot and heard the satisfying clunk, waited for the dial. After three rings, someone answered – not the reception guy, a woman.

'Hi,' Ingrid called. 'It's Ingrid from room 16. I stayed at Yorkies last night.'

'Yeah?'

'I wanted to know if my friend turned up, Joanne. Same room. She's Australian.'

'Hang on a sec.'

There was a pause and Ingrid could hear a hand being placed over the receiver. Still, she heard the muffled yell: 'Anyone here see Joanne come back today? Aussie, room 16.'

A pause, murmuring from another person.

Ingrid jumped up and down on her feet. Her money was running out fast.

'Love?' the other woman said. 'Joanne came back.'

Out the corner of her eye, Ingrid saw a vehicle with a

covered ute pull up in the station beside a bowser. A man got out and looked briefly to where she was, before turning to fill up with petrol. She focused her attention back to the phone.

The other woman spoke again. 'Want me to see if I can get her for you?'

'Yes,' she answered – but with one final clunk the money ran out.

'Shit!' she said. 'Shit, shit, bloody shit.' She tried to rummage around deep in her pack for her purse, knowing it was usually at the bottom, but couldn't find it; she needed more space. Opening the door of the telephone box, she pushed the pack out with her foot. Once free to move, she knelt in the dirt and undid the zips on the side to open it fully.

'You need a hand?' It was the guy who'd pulled up just before. Ingrid looked up at him; an older sort – weather-beaten and a big build.

'I'm right,' she said, turning back to the problem at hand.

'Suit yourself.' He headed into the roadhouse.

She found her purse. *Only notes, crap!* Remembering the night before, she fished out the jeans she'd been wearing and felt in the pockets. *If I don't find coins, I'm stuffed*, she thought. *I'll have to go in and get change from the old paedophile.* And then, some luck – twenty cents! She gave a little cheer. And what was this? A scrunchie! She'd been looking for it for ages. *Unreal!* She quickly tied her hair into a ponytail. Joanne had her other scrunchie, the black spangly one, but this one was her definite favourite.

Now, she needed more change. Change, change. She shoved the jeans back in and rummaged about for her Country Road windcheater, the one with pockets. Where was it? It took some time. She pulled at a sleeping sheet and a crumpled pair of undies came flying out.

'Where you headed?' It was the man again, back from the roadhouse, standing closer to her this time.

'Cutters End,' she said, grabbing the knickers in her fist. 'But fat chance of that now. My friend hasn't turned up, so I'll have to stay here or get back to Port York somehow.'

'On my way to Cutters now,' he said. 'Could give you a lift if you like. Only up the road.'

She looked up at him again.

'Isn't it three hours to get there?'

He snorted. 'Maybe if you write tourist books it is. It's two hours ten at the most. If you want to come, let me know but I've got to get going. Missus'll have the roast on. Beef.'

Ingrid thought about it while she lifted out her windcheater. She could be in Cutters End by 7 pm, wouldn't have to go back to the hideous Port York backpackers or face the creep in the roadhouse. Joanne could catch the early bus from Port York to Cutters End in the morning and they could be together by lunchtime tomorrow for a New Year's Day recovery session. She would even get to go to the New Year's Eve party at the Underground Hotel.

Ingrid felt around the pockets of her top. Another twenty-cent coin! She grasped it in her hand. It was like a sign.

The man waited a moment before turning and walking

towards his car. He *looked* like a roast, she thought. Thighs like two sides of beef.

Ingrid made a snap decision. 'Okay,' she called after the roast man. 'I'll come – but can I ring my friend to let her know first?'

The man shrugged. He lifted up the bonnet of his vehicle and looked deep inside.

Leaving her pack outside the phone box, she opened the awkward door once more and hurriedly shoved the coins in the slot. The phone was answered after two rings.

'Yeah?' Same woman.

'Hi, it's me again – Ingrid. Can you please tell my friend Joanne that I've got a lift. Tell her to get the early bus tomorrow morning and I'll meet her at the Underground Hotel in Cutters End.'

'Sure, love, you've got a lift – she'll get the bus and meet you tomorrow.'

'Thanks for that. Money's about to run out.'

'Can't have that.'

'Please tell Joanne.'

The phone went dead. Satisfied, she opened the door again, zipped up her pack, hauled it over one shoulder, and walked across to where the man had finished with the bonnet and was wiping his hands on his jeans. As she approached, he moved to her and took her pack. 'Jump in, mate,' he said. 'I'll put this in the back.'

She opened the passenger door and climbed into the vehicle. In the rear-view mirror she could see him lifting up a tarpaulin and placing the jerry can, then her pack, in the tray of the ute. He hooked up the cover again and climbed in beside her.

'Thanks for this,' she said. 'You're a lifesaver.'

She could see the old creep from the roadhouse staring at her through the window, the fading light on the glass giving him a ghostly air. She smiled back hard, giving him the finger as they pulled out. *Stuff you, you old sleaze*, is what she thought. *I'll never have to see you and your shitty shop again.*

Police Media Briefing: 5 January 1990, 11:00

An unidentified body has been recovered some five kilometres from the road, 250 kilometres to the north of Port York. Police are appealing for witnesses to come forward. At this stage, all lines of inquiry are being considered.

CHAPTER 2

October 2021

Detective Senior Sergeant Mark Ariti, four weeks into his long-service leave, was suffering a hangover. Not the worst, but bad enough. *I'm showing my age*, he thought. Once, he would have stayed out till 4 am then turned up to footy training. Now, unless he got to bed before midnight he was knackered.

The hoover lurching forward and back over the carpet gave him a seasick feeling. A hangover while vacuuming. Purgatory for those who'd only minorly stuffed up their lives. But still, the remnants of the Twisties weren't going anywhere and the carpet was relatively new. He wiped his forehead and manoeuvred the brush into a corner, where it gave out a sickening noise before turning into a high-pitched wail.

He flicked the vacuum off-switch with his toe, got the tube, gave it a shake. A Lego man fell out and he stooped to pick it up, feeling the blood rush to his head. A little Yoda stared at him and Mark looked at it for a moment before throwing it behind the couch. Even the Force wasn't with him today. Only thing with the power to heal was a souvlaki and a Coke. Lamb and garlic sauce.

Mark's foggy brain clicked into gear, registering the thought. Souvlaki for breakfast? Actually, that wasn't a bad idea. He wandered into his eldest son's bedroom. Sam, seven years old, was reading to his younger brother Charlie. The two of them looked like an advertisement. No sign of the tears and screaming earlier, the fight Sam had put up to stay at home rather than go to another day of Year 2. Sam pointed out a word to Charlie and the younger boy repeated it with care. It was heart-warming; he should probably take a photo or something. But this was not the time to ponder cuteness. Mark needed that souva. Besides, he knew the harmony could only be short-lived. In two seconds, mayhem would reign. 'Kids,' he said, 'in the car quick. Let's get going.'

'Kelly, I'm taking the boys in!' he called, while his sons wrestled with their bags.

His wife's head snapped around the door, glasses on the end of her nose and looking none too happy.

'What's that?'

'Thought I'd drop Charlie at kindy after I take Sam in. Might pick up something for breakfast.'

'Getting some hangover food, are you?'

'Yep.'

Her head whipped back behind the door before reappearing. 'Can you pick me up the papers?'

'Which ones?'

'All of them.' Kelly was a lawyer, currently working on a high-profile family violence case. Checking the papers regularly, she was able to keep up to date with emerging cases, the prosecutors involved, the dates for parole, the judges presiding, the allegations of harassment and corruption. Her work was brutal, the hours ridiculous. Christmas drinks at Mitchell & Co. Solicitors were never much fun.

He said yes to the papers and, picking up the keys, waited while Kelly kissed the boys before heading out the door. It was cold. He considered going back inside to get a jacket but knew that would only cause more delays and requests. He was a man on a mission. Souva with garlic sauce and a Coke for breakfast.

He dropped the boys off, first Sam at his pretentious boys' school – no tears now, a relief – and then Charlie at a nearby kindy. Once on his own in the car, he turned the radio to classic rock and sang along to the Divinyls. Fingers playing guitar on the steering wheel, he mused once more about the state of his hangover. Surely he'd only had five or six beers, how could anybody feel that bad? Drinks after squash with his teammates had turned into a mini session at the pub. He cast his mind back to uni days and the last year of school. Out all hours of the night at pubs and clubs with names like Velvet and Countdown and Rios. *Those were the days*, he thought fondly for a moment. Those were the days before kids and wives and mortgages and Yodas and vacuuming. In those days he wouldn't have given a toss about Twisties on the carpet. Was there even carpet in his old share house? He struggled to remember. He hoped not.

The Divinyls finished and Snap! started up. Shitty music, but great beats. Could lift a man's mood if he wasn't feeling so down. It wasn't that he was unhappy, just a bit low. Not morose at all. On the contrary. An intelligent, beautiful wife, two healthy sons and a nice house in the leafy 'burbs of Adelaide – by all accounts he had it all. He even had an inground pool.

He pulled into the main street and alongside the takeaway. Inside, Omar was leaning on the counter watching morning TV. In the background, loud Turkish music played. He gave a sidelong glance to Mark. 'Souvlaki?'

'Jesus, Omar, how well do you know me? This is getting a little familiar, don't you think? What if I felt like a falafel and tofu baguette?'

The big man wouldn't budge. 'Souvlaki coming up.'

Mark sighed and got a Coke from the fridge, peeled back the tab and had a long drink. Not for the first time that morning he thought that he needed to try to get healthy again, maybe start running or something. Squash once a week just wasn't cutting it. It wasn't that he'd got fat yet, but at fifty years old he could see the signs, he could see the signs.

After the episode with Detective Senior Sergeant Southern, Mark had acknowledged the gentle nudge by seniors to take long-service leave, but a month into it and he felt strangely deflated. Where was the customary trip around Australia with the family in a Jayco van? He wanted that obligatory shot of his boys holding a baby crocodile beside a cut-out of Bindi Irwin at the Australia Zoo. Instead, he'd taken on the childcare while Kelly focused on her job. Fair, but that didn't make it fun.

Omar handed him his souvlaki and he stepped outside to sit on the plastic chair provided. First bite and he relaxed. *Now this is what I need*, he thought, *this is what a man needs after five or eight beers and fifteen minutes of hard vacuuming. This will make all doubts about life fade away.*

His phone rang and the name registered as Angelo – his former colleague, now a bigwig in the South Australian force and rising. Mark paused before taking the call. 'Superintendent Conti, this better be good,' he said. 'I'm having an epiphany here.'

The line crackled and Angelo's voice faded in and out. 'Mark. I'm going to send you a photo and I want you to tell me if you can identify the person in it.'

Mark put down his food and waited, gazing at the phone.

A moment later, a grainy photo came through and he stared at it, a jolt of recognition forcing him to sit up straight and take a breath.

The phone rang again. 'You know her?'

'Clearly – I'm in the photo, aren't I?'

'Mark.' His old friend's voice sounded weary. 'Can you help us?'

CHAPTER 3

Ingrid Mathers had something about her, Mark thought, everyone could tell you that. She was clever for a start, and funny. She was good at impersonations: check-out chicks, Russian gymnasts, the local bishop; no one was sacred. People were drawn to Ingrid; gatherings were boring when she wasn't there. It made him think of himself at parties, eye on the door, waiting for her to arrive.

Mark remembered watching Ingrid before he recognised that he liked her: watching her work in class, hoping she wouldn't stuff up in tests, seeing her at her locker pulling out books, talking close with the other girls. Ingrid was kind too, he remembered that now. She partnered up with the kids in PE who had no friends, and she stood up to the bullies. White hair straight out of a Big M ad, and perfect teeth. Small eyes, a greeny blue. She was skinny but most people were back then. She had freckles and a nose always in a stage of sunburn. Not the best-looking girl in school, not the smartest, not the coolest; but at sixteen years of age he'd been stumped by her, shocked at the strength of feelings, which were a good part lust but something else too. In all his adult life, he'd never met anyone like her. And now, thirty years later. Ingrid Mathers.

When Angelo filled him in on the case and asked him what he required, he'd said yes without hesitation. He'd done so with a need to get straight in the car and drive, drive, drive. At home, he didn't have time to fill Kelly in on the particulars, just told her that Angelo wanted him in regard to work and he'd be home late. It wasn't unprecedented, but he felt the chill. He packed, gave her a quick kiss goodbye, and headed out the door just as his mother-in-law was arriving. She threw him a dirty look. 'Leaving again?' It hurt; she knew it would.

'Just for work, Rosalie, a day. No need to worry.'

'I hope not.'

He stepped back to open the door for her, but she bustled past, pushing it herself and ignoring him. He couldn't blame her, not really.

Two hours into the trip, driving in the police lease car on the highway heading east, Mark clipped a roo on his side window. The grey body ramming his car gave a sickening thud and for a split second he thought he'd hit a woman wearing a beige suit. The roo jumped wildly into the middle of the road and he braked, heart pumping. Natalie Merchant crooned. The roo stood, stunned, before lurching into a nearby paddock. Mark pulled to the side of the road and got out, breathed deeply, stretched, checked the window. It was cracked and the door dented too. He'd have to fill in forms, get some quotes, do some explaining to head office about the damage to their vehicle.

He flexed his fingers and walked, trying to shed the feeling of dread he'd had when the roo made contact. Bang! How fast it had happened; the grey blur, the dull thud and the brakes. For a few minutes he looked around half-heartedly for the animal, unsure of what he'd do if he found it dying. Kill it, but with what? A rock, bash its head in. There was no sign of it. A car raced by, windows down and music loud; it gave him a start.

At the next little town, Mark bought a coffee and a pie, and ate it while driving, bits of pastry flaking onto his jumper. Sauce dripped onto the upholstery and he tried to wipe it off. No luck. Another form to fill out. The coffee was bad but hot and made him feel better. Natalie Merchant finished, and First Aid Kit started up. The women's sad voices called to him like sirens and he drove and drove, the highway increasingly lonely, the landscape filled with yellow paddocks, long driveways and stone fences. He made it to the small town of Brae Inlet by midday, the sun hidden by ominous coastal clouds. Mark checked the address again and pulled up at the front of a weatherboard house. It made him sad, that beaten-down house, the shades closed and paint wearing like old skin.

He took a moment or two to collect himself before getting out of the car. A westerly battered; seabirds shrieked in the sky. Mark knocked on the door, drew a breath, pulled his shoulders back.

A woman answered.

'Hello, Ingrid,' he said.

CHAPTER 4

Ingrid took a step back, took a step forward and then was still. She took a while to register.

'Mark,' she said. 'Mark Ariti. I'm not sure why you're here, but hello.' She looked up and down the street and remained standing in the doorway, her dark silhouette surrounded by light. 'Is this some type of reality game show? Are there cameras in the bushes?'

'Now, why would you think that?'

'Because I haven't seen you in, like, thirty years.'

'That's right,' he said.

'And you come here looking like a, like you're on official business. Like a cop or something.' Understanding grew on her face. 'You *are* a cop, aren't you?'

'Yes, sorry. Acting Inspector.'

'No need to be sorry, I get it now. Well, I've got to go out in an hour.' She sounded resigned. 'Just let me know what I've got to do.'

'Maybe first ask me in? I'm freezing my balls off here.'

Ingrid stood aside to let him through, and he caught a whiff of something like a rainforest. He briefly thought of running streams and a canopy of dripping leaves. She shut the door and moved in front of him in the narrow corridor. Their arms brushed.

'Down here,' she said. 'I've got the fire on.'

A woodstove gave off welcome heat in the small room and he glanced around. It was the opposite of his own living room. Rugs on the floor, a sunken yellow couch piled with cushions, standing lamps and books all about. He recalled how much she used to read. A bookcase was jampacked with novels of every type, with more scattered on every surface. There was a bunch of flowers falling out of a jam jar and a red painting of a girl midway into a handstand. The rug closest to the fire was strewn with paper, and a half-drunk cup of tea sat on a wonky tower of art journals.

'Sorry about the mess.' She kicked a shoe under the couch.

'Don't worry about it.'

'Can I get you a drink or something?' She hovered near the door.

'Maybe just a coffee.'

When Ingrid left the room, he had a closer look around. Green paint on the walls was cracking in parts, and the floorboards needed a polish. The rug, a Moroccan style with patterns and swirls, was clearly worn. It would be a bugger to vacuum, he thought briefly, before turning his eye to the books. Classics, crime, architecture and languages. All academic stuff, but hey, wasn't that *Men Are from Mars,*

Women Are from Venus? He leant in and confirmed that it was. A heap of old newspapers, local ones, tied up with a piece of string. There were photos. One he recognised as her mother and father standing in front of the Eiffel Tower, another of two young children and one of a man, tall and thin with blond hair, squinting into the sun. He wondered briefly at the life she'd had since school.

'I'm sorry.' Ingrid returned. 'I've got no good coffee left. Will you have tea? Or a wine?'

He wavered; he felt like a drink, could do with one right now. But he was here under the banner of the force. Re-investigation. Just for two weeks, a secondment from his old department. Angelo had sorted it all with his workplace, with the various seniors and admin people – of course he had. And here he was, as Acting Inspector Ariti no less. There was no way he could have a drink. Mark glanced at Ingrid, standing in the doorway, her blonde hair wispy in the heat from the fire. 'Tea would be great, thanks. No milk.'

Ingrid turned on her heel and left once more. Mark flicked the papers on the floor with his shoe. They were pages and pages of sketches: coloured, black and white. He bent down towards one; a fruit bowl – pears and oranges. The likeness was good, very good. Another one, unfinished, of a single red line with the beginnings of a person at the top.

'Here you go.' Ingrid held up a cup of tea in a saucer with a biscuit on the side. 'I found you a bickie. Can't guarantee its freshness.'

He straightened up, face red as if he'd been reading her diary, when Ingrid nodded at the papers. 'Ideas for prints.

Today I got them all out and tried to decide which ones to work on. I've got to be sure about them before I begin mixing.' She sniffed. 'It's all a bit crap, I've hardly sold anything in ages.'

He sat down on the yellow couch – sank into it – and had to balance his cup and saucer while he rearranged himself. From somewhere else in the house Fleetwood Mac was playing. He took a sip of his tea. 'You're an artist?'

'I try to be.' Her words were flat. She sat on the floor cross-legged, effortlessly bringing the cup down with her. 'But most of what I paint is shit.' She took a sip and began to rearrange her sketches into a pile. 'I do a bit of teaching now and then too.'

'I like your house,' he said after a pause. 'It's just the sort of place I imagined you to live in.'

'You imagined my style of house?'

Steady, son, he told himself. 'I mean, you were always kind of messy.'

'Yeah, well,' she said. 'Old habits don't die.'

They sipped their tea. They dipped their bickies in the tea. They drank the tea.

Mark looked about the room again, trying to think of something to say. His eyes rested on a painting; a copy, encased in a cheap wooden frame. 'Hey,' he said. 'I remember that print from Art in Year 10 – what's it called again? Something about Odysseus?'

Ingrid followed his gaze. '*Penelope and Her Suitors*,' she said, and they both looked at the image of the woman at a loom, reaching down to bite a piece of string, while at her window a group of men stood with open arms, bearing gifts, beseeching.

'I used to think, why doesn't she just get a job?' Ingrid gave a snort. 'Move towns or whatever? All she does is wait. So pathetic.'

'Why keep it then?' Mark said, eyes still on Penelope, her red dress luscious in the darkened room.

'Maybe I've grown more forgiving with age.' Ingrid shrugged. 'Plus, I got it for five bucks at an op shop.'

'Bargain.'

They finished their tea and put their cups down almost at the same time. Ingrid turned hers upside down onto the saucer and examined the tea leaves.

'What exactly are you doing here, Mark?' she asked without looking up.

Mark cleared his throat, remembered why he was here, what had been asked of him. 'I think you know that, Ingrid. Superintendent Conti warned you someone would be coming.'

'Not you though, he didn't say that.' She grabbed a lock of hair and pushed it behind her ear. 'That was sneaky.' She snorted. 'What, so they found out you knew me and thought they'd send the ex-boyfriend around to soften me up, yield a little? I'm over this, Mark. I went through this a very long time ago and I don't see why I have to regurgitate all those memories again.'

'I know, it must be annoying for you . . . The case has been reopened and we're going back over all the old files, interviewing again, seeing if we can find anything new.'

Ingrid blew out air loudly and raised her eyes to the ceiling.

'If I could just ask some questions and take some notes, that would be great. But you know, you are under no obligation to say anything.'

'You-have-the-right-to-remain-silent.' Ingrid spoke in an American accent.

'Can I ask you a few things about your time near the roadhouse on New Year's Eve, '89?'

'May as well. You're here now.'

'Thank you. Now, Ingrid, can you please tell me what you remember about that day?' Mark reached for his notebook and pencil. Opened to a blank page. 'When you're ready.'

'Once again and for the record, I saw nothing suspicious that day. I got the early bus from Port York on New Year's Eve, I got off at the Mendamo Roadhouse three hours up the road, I waited for Joanne, I got a lift, I went to Cutters End and stayed at the Underground Hotel, I kept travelling as planned. I went to the police and told them all this thirty years ago. God! I'm so bored of it all.'

'We're just going over the facts again. According to some members of the public, the police didn't do a brilliant job of investigating the last time. This case has got a lot of people interested.'

'Thirty years after the fact?' Her voice was tired. 'Jesus, please tell me the force is this diligent on family violence.'

'The victim had fairly influential supporters.' It had been a surprise when Angelo told him who the woman was who was pushing for the inquiry. Suzanne Miller – even he knew her, the children's presenter on Channel 24. His boys loved her on *Fun with Shapes* at 4 pm each day. 'Suzanne Miller has been giving interviews left, right and centre, and the police have to be seen to be doing something about it.' Suzanne's husband was Eric Valer, former resident of Adelaide, now a mining executive in Sydney. They were loaded; they knew people.

'What do you want to know?'

'Just tell me what happened, be more specific if you can, on that day that you were waiting for a lift. Try to think of any cars which may have slowed down near you or if you spoke to anyone. Just anything, any minor details might help.'

Ingrid gave a long sigh. She began speaking in a bored singsong voice. 'I got to the Mendamo Roadhouse at about 1 pm on New Year's Eve. Walked up a bit and waited and waited for a lift. Nothing! The road was dead. Went back to the roadhouse, bought a sausage roll from the sleazy manager, and ate it by the side of the road. A car came past – a couple – and I waved at them, but they didn't stop. Walked back to the roadhouse, rang the hostel, then got a lift with some bloke named Don, or Ron, and went to Cutters End. I stayed at the Underground Hotel – you know all this. You know it!'

'Any other details which may help us? Please, Ingrid.'

'The sausage roll tasted like crap, does that help?'

'Tell me about the bloke you got a lift with, Don or Ron. What was he like?'

Ingrid shrugged. 'Normal. Didn't speak much, I think I slept a little. As far as rides go, it was a pretty easy one.'

'What do you mean?'

Ingrid laughed. 'Haven't done much hitching, have you, Mark? And it would be different for a man. For a woman, there's always the pressure to entertain, be funny, make them feel like they're pleased to have picked you up.' She put on a bright smile, raised her voice. 'Hi! How are you! Are you going north? Oh my God, so are we! A lift would be so great – you are a champion, this is the best! Thank you, thank you, thank you!'

Mark got the picture. 'Did he drop you at his house? You stop anywhere?'

'Nope, just at the Underground Hotel in Cutters End.'

'And that was on the same day, or early evening on New Year's Eve?'

'Yep.' Ingrid yawned.

'Is there anything, *anything* more you can tell me about him?'

Ingrid flapped her arms in a helpless gesture. 'I really don't know.'

'Anything.'

She looked at him, wanting to help. 'There is one thing, but it's kind of stupid.'

He nodded. 'Yes?'

'He kind of smelled like bacon. It was foul at the start, but I wound down the window so after a while it became manageable.'

'Well, thanks.' *Cracked the case with that one*, he thought. *Done and dusted.*

'Do you get what I mean? That smell? It's gross.'

'Yeah, I know.'

'Sorry, it's probably nothing.'

'It's something.' It wasn't. 'Why were you hitchhiking?' he asked. 'Why didn't you get the bus all the way from Port York to Cutters End?'

Ingrid gave him a blank look. 'Mark, don't you remember? It was the late eighties, everyone hitchhiked. We planned to hitch all the way up the Stuart; Alice Springs, Uluru, Katherine, Darwin. There were loads of people on the side of the road back then – you'd get lifts all the time and it was nothing to pick someone up.'

He remembered. People used to hitchhike to jobs, to friends' houses, get a lift back home after the pub. He even hitchhiked to and from school sometimes. It was common. Ivan Milat put an end to all of that.

'And the roadhouse owner?'

'Sleazebag, I told you.'

'Sleazebag?' Mark asked. 'What did he do?'

'When I paid for my sausage roll, he grabbed my hand and said something I couldn't hear so I leant in. He said it again: "Show us your pussy."'

Mark was quiet for a moment. 'Arsehole,' he said. He couldn't fathom it. He'd never said shit like that to a woman. Never. Didn't know anyone who had. 'Arsehole,' he repeated.

'Yeah.' Ingrid looked at the books on her lap, flicked through them. 'But a lot of blokes are, especially when you're young and attractive.'

Mark considered. He wanted to tell her that she was still attractive, possibly more so, with her ruffled, shorter hair and the lines on her face. He wanted to tell her that some men, while they couldn't deny the beauty of youth, preferred older women with stories to tell and a life behind them as well as in front. 'Anyway, the perv is dead. Lived his last few years with dementia, died in an old folks' home in Adelaide.'

'I feel for the nurses,' Ingrid said.

'Bet he did too.'

'Not funny,' Ingrid answered, but he thought he heard a smile. 'It's weird seeing you here, after all this time.'

'I know.' After a heavy silence he said, 'What about Joanne?'

Ingrid looked at her papers. 'What about her?'

'What was she like then?'

Ingrid turned to him and shook her head. 'Save us the bullshit, Mark – you know what she was like. Can't you remember your old Deb partner?'

He could. His mother still had a photo of the two of them on her mantelpiece in Booralama, crammed in among all the other ones of grandchildren and birthdays and babies and friends. In the photo, Joanne had a big perm sort of thing. A huge fluffy dress on her, green cummerbund on him, his thick hair gelled to the max and the two of them grinning like fools. 'I remember thinking it was odd you had gone away together,' he said.

'Now why was that?'

'She was more . . . experienced.' Jesus, he sounded like a sleaze now. He tried again: 'I don't know, she seemed older than the rest of us. I mean, I knew the two of you were close, but I just couldn't see you travelling together.'

'Yeah well, I wasn't exactly in the best of spaces, you may remember.' Ingrid gave him a weighted look. 'And she *was* my best friend.'

'You keep in contact with her now?'

'Every now and then. I hear she lives in a Sydney mansion.' Ingrid stabbed at the fire with a poker.

'You two have a falling out?'

'Not really. More that we just fell apart.'

'After the backpacking?'

'I don't know. Maybe. We went on that trip up the centre on the Stuart Highway, we'd been planning it for ages. It was good but, yeah – things were different.'

'She'd changed, hadn't she? Grown up or something.'

Ingrid rolled her eyes. 'We all have to grow up some time, Mark. You know how friendships switch and change.'

He remembered Ingrid crying when he told her they should break up. It was outside some party and she was drunk, sobbing on the kerb. All he wanted to do was go back inside to his friends. He'd patted her on the arm, tried not to notice the snot. He thought she looked ugly, there in the gutter with her mouth wide open and her face all red and twisted. He aimed for sympathy but felt revulsion. It was only days after that he sensed it, the dull ache that told him maybe he'd made a mistake. The low pain that wouldn't go away no matter how many girls he was with, how many parties he went to. He remembered riding his bike around to her house a couple of weeks later and her father telling him that she'd gone off travelling up the centre with Joanne.

'Did you receive the email about the reunion?' Ingrid asked.

'Not that I remember, why?' He wasn't good on social media.

'Thirty-two years since the end of Year 12 – it's in a couple of weeks.'

'Thirty-two?'

'Couldn't have the thirty-year reunion 'cos of the bushfires, and then last year was a total shitstorm with Covid and border restrictions, but this year – we're celebrating.'

Thirty-two years. The thought made him catch his breath. Was he really so old? The years bent and stretched before him. Ingrid, uni, travelling, girlfriends, friends, marriage, babies, work. Where did it all go? He wanted it to slow, put a stop to things. Mend things.

'Who's organising it?' Depending on who it was, he may not have got an invite. He hadn't always been the best of blokes.

'Maria Calomborous.'

He had a vague memory of a short girl with curly black hair and glasses. Stern. He used to call her Leo Sayer. 'I don't think she would have invited me.'

'I'll tell her to forward it to you.' Ingrid was friends with everyone. 'She's all right.'

'Do you think Joanne will go?'

Ingrid paused. 'Maybe. Listen, I've got to get going. I've got band practice.'

He looked at her in admiration. 'You thinking of starting a band?'

'I am *in* a band – Raise Hell Octavia. You'll be hearing about us soon. Wembley, the MCG, Elliston RSL, the Robe Town Hall.'

'Got other members has it, this band?'

'Of course. Me on guitar, Noelene from the post office on vocals and Libby, science teacher, on drums.'

Again, he couldn't tell if she was serious. Although she'd liked music at school, he couldn't remember her playing any sort of instrument. Now, Joanne – that girl could sing. 'You should get Joanne to come down, play a few guest songs.'

Ingrid snorted. 'What's with all the Joanne references? I've moved on, Mark, we all have.'

He nodded, agreed somewhat. Put his notepad back in his pocket.

'Will you be hanging around town for long?' she asked.

Again, that beating of his heart. From somewhere in the distance, a car alarm went off. 'No, I'll head back to Adelaide later on.'

'That's a full-on day.'

'Yeah.' Mark thought of Angelo, wondered if he'd been too quick to accept the Acting Inspector role. Long-service leave looking after the kids didn't seem so mundane all of a sudden.

'Anywhere good to get a feed before I go?'

'Not sure, really. I don't eat out much here.'

Mark felt a pang. Ingrid was lonely, he realised. She stood up, again that fluid movement from cross-legged to standing, and began to pull the curtains across the windows. Outside, he could see that it had begun to rain. 'You married, Ingrid?' He had to ask.

She did that thing, looking at her hands again. 'Yes, if you can call what I've got a marriage. Sander lives in Friesland.'

'The Netherlands?' He said it in an accent, didn't know why.

'Yeah.'

'You meet him there?'

'Yep, when I was travelling. We lived in Amsterdam for a few years before he moved back with me. Got married, lived in Adelaide, then finally here in Brae. I'd been pushing to move here for ages. Five years ago, his mother died so we went back for the funeral. He stayed, I returned.' Ingrid made circles with her fingers on the sides of her head. 'It hasn't been the most fun time of my life.'

'Can you work it out?'

She kicked another shoe under the couch. 'Maybe, we'll see.' He waited for her to ask if he was married, had his answer ready, but she didn't. Instead, she picked up his cup and turned it over on his saucer. The silence stretched. He could see it was time to go.

'Sorry I haven't been much help,' Ingrid said. 'You've driven all this way from Adelaide for nothing.'

'Only took around two and a half.'

'Still, there's the drive back.'

'Yeah well, been good to see you. May need to ask you a few more questions at some point. Can you send me your number?' Mark watched her scribble down the number on a piece of paper. She handed it to him and he felt the weight of her single life and his married one.

He nodded at his upturned cup. 'Anything interesting there? I'm about to win a fortune or something?'

She gave a dry laugh. 'Sorry, nothing like that.'

'Can't give back the badge just yet?'

Ingrid shook her head, holding out the saucer to show him. Two blobs on the plate, a mass of tiny leaves like flies or swarming ants. 'No fortune for you,' she said.

At the front door, he hesitated.

'Ingrid? There's just one more thing I need to ask. All those years ago. Why did it take you so long to go to the police?'

It felt cruel to ask it. Why bother?

'So, Mark.' Ingrid's voice was hard. 'You tell me. How long was it? A few days? A week?'

'Ten days.'

She shook her head, pulled her coat around her. 'Mark, I was eighteen. How much do you think I knew about police work? As soon as I saw the appeal in the paper, I went to the Darwin police station. Told them everything I knew, just like I'm telling you.'

He held his hands up in a gesture of peace. 'Okay, okay. I was told to ask.'

Ingrid raised her eyebrows and blew out air in a look of disbelief. 'You're smarter than you give yourself credit for, Mark. Try thinking for yourself.' She raised a hand and turned back into her little home.

CHAPTER 5

Outside, the wind whipped and swirled. Black clouds raced like chariots across the sky and rain battered. Mark pulled his jacket tight and walked to the car. Strange shapes of twisted trees hugged the road and he felt oddly bereft. How long ago the years seemed that Ingrid and he had been together, how distant the years between. He opened the car door, turned the key and sat for a while with the engine running. The windscreen was covered in dirt and rain; he turned the wipers on and watched them, their steady clunk reminding him of a heartbeat.

Ingrid had changed in the way that perhaps everyone did. Something bright had been chipped away. He supposed it was youth – that block of time that seems so fixed when you are young and all the world lies ahead. The windscreen wipers clunked along. Dirt stains remained. Mark started the car and pulled out onto the road.

On the way to finding a pub, he called Angelo and gave

him a quick rundown. His friend was blunt. 'So, in other words, you got nothing.'

'Well, what else could I have asked? I didn't want to press too much. God – I've only just caught up with her after thirty years.' He drifted off, not sure how to describe the way he'd felt cushioned from the outside world in that little room.

'Mention Joanne Morley?' Angelo asked.

'A bit. They don't talk much now.'

'Interesting,' Angelo said. 'Know the reason?'

'Christ, Angelo, how many schoolfriends have you kept in contact with? It's not uncommon, you know.'

His boss didn't answer for a moment. Mark pulled onto the side of the road, kept the engine running, and let the other man come up with suggestions.

'So, there was nothing else.'

He tried to think of something. Briefly considered telling him about the sausage roll. 'No.'

'I'll send you through the files.'

'Good,' Mark said. 'I need more details if you're going to send me all over the state interviewing people. I don't even know if I'm asking the right questions.'

He drove a couple of blocks into the centre of town and parked outside the only pub he could see. Out of the car, he stretched his legs and decided on a walk around town. In the early afternoon Brae Inlet was hard-bitten and mean. Treacherous footpaths gleamed wet and a flannelette shirt lay discarded in the gutter, the arm stretching over the kerb. An ice-cream shop, shut for the winter months, was covered in white gull shit and the old bank had a 'For Lease' sign. Ingrid had moved to a beach town on the howling coast, far away from family or friends. Why? He rubbed his hands, walked into a petrol station and bought a Big M.

'When's the weather going to warm up?' he said to the woman at the counter. 'Bit chilly.'

She gave him a steely look. 'You're on the south-east coast, mate. Harden up.'

He blinked, tried to think of something clever to say, but came up with a blank. 'Thanks,' he said, slumping out of the shop.

Mark walked across the river bridge and up to the beach. Waves chopped, grey and small. It seemed to him to be a shark attack sort of day, and he was shocked to see a group of women out swimming.

No doubt about it, he was an inland man, a child of brown rivers, rope swings and sleepy old gums. His big old town in the north-east of the state, Booralama, was known in the fifties for being awash with farming money. People left when it ran out, but the old buildings remained. A butter factory, a law court, two fading banks. His mother was the daughter of a sheep farmer, a boarder at Adelaide Ladies' College and a dab hand with the drenching. Devastating for her parents then, when she married Mark's father, son of Greek immigrants who worked on the Snowy Hydro before making their way to South Australia and Booralama. Mark thought of his father, a hardworking, serious man, long dead and remembered mostly for his dedication to the vegetable garden.

The ocean was a foreign land to Mark. Childhood holidays were spent mainly camping along the Murray. The beach made him nervous. Was that a fin out there? And what about the rips? His eyes darted over the waves, worried for the swimmers.

Mark walked back to the pub, eager to get out of the wind. Inside the hotel, a series of men were watching the races on a big television, a beer in front of them, carbon copies all. At least it was warm. The barman wandered over to him, eyes still on the screen. 'You right, mate?'

'Lemon squash, please.'

The barman brought the drink to him, still looking at the telly. A slave to it.

'You got a horse running?' Mark asked.

'Eh?'

This was not the country hospitality Mark expected. 'Got a horse running?'

The man looked at him surprised, began wiping the counter with a tea towel. 'No, mate, what made you think that?'

'Nothing.'

Mark looked at the screen; the horses raced on. The race finished and another one started up. In a line beside him, the series of blokes stared at the vision. Together, each represented the Seven Ages of Man. They were him in various stages of decline. They had a sip of beer in unison.

'You here for the weather?' The barman had returned, chastened perhaps by Mark's earlier reply.

'No, I'm here to see someone.' He hesitated. 'An old friend, Ingrid Mathers – you know her?'

The heads from the bar whipped around to face him like the laughing clown game at a sideshow.

'We went to school together,' Mark said. 'Haven't seen her in ages, nothing in it.'

The clown heads turned back to the races; only the barman remained.

'You know Ingrid?' he asked the barman again.

The man sniffed. 'Everyone does. She's about the best thing that's happened here since we won Tidy Town.' The barman became animated, listing Ingrid's achievements and attributes; member of the school kitchen garden program, editor of the Brae Inlet newsletter (delivered monthly to every household), initiator of the First Wednesday cheese and wine club, and a bloody-good-looking-bird-to-boot.

Mark wondered why all these accolades made him feel foolish. None of them should have surprised him; as a teenager Ingrid was involved in everything from debating to cross-country to Lions Youth of the Year. All of it should not have made him feel as if he'd somehow been cheated by her. And yet, the sight of the cup of tea balancing on the magazines, the faded rug and Fleetwood Mac, it had all conspired against him to paint a portrait of a woman in need, a waiting woman.

'Staying in town long?' The barman was drying glasses, edging towards his horse-watching clients and the television. 'Fishing comp on the weekend.'

'No. Just here for the day on business.'

'Yeah? What type?'

Mark saw no reason to lie. 'Cop business.'

'You here about the old case? One from the eighties?'

The barman poured himself a small glass of Coke, drank it.

'Yeah. Following up a few questions. All the people in the whereabouts at the time getting the same line.'

'Gone up north yet, have you? Up the Stuart? Lot of shit happened up that way and not the good kind, if you know what I mean.'

It always surprised Mark when he discovered how interested people were in cold cases and reinvestigations. Murders or mysteries that happened years ago, garnering no excitement, could whip people into a frenzy thirty years later. Something about black-and-white photographs, the blurred images of Jenny Kee jumpers in the eighties, the Farrah Fawcett hair and the details of a crime scene made people in their late middle ages shudder. It got them all thinking, *It could have been me.* Young women murdered thirty or forty years ago mostly turned out to be victims of the same people that young women were killed by nowadays: the husband, the boyfriend, the lover. 'Not yet, mate, I'm not one of the full-timers on the investigation. But I might – why?'

'Ingrid likes to ask questions, talk to people.'

Mark put his squash down. 'She spoke to you about this?'

'Well, why wouldn't she? We're all interested, mate. Missing persons, murders, local people and whatnot. And now you coming to talk to her, probably to find out all she knows – makes sense to me.' The barman sounded defensive.

'What did she say about the case?'

'Ask her yourself.' The barman turned, giving his full attention to the horse races. 'It's not for me to say what she's been discussing.'

Mark finished his squash and wandered to the dining section, two metres away from the bar. He ordered a bowl of chips from the same barman, who wrote the order down carefully, took it to someone out the back. From his table, Mark, the only one in the dining room, could see the conga line of red clown faces, each his future self, and he resolved to drink less. As a measure of his new-found resolve, he ordered another lemon squash with his chips. Mostly fruit, after all. Vitamin C, et cetera. But God it was awful, and terrible as a match for potato. Mark yearned for a beer, drank the squash and, virtue intact, ate alone.

He thought of Ingrid, talking to the barman about the case. He took out his phone, brought up her number and texted. *Ingrid, best not to talk about this case to the barman or anyone else, investigation pending etc. Mark.*

Moments later, the phone buzzed and Ingrid replied. *I have never spoken to anyone about this case. Give me some credit, Mark.*

Mark looked at his phone in disbelief. Either Ingrid or the barman was lying; why? He decided it was the barman, inventing intimacy, but an uneasiness remained – how well did he really know Ingrid after all these years?

Just as he was toying with the last few morsels of chips, the door of the pub burst open and, on the back of a severely cold wind, in walked a woman who was not Ingrid Mathers. Mark saw the barman's face fall and in the other man's visage he saw his own reflection.

The young woman, swallowed by a puffer jacket, ordered a red wine and looked around, clearly bored. She took out her phone and jabbed into it, talking loudly so everyone could hear. Something about meeting her here, picking her up, going to Fitzy's and then driving to Warnbeen and then to someone else's. Something about Sharon's and Mitch's and Daz isn't coming, he's at his mum's. Her social life exhausted him. Her world seemed centuries from his. All he wanted to do right now was to be home in Adelaide, stepping onto his hard-to-vacuum carpet and lying on the couch.

The girl put down her phone and drank her wine. She watched the horse races for a little while, and when one of the old men cried out in victory she gave a rousing cheer. The room brightened for a moment with the flush of youth. How powerful it was!

Mark's phone buzzed. Angelo, sending through the first of the files. Mark picked up his plate and, fishing about for his wallet, walked to the bar.

'You're not going to Warnbeen now by any chance, are you?' The woman was beside him, smiling. She glanced at her phone. 'My friend is coming to get me, but I know he'll be ages. And as much fun as this place is'—she tilted her head towards the television—'I've got friends to meet and places to be.'

'You're asking me for a lift?' Mark realised the incredulous tone in his voice sounded rude but didn't try to mask it. *All those high-profile murders*, he thought. The crime books, the *Wolf Creek*-type movies, the documentaries on ABC, the re-enactments on *60 Minutes*, the horror stories told late at night on camping trips – hadn't any of them sunk in?

The young woman flicked her hair. 'Yeah, what's wrong with that?'

Mark didn't answer immediately. He knew there was nothing wrong with asking for a lift, and there was nothing wrong with accepting one, with offering one, with declining one. But. He grappled for a response. 'Pretty dangerous, that's all.'

The woman looked at him closely and leant in. 'Why, are you a serial killer?' Her breath was warm and fruity, her teeth impossibly white. 'You certainly don't *look* like a serial killer.'

'How do you know what a serial killer looks like?' he said, before lowering his tone to mimic hers. 'Are *you* one?'

Her hair brushed the side of his face. 'Yes,' she whispered gravely. 'I want to do away with all the men in this bar by the night's end.' Her breath pressed close in his ear and he saw himself, cartoon-like, falling through the air, arms flailing. He took a step back, ear tingling. He felt in his pocket for his wallet. Took it out to pay, cleared his throat. 'I think you'll find most of these blokes will be very hard to prise away.'

She took a sip from her glass and laughed, teeth reddened momentarily by the wine. Mark was surprised to feel a twinge of fear, for him or of her he wasn't sure. 'In any case, I'm not going to Warnbeen,' he said. 'Perhaps it's best if you wait for your friend.'

She checked her phone again and took another sip. 'Can't blame a girl for asking,' she said, tapping the screen.

The barman returned. 'Gravy's going to Warnbeen in five,' he said to the girl.

The young woman's face brightened, and she turned to the men at the bar. 'Good old Gravy, you're a saviour!'

An old bloke, face like a grilled tomato, half-turned and smiled. The woman moved to a chair by the door and sat down, still glued to her screen.

The barman gave Mark a look. 'Gravy's all right,' he said.

Mark returned the look, nodded. 'You got a quiet place I can read some files?' he asked.

The barman jerked his thumb sidewards. 'Past the Ladies,' he said. 'Room there you can use.'

'Thanks, I'll only be an hour.'

'Free coffee by the poker machine. Instant, none of your fancy stuff.'

'That's fine.'

The man grunted and Mark turned away.

CHAPTER 6

In the room down a dank corridor marked 'Ladies Lounge', Mark sat on a drooping sofa and stared at the ceiling, where rising damp threatened in intricate patterns. The scene reminded him vaguely of a book he'd read when he was young, *A Wrinkle in Time*. There was a part in it when the main characters, three children, watched as darkness swallowed light. The room he was in had seen better days. In the adjacent bathroom, the smell of mould was winning against Pine O Cleen, and a general whiff of stale cigarettes lingered in the air.

His phone beeped, and he wedged it out of his back pocket. He'd missed several calls; a couple from Kelly and one from a friend asking him to play squash in the morning. No chance of that now. There was a text from Angelo letting him know he'd forwarded a few notes from Senior Constable Jagdeep Kaur, the colleague situated in Cutters End. From what Angelo had gleaned, via his contacts in the upper echelons of the South Australian force, Kaur was highly competent and on a transfer from North Adelaide to the Cutters End station for six months. Mark wondered briefly if she played squash.

He stood up and looked out the window. Trees whipped and the rain pelted down. The road was empty, save for one car parked outside the pub, brake lights blurred in the afternoon sky. Two figures emerged. A flash of bright hair and a red coat. The girl from the pub, the stooped figure of Gravy, and a third person in the driver's seat. The girl and the old man got in and the car pulled out slowly. Mark strained to read the numberplate for no good reason. The car disappeared into a dim distance.

Mark lay back on the sofa, propped up with lumpy cushions, and opened his emails. Angelo had sent him files, newspaper clippings and handwritten notes. There was no logical order, no lead or direction. He read:

Northern Territory Times, 10 January 1990

CUTTERS END FATHER FOUND DEAD ON SIDE OF STUART HIGHWAY

The charred remains of a body, discovered early last week, have been found to be those of 38-year-old father-of-two Michael Denby. Friends and family gathered at the Denby residence to pay respects to a man described as 'salt of the earth' and 'hardworking'. Denby was a 1986 recipient of a Commendation for Brave Conduct for his role in the rescue of a woman and her young daughter from a vehicle trapped in floodwaters near Port York. 'I owe him my life,' the woman told reporters today.

Adelaide Advertiser, 6 January 1990

The charred remains of a body were discovered early on Thursday evening by the side of the Stuart Highway, just north of the Mendamo Roadhouse. Police are urging anyone who was in the vicinity of the roadhouse or who travelled on the Stuart Highway between New Year's Eve and 4 January to contact them on Crime Stoppers 000.

Northern Territory Times, 5 January 1990

Chief Inspector Richard Nolan claims that police are currently working with witnesses to formally identify the remains of the body found. Names have not been released at this time. However, police indicate that a statement will be issued shortly.

Police Report, 5 January 1990

The burnt body of a male, aged 30–50, was discovered by local man John Baber at approximately 19:00 on 4 Jan. Baber notified local police who were called to the scene. A vehicle, suspected to belong to the victim, was left unlocked, bonnet up and burnt out at the scene. Heavy windstorms have made movements of the victim difficult to ascertain.

Police Report, 6 January 1990

Male victim has been identified as Michael Denby, 38, from Cutters End. Initial reports indicate that Denby died of injuries related to suffocation, caused by extensive burns to the respiratory tract, sometime between 31 Dec 1989 and 4 Jan 1990.

A typed note at the end of the report, dated a day later:

Victim also sustained a broken leg.

A handwritten note dated 11 January 1990:

Interview: Mendamo Roadhouse manager Gerald Cuxton. Recovered logbook from sales and accommodation. Victim Michael Denby, 38, found to have bought 20 litres of diesel, a packet of chips and a chocolate milk. Total cost: $23.60.

No CCTV cameras.

A scrawl at the end like an afterthought:

Last confirmed sighting of Michael Denby, NYE 1989, 15:00–17:00, Mendamo Roadhouse was by Gerald Cuxton, roadhouse owner who served him during that timeframe. Cuxton reported Denby mentioned engine troubles but otherwise was in good spirits.

Cuxton suffers from myopia, near-sightedness, and is unable to see clearly beyond the windows of his shop. C knew MD as a regular customer.

Mark rubbed his eyes; he knew most of this. He read more documents, mainly dead ends on the people who had come forward to say they were in the area at the time. They were mostly truck drivers and, apart from the observant

John Baber, who noticed fresh tyre marks running off the main road, none saw anything of interest. There were some handwritten notes taken by police after useless phone-ins. Mark could picture the tired cop listening to the person on the other end, frustrated and bored:

> *Person A saw a car being driven by a woman who looked like a killer.*
>
> *Person B saw a driver in a Sahara LandCruiser who was most definitely on drugs, two kids beside him – you should definitely lock him up.*
>
> *Person C had a feeling that he'd seen what happened in a dream and that the culprit is now in a hospital suffering heart pains.*

This was always the way when a case was made public. Every person sitting in their lounge room wanted to play a part. There was more; a busload of backpackers who stopped at the roadhouse on the morning of 31 December 1989 had reported nothing, although the Mendamo Roadhouse manager claimed one of them had stolen a packet of chips and a Coke. A woman, Judith Farley, had come forward to say she'd driven past a backpacker hitchhiking on the afternoon of New Year's Eve 1989: blonde hair, medium height, young-looking – late teens. And then, what he'd found out from Angelo that morning – that the person in question was Ingrid, who had later come forward to the Darwin police once she'd got wind that they wanted to question her. There was reference, too, to Joanne Morley, who had also been questioned along with others who'd travelled the road up from Adelaide to Alice Springs. From the scant information provided, it seemed that neither of the girls had reported anything strange.

So many people now to interview once more. People who knew the roadhouse manager Gerald Cuxton, John Baber, Ingrid, Joanne, other backpackers who caught the bus to Cutters End on that day, and now Suzanne Miller, main supporter of Michael Denby, who was demanding answers. No wonder Angelo needed assistance. This was the general strategy in the initial stages of any reinvestigation: talking to people, being deliberately vague, getting to know those in the file. There was the hope, always, that something new would turn up; an angle previously unthought of, a hunch confirmed.

Senior Constable Jagdeep Kaur had already talked to Denby's work colleagues, neighbours and extended family. Nothing of interest there. A good driver, reliable; a family man; sorely missed in the community. Mark flicked through images of the deceased: a solid man in life, tall with broad shoulders, looked the type to enjoy a beer. In one image, Denby held a small child on his shoulders, in another a young girl clung to his legs. A good father. Another shot: Michael Denby on the lawns of Kirribilli in suit pants, shirt and tie, proudly displaying his commendation medal. *A national hero for a couple of days, someone for the rest of us to look up to.*

In death, Michael Denby was not so easy on the eye. Upper body charred and disfigured, jawbone visible, face a shocking blur of patchy skin and flesh. The lower part of his body a broken mess – a leg lying at a strange angle, the blue jeans torn, clean white socks and solid boots. The autopsy report indicated that Denby had drugs in his system, some alcohol too – but not enough to kill him. A broken leg and extensive burns, particularly to the face, neck and palms of the hands. Suffocation caused by burns to the respiratory tract the probable cause of death. Verdict: Accidental death.

Another, more recent note, from Senior Constable Kaur in a tiny, neat script:

Guests of Roadhouse on 28–29 Dec:
Vic and Yvonne Gladstone, elderly couple caravanning – both now deceased

Guests of Roadhouse on 30 Dec:
Jason Dimler

Guests of Roadhouse on 31 Dec:
Jason Dimler
Joanne Morley

Cameras ordered? CHECK

No recorded guests for 1–5 Jan

Mark knew from his chat with Angelo that Joanne had stayed the night in the roadhouse on New Year's Eve after missing her meet-up with Ingrid. Even so, he felt a stab of surprise at seeing her name. Funny how the three of them, Joanne, Ingrid and now him, were caught up in the case.

This was not how he imagined any sort of reunion to be. Joanne, dark-haired, clever and cool. Out of his league always at school – but then again, Joanne was out of every male's league. Big clods of testosterone, it was no wonder she'd shunned each and every one.

Mark scanned over the old notes once more. Sufficient for the early nineties, but they'd never pass the requirements for records now. He gave a long sigh which turned into a cough.

Old cases were notoriously difficult to solve, despite the popularity of podcasts and documentaries which claimed to do just that. In those instances, some reporter usually managed to find a crucial piece of evidence that whole police departments had missed. The bungling police officer, a pie-eating, coffee-spilling loner; the lazy coroner; the forgotten witness – Mark hated that type of entertainment. What they didn't include was the mind-numbing paperwork, the reading and reviewing of boring documents, exhibits, transcripts and reports. The circumstantial evidence, the interviewing of people whose memories were exaggerated or, worse, fabricated to inflate their own importance. They didn't show that.

Outside, the wind made strange howling noises and he stood to go, opening a video link Angelo had sent him. A woman with wavy brown hair spoke into the camera, her voice easily recognisable as one of Australia's most-loved children's presenters. Suzanne Miller was at least a decade younger than he was, late thirties perhaps. It was easy to see why Channel 24 had kept her in employment for so long: a soothing singsong voice, wide smile and looks that appealed to all ages. In this video, Suzanne Miller called for further investigation into a crime which, she said, was a national shame. 'A young father,' she said (*Not that young*, Mark thought), 'A horrible death and no answers for over thirty years. There are *too many* unanswered questions. A body bearing suggestions of a violent death, and no suspects. This is simply not fair on his small close-knit community of Cutters End. Michael Denby, a hero, the man who saved my life and that of my mother. We want to know what happened to him. Is there a killer living among us? My family demand answers!'

Mark pressed pause on the video, Suzanne Miller's face caught fetchingly in a frozen screen. He hated this too, this type of appeal – the fear-mongering that led to reprisals and mobs with pitchforks demanding more of the police.

As he waved goodbye to the barman and the many ages of mankind, as he got in his car and drove out of Brae Inlet, his thoughts were not of Suzanne's ardent plea or the gruesome photos of Denby in death – rather his thoughts were of eighteen-year-old Ingrid, sitting by a desolate highway and biting into a sausage roll, long pickled in an ageing bain-marie.

CHAPTER 7

Ingrid couldn't draw. The four sketches of prints looked like surrender flags and she regarded them with a scowl. They were shit – what was she thinking?

A drawing of a small child standing in a field holding a flower? Boring.

A little girl in an apron running through the bush? Admit it, she was copying McCubbin.

The sketch of the bowl of fruit was technically the best, but the image was so overdone she wouldn't bother.

The red line: that one had promise but she screwed it up.

The rest were terrible. She couldn't waste whole days in the studio on these ideas.

Ingrid poured herself a glass of red wine and considered her options. She could go back to teaching (shudder) or find a job with the local council, something in art and culture. Unless she moved to the city, jobs in the arts were going to be pretty much non-existent. She enjoyed the workshops at the library, but they hardly counted as a living. There was the Netherlands and Sander of course; she could always go back to Friesland. Sander would like that. At least, she thought he would. But no. She still wasn't sure, she needed more time.

She rested her eyes on the small print her husband had given her before she left the Netherlands, a white tulip. It wouldn't have been her choice of art, but she liked it there, bright above the old piano. In vain, Ingrid tried to focus on her work once more, but the images swam before her eyes. It was no use trying to redeem them, they were no good. Her mind was too preoccupied to think of ways in which they could improve.

Ingrid slumped onto the carpet, lying with a cushion behind her head. She took a large gulp of wine and allowed herself, at last, to think of Mark. His visit was the reason she was so addled. Thoughts came flooding. Age had wearied him, she admitted, but the years did not condemn. Outside, a sea wind beat against the windows, but inside her little nest of a room, she was safe to remember. It was so easy to recall the first time she and Mark had kissed, on the street beside her friend's house on a hot summer's eve. Easy, too, to remember the feel of him and that smell of Brut 33 on wool. If someone asked her what her school days had been like, she'd probably lie a little, give some rendition about hard years, maybe some bullying or friendship issues – but in truth, they were golden. When she thought back to the schoolyard, she pictured girls in fits of laughter, re-enacting *Neighbours* and pretending to be ribbon dancers. She remembered the easy friendships, the warm intimacy of doing one another's hair, arms around shoulders, eating chips 'n' gravy down the mall.

But mostly, she remembered Mark. He was the first person she'd ever loved outside of her family. Someone so close that her parents had a meeting with them both about becoming too fixated at such a young age. Good-looking, funny and smart. A reader. Arrogant too, she remembered, and often absentminded. Sometimes dismissive and lazy. Popular? With some, not all. But loved up they were, loved up and passionate and all, *I love you, I love you, I love you and I'll never leave you and you'll always be mine.*

Ingrid snorted and a bit of wine splattered onto her rug. Her teenage life seemed almost sickening, like a *Sweet Valley High* novel or something. She was forgetting the crappy parts; the embarrassment of wearing the wrong outfit to a party, the worry that someone would notice you were wearing pads during your period or, worse, that you would get a blood stain on the back of your uniform. The bad haircuts, the fights with parents, the vomiting in bushes after drinking too much. Sleazy men, teachers a bit close, and negotiating confusing friendship changes. There were shitty parts to adolescence too.

Ingrid pictured herself at sixteen, a blithe jumble of youth. At that time, she'd been best friends with Jo. Joanne Morley, her rich and beautiful friend, the clever one with long brown hair and olive skin. Joanne, who all the boys obsessed over. Ingrid remembered her jealousy when Joanne partnered Mark in the Deb. The golden couple, it seemed, except when, at the after party, Mark had kissed her instead and asked her to be his girlfriend. Ingrid laughed at the thought. That was what actually happened back then. The asking, the accepting, like some Austen novel. In any case, Joanne wasn't upset – her best friend had any number of boys to choose from and opportunities aplenty. Rather, Joanne was happy for her – had made her a little card with love hearts and the words 'At last!' inside. Saccharine rather than sweet, with a passive-aggressive touch that teenage girls do so well. When Joanne went on exchange to America in their senior years, Ingrid missed her like crazy. Mark had filled the void.

I must call her, Ingrid thought. She wondered if her old friend was getting the same line of questioning as she was, wondered how she was coping. Ingrid imagined Joanne in her beautiful home, surrounded by glass and overlooking the ocean. She couldn't imagine how Joanne would react to all of this, because her friend was inscrutable and had been for years. They'd lost contact gradually. Infrequent catch-ups were awkward, their lives too different. The childhood friend she played dolls with, rode bikes with, had sleepovers with, who made cards for her and shared secrets, was now someone foreign. There'd been times over the past few years when she'd feel like calling Jo, telling her something she'd seen or something funny she'd heard. But Joanne was a closed book and, well, she didn't like to think of it.

Ingrid stretched her legs out, considered her socks. It would be easy to pull on a pair of boots, call off band practice and head down to the pub to have a sociable wine and so on. And so on. A Jason Isbell song drifted down the hall and she poured another glass. She could float right now into the pub, see how it all panned out. The thought wavered, hung in the warm room.

No. *Safer to stay right here*, she thought. *Stick to routine.*

But she would have to call Joanne soon.

CHAPTER 8

Driving through a dark sky on the way back to Adelaide, Mark wondered if Kelly would be up when he got home. In all likelihood she'd still be working. Her work! She lived for it, preparing cases against violent men, battling her way through meetings and conference calls. When they first got together, Kelly told him that she loved her job. It took him months before he realised what that meant. She was *passionate* about her work.

Still, he reminded himself, her job was the reason they lived in inner Adelaide and had an inground pool. Not one of those shitty plastic Clark models he had as a kid.

His thoughts were interrupted by a text from Angelo. The man was seriously getting his pound of flesh. His old colleague was upping the ante – now he wanted Mark to fly to Sydney tomorrow to meet with Joanne. While he was up there, Angelo would also try to arrange an interview with the woman Denby saved – TV personality Suzanne

Miller – what did Mark think? And when would Mark be able to talk to the current roadhouse manager and a few people in Port York and Cutters End? Next week? What did he think?

Mark didn't know what to think. He picked up the phone. 'Why me?' he said.

'You want my job instead?' Angelo's voice was tired. 'Reading files, checking inconsistent timelines, filing admissions with the bureaucrats, asking for more time and money? Hardly ever seeing your family, who you have recently come to understand don't like you much because of it? Please, say you'll swap.'

Mark remembered his early policing days. He couldn't stand the mundanity of the office, the long hours in fart-filled rooms, the emails, the form filling. 'No, I'm okay.'

'Besides,' Angelo continued, 'you know half of these people. They'll talk more, remember more for you. Little stuff they don't bother telling other cops. You're a skilled interviewer, qualified for this. All those courses you've done, put 'em to use.'

Those courses. A lot of butcher's paper and PowerPoint. What did it take to become Commissioner, role play?

'It's just two weeks,' Angelo continued, 'and you're being paid at Acting Inspector rates, remember. Go through the motions, Mark, help me to keep everyone happy. This is temporary but if you do a good job, well, world's your oyster.'

He hated oysters. Slimy bits of snot creeping down your gullet.

Mark looked at the clock. 'You should be paying me Chief Inspector rates for this day, Angelo.'

Angelo ignored him. 'I'll get admin to book your flights to Sydney?'

'Sounds like I don't have a choice.'

'There's a choice, mate.' Angelo's voice was grim. 'You can go back to your three months of long-service leave at home and then head back to Fraud.'

The men said their goodbyes and hung up.

Fraud. It was a good name for the squad Mark had worked in for the past four years. By day, sorting through evidence on white-collar crime, and by night, holed up in some cheap hotel with Detective Senior Sergeant Jane Southern, five years his senior and on transfer to his squad. Jane Southern. He tried not to think of her much and when he did it was in a rush of emotions: lust, shame and despair. Bound together by unhappiness, their relationship, however superficial, did more harm than anything else. He wasn't sure half the time that they even liked each other. The affair, short and destructive, blew up when Mark, in a fit of remorse, admitted all to Kelly. Cue recriminations, him sleeping in hotels, then the couch and only now, in the last month or so, in the marital bed.

The affair ended but the aftermath continued, and the sly looks in the tea room would take a while yet to dissolve. Fraud. He was tired of it and his seniors knew he needed a break. It was a relief to be out of the office, but he hadn't counted on the mundanity of home life. And then Angelo offering him this secondment on the reinvestigation, and at a higher pay grade no less. A career opportunity and, as always, something in it for Angelo, who knew Mark was familiar with people close to the case. If this case could be wrapped up, if Suzanne Miller and her influential husband could be satisfied, if the South Australian police force could be vindicated, then moves could be made and ladders climbed. Angelo had graduated the same year as Mark and now he was eyeing off a commissioner role. Who knew how high the man could rise?

As the dark paddocks rolled on by, gradually giving way to subdivisions and then traffic, he thought about his own lack of resolve over the years. He seemed to float along; things came to him and he accepted them as par for the course. His school years were a blur of Ingrid and fun, drinking with his friends in the park, smoking in the bush behind his parents' house, and watching girls dive from the platform at the local pool. Later, uni as expected, then he'd drifted into the police force after someone told him that he'd make a good cop because he could get over the wall easily in the fitness test. It was true: he'd easily climbed over the wall, passed all the requirements and, in less than a year, found himself pulling over speeding drivers. Experiences on the job soon jolted him out of his youthful reverie – the sustained verbal abuse from motorists, the harrowing visits to violent homes and the occasional car accident – but before long he'd moved to Finance, where the best part of his day was spent reading files on suspicious accounts.

Then, in his late thirties, meeting Kelly at the insistence of someone who said they'd make a great couple, kids, and then the move to the Fraud squad, and finally the affair. Now this. He'd fallen into it all, he'd played no active part.

Around 7 pm and hungry, Mark pulled over at a busy petrol station on the outskirts of Adelaide. He paid for a flat white and cheeseburger, hating himself for the image he projected: the middle-aged cop, the junk food. He sat at a table, pushed the burger wrappers aside and looked through his phone. He watched again the clip of Suzanne Miller on the news, appealing for justice. At the bottom of the screen as she talked, the number for Lifeline and suicide prevention rolled across. She spoke about Kylie Denby, Michael Denby's daughter, who had only been twenty-five when she killed herself, ten years after her father's violent death. A family ruined, a town still in mourning. This man was a national hero! There were questions still to be answered. What were the police doing? Absolutely nothing, that's what.

CHAPTER 9

Mark returned home to find Kelly slumped on the couch, a pile of files on her lap. He walked over, gave her a kiss, enquired after the boys. Both in bed, sound asleep. He had a shower, got a beer and joined his wife.

Kelly was drinking tea now, her thin hands wrapped around the mug and black glasses perched on the end of her nose. They each took turns to tell the other about their day. He asked her questions about the people and her work; she asked him about the particulars of the case. They listened carefully, making sure to acknowledge the other just as the counsellor had suggested. He drank his beer, looking out of the dark windows to the pool. Kelly worked steadily on her papers.

Mark thought about the case, scanned his phone and came upon the photo Angelo had first sent him, the one of him and Ingrid in Year 12. Angelo had told him that when the details of the case first landed on his desk, he'd looked through all the photos admin sent him. All the people connected with the case, all the possible witnesses, the people questioned at the time. Joanne's name came up, Ingrid's name came up. A mention of the town of Booralama. And that had rung some bells with Angelo. Then, there were photos of all of them. When he first saw the one of Ingrid and Mark together, Angelo nearly cried with joy.

Kelly turned, saw him looking at the photo. He held up the phone to her. 'This is who I've been interviewing today in Brae Inlet. Her name's Ingrid, we were at school together.'

Kelly held the photo at arm's length before bringing it in close. 'The two of you. You're so beautiful,' she said in a kind of wonderment, and he could see that it was true. It was youth – the pink and soft skin, the exuberance bursting out of the frame, the promise of things to come.

'She was my first proper girlfriend,' he said.

She nodded, smiled somewhere over his shoulder. It wasn't what he expected. Perhaps she was thinking of an old boyfriend. *We all have a past.*

Kelly read her files while he watched TV. On the screen, a woman backed into an alleyway, followed by a group of doped-up youths. He could see it wasn't going to end well. Crime, he couldn't escape it.

'Kels,' he asked, over the sound of the ensuing attack, 'any bloke ever, you know – made you feel unsafe?'

She gave him a look. He waited. A tired laugh. 'Do I have breasts plus a pulse plus a shadow? What do you reckon?'

He was quiet, contemplated again his own ease in the world.

She looked at her files, the one woman a week, the violence. 'It's a wonder we aren't out on the street smashing things,' she said.

'Well, why aren't you?'

'Who would get the school clothes ready? Who would organise the sleepovers?'

'Someone else.'

'Where is this someone else?' She cupped her hands around her mouth, made a cooee sound: 'Someone else! Where are you?'

'Jesus, Kelly.'

'Can you take the kids to school tomorrow?'

'I've got an early flight to Sydney.' He paused. 'But I'll reschedule. I could get the one an hour later.'

Kelly nodded. 'Good. I've got a lot on.'

'We should seriously think about getting a nanny while I'm in this job. Just for a few hours a day.'

'Maybe we should.'

'You think it's okay, me working on this case for a bit instead of taking care of the boys?'

'It's fine.' Mark couldn't be sure that Kelly was listening; it was always the way when she was engrossed in her work. He rubbed his forehead, yawning. Tiredness washed over him.

He looked over Kelly's shoulder at her work. A photo of a woman with a cut lip and disfigured nose greeted him. Kelly acknowledged his presence, lifted up the photo close to him for better viewing. It wasn't pleasant. 'Husband's saying he didn't do it,' she said. 'Her word against his.'

'There's always something,' he replied, straightening up and stretching. 'Locard's exchange principle.'

She gave him a blank look and he felt a flood of pride. He was a primary school kid again, getting student of the week. He filled her in on the old police theory, pleased that there was something in the world that he knew and she didn't.

'Locard's exchange principle – the perpetrator will always leave some sort of evidence on a victim or the surrounds. That evidence, it's the silent witness and you need it.'

'What about the fact that he has form in this? Hospitalised her last year.'

'Circumstantial. It'll help, but you need more, don't you? The cops will go back to the scene. Locard's exchange principle.'

Kelly reached out and touched his leg, giving it a small rub. 'I'm going to bed,' she said. 'You coming?'

He nodded, felt his heart fill, went to check on the boys. They were both still asleep, little fat things coiled up, warm and safe. One of them, half-crying, woke when he pulled the doona up. Mark sat on the side of the bed and, in a singsong voice, told his son a story about a mouse and a clock and other half-remembered things. The child drifted off once more. He kissed them both and walked back to his bedroom to find Kelly in bed, stretched out, sound asleep and gently snoring. He removed her glasses from the top of her head and placed them on the bedside table. Then, he took off his shoes and lay beside her on the bedclothes, one hand resting on his wife's arm. Through the gaps in the curtain, he could see the faint glow of a streetlight against a dark sky. No stars in the city. He rolled onto his side, closed his eyes.

Sleep didn't come.

CHAPTER 10

In Sydney, the sun shone and the people were a brighter breed; their teeth whiter, their postures more upright, their lycra more logo'd. On his way from the airport to the suburb of Bronte, the taxi driver gave him the drill; the natural beauty of the city, the warm weather as opposed to that dreary and sad southern city.

'I'm from Adelaide,' Mark said, flat.

'Which you prefer, Melbourne or Sydney?'

'Adelaide.'

The driver looked at him in the rear-view mirror, disappointed.

Mark felt the look.

'Adelaide's a great city,' he said. 'The best.'

'It's no Sydney.'

Mark tried to decide who was more painful, Sydneysiders or Melbournians? They were two kids in a primary school, constantly at war. The rest – Hobart, Adelaide, Darwin and

Brisbane – spent whole lunchtimes watching. Perth not with them. Probably enrolled somewhere else.

The taxi driver turned into a wide street, in what must have been a neatly timed manoeuvre, and all thoughts of competition died. Bondi Beach, so blue and beautiful you'd want to shed your own skin just to be near it. You could cry at such a sight – the surfers, the bikinis, the sand, the water, the sky, the sea, the life. At Bondi Beach, all arguments were rendered useless. The driver took his fare without a word.

Mark asked him to return in an hour – by then he'd have some more counter-arguments, although that looked unlikely on such a street, on such a day.

Mark stood outside the house. A big house, grand. *Palatial?* Maybe. He wasn't actually sure what that meant. Mark knocked on the door. It was a pleasure to knock on such a door: black, shiny and heavy, with a gold knob. He knocked firmly and sharply, the sort of knock such a door demanded, and the door was opened by a man who you'd expect to own such a door. 'Inspector Ariti?' The tall, bald man reached out his hand. 'Eric Valer, Suzanne's other half.' The two men shook and looked into each other's eyes, weighing the upbringing, the potential, the worth of the other.

'Is Suzanne in?' Mark followed Eric Valer down a long hallway, on a long rug, with long photographs of smiling people in squalid streets on the wall. *I love what you've done with the poverty,* Mark wanted to say and didn't.

'Not yet, she said she's on her way. Got held up with that interview in *New Woman*.'

Suzanne Miller, discussing the faults of the police again. Mark wondered if anyone ever went on record to say how wonderful the force was. How helpful, how clever, how hardworking and diligent.

'She's putting a lot of focus on this crime,' Mark said.

'Would you like a beer?' Eric had opened the door to some sort of fridge in the wall, a huge glass-fronted cabinet filled with wine bottles, beer and gin.

'No, thanks,' he said. 'On the job.'

'Of course.' Eric took a beer out of the miraculous cabinet, one of those honeyed boutique things, unscrewed it, took a large swig. He gave a look of apology, nodding towards his perfumed drink. 'You don't mind, do you? Been a long morning.'

'Of course not, carry on.' Mark wondered why he said 'carry on', as if he was in some British crime show – the poor cop come to interview the rich manor house owner. What was this, *Midsomer Murders*? 'Been in this place long?' he asked. *Guv.*

Eric put down his beer. 'Two or three years. Came up to Sydney for Suzanne's work – never looked back.'

Mark braced himself. Remembered the numbers for the refurbished Adelaide Oval, the Glenelg tram.

'But you know,' the other man was saying, 'I really miss Adelaide.'

Mark thought: *Well, blow me down.*

'Miss the footy, the restaurants, the hills . . .'

'You barrack for the Crows?' Mark asked. Smug.

'Port.'

Mark thought: *You think you know a man.*

Eric sat down in an armchair with cushions, lots of them, too many, big and fluffy and covered in blue patterns. He sank into the chair and gestured for Mark to sit on the other armchair, equally loaded with useless accessories.

Now this is the life, Mark thought. *This is what I should have done. Been rich and good-looking with a TV-star wife and an impressive front door.*

'I suppose you think Suzanne is going a bit far with all this bringing up the past,' Eric was saying. 'I've told her just to let go a little.'

'It's her right, she clearly thinks that justice hasn't been properly served.'

'Well, you're right,' Eric said. 'But surely there's limits on what can be done now. The man's been dead for over thirty years.'

'Were they very close?' Mark looked over Eric's shoulder to see a large pool, complete with a waterfall. A flamingo inflatable drifted past. Sydney.

'Not overly,' Eric answered. 'I think she hardly knew him, really. But she's grown up with this idea of him plucking her and her mother from a submerged car. Saving their lives. It's a hard image to compete with. When she looked into the circumstances of his death and his injuries a little more closely, well, she felt she had to do something. Honour his memory.'

'We're not sure any crime was committed, you know. The original finding was accidental death.'

Eric gave a deep laugh. One, Mark imagined, he gave among his rich friends while they were drinking boutique beers on boats. Boats they owned; bigger boats owned by their friends. The Packers or the Murdochs, the big-boated kind.

'What an accident! Extensive burns to the respiratory tract, face and hands, *and* a broken leg. From someone who lived in the bush all his life, knew the road and his vehicle well – seems pretty strange to me.'

'I've heard stranger things.'

Eric looked at him with respect. 'No doubt you have. It's a tough job you fellows have got.' Mark shrugged. 'That's why you need all the funding you can get. State-of-the-art technology, equipment, personnel.'

'That's what you're promising?'

'That's what the Liberal–National Party are promising. Tough on crime – could do with more toughness in Adelaide, what with all of your youth gangs.'

Mark stared at some place above the door, willing himself not to laugh aloud. There was always some gang to bring up. But most crime, of course, happened not in dimly lit streets or with bottles thrown, knives brandished. Most happened indoors. Quietly and sustained without media intervention. *A crime could occur in this house*, Mark thought, looking around. White-collar crime, family violence, a body in the backyard. No number of flamingos in pools could hide the fact: crime is everywhere.

'But anyway, here she is!' Eric stood up from his chair and Mark blinked back into the present. Suzanne Miller walked into the room, a picture of loveliness with floating curly hair and a bright yellow dress. She kissed Eric before holding out her hand to Mark and he scrambled to get out of the chair to shake it.

'Have you been offered a drink?' she asked him.

Eric wandered out of the room and Suzanne sat down in the chair he vacated. Mark sank once more into his. Suzanne Miller kicked off her shoes and lifted her feet onto the chair. She looked at him.

'Here to ask a few questions,' he said.

'Fire away.'

'Tell me about your relationship with Michael Denby.'

She sighed, flicking a long curl from the side of her face.

Before she could speak, Eric walked into the room again, carrying a glass pitcher of fresh orange juice and a canister of ice. He poured them each a tall glass, using steel tongs to add ice and mint to each one. He passed a glass to Mark and then one to Suzanne, placing a kiss on the top of her head as he did so. He walked out in a haze of perfection.

Mark took a sip of his drink. It was like Bronte in a glass, he thought. No Cottee's cordial in this house. No Quik.

'The first time I saw him was when I was five years old and I was screaming underwater. Michael was just a blurry face, reaching in towards me, lifting me up. That feeling of being brought out of the water, big strong arms carrying me to safety – it was, well, it was indescribable. And then diving back in to get my mother! He didn't have to do that. The rain, the water, the branches floating past, the car swirling and sinking – he went back into *that.* There were other people lining the banks who did nothing – or nothing until we were out – but he did.'

Mark took another sip of his drink. Waited.

'Mum kept in touch with Michael after he rescued us. How could she not? But Michael, he had a tough time. And then his daughter Kylie, she kind of went off the rails a few years after he died. Got into drinking, drugs. She killed herself when she was just twenty-five.'

'What about Michael's wife, you meet her?'

'Yes, but I was so young, I can barely remember her. She was kind, I think, and really quiet – not big and funny like Michael. But that's a sad story too – she died of cancer a year or so before Michael. The two kids were only little.'

'What do you know about the other sibling?' Mark only recalled reading about Kylie.

'A boy, Troy. Younger than Kylie, around the same age as me. He lives in South Australia, Port York. We've tried to connect with him a few times. But he's so messed up – his mother, his father, his sister – I'm pretty sure he's homeless. A few months ago, I heard he was with the Salvos.'

The Denbys. A family blighted by tragedy. Cancer, drugs, suicide, homelessness. Nurture or nature?

'Know the whereabouts of that Salvos?'

'No – but there could only be one Salvos in Port York, it's not exactly a thriving metropolis.'

Mark scratched the side of his nose, scribbling the name in his address book, and looked up again. 'Why are you bringing all this up now, Suzanne?'

Suzanne answered him in a long ramble that he'd heard in television interviews and magazine articles. She was in a position of privilege, people listened to what she had to say. She had a platform! She felt a responsibility, as someone whose life was saved by this man, to bring this national hero the justice he deserved. If she had brought this up five years ago, when she was just a guest presenter, no one would have paid any attention. But now, she had the chance to publicise this case, get some justice for Michael's children, one of whom was still alive – who never got over his father's gruesome death. 'It remains a real tragedy for our nation, for my family, and for the community of a small Australian town. The police must finally take proper action. The community won't stand for shoddy police work a moment longer.' Suzanne Miller spoke as if she was reading from an autocue.

The fault of the police again. Always the fault of the police; never of the perpetrators, never of the foolhardiness of human beings, never of misadventure, never of accident. Every time Suzanne Miller had a microphone, it was the police's fault.

Mark finished his juice. Gave the ice cubes a sharp rattle against the glass. 'I'll ask it again,' he said. 'Why are you bringing all this up now?'

She looked at him for a long time. 'What are you getting at, officer?'

'Acting Inspector.'

'What are you getting at exactly, Acting Inspector?'

'Word's out that *Fun with Shapes* is not rating too well.' It was true. Her employers at the television station were facing serious financial difficulties and local content was always first to come under scrutiny. It was cheaper to buy has-been shows from overseas and regurgitate them here. Reruns of *The Big Bang Theory* and *Friends* were now more profitable than shows made in the studio. He'd read up on that last night while lying in bed after Kelly fell asleep. Amazing what could be achieved in the lonely hours between 11 pm and 2 am.

'I hardly see what ratings have to do with the unsolved murder of the man who saved my life.'

'Don't you? With your ratings falling, you need to build your profile. Get people talking about you. Some people do it with weddings in Mexico, others go on *The Bachelor*. Some people create podcasts, try to get old murders solved. Have you been asked to go on *The Project* yet? It's a good story. "Television Presenter Seeks Justice for the Man Who Saved Her Life."'

Suzanne sat, stony-faced.

'I want to help you, Suzanne, I do – but you'll help me more by being honest. How much do you really believe there was foul play in Denby's death?'

Eric walked into the room, sensed something, pulled up short. 'Everything okay here?' he asked.

Suzanne sniffed, looked out the window. Finally she spoke: 'My mother loved Michael – he saved me, he saved her. That's something you just don't forget. We had everything because of him. And all Michael had was a medal and misery and death. So *you* explain his injuries. *You* explain the lack of scrutiny.' Her voice was rising now. '*You* explain why the police covered it up!'

Eric clapped his hands together. 'Well, this was a nice visit – make sure you come again, won't you?'

Climbing out of the chair, Mark said his obligatory thanks and walked once more down the long corridor towards the front door. As he opened it, he heard Suzanne's voice, calmer now, and turned to see her at the other end of the hall – a dark figure eclipsed by the light of the alcohol cabinet.

'You're right,' she said, moving towards him like a movie star. 'My time at the station *is* coming to an end; I need to make my mark, get back in the game, stay relevant. I can get justice for Michael with this story, raise my profile *and* showcase my media abilities.'

It was a good plan, it had merit. And she was finally being honest.

'On that day he rescued us, my mother was leaving my father. It was raining, raining, raining when my mother packed our car in the morning and we left our Adelaide home. I never saw my father again.'

'What happened?'

'Just before Cutters End, there's a dry river crossing, you'd miss it if you didn't know it was there. It wasn't dry that day though – water everywhere, shallow at first, but still my mother tried to get across it. She was desperate, I think, to put as much land between us and Adelaide as possible. The four-wheel drives were okay over the road, but our little car! We got to the middle and there was this surge of water, like a low wall. I remember the car slowly turning and dipping down where the river left the road. I was screaming. And then, there at the window was Michael Denby.'

Mark tried to imagine it. The noise, the panic, the relief.

'Did you like Michael, Suzanne?'

'I suppose,' she said. 'As far as people who save your life go. He was kind of mythical in our household. We saw him a few times before he died, and I think Mum gave him money for a car at one point. We owed him our lives and we couldn't forget that. My mother had the greatest respect for him, even as she was dying she'd talk about him saving us. I can't forget that.'

'Saviours,' he said, stepping out the door into the Sydney light, 'can't live with them, literally can't live without . . .' But his words were lost as the wonderful door slammed shut, its hinges impressive in their firm resolve.

CHAPTER 11

In the taxi again, same driver, Mark gave the address, leant back in his seat and closed his eyes. Two minutes later, the driver pulled up. 'Wakey,' the man said.

Mark opened his eyes. 'I could have *walked*.'

His nemesis grinned, held out his hand.

'This wouldn't happen in Adelaide,' Mark said, handing him his card.

Once the taxi was gone, he looked down the road and then at the house in front of him. Joanne had done well, he thought. A wide street, ocean-smelling and tree-lined, ran downhill, towards the beach. Here, every new house would boast a view. Minimalist gardens, designed by landscapers who lived in other suburbs, lay flat in front of every house, colour-coordinated and climate-aware, waiting for praise. No traces of wheelie bins on this street. No agapanthus, no gnomes.

Mark knocked on the door, waited. Pressed an intercom button – saw a small camera in the porch alcove and gave a little wave. Regretted the wave. Knocked again. Firmly.

Through the frosted window he saw a dark figure walking towards him. The glass made the figure appear long and ghostly, and as he waited, he felt for the first time a deep regret that he had agreed to do this for Angelo. These interactions, already awkward after thirty years, were compounded by the fact that he had an agenda. His presence would be, at best, an annoyance for Joanne. He wasn't sure what the worst would be.

The door opened and his old Deb partner appeared. Joanne in a navy dress, taut-faced and glossy-haired, with low heels, a thin gold necklace and earrings to match. Everything about her screamed money.

'Come in, Mark.' Joanne's voice was dry. 'You've got an hour – I have to drop my daughter at cello.'

Mark walked behind her, down one of those hallways again – this time completely white and devoid of artworks save a huge mirror and a wooden hallstand on which a large vase sat, filled with pale flowers. They walked into another room and stepped towards a view so beautiful it made him catch his breath. The ocean, wide and deep blue, stretched out before him. The whole side of the room was glass, the view dominated by the ocean, and then, on the back-deck level, by a pool – or two pools, which connected to each other via a graceful waterfall and large rocks. Mark stood at the window, breathing in the scene.

Behind him, Joanne was reaching into white cupboards, pulling out glasses, filling them with ice. She was still beautiful – even more so. Her long body was as slim as it was in school, and the small muscles in her upper arms demonstrated a fitness regime that worked well and was carefully maintained.

Joanne passed him a tall glass of orange juice clinking with ice.

Orange juice clinking with ice! he thought. *Is it a Sydney thing?*

He took it, thanking her.

'How are you, Joanne?' he said.

'I'm good as can be.' There was a short pause. 'And you?' she asked.

'Good,' he said. 'It was nice to see Ingrid again.'

'I bet it was,' she said, turning her head away from him.

'Do you see her much?'

'Is this part of your investigation?' Joanne clasped both hands. 'Should I sit down?'

There was a mocking tone to her voice. 'I suppose it is,' he said.

'And how on earth would it be?' Joanne was faintly amused. 'What are you possibly hoping to learn?'

'The police are going over everything. Everyone who had a sniff of information about the deceased, anyone who was within a fifty-kilometre radius of the scene at the time of death – we're interviewing them again. This is what happens when a case reopens, it's what we do.'

'All thanks to Suzanne Miller.' Joanne took a sip of her drink.

'To a large degree, yes.'

'Well, Acting Inspector.' Joanne clasped her hands together again. 'Begin.'

'Did you stay at the roadhouse on the night of New Year's Eve, 1989?'

'Yes.' Joanne gave a tight little shudder. 'Not the best one I've ever had.'

'Why?'

'The room was one of those cheap portables, stuck in the middle of nowhere. Just a bed and a cupboard, hot and dusty. The roadhouse manager was a bit of a sleaze – I locked my door.'

'Did he do anything in particular?'

'Just the usual, asking me about boyfriends, telling me I was too pretty to be on my own and so forth.'

'You talk to him for very long?'

'Just when I checked in and checked out. I didn't see him apart from those times.'

'Anything else you can tell me about him?'

'No, not that I can recall. Just your regular type.'

Regular. The word jolted.

'Why didn't you meet up with Ingrid?'

Joanne looked at him curiously. 'Didn't she tell you this already?'

Mark blushed. He didn't quite know why. 'I have to ask you.'

Joanne wiped at the immaculate bench. The surface gleamed. 'There was a mix-up. We were meant to meet up at the roadhouse and hitchhike to Cutters End together. We planned to go to a New Year's Eve party at the Underground Hotel. But I was late, so she got a lift. By the time I arrived, she'd already left. I stayed at the roadhouse and we caught up in Cutters End the next day.'

'Did you see anything strange up there? Hear anything? Denby died sometime in the window of time you were there.'

'I know that – law enforcement told me so at least five hundred times thirty-odd years ago.'

'See or hear anything out of the ordinary?'

'Nothing, sorry.'

'You don't recall seeing this man at the roadhouse or on the road?' Mark showed Joanne the photo of Michael Denby with his two children.

Joanne looked closely at the print and shook her head again. 'Nope.'

'Someone else was staying at the roadhouse on the same night as you. Do you remember anyone?'

Joanne frowned a little, remembering. 'I did tell all this to the police the first time, you know. It's been a while but I'm sure it's written down somewhere.'

'Yes, but I still have to ask.'

She sighed and looked at her nails. 'There was someone in the portable room next to mine. A man, bit older than me. He played weird music. Skinny, a mullet. We didn't speak.'

That haircut, a style? Business at the front, party at the back. 'Not a lot of mullets around here, I'd imagine.'

Joanne gave a brief smile and answered in the amused tone he recalled from school. 'No, not a lot of those in Bronte. We're all shiny bobs and short back and sides here.'

A light padding down the hall, then a teenage girl entered the room. Tall with long brown hair and a slight build, she was the exact replica of Joanne at school.

'My daughter, Annabel,' Joanne said, looking at the girl with affection as she rounded the kitchen bench and reached for a glass. 'This is Mark,' she said. 'We were at school together.'

Annabel studied him with dark eyes. 'Were you guys, like, together or something?'

Joanne laughed. 'No, not at all. Mark was with my best friend Ingrid at the time.'

'Ingrid?' The girl looked at her mother. 'You had a best friend?'

Mark felt a stab of surprise. Joanne hadn't talked about Ingrid? He thought of how readily he talked about his school and uni days to Kelly. Perhaps not about girlfriends so much, but friends and good times and the old days, he talked about those.

Joanne gave another of her brief smiles and nodded.

'I was your mum's Deb partner,' Mark volunteered.

Annabel looked confused. 'Deb partner? What's that?'

Joanne reached out and smoothed down her daughter's perfectly straight hair. 'It's a sort of ritual that schools in the country have. It's like a ball – the girls wear white frilly dresses and the boys wear suits, and they learn old-fashioned dances.'

'Like the formal?'

'Kind of.'

Annabel shook her mane and opened the fridge. 'I'd *hate* to wear a white frilly dress.'

Joanne looked at Mark and shrugged. 'Annabel is favouring the pantsuit at the present.'

The girl emerged from the fridge, apple in hand and

suddenly furious. 'Yet you won't let me *buy one* for this Saturday night! When I *need one*!'

'You don't need one.'

'I do!' Mother and daughter stood at equal height, opposite each other. Mark took a step back. Unknown territory.

'I'm going next door to Clara's,' Annabel announced. 'At least her mum actually talks.'

'I'm talking.'

'Clara's my best friend,' Annabel said with spite, glancing at Mark.

'Okay, Annabel,' Joanne's voice was mild, 'speak politely.'

'Whatever.' Annabel walked out.

'And you've got cello soon, don't be long.'

'Yeah, yeah.'

'Say goodbye to Mark!' Joanne called.

A young voice came from way down the hallway, sweet again. 'Bye, Mark! And bye, Mum!'

'Bye, darling,' Joanne answered, to the sound of the door slamming shut. 'That's my one and only,' she said with a wry smile.

'She looks like you.'

'She *is* me.' Joanne rolled her eyes. 'I wish she wasn't, but she is.'

'You were okay.'

'I was a cow.'

Mark thought about the Joanne he remembered. It was as if there were two versions. The one before her American student exchange and then the other, when she'd returned in Year 12, tough and remote.

'It surprises me that your daughter doesn't know about Ingrid. You two were so close.'

Joanne's face tightened. 'I'm not one to dwell on the past. School years were good, but they weren't the golden age.'

He supposed they weren't. 'Not going to the reunion then?'

Joanne shrugged. 'Probably not.'

They sat in silence for a while before he stood to go. He handed her his glass and she took it without speaking.

'Why were you late to the roadhouse, Joanne? When Ingrid was waiting for you?'

Joanne gave a deep sigh. 'I picked up the night before. Isn't that how we used to say it? *Picked up?* Some Swedish guy, a backpacker, I stayed at his hostel. When I got back to our backpackers the next day, Ingrid had already left. I had a hangover, I slept a bit . . . more than I planned.'

'Do you remember the name of the Swedish guy?'

Joanne gave him a hard look. 'Am I under suspicion of something, Mark? Or are you now the morality police?'

'You're not under suspicion. We're just checking everything again. Looking for things we missed.'

'How would who I slept with assist you in any way with the investigation?'

He wasn't sure. 'We're just following up every piece of information.'

Joanne shook her head. 'I can't remember his name. It was over thirty years ago. Can you remember every person you've slept with?'

He gave her a blank look. The thing was, he could.

Ingrid, last year of school. Ursula from first year uni, Karen from second year, Maya from his holiday job at the local pool. Natasha from the UK, Yona from Israel, Sofia – the Swedish backpacker in Cairns – and Sharon from Hamilton. He wasn't sure if he could count Kath Kirby, but if you did – then Kath Kirby from Camberwell. Bianca, girlfriend for four years. Marni, girlfriend for just under five. Then Kelly, and Detective Senior Sergeant Jane Southern. He knew all of them. Spent lonely hours at night thinking about each one; the regret, the yearning.

He cleared his throat. 'I'm sorry, Joanne. That was unfair of me. We don't need to verify everything. I'm being overzealous.'

Joanne looked at the small gold watch on her wrist and flicked her eyes to a clock on the wall. It was a none-too-subtle hint.

'I'll be off then,' Mark said. 'I'll call if we have any further questions.'

CHAPTER 12

Back home, a cool dusk gathering, Mark lounged with the boys on the couch watching a rerun of *Fun with Shapes* while Kelly worked in their small office, deep in a Zoom meeting. Their youngest, Charlie, chatted about the shapes and his imaginary friend, John-from-the-flower-shop. Mark listened absentmindedly, watching Suzanne Miller on screen. The woman was talented; warm and funny. In the segment they were watching, she drew big circles and little circles in chalk on white floorboards – making a show of trying to squeeze into the smallest shapes, taking care to listen to her unseen audience when the voiceover called, 'Not that one, Suzanne!'

Kelly walked out of the study and over to Mark and the boys, placing a kiss on each of their heads. 'We're going to court!' she said. 'There's enough evidence to prosecute and we've got a neighbour as witness.' On *Fun with Shapes*, Suzanne Miller was dancing to a jangling piano tune and Kelly joined in. 'I think we're going to win,' she sang in time to the music and pulling up the boys with her, 'I think we're going to win.'

Mark stood up, did a little dance with them before heading to the kitchen. 'Want a beer to celebrate?' he called out.

'Why not?' His family was still dancing with Suzanne. This was a version of them he had not experienced for a long time.

Leaving the boys and *Fun with Shapes,* Mark and Kelly headed out to the porch where they sat under the evening sky, the cool breeze doing little to dampen their spirits.

'So, you think you're going to get the bastard?' Mark asked, passing Kelly a beer.

'Yep.' Kelly took a long swig. 'Goes to court on Monday.'

'Good work,' Mark said. 'That's great.'

'And you?' Kelly's eyes focused on him. 'How was Sydney?'

He told her briefly about the day, about Joanne and Suzanne.

'It's like old times for you, all this catching up with ex-girlfriends and friends,' Kelly said, without a hint of jealousy. 'Have you actually found anything out yet?'

'No,' Mark mused. 'I don't think so. Sometimes I think that there's not actually anything *to* find out. But the injuries on the deceased man's body, the unidentified person Ingrid got a lift with . . . The whole thing is odd.'

'So, what's next?'

'Cutters End – I'll drive up Monday morning. Be gone a few days.'

Angelo had called him on the way home from the airport. His boss talked again about Senior Constable Jagdeep Kaur at the Cutters End station, conducting the case from that end. She'd been busy, meeting with friends of the deceased, people who caught the Port York bus to Cutters End around New Year's Eve, and others close to the case. Angelo wanted Mark, in his new role, to meet with Kaur, cross-check notes, maybe talk to some people together. Standard procedure for someone joining a new investigation.

'You're going away a lot,' Kelly said, but her mood was too good to be truly cross. 'Can you organise Mum with the kids?'

Mark nodded, realising that Kelly had forgotten or not really heard his earlier suggestion about the nanny. He gave an inward shrug; it didn't matter. His wife leant over and ruffled his hair in a friendly gesture before walking back into the kitchen.

The phone rang: his mother. Mark felt the familiar pang of guilt that she was calling him and not the other way around. His mother still lived in Booralama, the country town he grew up in. The rose gardens, the long, slow, winding river and the old gum trees – the town never failed to fill him with faulty nostalgia for all things young and free.

'Hello, Markos, darling.' She greeted him with the old term and they fell into an easy way of talking. His mother told him about her tennis, the garden, visits from friends and news from Prue, his sister in Canada. It was pleasant, a meandering conversation which rarely jolted or jarred. So it had been his entire life. He told her about the boys, Kelly, and seeing Ingrid. At this, his mother exclaimed. She'd always had a soft spot for Ingrid.

'And she got married, I hear? To a handsome Dutch man?'

'I think they're separated at the moment.'

'Oh.' His mother sounded disappointed. 'I always imagined a great life for Ingrid.'

Mark wondered whether his mother had ever factored him into that great life for Ingrid. He wouldn't know, because she would never tell. She loved Kelly too.

'I saw Joanne too, in Sydney today.'

'Oh yes?' Mark heard a slight edge in his mother's voice. 'And how was she?'

'Very rich.'

'Hmmm. Well, she always was someone who knew what she wanted.'

The tone was a little snide, but he knew that that would be as unpleasant as she got. Unlike other people around the town, his mother held back her views of Joanne Morley. There were lots of names people called Joanne behind her back despite her apparent popularity: arrogant, snob, bitch. It was in part the scourge of being a clever, confident, good-looking girl in a small town.

'Of course,' his mother said in a conciliatory tone, 'we shouldn't be too harsh, after the terrible time she had in America when she was on exchange.'

Mark felt a small twist, a dark unfurling in his mind. 'Terrible time?'

'You know, when her parents had to go over there and collect her after that business with the host family. When they all went on a *little holiday*.'

'Mum,' Mark was insistent. 'I don't know anything about this.'

'Sorry, darling, it was all a bit hush-hush at the time – you know the eighties and these things. Thank goodness we're all more open now.'

'What happened?'

'I thought you knew.' His mother's voice was conspiratorial. 'Joanne had a baby.'

CHAPTER 13

Monday morning: police car leased, fuel tank full, and the next four days in front of him. South Australia, heading north, 850 km of the wide brown land: a chance to reflect, to ponder life's big questions.

He'd asked for a flight, but Angelo had reminded him he was an Acting Inspector, not the police commissioner.

By mid-morning and halfway to Port York from Adelaide, Mark saw a hitchhiker on the side of the road. He slowed down a fraction; not enough to provide hope, but enough to catch a glimpse of a long-haired, tattooed man, a dirty singlet, bare feet and no backpack. Other than the man's own mother, who would pick up such a bloke? Mark felt his shoulders slump. The lives of others. He wondered if he would pick up another sort of hitchhiker, a young girl perhaps, with a heavy backpack on a hot day. He admitted he'd consider it, if only for her own safety. As a piece of advice, he mused, 'Don't judge a book by its cover' was a hopeful, moralistic piece of crap.

Mark listened first to the weather report – no rain and the hottest October on record – then switched stations to an interview with the woman who'd discovered the bones of King Richard III in a Leicester car park. DNA could absolutely prove that the bones were Richard's, and reasonably accurate suggestions could be provided for his cause of death – but the culprit's identity? Very difficult to ascertain after all these years. Especially as he was most likely killed in battle – and there could have been many who dealt the final blows.

As Mark drove, he wondered about final blows. The landscape around him widened and flattened, and as the afternoon drew close he reached the decaying town of Port York. No harbour to speak of, not a jetty, not a pier. The town swimming pool, closed for maintenance, was the only visible body of water. Mark moved slowly through tired streets littered with plastic bags. He'd never seen this part of his state. Fifty years as a proud South Australian and he'd never ventured north of Peterborough. Queensland, overseas, the Murray, but never here. It was forgotten. Like the aunt with failing health who sends cards to family but is never invited to Christmas, this area had a forsaken feel.

With the help of an old *Lonely Planet*, he passed the site of the backpackers, Yorkies, where Joanne and Ingrid had stayed the night before they left for Cutters End. It was long gone, now a sad shopping centre, with overturned trolleys and fast food wrappers lining the car park. Mark stopped the car, got out and stretched. The heat smacked him in the face, and he took one or two steps backwards. *Jesus!* he thought. A woman walked by – twenty or fifty, impossible to tell. She was a human sultana, lined and brown with arms like twigs.

He checked his phone, noted that the pub he wanted to find was only a kilometre away. He could easily walk it, could do with a walk, but instead he got back in his car and drove. *Stick that,* he thought, *I'll age a hundred years if I stay out here any longer than five minutes.*

The pub where Ingrid and Joanne met their Swedish friends on 30 December 1989 was still going strong. Mark walked in, ordered a lemon squash. Inside, the lights from the poker machines gave off a ghostly glow and their dull bleeps and pings made his head ache. A few men stood at the bar, but most were glued to the machines, transfixed and stupid. A tax on the poor, his mother called pokies, and he had to agree. But the lemon squash was cold and there was ice – small mercies.

He wandered to the other section of the pub, where a small stage signalled cover bands and Cold Chisel impersonators. He read faded posters listing past gigs: 'Trouser Snake', 'The Fat Chick from Wilson Phillips' and 'Dead Men Can't Sue'. There was also an ABBA revival band, an Elvis impersonator and Frankie J. Holden still to come. Good times in Port York, good times.

The dusty courtyard hosted a tired-looking bar, now closed. The air was still, devoid of any kind of life. He wandered again indoors, asked the barman about backpackers. The man surprised him by answering in a strong Yorkshire accent.

'I wish, mate, I wish. Only people come in here is your gamblers and your ex-gamblers seeing if they can hold off.'

'And can they?'

'They cannot.'

The young barman told Mark he was here on a working holiday with his new girlfriend, only she had left to go north and hadn't called or messaged him in two days.

'She had more money than me, so she said she was going to start travelling earlier. But I think she's left me for a Scot,' the barman said, eyeing a sodden beer coaster in sorrow.

'It doesn't worry you that you haven't heard from her?' Mark asked.

'Should it? I mean, she's an adult, she can do what she likes. I don't want to seem needy or possessive or anything . . .'

His hangdog eyes made Mark want to give him a pat. This was the part of youth he conveniently left out in his occasional longing for the Golden Age. The heartache, the uncertainty, the lack of funds.

'Maybe you should call her,' Mark suggested. 'Or just text to see if she's okay.'

The man took out his phone and looked at it. 'You think so?'

Mark stretched and prepared himself to face the outdoors again. He still had a long way to go to Cutters End – five hours at least. 'Give it a go, mate, what harm can it do?'

He left the barman still staring at his phone, walked past the zombies on the pokies and opened the door to a blaze of light and heat. It felt less like an escape and more of an apocalypse, but still, he was glad to be out of the pub.

A strange sound hit him as he neared his car; a howl, disturbing and out of place in the bright light of day. It was coming from the vehicle parked next to his. Mark approached and looked inside. There, head on the wheel, was a man, bawling. At first Mark thought he must be mistaken, but the hacking sobs, muffled yet distinct, could not be denied. Mark bent down, tapped on the window. No answer. The man was wailing; grizzled cries of someone whose life was not as he'd hoped or foreseen. Mark tapped again, louder, planted his badge on the windscreen. 'Hey!' He banged on the driver's side. 'You okay in there, mate?'

There was silence. A shocked pause. The man wound down his window.

'You okay?' Mark asked again.

'Yes?' A heavy accent. The man didn't look as if he'd been crying. In fact, he seemed annoyed.

'You okay, mate?' Mark asked for the third time. 'Thought I heard crying.'

The man held up an iPad and pushed the mute button. 'Got a movie on.'

Mark heard a car chase, loud music and the screech of tyres. An action movie in another language. All on the little screen. 'Someone just die in it, did they?' he asked. 'Bit noisy. Passers-by can hear you, might get a shock.'

'I turn it down.' The man's window wound up and he resumed his position of head on the wheel.

Turning to his own car, Mark now recognised the noises for what they were. The thought that they were anything else seemed unlikely and foolish. He tried to shake the thought of a man wailing. Couldn't.

Air conditioner on at full blast, Mark checked his phone for the whereabouts of the Port York Salvation Army depot. He still had time before the long drive up the Stuart.

First, he called Angelo and left a message relating where he was and what he was up to. 'Nice spot, this,' Mark commented, as he drove slowly through an intersection hugged by two-dollar shops and a sunken phone repair joint. A police car sped past, ambulance following suit. 'You can really get a sense of the spirit of the place. Angelo, mate, you might have to come here for a holiday, bring the kids. It's like Byron Bay, only in the outback and with no Hemsworths.'

Mark pulled up in front of the Salvation Army headquarters in a dirty, squalid street. Skips heaved with black plastic bags filled with clothes and a skinny dog pissed on the footpath.

He knocked on the door of the red-brick building and it was answered by a man around the same age as himself. Mark introduced himself, and the man smiled as they shook hands and grimaced at the dog, now taking its activity to the next level.

'I'm Chris,' the man said, standing with the door back so Mark could enter.

Inside, things were more orderly. Bags of clothes were piled up on long trestle tables and being sorted by volunteers, mostly older women. Assorted pieces of furniture lined the room and Mark followed as Chris dodged them, making his way to a small office. They sat on hardback chairs while Chris busied himself filling a plastic kettle to make them both a cup of tea. The squashed office appeared bigger for the fact that it was surrounded by glass, and Mark found himself turning in his seat to see the eyes of the volunteers on him. Some friendly, others bored.

'Big operation you got here,' he said.

'Can say that again.' Chris handed him a cup, the tea bag still immersed. 'This is the biggest depot outside of Adelaide and we can't keep up with demand.'

Mark gestured to the bags on the trestle table. 'You've got a lot of stuff to sort out – good that so many people are donating.'

Chris shrugged. 'It's great that people are well meaning, but to be honest, most of it gets thrown out. We've got too much to handle and no matter how valuable a person's moccasins might have seemed to them, there's not a great market for second-hand ones.'

Mark thought briefly of his own donations to St Vincent de Paul. Would anyone truly love his Port Adelaide football jumpers as much as he did? And the oversized Rivers top with a small hole in the shoulder? Perhaps not, but he'd felt so noble folding them into the Vinnies bag.

'Do you know a Troy Denby? Originally from Cutters End, now here in Port York. He apparently hangs out in the Salvos a bit.'

Chris gave him a steady look. 'He's not in any trouble, is he? You're not here to take him in?'

'No, no – I just want to have a word. You can be present if you like.'

'Is this about the possession charge last year? Because he is trying to get clean. He may have had the odd relapse, but we feel he is getting better.'

'No, nothing like that. This is in regards to a reinvestigation. I'm just after some information.'

Chris measured him up. Gave a nod. 'Good, well, I'll see if he's okay with it.' He stood and opened the door. 'Troy!' he called. 'Someone here to see you.'

Mark looked through the windows. A skinny man in his sixties raised his head from the workstation and squinted, running his hands over his scalp. The man said something to the woman beside him, then edged around the table and walked towards the office.

'That can't be the Troy Denby I'm after,' Mark said. 'The person I'm looking for is around the same age as Suzanne Miller and she wouldn't be much over forty.'

Chris turned his head so that the man walking towards them wouldn't guess at what he was saying. 'That's Troy Denby all right, son of the hero.' He gave an encouraging smile to the man at the door. 'And he's forty-one.'

Mark had to stop himself from exclaiming. Troy entered and the men nodded at each other while Chris made the introductions. Mark explained that he was there to ask a few questions about his father, about the reopened investigation, but all the time he was noting the wrinkles on the other man's face, ancient watercourses running down his neck and into his dirty t-shirt. Scabs in varying stages of ooze littered his arms and he picked at them as he waited.

'We wanted to ask if there was anything else you could tell us, Troy. The last time you were interviewed, you would have only been a child. You and your sister went to live with a family friend, didn't you, after your father died?'

'Ten years old.' Troy sniffed. 'Ten years old and my father murdered.'

'Well, we haven't ascertained that yet, mate. The original file indicates that—'

Troy bit his bottom lip and scratched at his arm. 'An accident! What a load of bullshit that is, accident! If you had known my father – never a man more good with vehicles. And the best dad a boy could have.'

Chris patted Troy's arm. 'The detective isn't here to question how your father parented. He just has to ask about your dad to find out if there's any additional information they may have missed the last time. You're happy they're reopening the file, aren't you?'

Troy's eyes spun around the office, landing on Mark. 'My father was the best dad. He was a good man, a hero! Something happened to him. No way a motor blew up in his face. No way. He was a good father!'

'Nobody's doubting that, Troy.'

'He made me a treehouse in the backyard,' Troy said sadly. 'Right up high in the tree. It had a little window and a ledge to sit on. Right up high it was, like – high! My dad built me that. Bought me a dog for my birthday too. Name was Rexy.' There was a childlike petulance to the man, which made Mark squirm.

Chris smiled. 'What sort of dog was he, Troy?'

'Little terrier. Rexy. Loved me and hated my sister.' Troy grinned and Mark was reminded of old days in the school yard, boys versus girls, *girls are weak, chuck 'em in the creek*, that sort of palaver which, as far as he knew, had died out.

'Did you and your sister ever talk about your dad, Troy?'

'Kylie's dead. She topped herself. Pills.'

'Did you see her much after she moved out?'

'Nah. Kylie was a bitch. Never came to visit me once after she came here to Port York, then Adelaide. Good riddance, I say.' Troy leant into him, a forced whisper through his blackened teeth. 'Heard she was on the game. Slut.'

'Now, Troy . . .' Chris's voice was stern.

'What about your mother, Troy?' Mark asked. 'You must miss her a lot.'

Troy's face turned away. 'Died when I was eight. Two years before Dad.'

'Were you close with her too, Troy?'

'More a dad's boy.' Troy scowled. 'But yeah, she was okay. Sick a lot.'

Mark recalled that Lynette Denby had died of cancer in 1988.

'And have you spoken with Suzanne Miller lately at all?' Mark asked.

Troy's hands fluttered about his lap. He rested one on the table and put the other over it to stop it moving. 'Once or twice,' he said. 'She's another one doesn't give a shit. Just wants the story, cameras and that.'

'You have to give people a chance, Troy,' Chris said.

The man was suddenly standing, arms in the air. 'Give people a chance! What the fuck is this? Who is giving who a chance?' He spun around, looking confused. Mark wondered if he even knew where he was.

'Fuck this – I'm out of here.' Troy flung open the office door, leaving the small room shaking. Out of the windows, Mark could see the volunteers look up from their posts with mild interest before going back to the sorting of middle-class detritus. All in a day's work.

Chris was righting a picture frame; a familiar image, the one of footprints in the sand.

'That happen often?' Mark asked Chris.

'Not as much. He's doing a lot better. Got a place to sleep at the moment, although he may be kicked out next month. We're trying to figure something out.'

'You know Suzanne Miller? She could afford to buy him a house anywhere he wanted.'

Chris looked at all the volunteers and workers at the trestle tables, manning the furniture. 'You'd be surprised how many people here come from really wealthy families or know benefactors in high places. We've had friends of the Packers, children of prime ministers in here asking for help.'

'Yeah?' Mark waited. Chris didn't elaborate.

'Fact is, we've got too many people to try to help, too many donated goods and not enough to assist in sorting out either.'

Mark thanked him and the two of them walked to his car. 'If Troy wants to talk further, here's my card.'

Chris took it, shaking Mark's hand. 'Troy is a troubled man. Ice addict, although he's trying.'

'He's had a sad life.'

'That he has.'

Mark could see that Chris was one of those rare breeds, a truly good man. 'You do important work here,' he said, nodding to the Salvos building. 'Thanks for that.'

'And thanks for the work that you do too. We have a good force in this country.'

Now this is a man I could have a nice lemonade with, Mark thought. He gave Chris a wave.

Chris raised his hand in a similar gesture. 'God bless,' he said.

It had been a while since anyone had blessed Mark. 'You too,' he said.

After filling up with petrol, Mark was on the road again. The landscape gathered around, swallowed up everything, became immense. On he drove towards Cutters End, listening to podcasts, singing along to familiar tunes and watching the world pass by. He thought about Kelly, wondered if she would like this place, wondered at all the places they'd never been together. When was the last time they'd been on holidays – Noosa two years ago? It felt like decades.

In just under three hours, Mark reached the Mendamo Roadhouse where Ingrid and Joanne had both stopped on their way to Cutters End. The former workplace of Gerald Cuxton, better known as 'old creep'. He parked, braced himself, and went inside.

CHAPTER 14

Beneath the painting of *Penelope and Her Suitors*, Ingrid sifted through papers. Maybe, she thought, maybe she was on the wrong track. On the wrong track and at the wrong time. She took a sip of white wine and contemplated the notes laid out before her. Compiled over months, over years in fact, they presented a dilemma – to act or not. *Head down, kick*, she remembered her old swimming coach yelling, urging her to speed up, to act. But she wasn't quite there yet.

On the small television in the corner of the room, a car chase was taking place. A hero-slash-villain in the leading car, scores of cop cars in pursuit. She flicked it off. Easy to predict what was going to happen: the cops would lose track of the hero-villain, upending cars and making themselves ridiculous in the process.

She looked at the papers once more and picked up a photo – studied it close. The problem was backing herself; if she was going to do this then she needed confidence. She took a gulp of wine – two gulps of wine – and surveyed her little room; the sunken couch perfect for reading, the cushions, the piles of books and magazines. It looked as if she was setting herself up here to stay, a single woman. Her gaze settled on the print of the white tulip, Sander's gift to her when she left Friesland after his mother's funeral. According to Google, the white tulip represented two things: love and forgiveness. Which one Sander meant when he gave it to her, she was unsure.

She returned to her papers, indecisive. Since Mark's visit, and perhaps just before, she sensed that her life was becoming unstuck. Her hand rested on the photograph from the old newspaper clipping. Nothing seemed definite and the resolve she'd enjoyed for a number of years was slipping.

She thought back to how she was at eighteen. After the trip with Joanne, she became flotsam in the wake of pub nights and beaches and outback towns where girls in missing persons posters all bore a resemblance to her. Joanne had flown home straight after Darwin, but Ingrid had drifted, drifted. Some time spent in Indonesia, making her way through the islands from Timor to Java, stopping in Bali to join the drinking games through Kuta. Her parents in Booralama remained hopeful she would begin uni at the start of the year, mid-year, the end of the year – any year! Instead: hospitality jobs, courses in a Cairns TAFE, and a year in Japan teaching English. And the boyfriends she had were nice enough, but when they left she felt nothing, and when she left, she felt only relief. And while she spent whole nights dancing to the Breeders and Ace of Base and

Primal Scream, there was Ivan Milat and Karmein Chan and Snowtown. They never ceased, the stories of violence and gruesome ends.

Ingrid cricked her neck, did a mountain pose. She was tired, but band practice called. Despite her early hesitation, she enjoyed it – the quick drive to Warnbeen, meeting the other women at Libby's house and then the rehearsals in her garage. Fun and loud. They were getting quite good. Each of them – she, Libby and Noelene – confessed to being terrified at the thought of performing, but Ingrid was firm. The goal of playing at the old Warnbeen theatre was agreed, date looming. Practice required.

Ingrid located her keys in the mess that was her kitchen bench and headed outside, hugging her puffer jacket close. It would be months yet before the far south-east coast really warmed up – but still, Ingrid loved the cold. While she had a fondness for her formative years spent in Booralama, for the wide rivers and hot, sleepy days, this part of the state was where she wanted to stay – she was sure of it. She and Sander had been happy here, mostly.

Ingrid got in her old Corolla and pulled out of the driveway. Yes, she thought – she was content here. She liked the townspeople, the classes she ran, the band. So why muddy the waters? Her mind turned to the photos she was looking at earlier and then felt a jolt when she remembered Mark's text, telling her to stop talking about the case to other people. He was referring, of course, to the Denby case. But it would only take a matter of time before he cottoned on. If she was going to act, it should be soon. She recalled the photograph: fading light, big hair and grins. Youth and hope and adventure. Then she thought of her band members, the two women she'd grown to love. *Head down, kick!*

Ingrid drove past green and brown paddocks, cows raising their heads to glance up, their big brown eyes slow and kind. Small farmhouses dotted the road, and as she turned into Warnbeen – her favourite sign announcing the town: *Warnbeen – you been? You'll come again!* – the rain started up once more, driving westward, towards the coast. No wonder the Irish flocked to this area in droves after the potato famine. It must have felt like home without the hunger.

She pulled into Libby's drive and saw the two women lugging a speaker towards the garage. Libby, ever the teacher, was shouting instructions while skinny Noelene, sadness etched permanently across her face, grimaced with the weight of the equipment.

Ingrid parked the car and hurried to help, Libby's words booming through the rain.

'Noelene, move your big bum this way, and Ingrid, bloody get here – can't you see we're dying?'

CHAPTER 15

Inside the roadhouse, it did not feel creepy. The place was light and clean and there were no magazines with nude women on the cover to greet him at the counter. Ita Buttrose smiled winningly from a *New Idea*. The woman behind the counter wore a crisp blue shirt with the words 'Providing customer service since 1932' on it, its firm statement a testament to the way she clicked at the till and handed out change.

Mark showed his ID and she nodded.

'You had any coppers come to ask you questions yet?' he asked.

The woman shook her head. 'None come here yet, but a woman with a funny name rang. Copper from Cutters.'

Senior Constable Jagdeep Kaur.

The woman continued, 'She wanted to know about the old owner, Gerald Cuxton. I sent her over his finances last week, the ones from the shop when we took over.'

'How long ago was that?'

'Be just over ten years now. Gone fast.'

Mark couldn't see how a decade would go fast in such a place. On his way into the roadhouse, he'd seen an actual tumbleweed pass by.

'You know why the coppers are asking questions?'

'Yeah, the dead bloke up the road. Long time ago.'

'They've reopened the case.'

Mark bought a Mars bar, seeing himself in the overhead TV when he paid. He sucked his gut in and counted the cameras in the store: two, plus two outside near the bowsers.

'You still got accommodation here?'

'No. We tore down the old portables, they were run down as. Sometimes people ask if they can stay here with their caravans, but we only say yes if there's a problem with their cars or something.' The woman launched into an explanation of how tourism had changed. People now booked their accommodation in advance; they knew exactly what their travel plans were and how they were going to get there. The only people stopping at the petrol station were those filling up and the tourists on buses taking a break. Hence the quality cameras. 'Get a lot of shoplifting, unfortunately.'

'Yeah?'

'Backpackers, mainly. Not good.'

He asked her if she'd met Cuxton, the last person to see Denby alive, but she said no. She and her husband had bought the place through an agent ten years ago and spent a fortune fixing it up, cleaning, clearing away the portables and bringing it, she said, into at least the twentieth century.

Her husband now worked in a mine nearby, coming back every Thursday night till Sunday to help in the shop. It was tough, but in a few years they hoped to have enough money to be able to sell at a profit and move to the Gold Coast.

Mark looked at the woman more closely. For all her professionalism, she was very eager to chat. He wondered what it would be like for her out here, all alone for most of the time.

'It is quiet, isn't it,' she said and, startled, Mark wondered for a moment if he'd spoken aloud. Together they looked out the sliding doors to the land beyond the petrol bowsers. Thousands of kilometres in every direction of a vast and uncompromising land.

'Once,' she said, 'I found a woman's shoe out there, in the scrub. Just one shoe.'

He felt a dark fluttering deep in his chest. 'A shoe?' he said. 'Strange.'

'A blue high heel,' she answered. 'I looked and looked for its pair. Damn near drove me mad when we first arrived – I searched for that thing for days. Found nothing.'

'Maybe it fell out of someone's bag,' he said. 'An animal could have carried it into the scrub.'

'Maybe.' She stared at him with a cool gaze. 'Maybe that's it.'

The sound of a vehicle turning into the station made them both jump. Outside, a Winnebago pulled up and one by one a family got out, the father last – short shorts and legs like mottled salamis. 'Howdy!' he boomed. 'After some gas and refreshments.'

'Americans,' the woman whispered to Mark out the side of her mouth. 'Loud, but they spend. Not like the bloody Brits.'

Mark raised a hand in farewell to her and stepped out of the shop. Dodging small American children, he made his way to his car and got in. Before he turned out onto the highway, he glanced back to see the woman looking at him through the glass, her inscrutable gaze leaving him unsettled and ill at ease.

CHAPTER 16

Finally, Cutters End. The Stuart Highway a blade cutting through the centre of town, railway line alongside it like a rival sibling. Two main streets, a petrol station, the town hall, council offices, a supermarket, dingy motel, a primary school and, in the back streets, houses with sad facades and secret interiors.

The opal mining boom was bust, had been for decades, and although the welcome sign read 'Cutters End, a town on the move!' Mark doubted it. This town, like many across the country, had the look of a dying dog waiting to be shot. But still, he knew all too well that dogs don't die easy – those pleading eyes, that sense of loyalty and long history. The faded pride of what they once were.

Night came fast. Mark booked into the Railway Comfort Inn, and set his bag onto a sagging bed that looked as if it had seen some serious action from heavy couples. Sheets a dull grey and a bedspread that reminded him of his sons' vomit after they ate too much cake. But who was he to judge? He rested his head on the pillow, felt his neck muscles jar with the hardness, and wondered if the Acting Inspector gig was worth it after all. He mouthed the words aloud – 'Acting Inspector.' Found he liked them still.

Mark's stomach rumbled. He had a shower and changed. There were three pubs to choose from for dinner and he balanced on his heels, wondering which one to pick. The Opal Inn, the Desert Dawn or the United. The Desert Dawn was just across the road, but he chose the latter, thinking it had more of a collegial feel.

It did not. As he watched a couple scream at each other near the jukebox, Mark yearned for the Opal Inn and the Desert Dawn. There, surely, were more convivial crowds. Still, the beer was cold and the chips were chips. He finished, left the bar and went back to his cheap motel room, where he fell asleep almost instantly.

The next morning, after a continental breakfast of warm milk and stale cornflakes, Mark fronted up to the Cutters End Police Station, the Australian and state flags hanging limp and faded in the morning heat.

Senior Constable Kaur was waiting for him, notebook in hand, when he arrived. They shook, engaged in the obligatory small talk.

'Jagdeep.'

'Mark.'

'Trip up okay?'

'It was fine,' Mark said.

'Hot enough for you?'

'Too right it is.'

'Been a hot month, usually a bit cooler.'

'Yeah.'

'Right, to work,' his new colleague said.

Mark managed to keep a straight face. Angelo did say she was highly competent.

'I've contacted all the people connected to Michael Denby in this town,' she said. 'His neighbours, former workmates, cousins, second cousins and third cousins.'

'Got something against fourth cousins?' Mark asked.

Jagdeep ignored him, continued without a pause. 'No obvious enemies. No one has anything bad to say about the man. He was by all accounts a typical bloke.'

'That's unhelpful.'

'What it *doesn't* mean, however, is that he was an angel. I don't put the bar very high for typical blokes around here.'

'You watch your tongue, young Jagdeep!' A male voice came booming around the corner.

'Piss off, Darryl,' Jagdeep called back to the unseen man, before turning again to Mark. 'That's Sergeant Darryl Wickman,' she said, indicating to the voice with a thumb. 'A pain in the arse, but all right I suppose.'

'I can hear you!' the voice boomed again.

'Aw, go and have a lie down, mate, you're about due your nanna nap!' Jagdeep hollered in response.

Mark looked at his watch. 'So, what sort of things did they like to say about him?'

Jagdeep read from her notebook. '"Good bloke", "likes his footy", "Port supporter", "liked a drink", "could fix any vehicle you like", and "liked dogs".' Jagdeep glanced up at him. Mark waited.

'See what I mean?' Jagdeep said.

Mark shifted on his feet. 'I'm not sure.'

Jagdeep stabbed at her notebook with a painted nail. 'This stuff could be written about anyone! It could be Darryl, for Chrissake!'

'Oi!' The invisible Darryl again from offstage. 'Leave me out of it!'

Mark nodded slowly as Jagdeep continued, barely taking a breath. 'I did a Skype interview with Denby's former neighbour, man by the name of Roger now living in the Philippines. Roger had very nice things to say about his old neighbour. Mentioned Lynette, Denby's wife, a number of times – said she made a great trifle and was always happy to help out at the golf club. Only had good things to say about the whole Denby clan, in fact. When I pressed him on Michael – personality, character, et cetera – he couldn't say a thing of substance. Not one! I also spoke to the best man at Michael's wedding, they'd grown up together in Cutters End. Same thing. "Good bloke" goes only so far after a while. I pushed. Asked him how much they actually caught up, like went for dinner, had some quality time. Know what his answer was?' Jagdeep looked at him, indicating with her hands that he should answer. She gave him a moment; he shrugged. She continued: 'Once every couple of years! And these people all claim to be best friends!'

Mark thought that perhaps Jagdeep was being a bit harsh. It wasn't every family or old friends who kept in touch. In his own case, his older sister lived in Canada – he hadn't seen her in years.

'Still,' Jagdeep conceded, 'they all said with some resolve that they thought Michael was a good father. That's something, I guess.'

It was what most people said at funerals in the eulogy. 'He was a good father. She was a good mother.' It was what was said in news reports after car accidents and natural disasters. Everyone who dies in car accidents or natural disasters isn't necessarily parent of the year, but they seem to become so after death.

'But everyone says that, don't they?' Jagdeep closed her notebook and looked up at him.

'They do.'

'He was a hero of sorts too.' Jagdeep waved at an old newspaper cutting on her desk. 'Rescued Suzanne Miller and her mum from their car during a flood around here in the mid-eighties.'

'Yeah, valiant of him,' Mark said.

'Yep. Makes it a little harder for people to say anything bad about him too.'

Still, it *was* brave. Takes a certain type. Mark thought for a moment what it would be like, during pissing rain, to see a car weaving about in floodwaters and a screaming woman inside. How many people would be like Michael Denby and wade, then swim, through the waters, smash a window and pull a child out first, then the mother, before dragging them to safety?

Darryl's voice boomed again through the walls. 'There's a plaque for him on the council wall. Mayor gave a talk on it one time.'

Jagdeep wasn't listening. Moving on already from the hero debate, she tapped her pen on the desk. 'No doubt you know that Denby was cremated, so no chance of further examination there.'

'And the autopsy was done by an old bloke, a Doctor Hirsch from Port York, now deceased.' Mark had read the reports, wanted to let Jagdeep know.

'Original verdict: accidental death. Easy enough to see why.'

It was. The burns, the motor, the cigarette butts, Cuxton's mention of engine troubles.

'But the broken leg,' Mark said. The image of Denby, dead, came to him. His burnt upper body, the left leg distorted. 'What are your thoughts?'

'Vehicle could have been running; after the motor blows up on him, it jolts over his leg – he's burning, he pulls himself out from under the wheel. Broken leg. Burnt, dies.'

'Could be,' Mark said. He'd run over possible scenarios a dozen times himself. 'Or, he's burnt from the motor, goes to get in the vehicle and drive off, pain becomes too strong, staggers out, vehicle runs him over. Vehicle stalls.'

'Interesting.' Jagdeep and Mark stood, contemplating.

'Another thing,' Jagdeep said. 'Why was Denby four or five k's off the road when it happened? Why not pull over on the side of the road, check out the engine there?'

Mark blinked. He hadn't even thought of that. 'Witness reports too,' he said. 'Not complete.'

'Saw that,' Jagdeep added. 'That woman you know, Ingrid Mathers, and who she got a lift with.'

Jagdeep *was* competent.

'All circumstantial,' Mark said.

'True.'

But questions to be answered.

Mark's phone rang; it was Kelly. He indicated to Jagdeep that he needed to take it and she nodded, walking into another room.

'Hello?'

'Mark, what's your password?'

'Nice way to greet your better half.'

'Sorry, but I need to know when Charlie's kindy excursion to the zoo is. It was sent to you and not me.'

Six months ago, fed up with being the one who dealt with all things children, Kelly gave the kindergarten and school Mark's email address, telling them to contact him and not her. Her idea was, she dealt with the sports and music lessons, so he could deal with education. Now she regularly had to hack into his account to find information for the boys. Only trouble was, he had to change his work password every four weeks, so it was difficult to remember.

'Is it Maxie92?' Their old dog.

'Nope, tried that.'

'Mark1971.' His year of birth.

'Nope.'

He remembered. 'GivenToFly.' Surely the greatest of all Pearl Jam songs.

'Thanks. Wait a sec . . . it works. How's your new colleague?'

'Good. I like her.'

'When you home again?'

'Thursday hopefully, maybe Friday. Give the boys a kiss for me.' He remembered her big trial. 'Hey, how'd it go with the case?'

'Still going. But well, I think. Still got a few more days in court.'

They said their goodbyes and hung up. Jagdeep walked out towards him again, keys in hand.

'Let's go, we've got an appointment to meet with John Baber.'

His mind clicked into gear. 'The man who found the victim?'

'Correct.'

So out of the police station they walked, and into the blinding heat of Cutters End.

CHAPTER 17

On the way to meet John Baber, Mark filled Jagdeep in on his meetings so far. Ingrid, Joanne, Suzanne and Troy. He told her, too, about his drink at the backpackers in Port York where Joanne and Ingrid had partied, and his meeting with the new manager of the roadhouse once owned by Gerald Cuxton.

Jagdeep nodded. She'd been looking into Cuxton and the roadhouse; Denby had been a regular customer. The road-house had undergone a number of changes since Denby's death – she was interested to know if Cuxton had installed cameras at any point. Interested, too, in any other witnesses they hadn't considered. She still had a few things to check out. 'How'd you find the couple who bought it?' she asked.

'It was just the woman, husband off at the mines. She seemed a bit . . . isolated.'

'Must be difficult living out there, all alone for most of the time.' Jagdeep drove fast over the rocky road.

'You're telling me. I'd go mad.'

He contemplated telling her about the blue shoe, hesitated, then jumped in with a kind of laugh and said it. 'She told me she found a blue shoe out in the scrub.'

Jagdeep was silent for a moment. 'You ask her when?'

'She said it was when she first arrived.'

Jagdeep stared out in front of her, eyes on the dusty road as they turned sharply down a driveway. 'You should report that.'

She might be joking. Report a shoe? He thought about all the tattered clothes he found lying around Adelaide. The shoes, the socks, the hats, once a suit. 'Yeah right,' he said. 'I'll write a report, file it, get someone onto it asap. I'll call it "Operation No Shoe Left Unturned."'

Jagdeep changed gears and braked. Mark lurched forward in his seat and turned to see her sitting with one arm on the side window looking at the landscape, dirt scattered with shrubs and stunted trees. A small house lay nestled at the end of a long driveway; they were parked at the top of it.

No streetlights near John Baber's house. No sealed roads, no shops, no neighbours.

'Since I've been here, I've heard things,' she said.

Mark waited.

'Women going missing. Clothing, objects turning up in odd places.'

'Okay.'

'People in small towns, they talk. It's probably just hearsay.'

Mark was silent.

'Still'—Jagdeep touched her turban, felt around to the back of it, tightening it, fastening—'I don't appreciate you playing the sarcastic senior metro-cop. I've been working on this case bloody hard. I might actually know a thing or two, you know.'

'Yes,' Mark said, chastened. 'I'm sorry.'

'Now,' she said, businesslike again. 'This questioning we're doing of Baber, you know the drill – keep it open-ended, non-judgemental.'

'I get it. This meeting with Baber is informal, get a more personal view of the case, see if anything comes of it.' Mark felt like saying he'd been a cop for longer than she had. Refrained.

They got out of the car and began walking down the driveway when the sound of a vehicle and a cloud of dust made them step off the road. A four-wheel drive slowed and a window was lowered. A man looked out at them, hat over his eyes. 'Sorry about the dust,' he said. 'I needed some milk, so thought I'd get some before you came.' He pointed to the house. 'Go right ahead, I'll park and meet you there.'

Mark looked at his watch: 9.30 am on the dot. Punctual.

Once parked, John Baber walked up to them, his tall stooped frame cutting a neat figure in jeans and a checked shirt. He held out a hand and shook with both of them, Jagdeep making the introductions.

'Come in,' John said. 'Let's get out of the heat.'

'Nice spot,' said Mark, by way of conversation.

John nodded. 'There's some lovely walks around here – little paths through the scrub and up over Ticklington Hill where there's a terrific view over the surrounds. Most of the paths are signposted. You should aim to go on one while you're here; the poached egg daisies are wonderful after a rain. Don't make the mistake of missing what's best about this area.' John continued talking about how the landscape changed after a flood, how it transformed and burst with colour. He opened the front door and stood aside, gesturing for them to enter.

Mark wondered about the scenic paths and poached egg daisies. Apart from half-dead shrubs and trees stark against the skyline, he'd seen nothing of colour. And certainly no hill. You could set a spirit level anywhere on the ground here and it would be dead straight. Perhaps the beauty of the place was a hidden gem, he thought, but he seriously doubted it.

Inside, the house was small, dark and neat. John led them through a hallway and into a lounge room where he left them to go and make cups of tea.

Mark and Jagdeep eyed the room. Curtains over the windows hid what Mark saw was a tidy garden when he pulled one aside to look out. A bookcase lined one wall and he stepped towards it to read some of the titles: Cormac McCarthy's *Blood Meridian*, *The Complete Tales and Poems of Edgar Allan Poe*, and Margaret Atwood's *Cat's Eye*. An old-looking set of Charles Dickens novels and a battered copy of *Frankenstein*. On a small coffee table was a photograph of a younger John Baber on his wedding day, arms around a laughing woman in white. In the background a group of bridesmaids stood smiling in puffy dresses, holding glasses of wine aloft.

'Does Baber live with his wife?' Mark asked Jagdeep, who was seated on the couch.

'Gillian died in March 1989.' Baber was back in the room, carrying a tray with three cups of black tea, a small jug of milk and some sugar. 'Car accident down in Adelaide.'

Mark offered apologies.

'You didn't know,' John said. 'Anyway, I like talking about her.' He nodded to the photograph Mark had been looking at. 'She was one in a million.'

'I've heard that,' Jagdeep said. 'Heard how well liked she was, how kind to people.'

For a moment all three turned to study the photo of Gillian in her wedding dress. She *did* look one in a million: that big laugh, hair getting caught in the wind. It made Mark think about his own wedding day – a freak storm, Kelly and her bridesmaids drenched, make-up sliding down their faces like clowns.

Mark waved at the bookcase. 'Was it you or Gillian into the literature?' he said. 'Some good books here.' He hadn't read one of them.

John rested the tray on the table. 'Gillian was the real reader,' he said. 'Although I studied and taught it a bit in the early days, I was never into literature as much as her. I have my dedicated favourites, but it's mainly non-fiction I read now. Gillian read everything.'

'So, you were a teacher – here, in Cutters End?'

'Yes, but I finished up in '89. After Gillian died, I had some time off and then took up driving full time.'

Mark nodded. It would be difficult to front up to a class full of students and put on a face day after day when all you wanted was to grieve.

'Still doing the driving?' he asked.

'Old bloke like me, retirement's a death knell. I'll keep working for as long as I can.'

Jagdeep watched as John began pouring the tea. 'So, John, you know why Acting Inspector Mark Ariti is here. The Michael Denby case has reopened and we have to ask a few questions.'

'Yes, I heard that you were looking into it again.'

'You'll probably have seen Suzanne Miller talk about it on TV, not to mention all the gossip going round town about the reinvestigation. But the fact is, we need to ask you to tell us again how you came to find the body and what exactly you saw. Just in case you mention something we haven't considered.'

'That sounds reasonable.'

'We won't tape this discussion, as it's just a chat for now – but I might take notes while my colleague here asks a few questions, is that okay?' Jagdeep held up a notepad and pen. 'I'm a note taker.'

'I understand.' John took a sip from his tea.

'You'll be able to read the notes at the end and sign them if you wish, and I'll remind you now of your right to say nothing at all.'

'That's fine. I understand. Fire away.'

'Can you give us a recap on how you came to find the victim?' Mark asked. 'Just start from wherever you think best.'

John answered in a quiet and deliberate way. His hands shook when he mentioned the crime scene, but his demeanour was calm and his words articulate.

'I used to work in Port York three times a week, did the supply run for the local supermarkets and hotels up here, drove the truck up and down the Stuart Highway every Sunday, Tuesday and Thursday. Ten-hour round trip. Rest of the time I'd be on deliveries, stations close to town, to the Mendamo Roadhouse, Aboriginal communities and whatnot. It kept me busy enough, but I've never minded being on the road.'

Mark nodded. He could see the appeal; time to think, time to listen.

John continued, 'On the day in question, it was the fourth of January, I was coming back up from Port York. I drove past the roadhouse and not much more than ten k's up the road, I noticed a vehicle mark veering off to the left side of the road. I'd seen the marks that morning and earlier in the week, but hadn't thought much of it.'

'No?' Jagdeep asked, pen at the ready. 'Why's that?'

'Well, it's not uncommon to see tyre marks like that,' John answered. 'People stop off by the side of the road for all kinds of reasons. To camp, to do their business, to have a break. When they do stop, it's usually not far from the road, but on that day it struck me, I couldn't see a thing. Thing was, after passing the tyre marks again on the way home that day, I realised that there wasn't a track coming back *onto* the main road, so whoever it was could have still been out there. It's windy that time of year, but not enough to cover tyre tracks completely – I should have been able to see the tyre marks come back to the road. It was hot – early January – and believe me, you don't want to be outside in that heat for too long. Every year there's cases of people dying out here – dehydrated, disorientated, lost. That time of year, there's not too many cars on the road – everyone knows that. People have settled somewhere for the New Year, businesses having a rest. Not a good time, if there's any, to be out in the heat. So, this time, on the way home, I checked it out.' John Baber looked at his hands, turning them over, examining them. 'I checked it out.'

The room seemed to grow smaller and Mark shifted in his seat. 'I know it's difficult,' he said. 'But can you tell us what you saw that day?'

John placed his cup and saucer on a side table; the rattle was loud and out of place. 'I saw, not too far into the scrub – say four or five k's – Mick Denby's vehicle.'

'You recognised it straight away?'

'No, not till I saw the broken side window, a roo had clipped it a week before. That's when I first thought it could be Mick's. It was burnt, not gutted – but there'd been an explosion of some sort.' John reached into his jeans pocket, took out a hanky and coughed into it. Mark held his breath, waiting for the man to continue. 'Sorry,' John put the hanky back in its place, 'been a while since I've said this aloud to anyone.'

'You're doing just fine.' Jagdeep nodded for him to continue.

'Mick was lying in the dirt, outside the left passenger seat. His face was, well, I knew straight away it was too late for him. The burns were bad. Looked like he'd been that way for a while. I checked anyway, just in case, then hightailed it back to the roadhouse where I called the police.'

'I know you've been asked this before, but did you notice anything strange about the crime scene? Anything at all?' Jagdeep held her pen and paper up again, mimicking a scribbling gesture.

'Not really,' John said. 'It was a sight I don't think about much, to be honest.'

Mark remembered the photos, agreed.

'You said in your original statement that the bonnet was up and you presumed that Mick must have been checking it,' Jagdeep pressed on. 'Why do you think that was?'

'My first thought was that it blew up in his face.' John glanced up at them. 'You've looked at that angle again, haven't you?'

The two police officers nodded. It was the conclusion from the original investigation. Cuxton's testimony that had Denby discussing vehicle problems, the nature of the burnt motor, the cigarette butt, the scorched hands on the man where he'd tried in vain to put out the flames . . . it still held weight. Real weight. All it would take was a fine hole in the fuel line – add an ignition source and bang! Only, the broken leg. The broken leg.

'I know we've gone over this before, but the Acting Inspector might want to hear it,' Jagdeep said, nodding from John to Mark. 'Michael had had problems with his vehicle's fuel system in the days leading up to his death, hadn't he?'

John gave a wry laugh. 'Michael was always having problems with his vehicles! Ask anyone in town who knew him back then. Mick wasn't too bad on fixing up motors, but he did not like to spend cash on doing it.'

What did that mean? Mark considered: the man was arrogant or hard up or a tight-arse, or all three?

Jagdeep flicked through her notebook. 'A number of townspeople at the time confirmed that Michael regularly talked about vehicle issues, and Gerald Cuxton stated that Michael had mentioned his motor that very day.'

What else is there to talk about? Mark knew plenty of blokes whose only conversation ranged from cars to football to fishing to shooting to welding to wives. He could relate. It didn't mean, of course, that that was all they *thought* about.

'What was your second thought?' Mark looked at John. 'After you'd had a chance to, you know, reflect?' He winced at the word *reflect* and noticed Jagdeep giving him a sideward glance. Possibly it was metro-cop talk.

John didn't seem to notice. 'It did cross my mind that he may have killed himself, mangled the job or something. I did think that for a bit.'

Jagdeep leant forward. 'Why would you think that?'

'I don't know . . .' John shrugged. 'His wife had died, his daughter was troubled, and I'd heard his business was going down the gurgler. It wouldn't be the first time someone committed suicide in this town. It happens more than you think.'

Mark and Jagdeep waited. *Police work, it's mainly waiting. Waiting and admin.*

'But the nature of the death – the burn marks, his face, all melted like . . . it wasn't suicide. No one would or could do that to themselves.' John closed his eyes for a moment and Jagdeep and Mark looked at each other. It was time to go.

They both stood and John, noticing, did not protest.

Jagdeep started to ask him something and Mark turned to her, but not before he saw the older man in a quick moment turn sharply to the window for just a second. Mark stepped back, saw the gap of where the two curtains didn't quite meet. Nothing.

'You see something?' he asked, voice thin.

'No, I . . .' John shook his head. 'Sometimes I think . . . it doesn't matter. Thank you for coming.'

'Just one more thing,' Jagdeep asked, putting her notebook and pen back into her bag. 'How well did you know Michael Denby? I notice you called him Mick, you knew about his wing mirror, et cetera. Were you friends?'

John exhaled, his whole body stooping with the effort. 'I wouldn't say that Mick and I were friends exactly. I mean, everyone knew about his bravery award – there's a plaque with his name on in town. The community was so proud; it put Cutters End on the map for a while there. Gillian, however, knew his wife very well – she treated her over a long period when she was ill. I knew Mick Denby mostly through her.'

'Gillian was a doctor?' Mark's voice rose at the end. The other two eyed him.

'I know it's very shocking, Mark,' Jagdeep said, straight-faced. 'But people get sick in the country too.'

Mark wiped an imaginary insect from his collar, thanked John and walked to the car, calling out a goodbye to him. The older man waved at them and stood waiting while they got in the car and drove off. A gentleman.

In the car, Jagdeep laughed. 'You can't help yourself. You think people up here are a bunch of rednecks, don't you?' She mimicked a Deep South accent. 'Y'all wanna see where the deceased abided?'

'I'm from the country too, you know,' Mark said, sinking in his seat. 'I grew up in a town not much bigger than this one. I know about isolation.'

'Yeah?' Jagdeep patted her turban, looking at herself in the mirror. 'Good for you.'

'You're from Adelaide, aren't you?' Mark asked, sulkily.

'City born and bred,' Jagdeep said. 'Used to think like you when I first got here. But I hid it better.'

In silence, they turned down a sealed road and continued back into town. Mark saw a golf course, each hole a shade of red dirt, and a sign: 'Keep Off the Grass'. A couple of glum-faced men in brown pants didn't look as if they appreciated the joke. Battling a hot northerly, they reminded him of a pair of cinnamon sticks. He snorted into the dirty glass window.

'What's funny?' Jagdeep asked.

He shook his head, continued looking out. 'What do you think John saw, when he glanced out the window?'

'A bird maybe? Or a feral cat. There's loads of them about . . .' Jagdeep tapered off and the question lay between them.

Low mounds of white scattered the world beyond; remnants of the opal trade, once thriving, now barely surviving. They passed a bus stop where a man stood waiting in a picture of resignation and Mark was reminded of *Waiting for Godot*, a play he'd studied in Year 12.

'Sad about Baber's wife,' Mark said by way of conversation.

'Yeah. Intersection in North Adelaide, young bloke on speed runs a red light, crashes into her car. Tragedy.'

Cutters End, a town of this size and tragedies in spades. It was the same in Booralama: car accidents, farm accidents, suicides and drugs.

'My motel's a bit tragic,' Mark said. 'Nickelback playing on CD in reception this morning.'

'How ever do you cope?'

Across the railway line and past the petrol station, Jagdeep drove by a shabby kindergarten and turned left onto a dusty street. She stopped the car and pointed. 'That's where the Denby family lived,' she said. 'Want to take a look?'

Mark nodded, got out of the car and put the ball of his foot on the edge of the kerb, raising his calf up and down. Jagdeep took note and nodded. 'Good to do that. The heat here swells the feet. Got to keep up circulation.' She did a few exercises herself, and for a minute or two they were perfect colleagues, each stretching and bending and flexing.

Michael Denby's former house was in a state of disrepair, a 'For Lease' sign hanging lopsided in the front yard. Jagdeep told Mark that after Denby's death, the house had been sold and then sold again. The current owners were now living in Adelaide and looking for renters.

Mark didn't imagine it would be easy for them. What would they say to attract tenants? 'Plenty of off-street parking'?

Blood circulated, Jagdeep led the way around the side of the house to the backyard. Together, the detectives peered through the windows into a run-down kitchen and a laundry with a sink stained heavily with rust. Beneath the flaking paint, the weatherboards were still in good nick. It was probably once a nice place to live in. They turned to the yard. Mark walked up and down it, inspecting the ground, kicking in the dirt.

Jagdeep leant against the side of the house, watching him. 'What's up?' she asked.

'Michael Denby's son told me that his dad built him a treehouse.'

'So?'

'You reckon there's ever been a tree big enough around here to build one in this back yard?'

Jagdeep looked about her, at the scrubby grass and a dying jade plant. She shook her head. 'Not a chance in hell.'

CHAPTER 18

On the way back into town the detectives discussed the lie, most likely the ravings of a delusional drug addict. After all, every kid wanted a treehouse whether they had a tree or not. Mark remembered his own attempts to build one for his sons, determined and hardworking for the first afternoon, less so after that, the idea more powerful than the reality.

But even so, with the son's skewed memory of the past, a picture of Michael Denby was emerging. The former hero, depressed husband, single father of a troubled teen and a son whose image of him did not match reality. Mark thought of the pills found in Denby's glove box. Suicide in this case was ruled out, but even so he remembered the statistics from a police course: men in rural Australia were 2.6 times more likely to commit suicide than their metro counterparts. Stress caused by drought, flood and bushfires, financial insecurity, social stigma in small communities, the 'living at work' feeling offering little opportunity for time away, and the big one – that old masculine stereotype of the laconic bushman. What a curse it would be for a bloke in somewhere like Cutters End to admit he liked scented candles or, worse, yoga!

Still, John Baber wasn't the rugged type. He was more refined than that, an intellectual even, someone who liked literature and neat houses with doilies on little stands. John Baber seemed to be accepted and well liked in the town. Perhaps, Mark pondered, he was selling Cutters End short. He should know, he reminded himself, how people were always underestimating country towns, for their potential, the shared knowledge within.

As they drove past a church and sad houses with fading paint, Mark thought of Banjo Paterson and how the poet had lived most of his life in Sydney. Easy to romanticise the Australian bush when you're drinking wine in Double Bay. Mark remembered the kids from his high school who left to go to boarding school in Adelaide and ended up living in the inner 'burbs, always the most vocal about how good life is on the land, always on about it when he saw them at the Adelaide Oval, at cocktail parties in their Unley Park backyards.

This land, the land around Cutters End, was more Henry Lawson country: relentless, harsh to the settler's eye, and unforgiving to those who faltered or were down on their luck.

'Want to see something?' Jagdeep took a right turn out of town.

'Okay.'

'Darryl took me here after I'd been in Cutters for a few weeks. Kind of blew my mind.'

'Yeah?' Mark couldn't imagine what it was.

His colleague entered a dirt track, wheels spinning up red dust and making it difficult to see out the window. After a few minutes the track ended and Jagdeep turned off the engine. 'Out you get.'

He obeyed and followed her, walking with some difficulty over the fine sand dotted with shrubs.

'Check it out,' Jagdeep said.

A shimmering hum of white heat for as far as he could see.

'Salt lake,' Jagdeep said.

The sight astounded him.

Cracks on the surface made the whole thing appear lunar. Mark squinted, trying to work out where it began and ended.

'How big is it?'

'It's 168 by 60 k's. There are bigger ones out there.'

The lake was beautiful and terrible.

'When the rivers in Queensland flood, the waters sometimes make their way to this lake. Pelicans fly here. Can you believe it?'

It was hard to. There was no moisture in the air, the salt made his throat ragged, and he needed a drink. Pelicans? Mark could imagine them only as mirages in this place.

It was impressive, seriously so – but Mark felt a pang of homesickness for Booralama, the river red gums, gentle hills and paddocks of canola.

Mark covered his eyes, felt his lids puff. There was a savage indifference to the place.

'It makes you feel small, doesn't it?' Jagdeep said.

It did. Minute. Afraid.

On the dirt road headed back to town, Jagdeep began talking about the rains of late 1985, when the salt lakes and channels filled – when birds flocked in their hundreds, when roads became indistinguishable and Denby became a hero. What it must be like to see the waters running along dry creek beds, to watch the birds arrive! And then, the floods.

They were brought back to the case.

'That award Denby won for bravery,' she said. 'Everyone in the town talks about it like they were so proud.'

'And fair enough,' Mark said. 'Not often someone in a town the size of Cutters wins a national award, gets their photo taken at Kirribilli and has a plaque with their name on it.'

'About the plaque . . .'

Mark waited.

'It's been vandalised twice.'

A pause. 'When?'

'First time a few months after it was put up, '87 then '88. White paint chucked all over it. The second time, "Hero" was scrawled on the wall above the plaque with a big question mark after it. Found a note on the incidents when I was searching for stuff about Denby. Not much made of it at the time.'

It could be nothing. Vandals were everywhere. Bored teenagers and paint and alcohol – the recipe for badly drawn tags all over town. It could be someone who objected to the national awards, someone who believed that they were compromised through politics or the media. The contentious date of 26 January – Australia Day to some, Invasion Day to many. It could be nothing. But.

'What do you think it means?' Mark asked Jagdeep.

Jagdeep slowed down and parked outside a tired cafe. 'Maybe not *everyone* thought Michael Denby was such a great bloke.'

'Yeah.'

Someone or some people had gone to the effort of vandalising the plaque. Someone cared enough to do that. Why?

'Want a Coke?' Jagdeep flicked her thumb at the cafe. 'We can drink it in the park.'

There was a chalkboard out the front of the cafe. The sign on it read, 'Why do women have cleaner minds than men? Because they change theirs more often.'

'Yeah, park would be good.' Mark fumbled about for some coins and Jagdeep waved him away.

'Find us a spot,' she said.

Mark walked into the park, next door to the cafe. A river red gum, trying hard to live. A faded playground, the swing set just like the one in *The Terminator*, and a sign detailing the town's history. A circle of mulga trees, plenty of red dirt. A bench seat. He sat. Stood again, bench seat too hot. Wandered to the history sign; it was under a tree.

The town of Cutters End has a fascinating history.

Opal was first discovered in this region in 1910, attracting hopeful miners from across the world. Cutters, professionals who cut and polish the gem, arrived soon after, rigging up old treadle sewing machines or even bicycles to create cutting and polishing gear. The most famous cutter was William Keane, a 46-year-old native of Shropshire who learnt to cut in Munich. His doublets and triplets (thin slices of opal glued to black stone) were revered throughout Australia for their brilliant colour and expert craftsmanship. By 1920 the opal mines in this region were largely depleted and the cutters found they had little to do. Forced to recreate their careers, many of them stayed in the area, building what is now known to be Cutters End. In recent years, small-scale opal mining has resumed in the area and the cutting trade continues.

A fascinating history, Mark thought. *Right up there with the Pyramids.* Two rough drawings accompanied the information: one of a man leaning into a cutting wheel, gem in hand, the other of a necklace around a woman's slender neck.

Jagdeep came up beside him and handed him the drink. He gave thanks, took it, tore off the tab and drank in long gulps. He hadn't realised how thirsty he was.

Jagdeep looked at the sign. 'Darryl told me that Cutters End was named because some miner named Cutter, devastated and broke, lost all his money here and didn't have enough to live on. Darryl said the bloke just walked off into the desert, never seen again.'

'Which story do you believe?'

Jagdeep shrugged. 'I've got to head back to the station.

Want to come? Or, I could drop you at your motel if you've got stuff to do there.'

Mark opted for the motel. A lie-down under the air conditioner, that's what he needed.

Back in his room, Mark opened his laptop and read a number of emails. A pressing missive from HR, an online module to complete for his interim position as Acting Inspector. One hour and thirty minutes later he was dull with corporate speak. The air conditioner blared out freeze. He turned it off and lay on the bed.

Mark slept and dreamt he was drowning in salt lakes, thick and vast. Woke sweating and confused. Found the fan switch and turned it on, the blades clunking into gear. *My God,* he thought – *it's either Mawson or Burke and Wills.*

After a cool shower Mark changed shirts, pondering as he did the swell of skin around his waist. In middle age, it seemed that the weight piled on, no matter how little or much he ate. He could see why blokes his age just gave up, lived on a diet of beer and steak and didn't bother with the gym. What was the point? He stood side-on, saw with horror the beginnings of a jowl, thought briefly about growing a beard. He sat on the small bed and changed his socks, put his shoes back on. This was the life he led.

Despite his looming weight and possible existential crisis, Mark was hungry and felt no need to go without food. But where to eat? He couldn't face the United, with all its discord and strife. The options were now the Opal Inn and the Desert Dawn. After a brief deliberation, he decided on the Opal Inn. That one sounded as if it had a bit of class. Situated on the posh end of the main street, it was no doubt the place where the bourgeoisie of Cutters End gathered to listen to jazz and discuss postmodernism. There would be red curtains, a dimly lit stage, and people reading books while drinking fortified wine. He could learn something. Maybe even what postmodernism was.

He walked to the Opal Inn, calling Kelly as he did so. His wife was subdued. She was tired, she said. The trial was coming along okay – but the neighbour, her star witness, was not allowed to present his testimony of seeing the violence displayed towards the victim by her husband.

Mark consoled. Kelly rallied; they still had a very good chance and the prosecution team was excellent. Her client, the victim, was amazing – so brave! They talked for a while before Kelly, to Mark's private dismay, put the boys on for a chat. He loved his sons but talking to them over the phone was not his favourite. All the questions and one-word responses. All the false enthusiasm. He said goodbye to his family and hung up just as he entered the Opal Inn.

Inside, there were no members of the bourgeoisie. The bourgeoisie, if they ever existed in such a place, had upped and fled to cooler and more remote climes. Instead, the Opal Inn was a gulag of shame. The sort where jaded gamblers, ex-footballers and wannabe pimps came to drink.

Mark joined one of the latter at the bar, gave him a nod in greeting, then a shake for no, no need to buy whatever it was the man was selling; no, not interested; no, piss off.

In response, the wannabe pimp nodded back, showed him on his phone a photo of a heavily tanned naked woman lying on a cheap bedspread, her face made up and haggard, breasts like two seals sunbaking on a barge.

Mark shook his head again. Wannabe Pimp persisted, held the phone up close, enlarged the image. Mark showed him his badge.

Wannabe Pimp backed up fast out the door.

Mark ordered a pint as he scanned the specials.

'Don't you worry about him.' The barman stood behind the counter, wiping something, the way that all barmen do. *Always wiping, must come with the territory.*

It took a moment for Mark to realise that the man was referring to the wannabe pimp.

'That's just Foobie Dixon, looking to start trouble.'

The barman passed Mark his beer and Mark took a sip. 'Foobie Dixon a pimp?'

'Nah, mate, he's a peddler of gossip and a know-all scum bucket.'

'Yeah?'

'Yeah.' The barman kept wiping. 'He likes to take photos, show them around town – create a bit of interest, get a bit of chat happening. And I'm not talking photos of your sunsets, your opal bracelets, your handstand into the wind.'

'Porn?'

'Not so much. More like images you wouldn't want to get around town, if you know what I mean.'

Mark wasn't sure he did know what he meant. 'So, does Foobie Dixon sell these images? Bribe people?'

'Nah, mate. Foobie's not right in the head. We all know he maybe gets around with cameras in places he shouldn't, but that's Foobie. Never done no real harm, as yet.'

'I'm a cop, you know,' Mark said. 'What you're talking about doesn't exactly sound kosher.'

If the barman was bothered by Mark's profession, he didn't show it. Instead, he burped softly out the side of his mouth and nodded. 'There's kosher and there's Cutters kosher.'

'Not in my book,' Mark said.

'Foobie's all right,' the barman said, firm now.

Mark shrugged and ordered the steak and chips. He looked around the bar. There were a few punters sitting on their own, staring into space, contemplating life. A couple poked their heads in the door, poked them back out again. Kenny Rogers and Dolly Parton crooned out 'Islands in the Stream' through a fuzzy speaker while Mark sipped his beer.

The door behind the bar burst open, and a woman came out singing and holding Mark's dinner aloft.

'How can we be wrong? Sail away with me . . .' she sang, winking at him and resting the plate on the table beside him. Her voice, made husky with perhaps forty hard years of smoking, wasn't too bad. 'And we rely on each other . . . ah haaa.'

With a start, he realised that the woman was the same one in Foobie's photo. She was still singing and smiling at him, giving a little dance for him, being fun. He didn't feel fun, not after those photos. He stared into his beer and she shimmied away, a little sadly but still upbeat like Dolly P.

This town, Mark thought. *This town is doing my head in.*

He ate his food, chewed it, swallowed. It was food and nothing more. The chips were better at the United. Dolly and Kenny finished and 'The Gambler' started up. Mark listened to the song about the secret to survivin' and thought how good it would be to walk away. The song finished and 'Islands in the Stream' started up again. The music was on a loop – two songs playing till the end of time.

He pushed his plate aside and bought another beer.

The door of the pub opened again and Mark was mildly surprised to see John Baber walk in. The older man strolled up to the bar, respectable in his tan pants and neat blue shirt. Mark watched as he leant on the bar, talking to the barman quietly and jotting something down in a notepad. The woman from the photo came out from behind the bar again, leant over and patted Baber on the hand. Mark could see that without the dancing and jiggling she had a kind face. John nodded at something, shook his head when the barman pointed to the beer taps, and turned to go. As he passed by, Mark raised his glass at him. 'Evening, John,' he said.

John Baber walked over, gestured at his plate. 'Having dinner?'

'Yep, not a bad feed.'

The other man gave a smile. 'There are better eating places in town, you know.'

'I'm sure of it,' Mark said. But he wasn't, not really. 'You in here for business?'

John looked at his notepad. 'Yes, I do the supply runs for the Opal. Have done for years.'

'That's a lot of driving. Up and down the same highway.' Same country, same road. The familiarity, there was a comfort to it.

'It is. Better now that I've got the van; more space, can listen to podcasts. When I first started I just had my regular vehicle – air con only worked when it was in a good mood.'

'Can't have been fun.'

'In summer, no. But I'll tell you what – the driving, it beats teaching. I like the scenery, the quiet.'

'What subjects did you used to teach?' Mark wasn't sure why he asked. Loneliness?

'Geography mostly, some English literature here and there.'

Mark hated English at school, all the essays and topic sentences and depressing novels. But even if he was out of the habit, he'd always loved reading. 'What's your favourite book?' he asked, seeing the other man pull away.

John looked surprised. '*Jekyll and Hyde*,' he said without a moment's hesitation. 'The study of doubles.'

Mark wasn't sure what he meant but couldn't think of anything else to say.

'Well, goodnight then,' Baber said. 'Good luck with the rest of your investigation.'

'Thanks. We may need to talk to you again at some stage.'

John gave a flat hand wave and walked out of the pub, his tall frame stooping at the doorstep.

Mark looked after him, wondering about all the books he had never read. There were so many worlds out there he hadn't accessed. It was inexplicable; he used to read all the time. But now, it was as if creativity and anything to do with it was dead inside him. Sport, kids, marriage, work. He may as well be a cardboard cut-out.

Mark decided to buy a novel the next time he was around a bookstore, or the airport. He thought about another beer. Decided against it, then bought one. He'd had more than he planned to and for the first time he noticed the carpet, a bilious pattern of orange and green. He closed his eyes for a moment before standing to go, taking his plate and glass with him to the bar. The woman beamed at him, took his dirty dishes and sashayed through the door to the kitchen. Mark pulled out his wallet to pay the barman. 'John Baber, he do a lot of work for you over the years?'

'He does,' the barman answered. 'Don't know what we'd do without him.'

'What sort of work?'

'Supplies, things we're short of. John's your man – down to Port York and back before you know it. Reliable as heart-burn; set your watch by the man.'

'He seems like a nice bloke.'

'Salt of the earth. And his wife! Now she was an angel, that woman, always taking in the less fortunate, listening to people. John was a mess when she died.'

'Michael Denby, the local man that died on the highway years ago. Did you know him?'

'Not well, moved here just before he died. There's another lost from this town. Gone too soon.'

In the background the woman flitted in and out of the bar, no longer smiling, her pleasant features weary with work and life.

Mark took his change, said his goodbyes and left. A hot night wind pushed him along the street to his motel. At reception, the woman was close-talking with a man bearing an impressive nose. They looked up annoyed as he sidled past them towards his room. 'Islands in the stream,' Mark said, pointing at them both. 'That is what you are.'

'Wanker,' Nose said.

Later that night, lying in bed and listening to the steady thrum of a generator nearby, Mark thought about John Baber, heartbroken after the death of Gillian. Never remarried. How would he feel, he wondered, if Kelly died? Devastated, yes, at the loss of his partner and mother of his boys – but something else too. A deep regret perhaps, that he hadn't backed her more fully in life and in marriage. How easy it had been to fall into bed with Jane Southern. In some ways even a relief. He hadn't waited a month after meeting her, no thought at all for Kelly at home with two young boys.

'You really are a prick,' he told himself aloud. 'You deserve this room and this pillow.' He shoved his head hard on the inflexible thing, falling eventually into a hot, uneasy sleep.

CHAPTER 19

The next morning, slick with sweat and an attitude none too pleasant, Mark fronted up to the police station.

Jagdeep waved him into the office behind the desk, a hot space of paper and farty chairs. Without looking up at him, she told him where the bathrooms were, where the coffee and tea was, and how to work the photocopier – it was a new one and fiddly at first touch. Mark took note. Jagdeep wrote on a pad, methodically checking against some papers in front of her. Mark watched. The clock ticked loudly overhead. He wondered at a fly banging itself against the window. Over and over, a kamikaze fly. Mark got a glass of water. He drank. The fly kept banging. Mark cleared his throat and said he was heading to the Underground Hotel, something to do at least.

In response, Jagdeep held one hand up for silence and with the other she checked her papers once more. Mark waited, then Jagdeep gave a low whistle and turned to him with a wide smile.

'I've been thinking about it nonstop,' she said. Mark widened his eyes in mock horror. She ignored him. 'The roadhouse – remember I said I was looking into it?'

Mark nodded.

'Turns out Gerald Cuxton *did* purchase video cameras. Good ones. He told police at the time that he never installed them, despite him whingeing big time about backpackers stealing from the shop.' Jagdeep slapped her hand on the table. 'Now, why's that, do you think?'

Mark's mind ticked over slowly. He opened his mouth.

'Look!' Jagdeep pointed to a piece of paper, waved it in front of him. 'It's an invoice for installation – some Port York bloke rigged them up for him. This was mid '88. So, where were they when the cops came asking?'

Mark felt a slow burn of excitement. Why would Cuxton lie about the cameras? What did he have to hide?

'Cuxton had poor eyesight, remember?' Mark said. 'Could only see things clearly up close. He needed those cameras. They must have been outside somewhere, perhaps to get a closer look at the cars and trucks getting petrol. He was worried about petrol theft too. They wouldn't have been installed inside the shop – footage isn't as good when pointed out the windows, or it wouldn't have been back then anyway. Or . . .'

'Or,' Jagdeep continued, 'they could have been installed on either side of the roadhouse, perhaps one at each end – focused on the bowsers and on the highway . . .'

'And if that's the case . . .'

'And if that's the case . . .' Jagdeep encouraged him.

'We could see exactly who entered the station around the time Denby went missing. Or, what cars were around the vicinity.'

Jagdeep gave a sigh of satisfaction. 'Now, of course, we've got to go back down there – see if we can find the videos, find out what he was up to and if there's any trace of Denby.'

'Didn't the owner say there were no cameras there when they bought the place?'

'Yeah – but we could find out who might have taken them, who helped Cuxton clean up or whatever. It's worth a look.'

It *was* worth a look, but, like so many trails of evidence thirty years on, it was almost inevitably a dead end. The tapes, for instance. Even if they found out where the cameras were installed or who took them, where was the footage? It was decades ago. Mark felt all of his fifty years and he wished he could share a little of Jagdeep's enthusiasm. *Youth*, he thought. *I miss the highs.*

Jagdeep collected the papers, putting them into her bag. She dangled a pair of keys in front of him. 'Ready for a quick drive?'

He wasn't; he needed one of Omar's souvas with garlic sauce. But even so, he answered in the affirmative. 'Yes, but after I email Angelo, give him an update. He likes to know everything, that man.'

Jagdeep clapped her hands, rubbed them together. She appreciated efficiency. Kelly would approve.

While he wrote to Angelo, Jagdeep and Darryl bickered back and forth through the wall about whose turn it was to clean the police vehicle. Jagdeep won and Darryl muttered vague threats that were not acknowledged. *Honestly*, Mark thought, *it's like sharing an office with the Two Ronnies.* Email finished, two cups of tea drunk, and police four-wheel drive shiny, Jagdeep steered out of Cutters End and onto the Stuart Highway.

Almost three hours later, along a barren scape scattered with salt lakes and spinifex, they pulled into the roadhouse once more. Two caravans took up all the bowser space; two sets of grey nomads living the dream.

A man in golfer's shorts and a GAZMAN polo shirt gave them a salute. 'Constables!' he called, eyeing the police car.

Mark groaned and Jagdeep frowned at him, pushing a button so that the passenger window wound down. The man hurried over, curried sausage legs carrying him to Mark's window. Why did they all have sausage legs? Baby Boomers and sausage legs. Something to look forward to for the men of Gen X.

'How can we be of assistance, good sir?' Mark asked.

The man rested his hands on his knees, trying hard to fit his head into the window as far as he could. He was like a big red dog, saliva gathering at the side of his face. 'Now, I'm no racist,' he began, with a knowing glance Jagdeep's way, 'but the Aborigines and greenie groups around here need a good talking to.'

'Yes?' Mark raised his eyebrows.

'They make the ladies nervous.' He thumbed behind his

head towards the caravan where the ladies did not appear. 'What with their painted signs on the backs of their vans about Ayers Rock and threatening us that we can't climb it.'

'They've threatened you?' Jagdeep leant over, made a show of taking her notepad out of her shirt pocket.

'Well, of a kind – yes.' The man's head was puce with exertion. 'At the Rock, you know, with the signs and the whatnot from the uni students. They're all over Alice Springs. Come up from Melbourne probably.'

'Someone *threatened* you?' Jagdeep's voice rose a fraction.

'Well, Beryl got told to go back to her own country. I mean, this is our country! I was born and raised here, I fought . . .'

'In the war? An Anzac?' Mark said dryly, looking ahead to the dusty window.

'Well, no, but I fought in . . . in Ash Wednesday!'

Jagdeep glanced at Mark. 'Well, that's almost as good.'

The man pulled his head out of the window and looked at them with new purpose. 'You can mock me all you like, constables, but there's going to be trouble in these parts soon. Buses coming up from Port York on their way to Alice with protesters, and the Aborigines all whipped up. People like us, we don't have rights anymore.'

Mark said he'd make a note of it. He'd seen blokes like this before, blokes with their fancy houses, their polo shirts with the horse thing on it, the Winnebagos and fat superannuation packages. Blokes who had never had to worry about getting a job or keeping one. Blokes who never went to uni but were bosses of people with PhDs. The type of bloke who he most feared he could become. He coughed, turned to Jagdeep.

'You going to report that?'

'Shit, no.'

They headed into the roadhouse, now busy with grey nomads and truck drivers. Behind the counter was the woman Mark had met before. Beside her, a young male was working, gawky in his movements, too eager to please, pushing change hard into people's hands. When the crowds had thinned, Mark held up his hand in greeting to the woman. She said hi, she'd be with them in a second and did they want to take a seat.

They wanted to take a seat. Plastic tables lined the windows and they sat at one, Jagdeep brushing aside a dead fly. A menu lay before them, nuggets and chips the hot food on offer. Mark wavered, remembered the bulging polo shirt, and refrained. No nuggets and chips for him. He ordered a coffee, Jagdeep the same.

The woman came over and sat beside Jagdeep. 'I'm Kay, by the way,' she said. 'Don't think I mentioned that last time.' They all shook.

'You got an assistant?' Mark gestured to the man-child at the counter.

They looked at him, now fussing with the Mars bars on the counter, trying to put them in a neat pile, failing to do so.

'If you can call it that,' Kay said. His name was Sean and he was the nephew of her husband, a nice kid – in a bit of trouble in York and up here to get away from the wrong crowd, earn his keep. 'He's all right,' she admitted. 'Good to have some company anyway.'

There were dark rings under her eyes. Mark wondered at the strain of maintaining a business in a place like this. Imagined it was her dreams of skyscrapers in the Gold Coast, big ivory towers and glinting edges, that were keeping her afloat.

Jagdeep asked her about the video cameras, telling Kay about their discovery that Gerald Cuxton had installed some, that they had the invoices, the documents to show it. Did Kay know about the cameras? What had happened to them? To the tapes that must have accompanied them?

Kay was silent.

Jagdeep tried again. 'The tapes in the cameras may hold important information for the reinvestigation into the death of Michael Denby. Gerald Cuxton was the last known person to see him alive, right here on this spot. Did you know about the cameras, Kay?'

'When we bought this place, it was completely run down. A real mess,' Kay said.

'The cameras are important, Kay,' Mark said. 'Was there any trace of them when you began your clean-up and renovation?'

Kay said nothing.

Jagdeep began again; during her investigation, she'd seen the invoices from '88, she knew the company who rigged the cameras, knew the type of cameras, the make. Cuxton didn't declare them to the police at the time, but records showed there were cameras at the roadhouse. Where were the cameras, Kay?

Mark looked at his partner with new admiration. She was persistent, but in a pleasant way, like a schoolteacher who's been around the traps. Did this make him the bad cop? 'Where's the tapes?' he said, hard, and Jagdeep frowned at him for his effort. *All right then*. He wiggled in his chair.

Kay fiddled with the tiny sugar packets and sucked in the air-conditioned air. She looked over to where her assistant was now sweeping, making wild movements across the floor with his brush. 'He's spreading shit everywhere,' she said glumly. 'I'll have to sweep again, no doubt.'

'What happened to the cameras, Kay? You know something about them, don't you?' Jagdeep was less agreeable now. Detention on the cards.

Kay rubbed her knuckles and looked at them, face flushed. 'Do you know how hard it is to get a business started out here? We're trying to build something in this place, actually make it nice for people to stop off here.' She waved around the shop, indicating the magazine rack with copies of *Australian Traveller* on the front. Beaches, of course; blue, blue water and a woman diving in a bikini. Never a roadhouse, a cul-de-sac, or some fat old bloke in a Santa hat.

'I mean, look at it,' Kay was saying. 'New tables, new floor, white paint. We've been trying really, really hard for almost ten years.' It looked as if Kay might cry and Mark had to stop himself from patting her hand.

'We know you have,' Jagdeep said, softer now. 'But you have to tell us, it's part of the investigation.'

In the background, the assistant smashed something with the broom. Kay looked over to him, a blank stare. Sean rushed to clean it up.

'When we bought the place, it was a mess,' she said flatly. 'We got a business loan and set up cleaning the place – it was filthy! First thing to do was stop ordering in those bloody porno magazines and get some things nice people like to read. We gutted it really, tossed out the old bain-marie, put in a new split system and had it painted and reroofed.'

'The old portables, the accommodation?' Mark asked.

'Revolting!' Kay said. 'First thing to go. We had someone come in and transport them away to some other shitbox place.'

'Why revolting?' Mark asked, an idea forming.

Kay looked at him directly. 'There were cameras in the rooms. Right up in the corners and painted the same as the walls, so at first it was hard to tell. Two of them were in the bathrooms, but the rest were facing the beds. I don't know if they worked.'

Jagdeep and Mark waited; they'd been around.

Kay continued, 'The cameras made us sick – and we didn't need the publicity of it if we went to you lot. We'd borrowed so much! There were two ads in the *Adelaide Times* about us! Why would we want some story about the sleazy ex-owner taping guests as they slept and did God knows what in there.' She reached for a serviette and blew her nose. 'Are we in trouble?' she asked.

Mark and Jagdeep gave each other a look. It was possible they were. This should have been disclosed years ago and certainly when the investigation reopened this time. It was all too often how crimes remained unsolved – not always through big lapses in police work, the obvious sign missed, but through things like this; the protecting of dignity, financial concerns, reputation.

Once, Mark had heard about a hit and run case. A young child, eight years old, run over by a speeding car – driver unknown. Years later, an elderly woman brought in her daughter's diary to the local police station. In it, her daughter had confessed to running over the child and then driving off in fear. The elderly woman explained that her daughter had died a month earlier and she finally felt as if she could show the diary to the police officers. She knew the contents of the diary, had read it just after the incident, but didn't like to tell anyone as she'd be thought a snoop.

'Were there any cameras installed other than in the rooms? Facing the road, or in the shop or whatever?'

'Two, I think. One on the bowsers and the other facing the road – probably so he could see if any cops were coming. He apparently used to tell customers that all sorts were out to get him. What a thought, he'd sit here in this shop and watch the monitor, all those cameras. Horrible!'

'What happened to the cameras and the tapes?'

'Destroyed the bloody lot of them and good riddance.'

The evidence, destroyed. Another lead lost.

'Did you ever ask Gerald Cuxton about them?'

'Never. He was a sleazy old prick and by the sounds of it, half-addled when we bought the place. I think he's dead now.'

'He is dead.'

'Yeah well, good for him. Wish we'd never bought this place. I don't know what we were thinking.'

They were thinking, Mark remembered, of a few more years' penance in the outback and then retiring to the coast. A wholly unoriginal dream.

The buzzer to the front doors rang and two young women entered the store.

Kay called for Sean to come and serve them. Sean didn't appear. Probably hiding from the girls, Mark remembered the feeling. The youthful shame of lust and acne.

Kay looked at Jagdeep and Mark. 'Sorry,' she said, indicating to the two women and sliding out of her seat. 'Is there anything else I can do?'

The officers shook their heads. Nothing to do now but drive back up to Cutters End, fill in more forms, then some more forms, and then go to sleep. Wake up, talk about the forms.

Kay left to tend to the women and Mark stood, stretching his legs. Jagdeep took out her phone and started texting. Mark saw the signs for the bathrooms, headed that way. He passed the young women at the counter, musing over lip balms. Kay gave him a wry shake of the head. *The business life.*

The bathrooms were out to the side of the building and, as he turned the corner, Mark was only partly surprised to see Sean sitting on the ground, smoking.

'Well-earned break?' Mark asked, stepping over his legs.

Sean grunted in reply.

'What's that?' Mark didn't like a grunt from the young. He was fifty, after all.

'I said, I'm shit at this job.'

Mark looked at him again, more closely. Sean was not as juvenile as he first appeared to be. Only his skinny, gangly limbs gave that expression. The face was older, sadder. He was perhaps twenty-five. 'Can't be that bad, mate.'

'It is.' Sean dragged on his smoke. 'I'll be back in Port York by the end of the week at this rate.'

'Well, you will be if you stay out here for too long.'

Sean ignored him. He picked at the skin beside his fingernails, studied his hands holding his smoke. 'This is my uncle's place, but I reckon they won't be here for much longer. Kay's not suited for life out here, that's what my mum says. Now, the other bloke, he was here for the long haul.'

Mark's ears pricked up. 'You knew Gerald Cuxton?'

'No, mate, knew *of* him.' Sean sniggered. 'A friend to all males aged sixteen and up.'

With a kind of dread, and already guessing at the answer, Mark asked him why.

'He supplied things.'

'What sort of things?'

'Videos, mate.'

'Videos?'

'Of girls, of people fucking.'

Mark sighed, felt a deep distaste for the world.

'How'd you get them, these videos?'

'Older brothers, people around town. Some dude sold them and they circulated round for years. I never bought any.' He looked mournful. 'Never had the cash.'

'Remember this dude? Who sold them?'

'Didn't know him well, I was just a kid last time I saw him. Simmer, or Dimmer. Mates with my brother.'

'Would your brother know his proper name?'

'He would, yes. If he was alive.'

Mark kicked at the dirt.

Sean finished his cigarette, butted it in the dirt. 'Overdose,' he said. 'Off his face on meth at the time.'

'Sorry.'

'I'm not, he was a prick.' Sean stood up, wiping his backside. 'Hey,' he said, looking and sounding like a kid again, 'will I get in trouble for telling you this?'

'You might get a medal.'

'Really?'

'No.'

Sean-the-kid-again looked crestfallen as he walked back into the store, giving a short goodbye wave as he left.

Mark leant against the wall of the roadhouse, felt the heat. It wasn't pleasant. If he was Kay, he'd sell the place, move on – accept the loss. All the deprivation here, the place reeked of it.

Unbidden, the blue high heel came into his mind again. Lying in the dust, somewhere out there.

Far off in the distance, he could make out squat trees battling the hot air, their limbs like scarecrows. They reminded him inexplicably of Ingrid, and at first he couldn't work out why. Then he remembered: there was such a tree, the silhouette of such a tree, on one of her prints. He thought about the wind-battered trees in her new hometown and the big river red gums of their old one.

It was better to think about trees than it was to think about Dimmer or Simmer or Trimmer.

He should have been an arborist.

CHAPTER 20

Distracted, Ingrid hummed a little tune. She fiddled her fingers, picked up a teacup and put it down. She adjusted the curtains in her living room window and mindlessly plucked at a guitar. It had been a good few days, productive. So why was she feeling like this? She moved her head from side to side, neck muscles straining. The thought of yoga made her grumpy. All that posing and stretching, where was the doing? Maybe she'd take up ocean swimming instead. At least there you were pitting yourself against the elements, or aligning yourself with them. It was kind of like picking a side, Ingrid mused.

She ran her fingers along her bookshelf, looking at all the works she had not yet read. She came to the print of the white tulip, stood staring at it for a moment. Ingrid felt her heartbeat quicken – she knew why she was feeling so restless, so distracted. It was Joanne, of course it was! So often, it was Joanne. For the umpteenth time that month she reminded herself that she must call her old friend. She picked up her phone, flicked through the contacts – found the number. Ran through possible things in her head to talk about: the reunion, her family, Sydney, Mark and the investigation? Ingrid groaned. *Just do it, Ingrid Alice Mathers*, she thought. *It's high time.* She dialled the number, waited. It rang and rang, and Ingrid contemplated the distance between her and her old friend. The years that had elapsed, the silent recriminations. No one was answering and she felt a great relief. She'd leave a friendly message, then go and read a book.

But as she went to hang up, a young voice answered, confident. 'Annabel speaking.'

Ingrid blinked. It was as if she had been swallowed by a wormhole and was thirty years younger. 'Annabel?' she said. 'You sound just like your mother used to!'

'Who am I speaking to, please?' The young voice was firm but curious.

'This is Ingrid Mathers, Joanne's old friend from school.'

'Oh!' Annabel's voice became warm. 'We had a man here not long ago talking about you. A policeman, I think. Mum told me you were her best friend.'

Mark. 'That's right,' Ingrid said. 'I sure was. Is your mum home?'

'I think so, just wait.' Ingrid heard the girl cup her hand over the phone and call out for her mother.

'She's coming in a minute,' Annabel breathed back into the phone.

'Oh thanks, Annabel, it's great to speak with you – I remember seeing photos of you as a baby. You were so cute!'

'I was bald, wasn't I?'

'Completely! Like a gorgeous little old man.'

Annabel laughed, delighted. 'It's so nice to speak to you, Ingrid,' she said. 'Perhaps you could come to our house one day for a visit.'

'Perhaps.'

'Mum said you're an artist.'

'Well, that's kind of her. Do you like art?'

'Yeah, but more fashion art. Know what I mean?'

'Yeah, I like fashion too.'

'I'm getting a pantsuit.' The girl clearly wanted to talk.

'Cool.'

'It's black. Mum doesn't like it.'

'Mums can be tricky about clothes.'

'She thinks it's, like, too tight?'

'If you've got it, flaunt it.' Ingrid wasn't sure whether that was the right thing to say to a teenage girl. 'I mean, I bet it would look great on you.'

Ingrid heard footsteps in the background and Annabel lowered her voice, speaking hurriedly into the phone. 'Mum doesn't have many friends. Maybe you could—'

Joanne's voice on the phone. 'Hello?'

'Hi Jo, it's me – Ingrid.'

There was a pause. 'Hello, Ingrid.'

'It was so good to speak to Annabel, she sounds just like you! She's funny and she has the same kind of lilt to her voice that you do, and . . .' Ingrid felt herself starting to rabbit on. Joanne didn't have many friends? Images of her old friend shifted in the back of her mind.

'Oh?'

'She sounds so much like you, I thought I was sixteen again!'

'Yes.' A long pause again. 'She looks like me too.'

'You'll have to send through a photo.'

'Yes. And – what were the two of you talking about?' Ingrid heard the genuine curiosity in Joanne's voice.

'Oh, well. Mostly her pantsuit.'

There was a dry laugh down the line. 'That bloody pantsuit. I've actually bought it for her – Annabel always seems to get what she wants.'

Ingrid laughed too, and felt some of the tension ease. 'Then she's just like you were, Joanne!'

It wasn't the right thing to say. Ingrid realised her mistake, tried to backtrack, but the other woman cut her off.

'Mark visited me,' Joanne said.

Ingrid sighed. 'Me too.'

'Bloody Mark.'

There was silence as the two women digested their shared history.

'He still looks good, though.' Joanne offered a lifeline.

'He does.'

'The questions he asked me, they were the same as thirty years ago.'

'Me too.'

'Only'—there was a pause—'he knows us. It changes things.'

'There's still nothing to tell.'

'Isn't there?' Joanne asked. 'Isn't there, Ingrid?'

'No.' Ingrid felt a tightness in her throat and a hot rush at the back of her eyes. God, she really didn't want to cry. 'All I wanted,' she said in a small voice, 'was to talk to you. It's been so long.'

Ingrid waited, picturing her old friend on the other end of the call. Considered, cool-headed Joanne, working out what to say.

'Like, I wanted to see,' Ingrid said, 'if you're coming to the reunion? Perhaps we could both wear pantsuits? You could borrow Annabel's . . .'

Another loosening, a soft laugh from Joanne. 'Maybe. I haven't been back in ages.'

'Good old Booralama.'

'Good for some.'

Ingrid detected the old bitterness. 'Oh, come on, Joanne, we'll have a good time. It's been so long since I've seen you.'

'Maybe. Look, I've got to go. Annabel has swimming and I've got pilates. I'll call you soon, okay?'

The phone call ended, as abruptly and unsatisfyingly as it had begun. But what had she really hoped to achieve?

Ingrid felt a rush of irritation at Joanne's cool attitude. Couldn't she at least try to act pleased to hear from her? She took out her phone again, started jabbing at the letters.

Why are you still so angry at me? she texted to Joanne, and then waited, staring at the screen. Moments later, a message popped up.

You know why.

CHAPTER 21

On the long drive back up to Cutters End, Mark fell asleep. In his dreams, strange figures came and went, flickering in and out of the light. Three trees under a heavy sky, a poem from his youth. When he woke, foggy and disorientated, the land sped by, dark smudges of trees and the headlights on the road giving off weird elongated shadows. The beginning of a starless night.

He shook himself awake, had a sip of water. The kilometres ticked over. He and Jagdeep discussed where and who next: the need to find Dimmer or Simmer, the asking around, enquiries in low places; the pokies, the church, the schools. The videos. It was their first real lead – tenuous at best, but a lead nonetheless. Mark called the cop station in Port York, told a young constable about Dimmer or Simmer. Said constable wrote it down, recorded it, and agreed to check if a person by that name was on their records from thirty years ago. Mark heard the frustration in the policewoman's voice.

He guessed five years and she'd be out – retention rates for country cops were low, cynicism high.

'I get the feeling our superiors really expect this death to be named an accident again.' Jagdeep's voice was tired. He offered to swap driving, but she declined. 'When I last spoke to my boss in Adelaide he said, "When're you going to wrap this up, can't be too much longer, can it?" I think he just wants me to tick a "verified" box on the last investigation and move on.'

Mark agreed with her. Angelo was much the same; speak to some witnesses, check out the old files, have it neatly tied up so the powers that be can get on with powering.

'It's the politics,' Mark said. 'The force wants extra funds in the new budget, so best to keep people happy, raise no shoddiness from the past.'

Jagdeep gave a snort. 'Plenty of that about.'

'I know, but now they've got Suzanne Miller talking about it on television, raising the gaps in the original investigation.'

The known gaps as it stood were thin at best: a broken leg in the autopsy report, some people who didn't think Denby deserved the title of hero, the as yet unknown man who gave Ingrid a lift.

'These videos, if we find them – they could yield some info, something that could widen the case.'

'They could.' Mark doubted it.

'Like,' Jagdeep added, 'we might see Denby trading something with Cuxton – money or goods or the videos. Denby could have been selling them too. We heard he had money problems – maybe he started working with Cuxton to raise some extra cash. Found something, Cuxton killed him. Or, maybe Denby tells Cuxton that he knows about the video business and Cuxton gets one of his dodgy mates to kill him.'

'Or, we might not find any videos.' The welcome sign to Cutters End appeared on the road ahead. Did he feel welcomed? Unsure.

'We have to!'

'Why?' Mark glanced at Jagdeep. 'Our job isn't to find a crime here, it's to reinvestigate the first case, the death of Michael Denby. It could be accidental or not.'

'But'—Jagdeep chewed on her bottom lip—'don't you feel that there's something missing in all this?'

'It's a mistake to run an investigation on feelings. We're about evidence, you know that.'

'I know, I know,' Jagdeep sighed. 'I just want these old cameras to yield something. It feels like we're getting nowhere and I'm running out of ideas.'

Mark recognised her frustration. A young cop working away from home, and largely on her own, on a case such as this one. Were they there just to tick boxes? 'What about we ask the media to give a call-out on the bloke Ingrid got a lift with? You never know who could see it. May jolt someone. Something to tick off and, as it fits in with the timeline of Denby's disappearance, it may actually be of some use.'

Jagdeep looked grateful. 'We'll do that.'

Back in Cutters End, Mark thought long and hard about trying the third pub, the Desert Dawn, but couldn't summon the energy. Instead, he bought himself a box of instant noodles and cooked them in his room. While the kettle boiled, he called Kelly and listened to her rage about the case. It had taken a turn for the worse; the history of her client had been brought up – periods of prostitution, questionable statements and problematic timelines. She could sense a shift in the jury; not as many sympathetic glances, an in-joke here, a flicker of boredom there. Mark knew the signs. Witnesses who were at first eager to have their spot in the sun or intent on doing the right thing soon grew tired of the grind. Kelly was fed up and didn't want to talk about it. He had a half-successful discussion with his younger son about *Fun with Shapes* and hung up.

Mark caught a glance of himself in the mirror, sitting on the edge of his bed in his jocks, eating noodles with a plastic fork, a gut threatening to give way. Midway to a mouthful, he felt that perhaps he had reached a pivotal time in his life. Surely it was all downhill from here. He was one step from watching car-chase movies till 4 am, waking the neighbours with hacking sobs.

He put down the noodles, threw the fork in the bin. He could be a new man. It was possible. He had a shower, then put on clean jeans and a blue shirt. Things could change and surely – with such a name – his transformation would take place tonight at the Desert Dawn.

Slick with new paint and a large photo of dunes on the wall, the Desert Dawn seemed to be on the up. There was a cheese platter on the menu, a chalkboard with fancy food choices written in loopy writing, and deep couches in the corner, inviting conversation.

The only problem was, Mark was the only one in the bar. Was the Desert Dawn a portal to the beginning of time? 'Hello!' he called out, his words ricocheting across the freshly daubed walls. 'Hello-o?'

A bottle of gin sparkled at him from an illuminated shelf across the bar. Perhaps it was like the apple, and if he had a sip it would ruin all of humankind. 'Hello?' The gin glimmered, evil in temptation. Mark started to feel ill; the paint fumes, the lack of sleep. Time travel was unpleasant.

He stepped out the front door again, feeling the night heat smack. The sound of a click behind him and then another. Mark looked to the side as a small man scurried past, rat-like, all scrunched up like Fagin from *Oliver Twist.*

Mark blinked and registered who it was. 'Foobie!'

The resident peeping Tom turned around and gave Mark a lopsided grin, edging back towards him.

'Got any more photos for me?' Mark asked. 'Photos of people in the town?'

Foobie fiddled with his phone, then brought up close to Mark's eyes an image of a large man in his undies, sitting on the toilet reading *Vanity Fair*. Mark shook his head, holding his hands up, shooing the image away.

'Photos of John Baber?'

The little man scrawled through his phone at speed and held up another photo. An image of John Baber appeared, loading packages into a solid vehicle, a sticker of the Sturt

Desert Pea displayed on the driver's side. Mark knew that blood-red flower, any self-respecting primary school kid from South Australia could tell you the name of it and its status as the State floral emblem. That information, and the song 'Along the Road to Gundagai' was about all he could remember from classroom activities in the seventies. Handy. Thanks, Mr Trickey, with your long socks and sandals. Mark looked at the photo again and recalled how fondly John talked about the land behind his house, the driving up and down the Stuart. Baber was a man proud of his state and its nature. Two more photos: one of John lifting a jerry can and the other a box of apples. In both, he looked relaxed, at ease.

'You know Michael Denby?' It was a long shot. 'The man who died off the side of the highway in—'

But the little man was already shaking his head, showing him instead two photos, both of women with big matted hair and bloodied faces, one with her eye swollen, the other with stitches along her jaw and a nose in plaster.

With a sharp intake of breath and in one quick motion, Mark took hold of Foobie's elbow and asked for the phone. The little man refused. Mark showed him his badge, told him about the right to take the phone for concerns regarding possible evidence of assault. Foobie whimpered. Mark used his strength, a bit more than he needed to. But he got the phone and the man scampered off.

Mark stood on the street, phone in hand, wondering what to do. The images of the women stayed in his head. One woman's lip had burst apart. He was no stranger to seeing faces bashed in – bleeding mouths and bruised cheeks were all part of the job – but Foobie's images rattled him. It was the suddenness; he was a man not used to being jolted.

A musical sound came from across the road and a woman walked towards him whistling, oblivious to him standing there on the footpath, phone in hand. She was young, early twenties, the world at her feet and swinging a set of keys on her hand. A bright gem in Cutters End, the first he'd seen since his arrival.

Hair swaying, still whistling, she was in that instant the epitome of all things good.

He smiled as she walked towards him and gestured for him to stand aside. She brandished her keys, bending at the door of the pub. 'You here for the Desert Dawn?' she asked. 'I'm a bit late, sorry.'

'It's unlocked,' he said. 'I've already been in.'

'Shit!' She put a hand to her mouth. 'I forgot to lock up? Jesus, don't tell anyone – I beg you.' She put her hands together in a praying gesture, and not for the first time Mark wondered at the strangeness of his situation.

'I won't tell,' he said. 'I promise.'

'You've saved my life,' she said. 'First drink on me.' She walked into the pub and he followed. As she went to the bar, she dimmed the lights and flicked some music on. The place took on what Mark imagined was a groovy vibe.

Without asking, she poured him a beer. He took it and drank like a man released.

She poured a small one for herself too and looked towards the door before sculling it back.

'People usually start coming around nine,' she said. 'Meals

are cheaper at the Opal, but we do the best cocktails, and the backpackers like the two-for-one deal on cock-sucking cowboys. I've been taking a quick dinner break because I just know no one will be here before nine, especially not on a weeknight. But to leave the place unlocked! My boss would kill me for sure.'

Mark looked at his watch; it had just turned 9 pm and, sure enough, the doors opened once more and four young men stumbled in, not too pissed, but well on their way. He watched while they negotiated who was buying. The chosen one pulled out a handful of fifties from his pocket and gave one to the woman, pointing to the slammer deal. Eight cock-sucking cowboys later and they'd be dancing or crying, hard to tell.

More people came in: groups of two and three, young people with accents and deep tans. Some older men, cutters by the look of it, and a group of tipsy middle-aged women on a hens' night, penis straws at the ready.

When she'd served them all, the whistling woman returned to him. 'You a miner?' she asked. 'You don't look like a miner.'

'I'm a cop.'

'You don't look like a cop either.'

He felt a stab of something like hurt. 'Really? What do I look like?' He suddenly felt a deep need to know.

'Dunno, but not a cop.'

More people entered the Desert Dawn. Someone turned the music up. The tipsy middle-aged women started dancing and he watched them, liking the way they interacted with one another, the way they joined hands when dancing, singing into each other's faces. He tried to picture Kelly there, dancing with them, her handbag in the middle of the circle, stumbling into a friend's arm. Tried and failed. Instead he pictured her as she would be now, at home reading reports on male violence.

He patted the side of his jeans and felt Foobie's phone there. The photos of the injured women looked as if they'd been taken from a window. There was a shine to the side of them, a line of light to the left of the frame that indicated some barrier between photographer and subject. Legal restrictions meant that unless Foobie agreed to unlock the phone himself, he may need a warrant. In any case, he'd need to send the phone down to someone who would go through the SIM and SD card to search for further images and anything else incriminating Foobie had in there. There would be forms to fill out, phone calls to make, and a good deal of waiting. Such was the excitement of the force.

'You know Foobie Dixon?' he asked the young woman, free for a moment after serving a new crowd of people.

'No,' she replied, looking sideways at him as she poured beers. 'I don't know anyone – only got here a few days ago. Was working in Port York before this.'

'You travelling?'

'Yeah, working and travelling. See a bit of the country and all that.'

He had a sudden thought. The Yorkshireman from the pub in Port York. 'You weren't working at the big pub there, were you, lotta pokies? Bloke from Yorkshire serving in there was telling me about his girlfriend he hadn't heard from.'

The woman gave him a steady look. 'Girlfriend?' she said. 'Yeah right, I only knew him a week. Jesus!' She nearly spat on the glass she was polishing. 'He called me his girlfriend?'

'He was really worried, said he hadn't heard from you in days.'

The look on her face when she turned to him was furious. 'I've called him, like, two hundred times! He never answers, I thought he'd ghosted me.'

'Maybe you've both got the wrong numbers or something.'

The woman looked deeply into a bottle of Kahlúa before pouring a shot and sculling it back. 'Maybe,' she said.

'You could ring the pub he works at, let him know you're safe.'

She looked at him askance and he straightened his shoulders, turned away. Odd to be playing the role of Cupid, but all too clearly he remembered the young barman's face, the feverish need to know, *where was she, was she safe* and most importantly, *does she still like me?* And that term, ghosting. It made him think of missing persons posters. White faces on fading paper, weather-beaten and sagging off the side of telephone poles all over the country.

The Desert Dawn was really pumping now, and he marvelled at how quickly a place could change from a dead zone to one where people danced and drank. In places like Cutters End, time seemed to warp. Perhaps it was because of the shifting horizon, the fuzzy outlines caused by heat and desert air.

A dead zone – a party zone. A dead zone – a party zone.

He'd had enough. He raised a hand to wave goodbye to the whistling bartender, but she was deep in conversation with two women, discussing a complex cocktail involving vodka and Midori. He walked outside, shut the door on the pumping music, and felt the silence of the town.

It was past his bedtime. Too late to call, but a text should be okay. He should have done it earlier. *Confiscated phone from Foobie Dixon. Photos of assault. Will need to send to tech asap.*

A message from Jagdeep came back at speed. *Anything Foobie-related, we go to Darryl.*

CHAPTER 22

The next morning, Mark woke in a sheen of sweat. For a moment he was confused as to his surroundings, but the painting of Jesus above the microwave – fair-skinned, wavy locks and gentle eyes – reminded him: Cutters End. *Christ,* he thought, getting up and heading for the shower, *if the Son of God actually did live here, he'd be so sunburnt with that pasty face it'd be straight off to the Royal Adelaide.*

On his way to the police station, he saw a fading sign outside the petrol station: 'Best Coffee in the World'. *Well,* he thought, heading over, *you'd be mad not to.*

The woman on the counter served him in slow motion. 'You the copper?' she asked.

He nodded; he knew small towns, the way news travelled fast.

'Here about the Denby bloke?'

He nodded again and wished she would stop talking. The woman passed him his coffee, her meaty arms dangling over the counter. 'You ever gunna look at the other ones?'

'What ones?' He felt that turning again, the twisting low in his stomach. The other ones. He looked up, arm knocking the side of a magazine rack, a magazine falling to the ground. He bent to pick it up. *Babes and Boars, Hunting Edition!*

'The girls what went missing here decades ago, the sisters.' His face blank, she continued, 'Two skimpies from down south, worked in the Desert Dawn – or Desert Cave as it was back then. Went missing, never seen again.'

'Skimpies?'

She nodded, her great jowls rolling up and down in an impressive swell. 'Topless barmaids.'

'Oh.' He took a sip of coffee and felt a rush of elation: 'Hey, this is really great!'

'Why would you have doubted it?'

The question was biblical; he couldn't answer. 'You know anything more about the girls – who they were, who they were friends with?'

The jowls took up their tidal journey again, side to side, side to side. 'Just know the story,' she said. 'Wonder about it every now and then.'

Giving a half-wave and making assurances that he'd talk to the others about the sisters, he walked outside, drinking his coffee, a truly miraculous brew at $4. *The others.* The thought rankled, sat somewhere heavy in his chest.

In the police station, Jagdeep was busy looking over files. She nodded towards his coffee cup. 'Good, isn't it?'

'Best in the world,' he answered, unsure now if the claim was false.

Jagdeep continued her file search, came to one and held it up to him – the words 'Phillip Dixon' on the front.

'That Foobie?'

Jagdeep nodded and wondered aloud why everyone called the small man Foobie. Mark didn't answer; he had long ago learnt not to question the reasoning behind why certain people were allocated nicknames. There was a friend from school he only knew as Spadger Ryan.

Jagdeep placed the file under her arm and walked through to the back of the station, beckoning for Mark to follow. In an adjoining room, an old man sat reading a newspaper with a magnifying glass.

Jagdeep introduced them. 'Darryl, Mark. Mark, Darryl.'

Mark blinked. He hadn't registered they'd not been properly introduced yet. The only time he'd had contact with Darryl was through Jagdeep, via a plaster wall.

The old man sat back in his chair and burped. 'What can I do you for?'

Jagdeep showed him the Foobie file and asked Darryl to give them an overview of the man.

Darryl put down the magnifying glass and coughed. Coughed some more. Jagdeep got him a glass of water and he drank. 'Looks after me, don't you, Jagdeep?'

'Piss off, Darryl,' she answered good-naturedly.

'Got a bit of the old emphysema,' Darryl said, looking at Mark. 'Had to cut down on the fags.'

Jagdeep picked up the Foobie file again – pointed to it and then to her watch.

'Foobie Dixon,' Darryl said. 'What's he done now?'

Mark told him about the images, close-ups of women with their faces bashed in.

'Why'd he show you those ones?' Darryl asked, leaning in.

'I don't know. I'd just asked him if he knew Michael Denby. Before that, he showed me photos of Baber.'

Darryl nodded, asked him to describe the photos he'd seen. The type of injuries on the women, their hair, the ones of John lifting the jerry can and apples into the truck. Then he asked about the photos themselves, their quality. Mark told him his theory of them being taken from outside a window peering in, the beam of light to the left of the frame.

Jagdeep spoke up. 'We'll need to get the phone to Adelaide, get someone down there to go through it. Could take a few weeks, and meanwhile we'll get Foobie in here for questioning.'

Darryl coughed again, hacking into a hanky. 'May not need to go to all that trouble,' he said. 'Tell me more about the photos.'

Mark looked sideways at Jagdeep who nodded. Mark repeated himself: the line on the side, the faded, glossy look. Darryl leant back, closing his eyes and shifting sideways in his chair, possibly farting.

'Might need to pay a visit to Foobie's,' Darryl said. 'Ask him to show us his collection.'

Jagdeep and Mark waited.

'Foobie's a strange character, but he's all right. Came here when he was a kid, sent to live with the Dixons when his own mother couldn't care for him.' Darryl looked straight at Mark and Jagdeep. 'The sixties, you know, kids given away left, right and centre.'

Jagdeep cracked the knuckles on her left hand and pointedly glanced at her watch again. Darryl continued.

'Strange kid, couple of years younger than me. Nowadays he'd have some sort of label, but then we just thought he was a bit off kilter. No harm done to him, none that I know of. In and out of the doctor's for most of his life, suffers from nerves I believe, and problems up here.' Darryl tapped the side of his head. 'Foobie's adopted parents were twitchers – birdwatchers – all sorts of cameras and binoculars and whatnot about the house. Foobie got into it after they both died, only it wasn't birds of a feather he was watching.'

The older man started hacking again, one of those dry, painful coughs – it made Mark's chest hurt to hear it.

'Foobie started taking photos of people in the town. At first, just down the street, at school, at work. No one minded too much, gave him a smile and whatnot. Said cheese. Later, his hobby took on more of your pervert flavour. Your photos through windows, photos of people doing stuff they'd prefer the public not to know.' Darryl gave a short barking laugh and moved sideways in his chair again. Mark took a step back from him. 'Foobie's parents had a darkroom in their house, so up until your mobile phones, he was developing all the photos at home.'

'He ever get into strife with the cops?' Mark asked.

Darryl ignored him. 'Poor old Foobie, he was soft in the head as I've mentioned. Didn't know what all the fuss was about when people started complaining about cameras in their windows at night, about seeing a mighty lens in their faces when going about their private business in the public amenities. When Foobie took a photo of the headmaster having it off with two members of the P&C and showed the offending image to the headmaster's wife, the shit finally hit the fan. That would have been over a decade ago.'

'Force called in?' Jagdeep asked.

'Too right we were called in. Made to go round to Foobie's house right then and there and destroy all the photos we could find.'

'No arrest?'

'Why would we arrest the poor bloke? All photos destroyed plus a warning not to take the private sort again.'

'Well, he's ignored that. Not only the two photos of the women, but I saw a nude one the other day too. Foobie hasn't stopped taking snaps.'

Darryl leant forward in his chair, looking hard at Mark. 'He has. Foobie only takes the garden-variety type now.'

'How do you explain the ones of the bashed-up women he saw then?' Jagdeep asked, jerking her thumb towards Mark.

'Foobie may be soft-headed, but he's not stupid. What do you think a photographer in possession of a mobile phone would do, if he heard that his precious hard-copy photos were about to be seized and destroyed by coppers?'

From somewhere in the back of Mark's mind, a cog shifted into gear, clicked. 'He'd destroy any incriminating ones.'

'And?' Darryl waved his hand in a 'go on' gesture.

'He'd take photos of the images.'

Darryl burped again. 'Correct. The images you saw of the women were not taken from outside a window; they were photos of old photos.'

Jagdeep was already getting her hat. 'Come on,' she said. 'Let's go pay the man a visit.'

CHAPTER 23

On the way to Foobie's, Mark rested his head on the window in the back seat. Jagdeep was driving, Darryl in the passenger seat. There was no need for him to come along with the others, besides a curiosity about Foobie and his photos. The Denby case required attention, though in what direction he was unsure. Remembering his earlier suggestion, Mark made a phone call to the *Port York Advertiser*, asked them to publish a 'Can you help us?' on the identity of the man who gave Ingrid a lift on the day Denby went missing. The journo wrote the details down, said he'd see what he could do. 'Going to find any weapons of mass destruction here, am I?' he asked. 'Got this degree from ANU in political journalism I want to put to use.'

'You never know, mate, could find Elvis.' Mark hung up, leant his head on the window again, and listened to Jagdeep and Darryl bicker – no malice in it, just a way to pass the time.

As a kid he'd leant like this on the long drive to Queensland for holidays, sleeping and half-listening to the cricket on the radio. Always he seemed to be getting a lift somewhere, being driven along to destinations not of his choosing. His older sister would sometimes whine about going somewhere else for holidays, to Bali or to New Zealand, but he was always content just to go wherever, rest his head and be carried along.

In later years, when he moved to Adelaide, he'd make the drive up to Booralama every Saturday to play footy for the local team. A long drive, three hours – same as the one from Cutters to the roadhouse. On those drives as a young bloke, leaving the city behind and heading home, he'd felt content to watch the land rush by. He was a country kid at heart, with all the loyalties and conflicts that come with it. And every Saturday, there'd be the catch-ups with friends he went to primary school with, boys he'd fought with and against and on account of, mates like Stitcher and Spadger and Leisurely Les. He wondered now what they were all up to. He vaguely remembered that Stitcher's brother had died in a four-wheeler accident on his farm, the vehicle having crashed and trapped him underneath. He was found by his wife five hours later, crows already lurching, his dog wrapped up beside him, tongue hanging out for thirst. Stitcher. Mark couldn't remember his real name. Felt he should know it and vowed to ask his mother next time they spoke. *Nicknames are mostly affectionate,* he thought, *but never used on tombstones. You enter this world and leave it with your real name, and that must count for something.*

Darryl calling his own name made him sit up straight. Had he been dreaming for a second? It felt like it. At Foobie's house, they parked in a neat carport and walked up a gravel path lined in hedges of rosemary. Olive trees dotted a green lawn; a garden bench and birdbath complemented the scene. Darryl knocked on the door and, while they waited for someone to answer, Darryl commented that the Dixons lived on the posh end of town. Old Adelaide money afforded them a life of twitching and travelling when the urge arose. Now both dead, their adopted son Foobie had inherited the lot.

Darryl knocked again.

'You ever think that we're vampires, what with all the knocking on doors and waiting to be invited in?' Mark asked. No one answered.

A dragging sound up the hall and Foobie answered, eyes frightened till he recognised Darryl.

The old man laid a hand on Foobie's shoulder. 'Foobie,' he said, 'we'll need to look at your phone with you, mate.' Mark was surprised by the gentle tone Darryl took: voice less gruff, demeanour pleasant.

Foobie shuffled down the hall and they followed him into a living area, blinds pulled down, the air close like a funeral parlour. They sat, Darryl in an armchair, Foobie beside him in another. Jagdeep and Mark shared a lumpy couch. As his eyes adjusted, Mark could see framed photographs all around the room. Beautiful landscapes of big desert sands, shrubs and trees native to the area, the township of Cutters lit up at night. The images reminded Mark that, contrary to what he previously thought, this part of Australia was not all desert and hot red sand, not all the time. There was foliage tough and old, hiding places for animals, mines and whatever else out there.

Foobie pointed to Mark. 'He took my phone.'

Darryl patted the man's hand down. 'We'll get it back to you, mate, you're not in any trouble.'

Mark felt Jagdeep bristle.

'We just need to check out those photos you showed the officer here.' Darryl motioned for Mark to give him Foobie's phone. He handed it over.

'We just want to look at the ones of the women who've been hit, that's all.'

Foobie stared at his phone for a moment before tapping in a passcode and swiping the screen. He held it up before Darryl's eyes. Darryl took the phone, flicked through the two images, held the phone up close – enlarged them.

'Where'd you take these photos, Foobie? They're old ones, right?'

Foobie nodded. 'Took photos of all the old ones. Every one.'

'Yeah, I could tell because of that reflection in these photos. And the borders of them don't quite fit the whole frame. Where'd you take these photos, mate?' Again, that fatherly tone. It didn't sit with the belching, laconic old cop Mark knew from the police station.

Foobie mumbled something and Darryl asked him to speak up.

'At Dr Baber's,' Foobie said. 'Long time ago.'

Mark pressed his shoulders back. Gillian Baber, the local GP. 'That John's wife?'

Darryl nodded.

Jagdeep spoke up. 'You sneak into her office or something, Foobie?'

Foobie mumbled again, only looking at Darryl. The older man leant in close. 'Foobie says that Dr Baber asked him to take the photos, said to share them around, show them to people.'

Mark sat up straight, felt Jagdeep do the same. He imagined the laughing woman from the wedding picture in John Baber's living room asking Foobie to take photos of women, presumably patients, who'd been bashed. Why? His brain felt murky, clogged. A doctor, asking for the images to be shared around – that was where the answer lay.

Jagdeep cleared her throat. 'Dr Baber couldn't tell the police or anyone about the assaults – patient confidentiality and all that – plus . . .'

The rest of her sentence lay unspoken, but they all knew what was left hanging. No one talked about family violence in those days.

Mark listened as Jagdeep surmised that Gillian Baber wanted the community to know what was happening to the women and Foobie was the one to do it; Foobie, her trusted patient and the one with a history of sharing unsavoury photos.

'You show anyone?' Mark asked. 'You let people see these photos?'

Foobie mumbled again, so they all had to lean in. 'I showed them, but no one wanted to look.'

'Showed them to who?'

'To everyone.'

Mark thought that if Kelly was here, she'd have plenty to say. How up until recently, domestic violence was considered a private matter, best left in the home. When people mourned for the good old days, they weren't considering that – the cult of silence which existed for all things deemed unbecoming in a civilised society.

Darryl was protesting with genuine hurt that Foobie had never showed him the images; he'd never seen these ones before. But then the older policeman recalled the instruction for destroying all the printed photos, the stern warning to Foobie not to return to his old peeping Tom ways, the threat to arrest him if he did.

'Did you destroy the hard copies of these images, Foobie mate?' Darryl asked, holding up the other man's phone.

'Yes. No one wanted to see them.'

The comment hovered. Would the police have acted if they had? Unclear, but Mark hoped they would.

'Well, why show me?' asked Mark. 'Why did you show me *those* images when I only asked to see photos of John Baber and Michael Denby?'

Darryl looked at him with interest, as if he'd only just entered the equation. 'Because,' he said, pointing to the phone, 'you showed interest. You were probably the first person to ask him to see them. No one ever asks to see Foobie's photos; if anything he usually just thrusts them in people's faces. But mostly because the images he showed you are of Lynette Denby, Michael's wife.'

CHAPTER 24

Darryl passed Jagdeep the phone and together they looked at the images again. In the short time that Mark had seen them the day before, he hadn't registered the big curly hair, the fuzzy tones emblematic of photos from earlier decades. Nor that the two images were, in fact, of the same woman – albeit that in one, her hair had been dyed a slightly darker brown. Foobie must have been asked to take two photographs at different times. The injuries were from hard punches, the chin stitches deep enough to have left a scar. Mark wondered about the reactions of the people Foobie had shown the original prints to. He imagined the averted eyes, hands pressing away the photos. No one good wants to see such things.

Darryl stood to go and they followed suit, walking again down the hall. At the front door they paused, Darryl pointing out a printed image of another landscape – a lone tree stark against the flat surrounds. 'Foobie's a real talent, aren't you, mate? He does a top job with the photos, does all the wedding shots for the coppers and their kids, don't you, mate?'

Foobie nodded, head down, but Mark thought he caught a sly grin on the small man's face. He thought again of the nude image of the bar lady. It didn't look as if it was taken long ago. In any other town or city, Foobie would be branded a pervert or a creep, but here in Cutters End, he was almost babied.

It occurred to Mark that no one had asked who tipped off Foobie and told him that the cops were coming to destroy his images – giving him time to take careful photos of them with his phone. Then again, maybe there was no tip-off; maybe Foobie took photos of the prints anyway. But looking at Darryl, at the way he was patting Foobie on the back, asking him to take photos at this year's SES Christmas party, he had some thoughts.

And Michael Denby's wife, those images. This cast a new and emerging light on Denby's character, for who else is the main suspect in the assault of a woman? Kelly would tell him straight away: it's the husband, it's the boyfriend, it's the brother, it's the son. He thought of Suzanne Miller and how she'd like to see the images, wondered how the *Fun with Shapes* presenter would spin that one.

Michael Denby. Add *probable wife basher* to the labels which stuck to his name after death: Aussie hero, good bloke, loving father, great with cars. Add too, *did not build treehouses* and *plaque vandalised.*

In the photographs he'd seen, Michael Denby in life did look like a good bloke. Big without being meaty, affable face, laconic stance. Mick to his mates. A Henry Lawson type. Reliable on the footy field, handy in a crisis, enjoyed a beer. Straight out of an advertisement for Tourism Australia, he'd be the kind of character overseas visitors loved to meet.

Darryl was still talking about Foobie, telling Jagdeep that it wasn't only landscapes and wedding shots Foobie did. Foobie religiously took photos of the New Year's Eve party at the Underground Hotel (still all there, as a matter of fact! The older ones were behind glass, not in such bad shape considering, worth a look if you've got time), a night that not only visitors to the town but also the whole community turned up to. None of those images had been destroyed in the original purge, only those in his home – such as the one of the headmaster in the infamous three-way. 'Got that one embedded in my memory like a virus,' Darryl chuckled. 'Some things you just can't get rid of.'

Jagdeep and Darryl talked about the fact they'd have to copy the images of Lynette Denby before they could hand Foobie's phone back, how they knew a cop in Port who'd likely get the job done faster. They'd have to do it for all the phone photos probably; who knew what else could be on them? Mark, head hurting from the heat and constant talk, asked them to drop him off at the Underground Hotel, said he'd check out the photos Darryl mentioned. Look at the images from the 1989 New Year's Eve party – you never know.

'Done that already,' Jagdeep said. 'Nothing of interest.'

Darryl turned around in his seat. 'I remember that party, now that was a good one. My son was born a few weeks before, Jeffrey. Gay.' Darryl gave Mark a stern look. Mark shrugged. Darryl continued, 'Lives with his boyfriend in Robe.'

'That's very nice, Darryl, but what about the party?' Jagdeep took a corner hard and pulled up beside the Underground Hotel.

'The party . . . We usually checked in, in case there was any trouble.'

'And was there?'

'None that night, except for a dead generator which soon got fixed, no electricity before that. It was John who got it going again. When he finally arrived, the whole place cheered like idiots. Place lit up like Hong Kong after that. Days later, shit hit the fan with Denby's body being found.'

Well, Mark said. He'd like to take a look.

The Underground Hotel looked as if it hadn't changed in decades. The only hint it had entered the new millennium was the 'Free WiFi!' sign written in faded paint on the front window. At the front desk, an ageing backpacker, too many full-moon parties behind him, waved him through the doors to beyond. A pool, tiles cracked and peeling, the water needing some chemical attention. Where were the people? Surfers? Rooms with triple bunk beds, stained mattresses and signs for camel trips, diving trips and cheap meals on the walls.

In the bar area, a large barbecue took up space, fake palm trees lining the courtyard. Down the stairs an electric light read 'Cave Lounge' and here, photos lined the wall, every inch taken up with them; a visual onslaught. Mark took a moment to navigate the pattern – for there *was* a pattern – shots taken every New Year's Eve for the past forty-odd years. The more abundant images were from the time before the digital age. After that, the old gallery lost its appeal.

But from the late seventies and all through the eighties and nineties, the photos were prolific and straight from the darkroom. Despite the fact that these ones were housed behind glass, the corners of the old photos were yellow, the colours fading and some difficult to decipher. Young men with big curly hair and short footy shorts grinned at him from their coveted spot; girls in ruffle skirts waved. *Good times,* Mark thought, *good times.*

He headed for New Year's Eve, 1989. A decent turnout. On that evening, it seemed, most of the town had turned up to celebrate the new decade with the backpackers. Mark stood close to the wall, looking at each photo for that year's party: a group of blonde women lounging by the pool, two tall guys, glum with VB cans in hand, an older woman in relative darkness stirring what looked to be a bowl of punch. A photo from later in the night: fairy lights hung up around the place, flashing lights across the bar and people with their arms around each other, smiling for the cameras, a group shot – people cheering, arms in the air, 'Happy New Year!'

And there was a young Darryl in uniform, grinning widely at the lens. There was John Baber too, lifting something from the same vehicle Mark had seen on Foobie's phone, young people around the man, helping. The generator, Darryl said John helped get it going.

Mark scanned each photo from the 1989 party again. Same feel to all the years before it, '89 a little larger due to the new decade. Drunk young people celebrating life. But no Ingrid – no Ingrid in the photos when she said she'd arrived there that evening. Too tired, perhaps? Hungover still from the night in Port York and the long day worrying about Joanne? It was feasible. Possible that, while all the drinking was going on, she was curled up in one of the dodgy bunk beds somewhere, trying to block off the noise with pillows over her ears. Possible, but difficult to reconcile with the Ingrid he once knew.

Old girlfriend still in mind, Mark walked slowly past the other years, looking at all the young people frozen in time. He hovered over the New Year's Eve party of 1999 heading into 2000, another big one. People in the pool this time, doing bombs. Obligatory group shots, images of young people in various stages of drunkenness, a sign reading, 'Y2K? Why Worry!' Standard for a party on that night, but something about the year made him stop and pore over the photos again.

The Underground Hotel in the frames appeared much as it did now, nothing to pique the interest there. He scanned the people in the photos once more. Paused at one in particular, leant in, looked at it again. From deep in the back of his mind, he felt a twist of recognition. A young man, standing between two women, his smile uncertain – a hand up as if to say, 'No photos, please.'

Mark felt a queasiness in the pit of his gut and rubbed his eyes. The young man – blond and tall – was somehow familiar.

He needed water. The photo cave was oppressive in its heat and he stumbled out into the bar garden, searching for a drink.

Finding a tap and angling his head under it, Mark took large gulps, finishing off by putting his whole head under the stream of water, shaking his hair about like a dog. He stood up, newly refreshed, and the thought came in a rush: the young man in the photo was Sander, Ingrid's estranged husband.

CHAPTER 25

No reason to raise alarm bells, but the man in the photo was Sander from the Netherlands. Ingrid hadn't mentioned him travelling to Cutters End – didn't need to, but still. It was something to file away. Something to stew over, perhaps needlessly, while he went about his work.

Out of the Underground Hotel, the heat gave him another clout. He stood for a moment on the street, working out which way to get back to the police station. Not a big choice, right or left. He took the right – trusted his instincts, confident in them, walked past a hardware shop selling raincoats and a butcher's, where a group of dead flies lay congealed in the corner of the sign that read 'Fresh Fish'.

He heard the tooting of a horn and glanced up to see a ute being driven slowly beside him. 'Want a lift?' It was the whistling woman from the night before, leaning across her seat and beckoning. He climbed into the passenger seat and said his thanks. The air conditioner blared and music played faintly on the radio.

'Too bloody hot out,' the woman was saying. 'Where you going?'

'Police station.'

She slowed down, did a U-ey and drove back the way he came. 'You were headed in the wrong direction, mate,' she said. 'On your way to the brothel, were you?'

He looked at her, unsure if she was joking.

'Never mind,' she continued. 'Wanted to see you anyway, to say thanks. I got in touch with Gavin – turns out I *did* have the wrong phone number.' She tapped her fingers on the steering wheel. 'I'm such a bloody dickhead! Anyway, he's coming up here in a couple of days and we'll make our way up the centre, maybe then across the Kimberley – get some work in Broome.'

Mark sat back in his seat and listened to her travel plans. *To be young again*, he thought. To be young and newly coupled, to be young and free. He closed his eyes, enjoying the energy in her voice and the hope in her plans.

'Then,' she was saying, 'Gavin is flying back to the UK for a bit, so I'll probably hitch down the West to Perth.'

He opened his eyes. 'You'll hitchhike?'

'Yeah,' she said. 'What of it?'

He didn't answer, thought instead of the young girl in Ingrid's hometown wanting to hitch, and his relief at her getting a lift with Gravy. Hitchhiking was on the rise again. A lull perhaps, after Milat, but now gaining in popularity as travel became expensive and young people forgot the horrors of Belanglo. It would all happen again.

Whistling Woman pulled up in front of the police station;

he said thank you and got out. She gave a friendly toot-toot and sped off down the road.

Inside, Darryl had retreated to his back office. Mark filled Jagdeep in on the photo cave wall, Ingrid's absence from the 1989 New Year's Eve party, Sander there in 1999. Jagdeep listened, filing it somewhere internal.

'You think she'd be the type to attend the backpackers' party?' she asked, flicking through some other files.

'Yep.' From what he could remember about the early days, Ingrid was never one to miss a party.

'The husband being there is interesting, but not much in the way of helpful,' Jagdeep said. 'But even so, record it.'

Mark took out his laptop and wrote it down, including other information: Lynette Denby, Foobie Dixon and the like. Angelo would want it all in a full report at some stage soon. Something to hand to his superiors and for them to hand to theirs.

'Here it is.' Jagdeep held up the police notes that recorded who was staying at the roadhouse on the night of 31 December 1989 – 'This is what I was looking for.' She explained that, after her musings on nicknames that morning, she got to thinking that most of them were derived from the family name: Smithy for Smith, Blacky for Black, Conners for Connelly.

Mark waited; this was obvious stuff. 'They're not nick-names,' he said.

'What are they then?'

'Abbreviations.' He went to tell her about Stitcher, decided against it. It wouldn't be worth it to explain that as a young kid in primary school Stitcher used to go to bed in his school uniform rather than his pyjamas. When his mother found out and asked why, the little boy reportedly said, 'A stitch in time saves nine!' Cue a lifetime of Stitcher. Even his own wife called him that.

'Look, here.' Jagdeep was looking down at the police notes.

Mark stepped behind her and read over her shoulder. He'd seen the notes before:

Guests of Roadhouse on 28–29 Dec:
Vic and Yvonne Gladstone, elderly couple caravanning – both now deceased

Guests of Roadhouse on 30 Dec:
Jason Dimler

Guests of Roadhouse on 31 Dec:
Jason Dimler
Joanne Morley

Cameras ordered? CHECK

No recorded guests for 1–5 Jan

'I went back and checked earlier stays too – everyone for the whole of 1989. Not many guests in the scheme of things, but one name pops up almost every six weeks.'

Mark looked at the paper again and felt a jolt of realisation at one name. 'You're a genius,' he said. 'You're a bloody—'

'Jason Dimler – Dimmer. Our video distributor, most

likely.' Jagdeep turned and gave him a grin, the first proper one he'd seen on her. It transformed her face, made her a kid who has just come first in hurdles, a big blue ribbon taped to her front.

He tapped the top of her chair. 'What'd the cops have to say about Dimler in the first round of interviews?'

'Back in '90? Not much, as you'd expect. A resident of Port York, twenty-two years old, itinerant mine worker, liked a drink, liked a smoke.'

'They get an address?'

'Yeah, I'm onto it.' She tapped the address into Google, face falling as she read out that Dimler's former home on the outskirts of York was now a vacant lot.

Mark shoved in beside her and tapped the number of the York hotel with the Yorkshireman working in it. Pubs, the agora of every country town. What was he even doing, he thought, calling the cop station previously? He should have known that the bar was where you sought your titbits, your experts, your credible theories.

The man he now knew as Gavin answered, and when the Yorkshire lad realised who he was talking to, he became enthusiastic – describing the mix-up in phone numbers, the relief at knowing he wasn't dumped by his Australian girlfriend after all. Mark listened, nodding and smiling. Gavin continued: it was almost like fate that Mark had wandered into the pub that day; his granny back home in Easingwold told him when he left the UK that he'd meet someone in Australia and now he had. Australian girls weren't half bad, he said. In fact, his mate had—

Mark cut the young man off, asked him if he knew someone in his fifties named Jason Dimler, or Dimmer. Gavin, eager to please, said he didn't, but he'd ask the regulars and call him back.

Mark hung up, feeling pleased with himself, and asked Jagdeep if she'd like a coffee, the best coffee in the world. She said she would. Darryl's disembodied voice called through the wall that he'd like one too. The place felt collegial.

At the petrol station, the coffee was as miraculous as that morning; a blend of honey and almonds – a hint of cinnamon? All those coffee wankers in Adelaide didn't know what they were missing, he thought. Some would probably drive the thousands of kilometres just to have this brew, dick-heads that they generally were. And he wasn't even including Melbourne types in the equation; they'd hire private jets to be served such a cup. He beamed at the meaty woman.

'You asked about the sisters yet?' she said. He retracted his beam, shook his head, felt a stab of guilt. He was a bad citizen. Nodding a goodbye, he balanced the three drinks and left.

Back at the police station, coffees providing cheer, Mark asked about the girls.

Jagdeep shook her head. 'Ghost stories almost, gives me the creeps. Remember your blue shoe in the scrub? That sort of stuff.'

Darryl wiped his mouth with the back of his hand and gave a discreet burp. 'I remember the girls,' he said. 'Sisters from the south-east, skimpies at the Desert Cave – went missing after they left the job, never seen again.'

'Theories?'

'Lots of theories, mate. Some said they'd hightailed it to Darwin, got a boat to Indonesia and left the country. Others thought that maybe a customer offered them money elsewhere, Perth perhaps, and they changed identities. I remember them, was just a young copper then. Good-looking sorts they were, always heading back and forth to parties up and down the highway; very popular in town. Sometimes had oddballs on their tails, so to speak.'

'Oddballs on their tails?' Jagdeep screwed up her nose. 'What's that?'

'Weirdos, hangers-on – creepy blokes,' Darryl said. 'No-good types.'

'Sleazebags,' Mark offered.

'I get the picture.' Jagdeep sat back.

'What did you think happened?' Mark asked Darryl.

'Me? What every copper thought then – abduction and murder. The sisters finished their work, said they were getting a lift to Adelaide, then no one ever saw them again. No cameras on the streets or in the pubs then. We followed it up as best we could – interviews, re-enactments, a bit of media – but the sightings in Cairns threw things out of kilter. A couple said they'd seen them there and we lost our momentum. The skimpy angle didn't help; people down south thought that it meant prostitute, and girls like that don't make for good news stories.'

'When was this?'

'Around '87, '88 – lot of backpackers then, plenty of people reported missing, most found within a week. Press barely looked at it.'

The three police officers went quiet, sipping their coffee.

Darryl spoke again. 'Copper older than me, dead now, he was interested in that – in the missing girls. Used to spend his free time reading up on the cases, making calls and whatnot. There were a few others he was interested in too, earlier than the sisters, nothing confirmed. When Milat was caught we thought that maybe he'd slow down, but he didn't – old-school copper. Said there was a Milat in every town if you looked hard enough.'

The coffee didn't taste so good any more. Mark sculled the rest of his and threw the container towards the bin. Missed. Jagdeep did the same; it went straight in.

Darryl stood up and walked slowly back into his office, left leg not quite keeping up with his body. The phone rang: Gavin, his Yorkshire mate. 'Hey!' the man gushed. 'How are you, mate?'

'Same as about ten minutes ago, mate,' Mark said. 'Find anything?'

'Bloke here reckons a Jason Dimler lives at the caravan park south of Port. Keeps to himself, the guy says, but a decent enough bloke.'

'Got an address?'

CHAPTER 26

Too late now to drive down to Port York, the detectives worked out a time and which vehicle they'd take the following day – Mark would then continue on to Adelaide after the chat with Dimler. It occurred to Mark that he was overdue for an update with Angelo. Sighing as he jabbed at his phone, Mark stepped out of the office.

His old colleague picked up the phone on the first ring. 'Mark, you find anything yet?'

'A "How are you, mate" would have been nice.'

'How are you, mate?'

'Good.'

'You find anything yet?'

Mark tried to remember why he and Angelo had ever been friends. Something about both liking beer and Bob Dylan, perhaps?

'I can't talk for long, at a function.'

Mark pressed his ear to the phone; he could hear music

and laughter, people talking. He thought about his own excitement at the $4 coffee. Perhaps he should have tried to rise up the career ladder after all. He attempted to give a brief overview to Angelo. Included the revelations about the video cameras, Jason Dimler, John Baber, and the images of Michael Denby's wife. Left out the bit about Sander on the photo wall.

On the other end of the phone, Angelo grunted. 'Sounds like you've been busy, mate. Done enough to satisfy the naysayers, I reckon. Gone into the detail, asked the questions. On Monday after happy family times, you can send in your report. Go back to losing at squash.'

'I could fly home from Port York tomorrow.'

'Or, you could drive the whole way.'

'How much does that wine you're drinking cost, at your little party there?' Mark asked, listening to the glasses clink in the background.

'It costs nothing when you consider what funds we'll be getting from the government after this election, mate. Stocks are being sold as we speak, tins are rattling, cap in hand is growing heavy. This, my friend, is called networking.'

'Networking my arse.'

'One more thing. Let your colleagues up there know that the forensics from Adelaide will be on-site by Saturday. All approved.'

They said their goodbyes and hung up. Mark walked back into the office, feeling as if he'd been picked last for Year 9 volleyball. He asked Jagdeep what Angelo meant by the forensics.

'We arranged it before you got here,' she said. 'Forensics, to re-examine the site where Denby was found. Probably won't find anything, but you know, Locard's exchange principle.'

'Didn't think to tell me?'

Jagdeep stared at him and shook her head. 'The ego!' she said. 'You've only been here five minutes, we've been working on this for a month.' Still, she caught his wounded expression, picked up her jacket and gave him a pat on the shoulder. 'Come on, no need to crack the sads. We've done well today; Foobie's photos of Lynette, the Dimler connection, now this funding for the search – and it's your last night here, we've got to celebrate.'

'How do you do that?' Mark didn't feel like any of the three pubs tonight. In his three nights here, he felt that each one had made him slightly less of a human being.

'Kebab shop,' Jagdeep answered, and he was immediately cheered.

Darryl said he wouldn't come but limped out of his hideaway office to shake Mark's hand. 'Got something to give you too,' the older man said. 'Been photocopying the old copper's notes – stuff he collected over the years on the kids who went missing around here. You might be interested to look at it sometime, bright fella like yourself, plenty of time on your hands.'

'What about Jagdeep?'

Darryl smiled with real fondness at his young colleague. 'She's been busy with the Denby file, but it's all here if she needs it. Maybe you both can work on it. Get you'—he looked at Mark with hope—'up this way again.'

'You never know.'

Mark took the overflowing folder in one hand, shook Darryl's with the other.

The kebab shop wasn't much at first glance. A faded sign, Christmas decorations a good two months early or ten months too late hanging from the till, and a comatose man behind the counter, reading *The Barefoot Investor*. Mark realised he was hungry, ordered chips and the beef and chilli sauce, no tomato. Jagdeep the same. They each got a can of Coke from the fridge and sat down on the plastic chairs by the window. The kebab was good. Not as good as Omar's, but still, it was the best meal he'd had since his arrival in Cutters End.

He finished, wiping the serviette over his mouth and leaning back, a happy man.

'You married, Jag?' he asked, feeling, in the after-kebab glow, that they were surely now at the name-shortening stage. Why, he could have even lit up a cigarette.

Jagdeep, still eating her final mouthful, shook her head. She held her hand up with the signal for 'wait' and had a drink. 'Engaged,' she then said. 'Wedding at the end of this year.'

Mark noted the flash of diamond on her finger. Funny, he thought. For some reason he didn't imagine her as the diamond type of person. But then again, weren't diamonds known to be hard, difficult to break? 'What brings you to Cutters End?'

'Got seconded here. Darryl's nearing retirement and needed a hand. I pretty much volunteered for it. Extended family driving me mad, needed some space. I've got four younger brothers and two aunts who can't stay away.'

'Jesus.'

'Yeah, and trying to plan a wedding plus work in all that? Madness. Anyway, I agreed to a six-month stint in Cutters End. It's not too bad. I like Darryl and this case has made things more interesting. Still get down south every few weeks.'

'Doesn't your fiancé miss you?'

'He's a FIFO worker – fly in, fly out with the West Australian mines. Engineer. He knows the drill, pardon the pun. Lot of couples around here in the same boat. Our plan is, work hard early, find a nice place to buy in Adelaide, and have a family in a couple of years.'

'Sounds good,' Mark said. It did sound good, all these plans for the future. He hoped every one of them would pan out for Jagdeep and her FIFO fiancé.

Jagdeep wiped the sides of her mouth with a serviette, scrunched it up and threw it in the bin. A perfect throw again. 'What made *you* come here?' she asked.

Mark ran through the list: he knew people identified in the case as potential witnesses, he was apparently good at witness interviews, he was in a position to travel, he was on long-service leave and needed a new direction. 'My mate Angelo, a Super, thought I needed a change, plus as you're aware, I'm familiar with some of the people involved. Got this job as a temporary promotion.' His old friend guiding him, leading him along – Mark continuing to drift as always.

'Jobs for the boys.' Jagdeep turned away.

'Hey, I've been a cop for over twenty-five years, remember – about time I got a promotion.' Mark heard his own voice rise in defence.

'You play football with a commissioner, did you? Went to school with a bigwig?'

'Jesus, Jagdeep, I'm just doing my job.' Mark reddened. Truth was, he *had* played football with Angelo.

Jagdeep's whole body sighed. 'I know,' she said. 'But for some people – blokes and Anglos – things are just easier.'

He couldn't deny it. Things were easier for him. His light skin, his sex, all of it. They sat in silence, gazing at the remnants of kebab and Coke. He wondered whether or not to tell her about his Greek heritage. Decided against.

Jagdeep cleared her throat. 'Got a wife and kids, Mark?'

Mark nodded, grateful. 'One wife, two sons.'

'All okay in that area too?' She was wiping the table with a spare serviette, not looking at him.

He considered her for a moment before taking the plunge. 'We're going through a rough patch.'

'You have an affair or something?' She looked at him steadily. 'Sorry, but it's just that I swear every cop I know, excluding Darryl, seems to be having an affair. Must be in the job description, but it's something I don't want to catch.'

Perhaps she was right. The force did seem to be filled with unhappy men and women. The difficulties of the job didn't seem to be enough of an excuse; plenty of professions had stress and emotional baggage, ambos for instance. But the force. Mark wondered if it was something to do with wearing a uniform; the shared vision, the sense of us versus them. Certainly, when he was holed up with Jane Southern in three-star hotel rooms across Adelaide, he felt that in some way. But it wasn't the whole story.

'We both had affairs, it wasn't just me. Kelly with some visiting lawyer bloke and then me with a colleague. You can't just blame the force.'

Blame marriage, he wanted to say. Blame an institution which demands fidelity but doesn't offer a blueprint against the mind-crushing boredom of waking up to the same person day after day, and the tedium of kids and routines, and the treadmill of life. But then. When Kelly had her affair and told him, he'd been devastated. He felt cheated – not in the obvious sense, but in the way that all this time he'd been faithful and she'd been the one to break, not him. She wasn't in love with the guy, she'd said. It was a drunken thing with a colleague. This hurt too – a drunken thing! Kelly never got drunk with him. It seemed like years since they'd stayed up late, listening to music and drinking wine, or stumbling home from some gig. His reaction: an affair with Jane Southern who, it couldn't be denied, he'd been eyeing off for months. It wasn't lust so much as payback.

'Why stay together?' Jagdeep asked. He could see her point. After that – what was it all for? He'd asked himself the question more than once.

He paused. 'The kids, at first – our boys are young – but then, other things. There's still something there. At least, I think so. We're in counselling and all that.'

'I hope it works out.'

'Me too,' he said. And he realised, *Yes, yes I do hope it works out.*

'If Adi cheats on me, I'll kick him in the balls.'

Mark grinned, remembering the ferocity and optimism of young love. 'You do that,' he said.

That night, the generator humming like a heartbeat, Mark couldn't sleep. Jagdeep's observations on the force, the photos, the videos, the missing girls. Kelly and the boys. He turned over, flicked on the bedside light and located the file Darryl had passed him. A truckload of papers fell out and he had to lean over the side of the bed to get them, the remains of the kebab churning unpleasantly as he clattered about, collecting the papers and photos.

Once upright, he tried to assemble the papers into some sort of order, by the dates listed at the top of each page. There were sheets and sheets of typed notes, interviews – the official and the non. Descriptions of cars, people, cut-outs from newspapers. So much to read. He found what he was looking for: articles. It was 11.40 pm.

Darwin Advertiser, 21 July 1988

SKIMPIES MISSING!

Two popular skimpies from Cutters End, South Australia, have gone missing. The skimpies, sisters originally from Warnbeen, SA, have not been seen for three weeks. Patrons of the 'Desert

Cave' are reported to be devastated that the sister act is over and hope that the bubbly girls will be found soon.

Mark sighed. Deeply. Read on:

Adelaide Times, 6 July 1988

SISTERS MISSING

Sisters Adele and Raelene Cunningham from Warnbeen, South Australia, have been missing since last week, 28 June. Friends and relatives say it is highly unlikely that the pair would go this long without contacting loved ones.

Adele Cunningham, 22, is described as around 164 cm, of slim build with brown curly hair. She was last seen on the road north of Cutters End, SA, stating to friends that she and her sister were seeking work in Darwin. She was reported to be wearing light blue shorts, white runners and a navy t-shirt.

Her younger sister, Raelene, 19, is described as around 160 cm, of medium build with brown, short hair. Reported to be wearing a denim skirt, high heels and a blue blouse, she was last seen with her sister on the road north of Cutters End.

It is believed that the two sisters were previously working as topless barmaids, known as 'skimpies', in the town, and had left their workplace on good terms. Anyone with information is asked to call Missing Persons or the police on the following number.

Warnbeen, Mark thought. That windy, sea-swept town near Ingrid's house. With a start, he recalled the Brae Inlet barman discussing his interest in the case with 'missing persons, murders, local people' and Ingrid asking questions. Later, Ingrid's angry text denying she'd been talking about the Denby case. Mark rubbed his head. She hadn't been talking about Denby at all. Rather, she'd been asking questions about the sisters. But why? He read on:

> *Owner of the Desert Cave, Ronald Keenan, claims the sisters seemed happy on their last day at work. 'Both girls were popular and well liked by patrons of the Cave. We've had a fundraising event here at the pub to generate funds for the search. Our thoughts and prayers go out to the Cunningham family.'*

A photo accompanied the article: the two girls leaning on the side of a LandCruiser, big hair swept up and vague smiles on both of their faces.

Other pieces of information: more photographs, interviews with staff at the Desert Cave and the sightings in North Queensland, unconfirmed but firmly acknowledged by the press. Even the mother of the two girls agreed in a local rag that the hazy image in the CCTV footage outside the Cairns hotel looked like Raelene. The father of the girls commented that he hoped they'd met two nice blokes and taken off overseas. Any other option, he said, would be too horrible to contemplate.

Mark zeroed in on the CCTV image, then looked again at the pictures supplied by the parents to the police for the missing persons photos. They were similar, but not conclusive. A lot of young girls have medium builds and brown hair.

When it came down to it, hope was a killer.

In the early hours of the morning he woke, startled by the sound of a cat outside his window. In the stillness, it sounded like a woman crying. He lay, eyes open, waiting for daylight. Why, he thought again, why was Ingrid interested in the case of the missing girls? He rubbed his eyes, turned and looked at the files scattered on the floor. Pages and pages he hadn't read yet. Witness statements, the psychic theories, the wackos from the public who wanted a piece of the action, media reports, police reports, sighting reports. Mark's whole body sighed. There was a rush of blood to his head as he bent down to pick up some of the papers, and one of the headlines first appeared to him a little blurry.

He read it. Read it again. Straightened up and read the whole thing once more:

Adelaide Times, 18 October 1982

DISAPPEARANCE

20-year-old Dutchwoman Anne Modderman has been missing since 13 October, when she was last seen leaving the Adelaide Commercial Hotel at 8 pm. According to close relatives, it is out of character for her to be missing this long without calling someone.

Anne Modderman is described as being around 170 cm, of slim build with straight blonde hair. Her bank accounts have not been accessed and her belongings at a nearby backpackers were not collected.

Friends of the young woman report that she was planning on heading to Perth and then up the west coast.

At the time of her disappearance, Modderman was wearing a green denim skirt, a white jumper and sandshoes. Anyone with information is asked to call Missing Persons or the Police on the following number.

Why was an old Cutters End cop interested in this case? It was for the Adelaide coppers, not the Cutters ones. Not even Port York ones. But still, Mark thought, the old bloke may have found something. He shuffled through the papers, alert now, senses ringing. Another one, this time a police report:

Police Report, Adelaide Central, 15 October 1982

A missing persons report was filed by 21-year-old Dutch backpacker Mieke Janssen at 09:00 on this day, 15 October 1982. Janssen last saw her travelling companion Isa Modderman at around 20:00 on 13 October 1982 when they were both drinking at the Commercial Hotel, High Street, Central Adelaide.

Janssen reports it is highly unusual for Modderman to travel anywhere without alerting friends and family. Of particular concern to Janssen is the fact that Modderman did not take any belongings with her.

Janssen has been advised not to leave the state and police will conduct further inquiries.

Mark noted the date of the report again. Two days after the woman disappeared. Not likely in those days that police would be overly concerned. People came and went; 90 per cent ended up being found within forty-eight hours. He checked the names again – Anne Modderman in the newspaper report and Isa Modderman in the police report. A mistake? Not a helpful one. Names and initials were of vital importance in missing persons cases.

Adelaide Times, 20 October 1982

MISSING BACKPACKER

Adelaide Police are appealing for public assistance to help locate missing Dutchwoman, Anne Modderman.

The 20-year-old was last seen outside the Commercial Hotel in Central Adelaide on 13 October, around 8 pm.

An alert has been put out for Modderman's whereabouts across South Australia. Interstate police have been notified.

Police and family are concerned for Anne's welfare due to her responsible personality and the length of time she has been missing. Her family state that it is unlikely she would have forgotten to phone home for her father's birthday a week ago.

An image of Anne has been released in the hope someone will come forward with information about her current whereabouts.

Anne had expressed hopes of working in Perth over the coming summer. The search for her has been extended to Western Australia. Anne's parents are travelling to Australia to assist with the search.

Anyone with information is urged to call Adelaide Police Station on the following number.

An image of Anne or Isa Modderman accompanied the appeal: she was tall and fit, blonde with a broad smile. In the photo she was laughing at something, her mouth open in delight. She might as well have been saying, 'Look at me! I'm having the best time of my life.'

The photo made Mark immeasurably sad. They always did. He thought of the one of the sisters by the vehicle, smiling into a desert wind. What were photos anyway? Memory imprints, not always true. It was what was happening behind the camera that was truly of interest. Who was watching, what they were thinking.

Mark looked at the smiling Dutchwoman and recalled the date of her disappearance. 13 October 1982.

In that same month, in that same year, Lindy Chamberlain was wrongly convicted of murdering her baby Azaria at Uluru, Northern Territory. 'The trial of the century', the papers called it. Australians heard of little else for years.

This disappearance, this case of the Dutch girl, was in all likelihood forgotten or, at the very least, pushed to the bottom of a to-do pile. All hands on deck for the Chamberlains – old coppers talked about it all the time. He wondered whether Anne or Isa was ever found, rifled through the papers, saw nothing.

But there, in the very back, was a handwritten note in careful script from the Cutters policeman:

Donna Arlington, 1980 – Alice Springs

Carly North, 1980 – Katherine?

Isa Modderman, 1982 – Adelaide

Adele & Raelene Cunningham, 1988 – Cutters End

Mark felt the closeness of the room. He clawed at his t-shirt and ripped it off. Opened a window, let fresh air in: warm – not cool enough. Outside, the sky was streaked with orange. Soon, Cutters End would wake.

Mark looked at the old policeman's handwritten note. He'd been keeping track of the missing women. But who were Donna and Carly? Something raced by the window, a bird or the cat again; still it made him jump. He stood up, drew the curtains aside. In the darkness, small shrubs looked like people crouching. He stared at one of the clumps for a long moment, half-expecting it to move. Anyone could be out there. A whoosh past the window again and he stepped back, startled as the cat peered through the windowpane at him before darting off. Mark sat down on the bed, heart racing. He stared at the notes, an idea forming.

The places on the list, all of them were along the Stuart. The highway that sliced the country in two, a thoroughfare for travellers, business, and those who favoured silence in a vast land. If Michael Denby hadn't been discovered by John Baber, he too could have been added to the list. A person, disappeared.

Maybe the old cop was interested in missing persons up and down the Stuart.

CHAPTER 27

Ingrid and Noelene bobbed up and down in the gentle lull of the waves. A perfect day for swimming, if you were from the far south-east of South Australia. Clear sky, no wind and the water a brisk fifteen degrees. With a full wetsuit, Ingrid was warm enough and content to float, looking up at the chilly blue of a morning sky. She thought of Joanne and the phone call they'd had earlier. Joanne admitted the anger had faded. Age does that. 'Fact is,' her old friend had said, 'despite everything, I miss you. And no matter what happens, we have to stick together. Always.'

Hearing that made Ingrid almost cry. For so long, the two of them had been estranged – and for what, really? For matters of coping, for learning how to live. Joanne told her over the phone that it was Annabel who'd encouraged her to call. At sixteen, friendships are vital – but at fifty, the women knew, they can be life-saving. Before hanging up the phone,

Joanne and Ingrid had agreed to meet in Booralama and attend the school reunion together.

Ingrid floated and thought about friendships, old and new.

Noelene, sixty years old, was talking again about the upcoming performance of their band, Raise Hell Octavia.

'I'm just so nervous that I'll stuff up,' she was saying. 'There's that part in "Boys in Town" where I mix up the lines.'

'You'll be fine,' Ingrid said. 'You've got a beautiful voice.'

'Oh, Ingrid.'

'It's true.' Ingrid meant it. 'Sing it for me, Noelene, go on – please.'

Noelene began, tremulous at first and then with more confidence. Ingrid listened as she floated, watching sky birds dip and wheel in the blue above.

When she finished, the women were quiet.

'It's such a sad song,' Noelene said.

'Yeah. I think Chrissy Amphlett went through a really bad patch.'

'Thanks for encouraging me,' Noelene said. 'These past five years since I've known you – you've really brought me out of my shell. Before that, well, before that I was – you know. On the brink.'

Ingrid caught the expression on Noelene's face, that haggard look – deflated. 'Tell me a story about Adele and Raelene,' she said.

Noelene gave a short laugh, more of a bark. 'You like hearing about them, don't you?'

'I do. I like the sound of them. I wish I had sisters.'

Noelene ducked under the water and came up again. 'They *loved* music.'

'Yeah?'

'They would have laughed to see me doing this! Their big sister Noelene in a band? I can just hear Adele – "*No way!*"' The older woman was quiet. She lay back again and floated. 'I miss them so much.'

'You going to tell me a story about them?'

'No. I don't feel like it today.'

'Okay.'

'It's just that, I like talking about them but afterwards I almost feel worse. It's the not knowing.'

The women felt the waves lifting them up, letting them down, gently and with only a vague sense of the force that lay below.

Noelene splashed some water about, the droplets like jewels across her lined face. 'Why don't *you* tell *me* a story? You know everything about me, and I know hardly anything about you! Tell me a good story from your past.'

Ingrid looked at her, her friend's head half in the water and the grey hair floating around like an old mermaid. How fortunate she was to have found her. And Noelene was so open with the events of her life, the tragedies. Surely, she deserved something back.

'Okay,' she said. 'I'll tell you something. It's about when I was young, twenty-two or twenty-three, and just drifting around the country, no direction. Bit like Chrissy A.'

Noelene laughed, started heading back to shore. 'Tell me while we're going back in,' she said. 'My arms are getting tired. We can rest in the shallows.'

'Okay.'

And Ingrid told Noelene a story from her past.

Not the most significant one, perhaps, but one which signalled a change in direction and led her, she was aware, right to this very moment.

'I had this old friend. Joanne. After school, we travelled together but lost contact. She headed to Sydney, I kept on travelling around – odd jobs and so forth. She was always much more focused than me.

'Anyway, this one time, I was in Sydney and I thought I'd visit. She was living with her new boyfriend in Bronte, this beautiful place right on the coast. I rocked up to their house already half cut with a packet of fags, ready to reminisce.'

Noelene nodded, enjoying the story. By now the women were lying in the shallows, oblivious to the morning walkers and the surf school setting up down the beach.

'There was, however, no catching up on old times.' Ingrid gave an ironic laugh. 'The first thing Joanne told me when she answered the door was that I had arrived in the middle of a lunch party. She said she was entertaining new friends, could I come back later?'

Noelene gave a low whistle. 'Harsh,' she said.

'"A lunch party!" I cried. "What the hell is a lunch party?" Then I called down the hall, "Are you all enjoying cucumber sandwiches, laydeeeeeeez?" But my old pal didn't find it funny.' Ingrid grimaced. 'Instead, she shuffled me into this spare room and told me to get a grip.'

'No!' Noelene said, and shook her head.

'Yes. And I tell you, Noelene, it came out as an accusation.

I felt this terrible sense of shame. "Get a grip" is a difficult thing to hear for someone like me in her early twenties who has no idea what she's doing in life, who's drifting, who feels sick with guilt every single day.'

Noelene clucked in understanding. She rested for a moment, her cold hand on Ingrid's wetsuited arm.

'So, I stormed off down this long, steep hill to the beach. I was furious! Disgusted in myself and at my shitty life. I took off my shoes, jeans and jumper and swam out past the few swimmers and surfers.'

There was a pause, and the women sat up and looked out to sea.

'Whoa, that's rough,' Noelene said.

'Not finished yet,' Ingrid replied. 'So, I was just lying there, floating. It was so nice, you know – up and down, up and down. Then, a rush of water beneath shook me, and as I turned on my stomach to see what it was, a flash of white raced below. Another rush of water and this time I saw the body of a shark. I saw its eye! I froze. I seriously froze.'

'My God!' Noelene said. 'What did you do?'

Ingrid could remember it clearly, how a voice within her screamed *Go!* and how in a blur of fear, she saw her initials, I.A.M., imprinted in her mind. They just came to her and at the same time, she began to move – arms mechanical and face to the shore.

'I swam like crazy to the beach!'

In the corner of her mind, she remembered the desperate movements of the other surfers and a grey fin disappearing into the swell. *Head down, kick!* The scream became a mantra and she powered through the water, arms pumping, legs kicking strong into the shallows where she ran, aching, up the beach, collapsing on the sand.

'And when I got there, all these surfers started coming in and we couldn't believe it, we just started laughing. It was like, this amazing experience. Terrifying – but galvanising too.'

Noelene was laughing. 'That's a great story,' she said. 'But I can't believe you told it to me while we were in the ocean.'

'Haha. Thought you'd appreciate it.'

Later, back in her little house with the fire lit and the lamps giving off a rosy glow, Ingrid wondered why she chose that story and the other things about it she didn't tell. How, after that day on the beach and later that night, when she was slipping and sliding beneath the surfer in some Bondi bedsit, he asked her if she wanted to join him in Byron Bay for a couple of weeks. But as much as she could appreciate his lithe body and easy charm, she was already planning ahead. That eye, the fear, and then the initials of her name in her mind, like a sign.

Ingrid took a sip of wine and thought briefly of calling Sander. Above her in the painting, Penelope bit on her thread, oblivious to the suitors outside. *She must be so bored,* Ingrid thought, looking at the painting. *She should go for a swim in the Aegean or something.* Ingrid had another sip of wine, gazed at the Greek woman working, and thought more fondly of her. After all, she couldn't be too harsh on

Penelope. The woman was plotting even as she waited for her husband. Far from being idle, she was weaving and unravelling, weaving and unravelling.

But Penelope couldn't wait forever; no one could.

She wiped her brow and put her glass down. Here it was, Ingrid could feel it again – a darkness unfurling, the spreading outward of anticipation or fear. She picked up the phone and called her friend's number.

'Noelene,' she said. 'Can you come around? I need to tell you something.'

CHAPTER 28

Friday. Bag packed, in the car on the way out of town, Mark felt a hint of regret. Not for Cutters End itself, with its streets like sandpaper and the shops tired and drab. Not for the pubs, with their general vibe of hell. But rather for the fact that he'd never taken one of the walks John Baber told him about.

Now, driving down the highway towards Port York, he could see the varied tones of the land, the rich chocolate browns of the hillocks, the pale dusky sand, the olive green of the shrubs and clouds like chariots. He would have liked to go on a walk with Baber and listen to the quiet man tell him the names of the plants and the places beyond. But that was for another time.

Jagdeep and Mark didn't talk as they sped by the roadhouse. He caught a brief glance of Sean out the front and noted the welcome sign, faded.

Mark's phone rang: the journo from the *Port York Advertiser*.

'Tell me,' Mark said. 'You've solved it. Who *was* there on the grassy knoll?'

The journo laughed then coughed. 'That's for next year's assignment, mate. As for this day, I've been working out where to put your "Have You Seen?" It'll be in tomorrow's edition and we'll help you find your mystery driver.'

'Be good.'

'Thing is,' the journo said, 'I had a little delve into media reports on your case – went back, looked at the victim, Denby.'

Mark put the journo on speaker. Jagdeep bent her ear to listen.

'You know he was awarded a medal for bravery, right?'

'Yeah.'

'Thing is, when you get nominated for one – in this case, by the Miller family – you've got to have other people back it up, put forward glowing statements about your general character. They're always made available to the public.'

'Okay . . .'

'Interesting sidenote: Denby didn't get a whole lot of supporting statements. Two, in fact. One from a guy who knew him at school and another from Adelaide who was in business with him briefly. None from Cutters End. The paper wanted to publish all the praise, pump the man up – but they could only get hold of these two statements. Why's that, you reckon?'

Mark glanced at Jagdeep. 'Couldn't tell you.'

'And then, Denby's funeral. The paper had a small piece on it accompanied by a photo. You'd think for such a hero the whole town'd turn up, wouldn't you?'

'Yes, you would.' Jagdeep rolled her eyes at Mark.

'Well – I'd like to think I'd get a few more at my funeral than he did, and I'm a prick. The photo shows about six people looking sad and two others bored shitless.'

'Thanks for letting us know.'

'This investigation getting sticky?'

The man had a true journalistic nose.

'No, mate, just reinvestigating again.'

'Fair enough. Look, you find any more, let me know, okay? Name's Hugh.'

Jagdeep mouthed an emphatic 'Not a chance,' and Mark shook his head with vigour.

'Sure thing, Hugh.'

The journo hung up. Busy sniffing other matters, chasing other dodgy leads.

More evidence that Michael Denby wasn't as popular as he seemed. Cutters End people were nonplussed by his achievements. Jagdeep indicated her notebook; Mark recorded the conversation. More details. Circumstantial, but growing.

In Port York, they stopped off at a cafe for lunch. The man serving them said he could make them a cappuccino but without any froth. Jagdeep declined; Mark said yes out of interest. It wasn't too bad, but he missed the froth.

While he drank, Jagdeep filled him in on the forensics search of the site, arranged weeks ago. With new technology such as 3D imaging, whole crime scenes could now be reconstructed in minute detail. Everything from bloodstains to bone fragment evidence could be mapped and then analysed for police and court. The latest findings in

DNA science would also help if the forensics came across anything new. It was Suzanne Miller's influence, Jagdeep and Mark agreed, that had galvanised the force to find funding for the search. People like her and her husband moved in the type of circles that listened. Mark thought of his old mate Angelo, wining and dining it with the cream of politics and the force. It probably did pay to network. Just seemed like a shit of a job.

On the road out of town, they drove into a camping ground which had seen better days. Tired caravans leant like war veterans into flaking carports and an outdoor barbecue sat overgrown with blackberry vines. No jumping pillow at this joint. No games nights, no kids' club, no cashed-up grey nomads living the middle-class dream. Jason Dimler's place of residence: an old Jayco van with a rusted roof, a sagging annexe and a door shut with string.

They knocked. Knocked again. 'You smell that?' Mark sniffed the musky air, dense with weed. A tall figure came to the door, stooping to answer through the metal and twisted flywire. A cough. 'Coming out,' the voice said, and out stepped Jason Dimler – Nick Cave-like, without the suit and smoking a fat joint. He clocked Jagdeep's uniform. 'I use this for medicinal purposes,' he said, cocking his head back towards the van. 'Got the paperwork.'

'We're not interested in weed,' Jagdeep said. 'We're reinvestigating the death of Michael Denby at the start of 1990, up near the roadhouse? Just want to ask you about your association with Gerald Cuxton, former roadhouse owner.'

'And distributor of illegal videos,' Mark added.

At this, Dimler straightened, his long frame extending like a tent pole. 'I never made any videos. And I haven't seen Cuxton for years. Heard he died.'

'You Jason Dimler, friend of the now deceased Gerald Cuxton? Regular visitor of the roadhouse?'

'Maybe.'

'What can you tell us about the videos Gerald used to make, where he kept the tapes, stuff like that?'

'Am I in trouble?'

'If you don't tell us what you know we can take you down the station, continue the discussion there,' Jagdeep said. 'We can talk about your use of weed too, ask to see those medicinal forms.'

Dimler sighed, butted out the roach and took a packet of fags from his back pocket. He offered one to Mark and Jagdeep before shrugging and lighting up.

'Cuxton was a fuckhead,' he said, breathing in the smoke. 'Sick bastard when I think of it. Paid me to set up cameras in all the dongas, then sell the videos to kids in Port and Adelaide. He used to edit them, black out faces and whatnot, no sound. Once, some bloke whose wife was in one came around and gave Cuxton a what for – same bloke ended up in hospital with a broken leg and very few teeth.'

Dimler took another drag; the others didn't interrupt. 'Videos sold like fucking hot cakes: kids, old perverts, travellers. Mostly not much in them – not everyone gets a root in a donga – but enough, you know. And always tits from the showers.'

'Why work for him? Set up the cameras, sell the videos?'

'It was work, mate. Look around you, not much employment here – 'specially not if you've only got Year 8 and a habit to maintain. Didn't make me feel noble, but it paid.'

'So, what happened to the videos made around the time of Denby's death?'

'Destroyed, mate – big fucking fire and a lot of fucking petrol straight after word got out about the dead bloke up the road. Cuxton was a fuckhead, but he wasn't stupid. He knew the cops'd be sniffing around, maybe even staying there during the investigation. After five or six months, when the heat died down, he put the cameras back up. Started up selling again, but they were never as popular – videos were becoming old-school, you know?'

Mark rubbed his head. Soon, he would be out of here – in his air-conditioned lease car down to Adelaide and home. It couldn't come quick enough.

'Did Cuxton ever mention Michael Denby?'

'Not that I know of.'

'You ever have dealings with Denby yourself?'

'No. I mainly sold the videos in Port York and mostly to young blokes. Denby could've been buying direct through Cuxton, wouldn't know.'

'You ever see Michael Denby'—Jagdeep showed Dimler a photo from her phone—'on New Year's Eve 1989?'

'Long time ago, mate, but no – not that I recall.'

Jason Dimler was a good interviewee. Clear and precise. No hedging about or eyeballs to the sky.

Mark tried a different tack.

'You notice a girl staying in the room next to you that New Year's Eve?'

'That would have been around the time Denby went missing, eh?'

'Yeah.'

'Nup. However, and full disclosure here, memory's not too good, you know? Struggle sometimes to remember dates and faces. Funny that.'

Yeah, Mark thought, looking at the man who resembled Nick Cave in more ways than one, *funny that.* Jagdeep's shoulders slumped. *What a bloody waste of time.*

'Still got some tapes, but,' Dimler nodded. 'Yeah, ones from the last few days of the big burn. Didn't have time to get rid of the whole lot. Two or three years of tapes. Jesus, I nearly died of the fumes.'

A flicker of excitement ran through Mark. 'You got tapes from all the cameras?' *The one from the road, the one from the road*, he thought. *Let there be one from the road.*

'Yeah, from the last few days around New Year's, probs, from all the cameras. Don't bother to go destroying only some angles and not the others, mate.'

'We'll need them now, please, all you've got.'

The man was in no position to argue. Bending back down inside his van, he shuffled about for a few minutes, mumbling, lighting up another smoke.

Mark and Jagdeep stood outside, waiting in the dirt. There was a lot of banging and crashing and swearing. Eventually, after fifteen minutes, the tall man reappeared, this time holding a washing basket of black videotapes.

'Here's your first lot. Wait a minny and I'll get the rest.'

Jagdeep looked in dismay at the basketful. As Dimler turned to head into his van again, Mark had a sudden thought.

'Jason,' he said. 'Did you know Michael Denby's kids? Had a son, Troy, and a daughter, Kylie. She was about your age, or a bit younger, lived in Port York for a time. Killed herself.'

The lanky man leant against his van door and gave the question a bit of thought. 'Couldn't tell you about the son, but Kylie, yeah, I knew her. Nice girl. Bit troubled and that.'

'What do you mean?' Jagdeep sounded tired.

'Death of her mum and dad, drugs here and there. Problems with housing. Moved down south soon after. Didn't see her after that.'

'She ever talk about her father?'

'Never talked about that sort of stuff. Only knew her to have a chat. Sad that she killed herself. Dunno what it is with all these young kids topping themselves. You can't tell who hides trauma, can you? The face, it's such a good actor.'

Dimler looked thoughtful for a moment and Mark stood back, impressed with the insight. What exactly could someone like Dimler have been if he'd gone to a private school, if he'd had opportunities and money? A different Dimler, but still Dimler nonetheless.

As he pondered, the tall man turned back inside, crashing and pulling at things before stumbling back out again with another load of videos. Jagdeep's face fell even further.

'That's for the last few days of taping before we started up again after the shit died down.' Dimler nodded as they began shifting through them, looking on the side for dates. 'Some dated and some not,' he said. 'When the body was found, any sort of organisation went out the window in the rush to get them disappeared.' He coughed and spat to the side. 'Be needing those two baskets back too. For laundry and that.'

Jason Dimler and laundry; the two didn't match. Even so, they emptied the tapes into the police car and handed back the baskets.

'Not in any trouble now, am I?' Dimler asked. 'Full cooperation and that.'

Jagdeep looked at the scores of tapes. 'We'll see,' she said.

CHAPTER 29

A spare office was found for them by a tired cop at the Port York station and they settled into their new room, files laid out, tapes on the table in some sort of order. First, they ran through the tapes looking for road shots. It was boring work. The old VHS police video player swallowed and spewed out the tapes like a weary soul nursing a hangover.

In a painful process, they worked through the videos to determine which ones came from the road camera and which from within the dongas. A slight deterioration marked some of them, but the old videos held up remarkably well. Jagdeep confirmed that there were six cameras in all, four in the rooms and two outside. One facing one set of petrol bowsers and on the road pointing south. Whoever Gerald Cuxton feared or suspected came from that way.

Then, sorting the tapes into order. Any tapes before 31 December 1989 were put to one side. That left thirty-eight tapes – from 31 December to 5 January.

The next step was to watch the tapes from the road camera, but by that time both Jagdeep and Mark were fading fast. No amount of tea or coffee could keep them awake and they walked the block to their hotel, agreeing to begin early the next morning.

It was only when he woke in a stupor at 11.45 pm that Mark realised he hadn't told Kelly he'd be arriving home the following day and not that very night. He tried calling, left a sucky message. Hung up feeling like a shitbox, which was pretty much the same as knowing he was.

The next morning, sky like a bleached canvas, they walked to the police station once more. A cop on duty there kindly offered to pick them up breakfast, and came back later with two pies and a couple of iced-coffee Big Ms.

'Do I look like a tradie?' Jagdeep grumbled, squirting the sauce on her pie and inadvertently on her top.

The road videos were tedious, the timeframe uncertain. It was torture to watch the screen, slow down on the cars, searching for hints of something they weren't sure of. What they were hoping for was a hunch, a gut feeling – that flicker of unease.

Mark had a mate who liked to go hiking in the high country. A real outdoor-ed, Bear Grylls type without the hype. One time, he told Mark, he spent two whole days hiking in the mountains and came across a wide stream, deep and clear enough for swimming. It was great, he said. The sounds of the Australian bush, the water, the birds, the solitude.

Then, when night came, he lit a fire and sat in his chair beside it, facing the river and watching it darkly gurgle and flow. It was weird, he said. But when darkness struck, he immediately felt the hairs on the back of his head stand up. A feeling of fear came to him and he had no idea why. He stood up, turned behind him, shone his torch into the bush beyond, but nothing. Once more, he sat in his chair and tried to enjoy the river, and once more, the feeling of fear came over him. He felt, inexplicably, that someone or something was watching him. 'Hey!' he called out into the bush. 'Hey!' It gave Mark the creeps just to think of it. His mate said that after a third time of trying and failing to sit and enjoy the river he got up, picked up his chair, and moved it to the other side of the fire, so that he was facing the bush, with the river behind him. Instantly, he said, the fear went away. When Mark asked him what his theory was, his friend said he wasn't sure but put it down to some primal instinct – a need to have a clear vision of where your danger is going to come from. With the fire and bush in front of him, his power somehow increased.

Instinct. That's what Mark was waiting for as he watched the road videos, the camper trailers, the caravans, the road trains passing by and mostly not stopping at Gerald Cuxton's petrol station.

Time slowed and Mark became fidgety. A bus pulled up on 31 December around 11 am and a group of people got out, mostly young. Jagdeep scanned the images to see if they could make out Ingrid, but no. The camera was focused firmly on the road, and only the parking area and the edge of a petrol bowser were visible. Only the dark figures of the group walking towards the shop. They tried zooming in, but it was no good. *Ridiculous!* Mark thought. Why waste all this money on a camera facing towards the road? Police was the obvious answer, but still.

Jagdeep said she could send it for analysis; maybe the tech guys could see if there was anyone of interest in the group. Mark shrugged; why not.

Later on, around 4.20 pm in the same tape, Mark noticed something – a covered ute driving up the road, stopping at one of the bowsers. He grabbed at Jagdeep's arm. It was Michael Denby's vehicle, the rego plate clear.

The camera showed only the back half of the vehicle. They rewound the tape, putting it in slow motion: there's Denby's ute driving up the highway – there it is pulling into the first bowser, a hand reaching out to grab the petrol nozzle, and then filling up the vehicle tank and jerry cans. There's a pause, presumably while Denby goes in to get his snacks and drinks, and pays for the petrol. It's a few minutes till he comes out again – having had a chat, they knew, with Cuxton about his motor. A thick leg comes into shot; Denby is putting something in the back of the ute, or rearranging it, or something. Then he gets in and is gone. It's the last time he will drive this stretch of road.

The police officers looked at each other. It was like seeing the hint of a ghost. The big legs, one of which would later be broken, and the ute, half blown up down the track.

How long did Michael Denby have to live? Two hours? Twelve?

They turned to the other videos, their enthusiasm revived. But not for long.

One hour and thirty minutes later, in the back of the police station in Port York, Mark and Jagdeep were still sifting through tapes, backwards from 4 December.

Mostly, the tapes were mind-numbing. People getting in and out of cars, people stretching, filling petrol, checking tyres, leaning against vehicles, walking to and fro.

They came to the tapes set up in the portables. Began watching. What for, exactly? The day took on an air of defeat.

'Why even buy an illegal tape set up in a donga?' Jagdeep said. 'Who would want to watch that shit?'

Mark thought: *Hope.* Every young boy who bought a tape was probably told they were getting a bird's-eye view of Swedish backpackers hard at it, preferably with each other. For the most part, the kids were badly ripped off.

Almost nodding off now, Mark and Jagdeep watched the grainy footage of a basic room, basic bed, basic bathroom.

Mark yawned, glancing at his watch. 'I've got to go soon, get home to Kelly and the kids.'

He began putting his notes in a bag, then checked around to see where his jacket was.

'Hey, Mark.' Jagdeep was staring intently at the screen. 'You'll want to see this.'

He turned to see Joanne in the frame, long hair covering her face and her thin build stepping up into the small space of the donga. It shouldn't have been a surprise to see her there, they knew she stayed at the roadhouse on the thirty-first. But he had that eerie feeling again, as if he was watching a ghost.

On the screen, Joanne sat on the bed, put her hair up, let it down again.

'I'm not sure I want to watch this,' Mark said. It felt wrong to be spying on his old friend.

'Sure,' Jagdeep said. 'We're pretty much done here anyway.' But as she went to flick the off-button, the door of the donga opened again.

Mark and Jagdeep sat stunned, heads bent close, as on the screen Ingrid entered the room.

Ingrid, who was supposed to be three hundred kilometres away in Cutters End by then.

'Holy fuck,' Mark breathed.

In grainy black and white, they saw Ingrid sit down beside Joanne, then stand, her back towards the camera, facing Joanne. They looked as if they were deep in discussion, Ingrid shaking her head, before Joanne pushed past her and went into the bathroom. Mark closed his eyes for a brief second, a spreading sickness in his chest.

'Oh God,' Jagdeep was saying, 'she's laughing.'

Mark snapped open his eyes and leant close in again, his face almost touching the screen. It did look as if Ingrid was laughing; her mouth a rectangle, head thrown back and hands on her sides. Facing the camera, it felt as if she was addressing them.

'I've been here the whole time,' she may as well have been saying. 'Didn't you know?'

CHAPTER 30

1994

'Head down, kick.' When Ingrid returned to her family home after her travels and the failed visit to Joanne in Bronte, she had been energised – new ideas crackling, bubbling. Finally, she knew what she wanted to do. 'Head down, kick,' she told herself as she went about her research in the library and online. 'Kick,' she told herself, every time she felt unsure what it was she was doing and the reasons why. Seeing the shark, swimming to shore and the relief afterwards had given her a release. Not that she had been in any real danger – the lifeguard told her and the hyped-up surfers that it was probably just a curious bull shark. But when her mind told her, 'Head down, kick,' and her body obeyed, that was the thing. The action, the release. It was as if a different person emerged from the water than the one who had entered it. A baptism.

In the months that followed, Ingrid found she had a knack for research, an ability to find obscure details in articles, to spend long hours poring over maps and analysing photographs. All she needed was a name or even the hint of one. Who knew it was within her? Not her. When asked what she was doing, she'd answer, 'Studying,' and this was enough to satisfy her parents and most friends. It *was* studying, just not for credit points.

She bought a return ticket to London and left Australia on a bright day in February.

On the plane over, she looked out her window and observed that from above, clouds look a little like churning waves. Easy to get lost in them, drown if you didn't know what you were doing. In London, she met up with schoolfriends living in a Cricklewood share house and stayed with them for a few nights, drinking in local pubs and dancing in Soho clubs. It was fun, but she only really began to feel as if she was away from home when she caught a train down south and went hiking in Kent and Sussex.

Her friends had told her a lot about England, but not that it was beautiful. The green fields and forests of oaks, big rivers running clear and full, the bridleways and kissing gates – she didn't know much about these. It was a marvel to her, how almost every patch of land seemed to be managed in some way but still retained its beauty. Wooden fences, sheep, hay bales, houses, villages, castles, manors, roads and signposts. Every part of the UK was taken up; it would be almost impossible to get lost there and this gave her great comfort. How easy it would be to get a job in one of the little pubs, rent a room in a village and live quietly for a few years. The idea was tempting and, as she drifted past a sign on a pub named the White Hart, in a village called Penshurst, she almost gave in. She could live in one of the rooms at the top of the inn, go for long walks, get to know the country. She could change her name, be someone else entirely. Maybe something like Eloise, or Henrietta, or Alexandra Winter. That would be great. No one would ever know who she really was, and Winter was a very cool surname.

A lorry drove past, beeping its horn as the owner waved goodbye to someone. The noise made her jump, feel shivery in her legs.

The next day, she booked her flight to Amsterdam.

Hundreds of thousands of people. It was as if every tourist in the world zipped up their suitcase on wheels and arrived in the Netherlands on the same day. Tourist groups with the same coloured umbrellas, groups taking photos, bachelor parties, hens' parties, lecherous divorcees slinking among red alleyways, tour buses, bike tours, tulip tours, sex tours; Amsterdam was exhausting. Beautiful no doubt, but exhausting.

As she sidestepped pools of vomit while crossing a canal bridge, Ingrid checked her phone for the address once more. Four blocks along and she was in a quieter part of the city. Lights from the houses were beginning to flicker on and the reflection in the canal was peaceful and calm. Ingrid stood in front of a tall, slender house, brown bricks with long windows and series of steps leading up to the first floor. The house looked like a graceful lady, stooping with age and experience. The image somehow made her feel reassured and Ingrid mounted the steps, knocking firmly on the door in a show of confidence. A few moments passed, then a shadow appeared behind the glass panel, the door opened and a tall woman appeared, around thirty years old. With light brown hair cut fashionably short and a black dress complete with a grey stone necklace and earrings, she was impossibly stylish.

'Ja?' the woman asked.

'I'm wondering if Mieke Janssen lives here.'

'Are you here to complain about the rubbish?' The woman spoke in perfect English. 'Because I have nothing to do with that side of things. I'm working on the Corey project.'

Ingrid had no idea what she was talking about. She shook her head.

'I'm here to see Mieke Janssen.'

'I am Mieke.'

Ingrid shifted about in her Birkenstocks and went to speak again. The older woman interrupted her, held up her hands. 'If you are here about the dirty streets, go to Janke for that. I can give you the council address, but you really must stop coming to my home.'

'I don't know what you mean, I'm not here about the rubbish or the campaign,' Ingrid said.

'You're not?'

'No.'

'Thank God!' The older woman stepped out of the house and stood on the top step, next to Ingrid. 'It's all I have to deal with these days. Rubbish and Corey, Corey, Corey.'

'I'm here about Isa Modderman.'

There was a sharp silence. Wind whipped. The canal's surface became jagged with colour.

'Are you the police?' The woman's voice was hard.

'No, nothing like that.'

'Is there any news?'

'No.'

'So, maybe you want to write a book or an article or make a documentary?'

'I want to know where her family lives.'

Mieke took out a small case of cigarettes from a pocket in her dress and lit one up. She didn't offer one to Ingrid. 'You won't tell me why you're in the Netherlands?'

'I can't, not till I've spoken to Isa's family.'

The woman took a long drag of her cigarette and blew out slowly. She looked towards the canal, where the lights reflected a yellow glow as more houses and shops opened up for the night. 'I haven't spoken to them for at least ten years. In the beginning I stayed in contact, but it was just too difficult for them. I reminded them too much of her, you see.'

'I just want to speak to them, nothing else.'

Mieke closed her eyes. 'Your accent,' she said. 'It's hard for me to hear.'

'Yes.'

'I actually knew her as Anne. Isa was her official first name, it's just everyone knew her as Anne. We don't have the tradition of middle names like you do, but sometimes we have two first names. I'm not sure how much it helped or hindered – sometimes the press went with Anne and sometimes with Isa.'

It had hindered. Months of looking for the wrong person, following ghosts.

'Will you let me know where her family lives?'

Mieke gave her a sideways glance. 'I think I will,' she said. 'You don't look like a reporter and you've come a long way.' She went back inside and came out again with a small piece of paper. 'I don't know the Modderman family's exact address, but I know they went back to Friesland. Good luck.'

Ingrid took the piece of paper. 'Thank you,' she said. 'I hope you find Corey.'

The woman looked surprised and then gave a laugh. 'Corey isn't one person,' she said. 'It's the name we are beginning to give to the new type of tourist around here – usually English, usually a male aged eighteen to twenty-four, usually drunk and stumbling around the red-light district.'

'Sounds like a nice person.'

'I'm on the Amsterdam tourism board. We're looking at ways to mitigate the Corey problem. In years to come, I hope there will be a fully funded campaign. For now, it's just me battling on.'

Ingrid headed down the steps, turning before she walked up the canal path once more. 'I can see that tourism is a problem here,' she said. 'It's kind of awful.'

Mieke butted out her cigarette. 'There are worse kinds of people than a Corey,' she said. 'You should know that.'

CHAPTER 31

Friesland, 1994

When she first saw him, he was running. At first a speck in the distance, way down at the bottom of a field of daffodils, and gradually a tall, thin pencil, and then he was running past, sweaty and slowing down, distracted by his watch.

'Good time?' she asked.

He glanced up at her, standing on the edge of the path, and frowned; he nodded towards the daffodils. 'You want me to take a photo of you?'

Ingrid looked at the camera she was holding at her side. 'What? No,' she said.

He bent down to tighten his shoelaces and she could see him studying her out the corner of his eye. *Perhaps he thinks that I'm going to mug him.*

She cleared her throat. 'What I meant was,' she said more slowly, 'are you completing your run,' she mimicked running, 'in a good time?' She pointed to an imaginary watch.

The young man straightened. 'Goodbye,' he said, voice clipped, and began running once more.

Ingrid sighed and continued walking, shoulders hunched, in the same direction as the runner along the path out of town. She thumbed the slip of paper in her pocket that had the address and thought about packing the whole idea in. An old lady walked past, pushing a trolley, thick legs working overtime, brown shoes worn thin.

The night before in the Friesland backpackers, Ingrid lay on her top bunk and felt the weight of distance bear her down. Europe, so far from home. Her country town by the river may as well have been on another planet. The beds in her dorm were bare, backpackers and tourists preferring the nightlife and reputation of Amsterdam. No couples trying to quietly shag, no loud snorers, no giggling drunks at 3 am. Ingrid missed them all. *Come back!* She thought of the times she'd cursed drunken lovers in bunks below her, the time she'd yelled at people who were threatening to spew. *Come back, all is forgiven!*

The mattress she lay on creaked sadly every time she turned. What she wouldn't give for a couple of Coreys to walk in, just so she could listen to them talk. It was funny, all those times at school spent dreaming about the day she'd go backpacking – the places she'd see, the people she'd meet, the nights out raging she'd have. That game with her friends, spinning a globe and putting a finger on what country they'd end up living in. It was all about adventure and the richness of life. What she'd never imagined was loneliness or that travel was really another word for escape.

She looked at the bunk across from her. What she wouldn't give for her old friend Joanne to be lying there! Not the Joanne of beachside Bronte with her tiny earrings and discreet gold necklace, but the old Joanne from Year 9 and 10. Joanne, who dared them all to swim a lap in their school uniforms in the seniors' pool. Joanne, who of course was the first to do so. She was so daring and cool – Ingrid would have done anything for her, anything!

Ingrid hugged herself, ran her hands up and down her body, grabbing at the thin material of her nightie. It would be so nice to have a boyfriend. Someone to tell her she was okay, that what she was doing was fine. Horrified to feel a sob coming on, she pressed her face into the pillow. All this wandering and wishing – and what for, after all?

Now, walking down the daffodil-lined path, Ingrid had the same thought. What for? She passed two tourists who clambered down the path into the daffodils and started taking photos. Were they Coreys? She didn't know. But they were idiots, trampling on the yellow flowers and posing with their prepared smiles.

Ingrid felt the paper in her pocket again, wondered about her recent faltering resolve. Thought about the years of drifting and stalling and not sleeping, and then remembered with a jolt the shark's eye and the grey body whipping by. Her strides lengthened; she forced herself to breathe in and out in a rhythm. She looked straight ahead, and her body moved as she willed it. *Inhale, one, two, three, four, five and exhale, one, two, three, four, five.* She may have given up competitive swimming at the end of school, but the lessons it taught her really may have saved her life. *One, two, three, inhale.*

The path turned and she entered a little village, grey stone houses on either side, muddy front gardens juxtaposed against the brilliant yellow of the daffodil fields behind. She studied her paper again, counted the house numbers and stopped outside sixteen. It had been as simple as looking in a telephone book and asking the woman on reception at the backpackers to find her the exact address. No different from all the rest, the house was neat and grey and without character. A small red car was parked out the front; a bike leant against the wall beside the door.

She knocked. Heavy footsteps came down the hall and a tall, dark figure appeared behind the frosted glass. She stood back a little, half-afraid and suddenly at a loss for what to say.

The door opened and Ingrid began to speak.

'You!' the person said. 'What is it now?'

'I'm here about Isa.'

The man she'd seen running studied her for a long time. 'Are you Australian?'

'Yes.'

He sighed, turned around and began walking back down the hall. The door was left open. She stood for a moment on the step, hesitating.

'Can I come in?' she called out.

'If it is about Anne,' the voice called back, 'then yes, you can. But I don't know how long we'll let you stay.'

Ingrid took a breath and stepped into the hall.

CHAPTER 32

Mark called Ingrid on the drive from Port York to Adelaide. No answer. He called again: nothing.

Radio on, he drove. Miles and miles of flat earth and scrappy shrubs and heat baking the earth like some hellish furnace. October, should it be this hot? He wound down the window and stuck his arm out, waving it in the headwind. It was easy to see how people could die out here. Each year, people walked their way to death, lost and confused. He recalled stories from years past, people driving off the side of the road to camp, getting bogged in the sand, becoming disorientated and walking in the opposite direction from the road. He'd always wondered why they didn't just follow the tyre tracks, but now it was obvious: the wind. The hot westerly winds swept over everything. Even now, with his arm waving in the air, he could see a fine layer of red dirt on his skin. *Sand will cover us all in time*, he thought. *But out here, you can see it coming.* And what a way to go. Mad with thirst, weak with heat, and the sand cutting into you, getting in your throat, making you hoarse. Yelling wouldn't work out here. Mark imagined someone clawing the desert air. He brought his arm inside, wound up the window. Rang Ingrid again, and this time she answered.

'Ingrid,' he said.

'Mark.' She sounded harried.

'You'll need to tell me why you lied about staying in the roadhouse.'

'What are you talking about?' It sounded as if she was carrying something heavy, her voice slightly out of breath.

'We've seen video footage. There were cameras in the rooms at the roadhouse – you didn't think about that? You were there, when by your own testimony you had already hitchhiked to Cutters End and were staying in the Underground Hotel.'

A silence. He imagined her thinking, brow furrowed, looking at the floor.

'So what?' she said. 'So what if I was there? It was thirty years ago, Mark.'

'Even so, you—'

'Can *you* remember thirty years ago?'

'Well, for something like that I think I'd—'

'Do you remember pushing me into a wall?'

Mark took a moment to register the words. He indicated left, pulled sharply over to the side of the road. 'Say that again?'

'I said, do you remember pushing me into a wall? It was after the pub one night, I had a bruise on my shoulder for weeks.'

Mark felt his heart beating. He held a palm to his forehead, closed his eyes. 'I think that is something I would remember, Ingrid. It's not true.'

'Isn't it, Mark? Have a think. Think back to all those years ago at school when you were some big football hero and I was your little lackey girlfriend.'

'I don't remember it that way.'

'Difficult to remember things we feel uncomfortable about, isn't it?' Ingrid sounded as if she was on the edge of tears. 'They're there though, hidden under scabs.'

'I never pushed you, Ingrid.' He wouldn't forget something like that. Surely.

There was a sigh on the end of the line. 'What do you want from me?'

He looked out to the long road ahead, end or beginning nowhere in sight. 'We need to know why you lied about staying in the roadhouse on the night of New Year's Eve. Why tell us you got a lift with someone who smelled like bacon?' *Jesus*, he thought. The whole thing sounded ridiculous.

'Mark.' There was a hard edge to her voice. 'I hitchhiked a lot. I stayed in a lot of places, it was a long time ago.'

'But you said the same story to the police ten days after the body was found.'

'I didn't tell them about the smell. I told you.'

'Why did you tell me that?'

'I don't know – his car smelled of bacon. Why wouldn't I tell you that? You were desperate for something new, so I told you that.'

The conversation was becoming absurd. All these lies and mistruths and half-truths, he was tired of it. Mark tried once more. 'I'm going to report this; my colleague probably already has. You've lied, Ingrid, at a time when a man went missing and was found dead not ten kilometres from where you were. And now. Right now, you're lying.'

'I've had enough of this, Mark.' She hung up and he closed his eyes for a second. This case was spiralling and he didn't know where. Enough of drifting, he was in a whirlpool now, spinning round and round and going places he didn't want to. He'd have to speak to Joanne next and report all this to Angelo.

The phone rang again. He looked at it. Kelly. He picked up.

'Will you be here tonight?' she asked. No preamble.

'Yep, later on.'

'Can you pick up the kids from Mum's? I'm going out.'

'Who with?' He hated the way he sounded. Churlish.

'People from work.'

'Have fun.'

'Hardly, we lost the fucking case yesterday.' Her voice was cold, dismissive.

'I'm sorry, Kelly.'

'Yeah, yeah. Everyone's sorry. We're all sorry. That's why we're going to drown ourselves in drink.'

'Okay. See you later then.'

She hung up without saying goodbye, the second woman in two minutes to do so, and he turned on the indicator again, pulled out onto the road. Really, he thought, it was no use even paying attention to road rules in places like this. You could do all sorts of things here and no one would know.

There wouldn't be a soul who could come back thirty years later and say, 'Look here – I know what you did.'

CHAPTER 33

Friesland, 1994

Ingrid stepped into a room filled with books and flowers. The contrast with the drab exterior had a blinding effect, made her blink like a prisoner out of solitary.

The man Ingrid had followed was standing by a fireplace, talking with an older woman in an orange dress, her grey hair swept up in a bun and pinned together with a shiny brooch.

'My mother, Julia,' the man said, gesturing towards the other woman.

'Who are you?' Julia said, her clipped English perhaps better than her son's.

'My name is Ingrid Alice Mathers. I have the same initials as your daughter.'

'That makes you an expert?'

'Her initials are kind of what got me started on all this. Us having the same, the I.A.M., it, well . . .'

'Go on.'

'I think I may know what happened to her.'

'*May* know?' Julia arched her eyebrows and looked sideways at her son.

The son picked up a snow globe and shook it. Bits of white flakes scattered and fell over a little boy and girl holding hands. 'We have many people coming here who tell us they may know what happened to my sister. Psychics, mainly.'

'Are you a psychic?' Julia turned to her, blue eyes narrowed, hard.

'No.'

'Remember the last one?' Her son turned to the woman. 'She told us that Anne was in South America, living in a cult.'

'I remember.'

'And then there was the man with the photos.' The son studied the snow globe closely. 'He said he had evidence of Anne living as a sex slave in Romania.'

Ingrid cut in, 'I don't want to—'

The man ignored her. 'He wanted ten thousand guilders for the photos. Moeder and I did not believe him, of course. We called the policeman and he was escorted out of town.'

'That's terrible, that's . . .'

The man put the snow globe down carefully. He pulled his hands through his hair and looked out the window. 'My father, however, *did* believe him. He was always believing them. He gave this man the money and received in return an envelope with photos of Filipino children in a cage.'

His mother clasped her hands together and he walked across to her, standing behind the back of her chair. 'Just leave,' he said, more tired than annoyed. 'If you are a psychic, leave. If you are a con woman, leave. If you are a journalist – leave immediately. We are done with people like you.'

Ingrid turned to go. There was nothing here, she thought. All resolve and her half-baked ideas seemed amateur and childish. She pushed a lock of hair behind her ears.

'Goodbye,' she said. 'I'm sorry for bothering you.'

But the older woman spoke. 'You should wear it loose,' she said, touching her own grey locks. 'You have very pretty hair.'

Ingrid reached up to her ponytail, felt the length of it. 'It's too messy,' she said. 'It just blows about all the time. I should shave it off.'

'Girls are always trying to hide their hair – why? I never did.'

Ingrid stood, her eye on the son, not sure of what to do. She gave a small shrug.

'How old are you?' Julia spoke more kindly now. 'You look very young.'

'I'm almost twenty-four.'

'One year younger than Sander here. Such babies still.'

Sander gave a long sigh. 'Mama, she has to go.'

His mother ignored him. 'What did you want to tell us? You don't look like a psychic, not enough cheap silver and you've pretty hair instead of ugly purple dye.'

'I think I know what happened to Isa.'

There was a moment's silence. 'You really *do* think you know,' the son said.

'Yes.'

'Well, tell us then. I'm curious now.' Julia settled back in her chair.

Sander shook his head and leant against a bookshelf, refusing to look anywhere near Ingrid.

'Tell us then,' the woman repeated. 'And tell it properly, don't leave anything out – we've already imagined the very worst.'

She told them. She told them properly. She left nothing out.

CHAPTER 34

Back home, Mark poured himself a whiskey and took it out onto the porch. His sons asleep after sausages, a bath and some half-hearted bedside reading, he scrolled through his phone and thought about his past; the days in 'Coppers Christi', the residential college for police in training, and the heavy nights drinking out on the town. Always out on the town. On the prowl, on the pull, on the booze, on the grog. On something, never with.

His best mate at the time, Richo, had a way with women – constantly in between breaking up with girlfriends and finding a new one. Mark sometimes said that he ended up with Richo's leftovers, women who didn't quite make the grade of his mate's lofty standards. But what was that sort of thinking? Mark pondered now. All that talk of leftovers and making the grade and the meat market – it made him ill to think of his sons in ten years.

And worse, a deep struggle to remember . . . other things. A video late at night with a group of blokes, them watching it, watching Richo having it off with some girl he'd met at a pub. Who was that girl? None of them bothered to consider or ask if she'd consented to being filmed. There at Richo's house, in the dim light with the blue of the television flickering and their stomachs full of booze and a dark connection that spoke of something between sex and violence, none had questioned why Richo videoed himself having sex with some girl, and none questioned themselves watching. Always the watching and never the doing. But did the doing spring from the watching? Always on and never with.

He tried to remember pushing Ingrid, couldn't recall it. There were arguments at times – youthful tears, snot and yelling – but pushing? He wasn't the sort. A push takes force and he wasn't forceful. Ingrid was lying. She must be lying, about all manner of things.

Had he used force? The thought wavered, wouldn't go away. He sipped his whiskey and looked out into the night. A car drove slowly past his house, the engine a mellow hum. Mark could make out a figure bent over the wheel, head stretched forward as if straining to see. And what was there to see? At this time of the night, not much. A quiet street, respectable gardens with polite letterboxes out the front. Small facades hiding wealth – the renovations, the decks, the double-glassed doors. All secrets lay within, not out front.

The car did a U-turn, drove past again, almost at walking pace, the driver still bent like a magician's fork.

Mark finished his drink, chucked the ice over the porch into the garden. He could have thrown it at the car if he'd wanted to. When he was thirteen he used to do such things. It was fun, throwing things at random, just to see what would come next.

He stood up, bent over the porch railings and watched the tail-lights of the car blink as the car turned onto the main road. The person must have been lost; false directions, faulty reading of the map.

A thought niggled at the back of his mind and stayed there. He'd missed something, but it was just there – a realisation away. He tested the back of his mind again, tried to clear the fog, tried to see the faint lights. Nothing. They faded into the night.

He'd already had the call from Jagdeep, who had phoned Joanne in Sydney. Nothing to report there either. Hazy on dates, vague on details – Jagdeep thought Joanne a snob who was hiding something. When Jagdeep had said that 'the investigation into a historic crime involves examination of prior times and dates,' Joanne had said, 'You mean *an* historic crime.'

'What a bitch,' Jagdeep railed down the phone to Mark. 'I'd hate to have been in your social group of friends at school.' Joanne told Jagdeep that she had no recollection of Ingrid staying with her at the roadhouse on New Year's Eve. They'd been travelling together for a while and before that, they were always at school together. After a while, most nights merge into one, Joanne told her, and Jagdeep admitted she had to agree. But – missing out on a party on New Year's

Eve when you're eighteen? Would that disappointment have blurred as easily? Jagdeep had doubts. Of course it didn't mean anything significant yet. The two women, however, would need to explain further.

He looked at his empty whiskey glass, poured another; dark brown like solid earth. All nights did seem to blur into one. His past was like a squeeze box, pulled out the length of a beat, then collapsed into a single tune. In truth, the golden years were beginning to fade. All that nostalgia was probably based on photographs and not actual memory.

He looked at his phone; Kelly still hadn't called. He stood and jumped up and down on the spot. That niggle, he couldn't shake it. If only he was smarter, more alert, more on the ball.

More like Joanne – the thought came to him in a rush. Joanne was always the smart one, quick-planning and calm. She would have made an excellent cop. A memory: Joanne in maths, Year 10. The teacher had written a complex problem on the board and was waiting for them to answer it. Joanne, meanwhile, was looking bored – tapping her fingers onto the wooden desk she shared with Mark. The teacher told her off: 'Are you going to do any work or just sit there daydreaming?'

'I don't daydream,' she'd said coldly. 'And your answer is forty-three.'

The teacher was taken aback and Mark, sitting beside her, felt the chill.

The phone rang. Jagdeep again. He took his glass of whiskey and walked inside. 'Yes?' he said. 'What's up?'

Her voice was scratchy over the phone. Mark asked her to repeat herself, asked her how she was, but she cut him off, her customary bluntness always a jolt.

'They've found something, the analysts,' she said.

He waited, a heaviness in his gut. He knew she was referring to the search of the site where Michael Denby was found dead.

'A new development.' Her voice was cutting in and out, so Mark had to step inside his bedroom, shut the door and cup the phone to his ear. Jagdeep kept talking: 'Ago . . . analyst says . . . new, no ID . . . the press will need to be . . .'

'Slow down!' he said. 'I can't hear you properly.'

'Sorry, it's my phone. Been playing up.' Her voice was now suddenly calm and clear. 'Look, there's been a development. Hush hush till it's official. You're going to need to go and pick up the report from Forensics.'

'What did they find?' He'd missed it when she said it the first time.

'Human bone fragments recovered from the site, possibly from the forearm.'

He waited, hearing the dread in Jagdeep's voice. 'The bones are not Denby's, Mark. They're from someone else.'

Mark was silent. His colleague spoke again, her words punching the air. 'Can you hear me?'

He could. He could hear her just fine.

CHAPTER 35

Friesland, 1994

After Ingrid left the Moddermans' little house, she went back to her dorm room and lay on her bed. She imagined herself a prisoner in the Tower of London, in some dank cell with coldness seeping through the walls. She could picture it: the footsteps up the stairs, the rapping on the door, the jostling of men, the manacles, the fear, the shame.

She huddled up in her sleeping bag and looked out the window to the flat fields beyond, the yellow of the daffodils dazzling against a grey sky. She missed home – her childhood home, that was – the dry country town with its wide, slow river and drooping gums. She'd never swim in the North European rivers, with their dark silver currents deadly as a knife.

Before she left the house, the older woman turned away from her without speaking. The space between her feet and the woman expanded – she may as well have been on a distant hemisphere.

Sander stood, head bowed for a long moment before he walked over to her, took her by the elbow and escorted her out, as if she was too unseemly to be present in their company. As she stepped out the door, he asked her in a quiet voice where she was staying and what her plans were, because, well, they would need to know. Ingrid told him: the next morning she was headed back to Amsterdam, to the Hans Brinker Hostel, where she'd try to get some work to raise money for the trip home. There was some work on reception there, she added, her voice trailing off then gaining strength. She would stay four weeks at most, so if anyone needed to see her there or ask questions or whatever, that was where she'd be.

But lying on the top bunk, looking at the fields growing darker and the yellow ever more brilliant, Ingrid only wanted to go home. Preferably back in time too, to when she was a kid leaping off rope swings and riding her bike.

Before she closed her eyes to sleep, ears open to the sound of thudding feet, she thought of the sleek grey body of the shark, how flexible and quick it had been. On another day, she might have mistaken it for a dolphin riding the waves. That was the thing, Ingrid thought; you never knew what someone or something was till it looked you in the eye, till it declared, 'Look at me, this is what I am, make no mistake.'

The next morning, Ingrid travelled back to Amsterdam and signed up to work at the hostel. As backpacker places went, it wasn't bad. She'd been in ones where going to the bathroom on a Sunday meant an evil game of dodge the spew. There was no jelly fighting like there was in the

Cairns backpackers, and for that she was glad. Jelly was terrible to clean up. She was still waiting for the knock at the door, still ready to stand and say, 'Yes that's me,' but one day passed, two days, and nothing happened. On the third day she was trying to explain to an Australian couple how best to get to the Anne Frank museum, when Mieke, the woman she'd first been to see, entered reception. As she shook down her coat and looked about her with cool interest, the Australian couple shrank as if before greatness. *That's the thing about Australians*, Ingrid thought. *We like to believe that we're egalitarian, but really, we're still in thrall to the bigwig.*

'Can I help you?' Ingrid asked.

Mieke flicked her hand towards the couple in a gesture for them to finish their business, but they backed off at speed. Ingrid half-thought they would salute.

Mieke looked around her, to the posters advertising pub crawls, African safaris, share houses, cheap tickets to Lima, and a handwritten sign: 'JEZ WHEN YOU GET HERE COME FIND ME, I'LL BE IN THE BAR OR SLEEPING, SIR RAZ.'

'Who is Sir Raz?' Mieke asked, with genuine interest.

Ingrid shook her head. 'I'm not sure.'

'Would you say he is a Corey?'

'I don't think you'll find him at Rembrandt House.'

Mieke sat down on the chair opposite Ingrid's desk and crossed her legs. *This is it,* Ingrid thought, *the door will now burst open and there'll be television cameras at the window.* 'Sander called me. He told me about your visit.'

Ingrid looked hard at the Sir Raz sign. You could find anyone if you wanted, she thought. Sir Raz would be found.

'I came to see if you would like a job,' Mieke said, noting Ingrid start. 'This Corey project is taking up all my time and I wondered if you would work through the papers for me – submissions, ideas, some translation. It's really just filing, but I do need help and you sound as if you need the work.'

'I'm only planning on being here three or four weeks, till I get enough to go home,' Ingrid said.

'Well'—Mieke tapped the desk twice—'now you can do it in two. I'll pay you the proper rate and I doubt you're receiving that here.'

It was true. The amount she was earning barely covered food and board.

'Why are you helping me?'

'Anne, or Isa as you call her, was my good friend; I like her family. I'm in a position to help you and so I will.'

So it happened that three days a week, Ingrid went to Mieke's house to work. It calmed her, the walk from the hostel to the house by the silver-grey canal. The streets became familiar and after the backpackers, Ingrid found that she enjoyed the quiet of Mieke's place. The coffee in small cups, the *speculaas*, the rustling of papers and files.

On the second week, Sander showed up at Mieke's house towards the end of Ingrid's shift and offered to walk her back to the hostel. He was sorry, he said, about the way she was treated at his family home. It was just the shock, he explained. As they strolled, Ingrid hesitant, Sander talked no more about her visit and what she had revealed. Instead, he spoke about the city, about his share house, about the game of *fierljeppen*, or canal jumping, he used to play as a boy. Walking and listening, Ingrid felt a loosening, as if somewhere inside her, extra string was being released from a spool.

It was pleasant, listening to him talk, and when he said he'd see her the next day she didn't object. Two weeks longer in Amsterdam turned to three, and it began to seem normal that, besides the walk, they'd also stop for a drink and something to eat. Mieke asked if she'd like to stay on for another month and Ingrid agreed. When one night Sander kissed her as they said goodbye, it seemed only natural that he should stay in her room at the hostel, and then the night after that, she at his. In those days, she felt that she could already see the trajectory of how it would go. The gentle rise and fall, the kind gestures after lust, and always beneath, always the Sturm und Drang – the turbulence of life. But at that time, in those days when she worked with Mieke and walked with Sander, Ingrid focused mainly on the forgiving embrace of people from another land.

And when one day, eight weeks after they'd first met, she received a notification that her work visa was overdue and told Sander she'd have to go home, he suggested she get sponsored by Mieke, to try to stay. They asked Mieke; she agreed. Ingrid and Sander moved in together, a small apartment near the red-light district. They were happy, she remembered. Fixated.

But after a few years, she found that she missed the wide open spaces, the big skies of Australia. She began to remember why she'd come to the Netherlands in the first place, all the things she still had to do. Occasionally, she thought of the eye of the shark, a predator she strove to be free from. So when, after almost five years in Holland, she asked Sander to come home with her, she felt an immense relief that his answer was yes.

CHAPTER 36

Mark woke to the sound of Kelly vomiting in the front yard. At first, he thought it was some wild animal howling in the wind, and then he recognised the familiar, anguished tone of the drunk in a fallen state. As he stumbled about in the dark, finding the lights and making his way to her, Mark noted the time, 2.45 am, and the voracity of the spew. It told of a night of hard drinking, most likely brown spirits. Probably dancing, maybe a smoke or two.

When he opened the front door, Kelly was on her knees, half-crying in between the doleful swallow and purge. He did the right things – held her hair away from her face, rubbed her back – and when she was finished, helped her inside. She limped beside him like a puppet, lifting her arms up so he could remove her shirt, then dropping them hard at her sides. 'Fucking fuckheads,' she dribbled. 'Law is so crap.' And listening to her, he had to agree.

When he laid her on the bed, she pulled him to her and

whispered hot in his ear, 'Next Tuesday,' and even as he recoiled from her vomit breath, he felt a kind of longing for the following week. What was next Tuesday? Not their anniversary. He pondered for a second while she crawled into a ball and continued moaning about the state of the law. Not her birthday or one of the boys'. Not his.

Kelly lay on the bed in her undies and bra, her blue socks wrinkled and her face a sea of snot and tears. She reminded him suddenly of a young girl, and he covered her up with the doona, placed a bucket beside her head. How easy it would be for someone to take advantage of her, he thought, and for the first time, rightly or wrongly, he was glad he had no daughters.

It was 3.30 am – no rest for the wicked. He couldn't sleep in the room with his wife, not with her vomit breath and the low moaning of a person on the brink of a hangover sent straight from hell. He pulled a blanket out of the cupboard and took himself into the lounge room, where he settled on the couch and listened to the sounds of his house. *Next Tuesday*, he thought before drifting off to sleep. Surely by next Tuesday the world would appear less haphazard, and all within it would be methodical and calm.

Daylight hours brought no relief for his wife. When he poked his head in to see her before he went to work, she lay in a sea of agony, white-faced and sombre. 'What happened?' she asked him. 'I can't even remember getting home.'

'You were off your face. And what's next Tuesday?'

Kelly, holding a bag of frozen peas to her forehead, looked confused. 'Tuesday?'

In the room down the corridor, Mark could hear one son beginning to wake. 'Got to go,' he said to his wife. 'You'll forgive me for not kissing you goodbye.'

Kelly looked at him with a blank face and laid her head down on the pillow.

'See you later,' Mark said, and a limp hand rose from somewhere beneath the covers to give him a farewell.

On the way to the Forensics office in central Adelaide, Mark rang Angelo. His boss had already heard from Jagdeep about the video with Ingrid and Joanne, and was keen for further questioning. Angelo knew, too, about the search of the site and the meeting Mark was about to attend.

'Jesus, Angelo,' Mark said. 'What am I here for?'

'You're my eyes and ears,' Angelo said.

'While you're off hobnobbing with the elite?'

'Exactly. Hobnobbing is what I do.'

Angelo asked him if he'd heard; Suzanne Miller was out of a job. The channel she worked for had given her the flick for a younger presenter, someone who was more relatable to the young folk of today.

'When you say "young folk", you sound as if you're ninety,' Mark said.

'I feel it.'

Mark thought about Suzanne Miller, with her flowing curls and megawatt smile. Surely kids couldn't care less about who presented *Fun with Shapes*, as long as it was someone who could dance and look as if they were having fun. It was more likely the executives of the station had given her the heave-ho because of her age. Younger women with fewer lines, firmer chests, lower wage brackets and on the brink of their careers – they were the ones the bigwigs wanted. Those more likely to say 'yes, please' instead of 'piss off'. *Poor Suzanne*, he thought. Scrambling for some media attention by dredging up the past; surely now all the future held was a half-decent podcast and an invitation to *I'm a Celebrity . . . Get Me Out of Here!* She'd be eating the arse out of an armadillo in less time than it took to say 'triangle'.

'What about Suzanne's husband?' he asked. 'How did he do in his lobbying?'

'Too early to tell.'

'Well, we won't be hearing from Suzanne again, then.'

'Probably not. But she got the ball rolling on this whole investigation, she's the reason we're all in this mess.'

Some mess you're in, Mark thought. *You and your Mercedes-Benz.*

'Talking about mess.' Angelo cleared his throat, Mark waited. 'You may find in Forensics today there's a little awkwardness, couldn't be helped.'

Mark felt his stomach drop to his knees. Forensics, he should have known.

'Anyway,' Angelo continued, 'be needing a full report in the next week. Send everything you've got, every minute detail, every time you or someone you met picked their jocks out of their arse. Then we can move on to other, more important matters.'

'Like funding allocations for the force after the election?' Mark guessed that was what Angelo had been working on. All the fancy dinners, the politicians, the background knowledge on Eric Valer.

'Exactly.'

Mark turned into the Forensics parking lot and switched off the engine. He told himself that fifty was the new thirty, that he was in a good place, that the past is the past is the past. He patted down his hair and entered the glass doors, and two officers were waiting to meet him. One, a younger male he didn't recognise, the other, a female he did.

'Acting Inspector Mark Ariti,' she said, shaking her head. 'You again.'

'Detective Senior Sergeant Jane Southern,' he replied, reaching to shake both their hands. 'Me again.'

Jane, he noted, looked the same on first glance. The short dark hair, the tall lean build, the fitted suit and low heels. But as she and her partner filled him in on the way to the lab, on the procedures they'd followed, the trip taken by the SA experts to the location of Denby's death, and the papers which would now need to be filed, he saw that she looked tired, drained even. There were dark circles under her eyes and she'd lost weight, if that was even possible. He was used to seeing her wearing red lipstick, but today she seemed subdued.

In the lab, the two detectives showed him the microscope, and he peered in and saw a confusing array of lines and dots. 'That means nothing to me,' he said, surfacing. 'I don't even know if I'm looking at something in my eyelid.'

The male officer, whose name escaped Mark, began to explain before Jane cut in. 'All you need to know is that we found evidence of blood from the deceased and possibly some hair fragments which match Denby's DNA. But we also found something else.' Here she paused and Mark waited. 'The analysts found bone fragments too – and not Denby's.'

Mark widened his eyes, aiming for surprise. He saw Jane look at him and narrow hers.

The expert continued: 'That in itself is interesting enough, but our SA analysts – and this is why it took them some time to disclose the fact – believe that the bones have been lying there for some time. A decade or so before Denby's death, in fact.'

Mark felt a slight rise of panic in his chest, though he hardly knew why. A decade *before* Denby? He saw Jane still watching him closely and he took a breath. 'Do we know anything about the bone?'

'Possibly finger, forearm matches. And female, probably young. Beyond that – we won't know much more till we get some DNA matches from the Nat database; missing persons, et cetera, et cetera.'

That could take a while. Mark made a note to ask Angelo to get them to speed up the results.

The male officer handed him their report. 'The press have apparently got hold of most of this information already,' he said. 'Some journo from up north was sniffing around the search site, asking questions.'

Mark thought of the dogged Hugh from the *Port York Advertiser*. Snooping around, a growing excitement.

Weapons of mass destruction? Not quite – but a bomb of sorts.

The forensic report was complex and he stood for a few minutes, trying to decipher the codes and medical terms. At the bottom of the page, neatly typed:

> *Site search and analysis revealed older evidence linked to an individual other than Denby. Fragments of bone, found 1–7 cm apart. Possibly finger phalanges and radial. Female, age not yet ascertained, likely late teen. DNA samples revealed traces of blood in a radius of one metre. No spatter formation.*

Mark signed the necessary form to state he'd received the report from the lab, and put all papers in an A4 envelope Jane handed him.

Outside, the city was sharp with thin rays of sunshine and office windows gave off harsh, glinted light. After making small talk – football, the election, Angelo's ascent – the younger officer said his goodbyes and turned back inside.

Mark looked at Jane. 'Coffee?'

Jane hesitated for a second before giving a brief nod, and together they walked to a place a couple of doors up from the lab, decided on a table and sat down.

'I never know whether to sit at a table or at one of those bench things by the window,' Mark said. He looked at a group of businessmen hesitating with the choice. 'It's a real problem.'

'Tell me, where does the United Nations sit on that issue?' Jane asked, and they both smiled.

'It was a surprise seeing you here today,' Mark said.

'I was warned,' Jane replied. 'And I wasn't too happy – but then I thought, well, we can't go on ignoring one another for ever.'

'I was surprised you left Fraud so soon after I went on leave.'

'Really? Why would I stay?' Jane glanced out the window. 'It was only ever temporary and without you it wasn't too pleasant, what with all the talk. And,' she added, 'I don't like being called a cougar.'

'You got called that?' Jesus, she was hardly much older than him.

'What did you get called? A toy boy, I suppose?'

'Me? I got called a lucky bastard.' Immediately Mark felt his face grow hot. He shouldn't have said it. But it was true. Of all the gossip after the affair, that was the phrase that most stuck. All the overweight married cops in Fraud coveting their Super and planning the next cruise – Jane Southern may as well have been a mirage. When they told him he was a lucky bastard, they said it half in sadness and half in wonder. The yearning, the loss – men don't change much from adolescence. His female colleagues hadn't been so admiring of the affair. Kelly, though they barely knew her, was first and foremost in their minds. The photograph of her on his desk eyed the women in his office sadly, and they answered that look. Women stick together. It's a good thing. But he shouldn't have told Jane just now that he had been called lucky.

Mark focused hard on his menu, then ordered a flat white from a waiter with a stupid moustache thing on his chin.

'Are you still with Kelly?' Jane asked.

'Yes, we're working things out. We're trying.'

'That's good.' There was a moment of silence.

'You work things out with Rod?'

Jane smoothed the table with her hand. 'Rod left me.'

'I'm so sorry, Jane.' He *was* sorry. It didn't seem fair that she was now alone when Kelly had stayed with him. He remembered reading an article that stated it took, on average, two years for a man to find a new partner after their old one had died. For women it was an average of five years or never. Men really were arseholes. His eyes followed the waiter and his chin moustache thing. Dickheads too. Why would a bloke leave someone like Jane? For a brief affair? Give me a break. It's hardly a hanging offence. Suddenly, he felt very tired.

Moustache presented them with their coffees, telling them to *Enjoy, guys.*

Jane took a sip of hers and looked at her watch. 'Listen,' she said. 'There was something else the analyst told me, unofficially of course.'

Mark believed it; men told Jane things. He had told her things. Things that made him blush when he recalled them now. He drank his coffee. He listened. Tilted his head closer to her.

'The analyst told me his initial thoughts were that we should spread the search wider. Go out, look for other evidence.'

'Why would he say that?'

'Because'—Jane leant in over the table, her perfume a woody mix of flowers and bark—'he found *another* piece of bone. Not official yet. Too early to tell if it was from the same woman as the other fragments, but he has his suspicions. Go wider, he said.'

Two different bone specimens? The female's from a decade earlier and now one more? Mark closed his eyes. Suzanne Miller could not have possibly known what she had uncovered. Locard's exchange principle; the theory held tight, offered possibilities and dread. Belanglo, Milat, *Wolf Creek* – all the old fears came back.

Jane finished the rest of her coffee and stood. 'I'm not sure we'll be seeing each other again, Mark – or should I say Acting Inspector? But good luck with everything.'

'We may need to talk further on the bones when the new findings come out.'

Jane took a lipstick out of her pocket, applied it quickly and without fuss. 'You know where to find me,' she said.

CHAPTER 37

1999

When they landed in Australia after almost five years in Amsterdam and in time for Christmas, Ingrid felt the hot slap of a dry wind that told her she was back. Adelaide was in the midst of a heatwave, five consecutive days of temperatures over forty and boiling nights which made for fevered dreams. They spent the first few days in Ingrid's hometown of Booralama, where Sander swam in the brown river, hurled himself off rope swings, and drank icy beer with overweight uncles. His pale European face stained a blotchy red on the second day, and his lips peeled and blistered. Jet lagged, thirsty and covered in flies, Sander could be forgiven for hating the joint. But, as he sat with her father eating a sausage in white bread and drinking another VB, Ingrid could see that he wasn't hating it at all. On the contrary, Sander seemed to thrive with a nervous energy undetectable to Ingrid in the Netherlands.

One stifling night, coming to bed after rabbit or roo shooting with Uncle Frank, he wondered in a drunken voice at how friendly and open Australians were. This had surprised him, he said. He was brought up to believe differently, thought Australians were largely incompetent, lazy and reluctant to admit error.

'But that was just the police force back then,' Ingrid said, wiping his hair from his sweaty forehead as he lay beside her. 'We're not all like that.'

He was quiet. 'Frank told me that you are a good shot.'

It was true: growing up she used to be a dab hand with a .22 calibre rifle. Tin cans and rabbits mostly.

'I was okay.' Ingrid remembered standing on the back of the ute at night, headlights on, searching for roos. As a kid, she loved the speed, the weight of the .22, the thrill of the hunt. Now, the memory filled her with a deep distaste.

The following week, Ingrid and Sander hired a car and drove along the south-east coast, all along the winding roads beside the lagoons and the wild ocean. One night a storm threatened and they huddled close in their tent, watching lightning sear the sky above a choppy sea. On the fourth day they reached the little town of Brae Inlet near Warnbeen, and rented a cabin in the caravan park across the road from the beach. Ingrid showed him newspaper clippings and notes she'd made, the ones she'd kept at her family home all this time. Sander flicked through them, distracted and vague. He didn't know she'd done all this research. When Ingrid said that she wouldn't mind living in such a place as Brae Inlet, he became angry and questioned her motives. She yelled, he yelled, and in a move that shocked them both, Sander threw a wine glass hard against the wall, smashing it. A small shard flew out, cutting Ingrid on the foot. Red wine ran down white paint and Ingrid stood startled, looking at the blood welling near her little toe. It seemed to her to be from a different foot, not hers.

Sander sat with his hands wrapped around his head, murmuring apologies.

Ingrid did not say a thing. She swept up the broken glass. She sponged the blood away from the floor and wiped the walls. She placed a plaster neatly over the cut. In time the small wound left a scar, but of their fight, that was the only trace.

Sander went for a walk on the beach and came back to find her lying on the bed. He lay beside her, wrapped his big arms around her body, and told her he was finally ready to travel north.

On the way to that place, desolation etched in the Dutchman's face, Ingrid drove while Sander stared out the window at the wide brown land. When he asked to stop and get out, she remained in the car, watching him while he paced, with head turned to the ground and hands gripped together like a priest reading the last rites.

At the roadhouse, Ingrid let Sander go in to pay for the petrol. It wasn't an old man serving, he said – it was a young man, shiny like a Christmas decoration. According to the shiny guy, an old man did still own the place: Coke bottle glasses and grossly overweight. Not a good boss.

Up the Stuart they drove, and Ingrid stopped where she thought she should stop, and they both got out and wandered around the scrub. They didn't speak. After a short while they found a stunted tree and Sander bent down, reading the bark on it, looking for signs. He rested his cheek on the tree for a long time. Ingrid didn't go close, kept her hand over her mouth, willing herself not to be sick. Difficult to know if it was the right tree, but the landscape overwhelmed, made her heart thump and head ache.

After that, Ingrid decided she didn't want to go any further, so Sander dropped her at the roadhouse where she caught a bus to Adelaide, and then another to the small town in the south-east of the state. She took her clippings and her notes and her research with her. *I.A.M.!* she thought – her old inspiration, her spur, but it was harder now that other people were involved.

I.A.M.! That mentality – it's a solitary pursuit; only you can save yourself from the shark. It's hard to rescue others, or help others, or lift them up on your raft. Sometimes it's best you don't.

Sander kept driving; first to Cutters End, where he spent New Year's Eve 1999. There was a party at the Underground Hotel where he stayed, and he joined two friendly Croatians at the bar for an hour or so. They suggested he travel up to Alice Springs and Uluru with them, but he said maybe another time. Instead, he drove back down the highway and stopped to look once more at the little tree. Such a small tree, he thought, minute against the enormous sky and the distant horizon. He thought perhaps it would be the opposite, but the tree made Sander love Ingrid all the more, and he drove all the way down to the small town where she was and asked her to marry him and forget about it all.

On one condition: he would live in Australia, but Adelaide first, not in Brae – at least for a few years. They needed to get on with their lives. In hindsight, it was a simple thing to ask.

CHAPTER 38

Back at home, Mark read the paper online:

OUTBACK INVESTIGATION WIDENS

Bone fragments have been found on the site of investigation into the January 1990 death of Michael Denby, the man who saved the life of a young Suzanne Miller.

Following findings, a spokeswoman for South Australian police said: 'Although it is too early to say precisely how old these fragments are, initial forensic investigations suggest they are not recent and are likely to be up to a decade older than any remains of Michael Denby. Specialists are being deployed to recover and examine them.

'We'd ask people not to speculate online about the nature of the bones while this process is underway. Such actions could jeopardise the investigation and any future court case.'

Nearby roadhouse owner, Kay Forster, said that since police arrived, there had been a lot of activity. 'They are searching the land just up from here and we've been told that human remains have been found,' she said. 'It's very concerning – this is such a peaceful place, we've never had any trouble here at all.'

Mark turned off his iPad, cleared the table, picked up the recycling and took it to the bin outside, wheeled it to the front of the kerb. Life goes on and bin night cannot be ignored. A neighbour walked past and he stopped for a chat, stooping to pat the man's little dog.

'Is Kelly all right?' the neighbour asked. 'Haven't seen her out walking for a while.'

Mark looked at the man, whose name he could barely recall. *All these observant people*, he thought. *They should have been cops.* Again, that feeling he was on the outside of things, looking in. 'Kelly's fine,' he said. 'Just a bit snowed under with work.'

The neighbour looked at him closely. 'Yes, that must be it,' he said, and kept walking.

Back in the house, Mark went into the study and paused in the doorway, watching his wife. Kelly was bent over a laptop, typing hard. She jumped when Mark asked her if she wanted a coffee, and then shook her head. 'I'm contacting people about the case,' she said. 'We've got to work quickly if we've any hope of an appeal.'

'But isn't it all over? You need a break from it, Kel.'

She turned to him, suddenly furious. 'You think it's over?' She grabbed a photo from her desk, the one of the woman with her face punched in. 'You think this is over for her?'

She pointed at the woman. 'God, Mark, you seriously don't get it, do you?'

He stepped back; it was as if she had slapped him. *Do something*, she may as well have said. *Fuck off*, she meant.

He backed out, went to close the door as she spoke again, sniffing. 'Someone from your school rang, a Maria somebody. She wanted to know if you're going to the reunion. It's next weekend, you should have replied by now.'

Mark closed the door of the study and left her to murder the keyboard while he sat with the two boys on the couch. Kelly was speaking on the phone to someone, voice raised, angry. 'I asked you not to send that!' she was saying. 'I specifically asked you not to, Robyn!'

A thought came to Mark: the images of Lynette Denby, face smashed, eye flooded in red. He thought of Darryl recalling what his old colleague in Cutters End had said, that there was a Milat in every town if you looked hard enough. He pictured the old cop in the dingy station, researching the disappearances of the sisters, of the Dutch girl, Isa or Anne, going over the evidence again and again. Those other names, too: Donna Arlington, Carly North. That was police work. The rereading, the files, the going over.

He removed his arm from around one of his sons and collected from the bottom of his suitcase the manila folder Darryl had given him. A Milat in every town. Moving rooms, he settled himself on his bed, door open so he could see the boys. He opened the file. The papers, most of them familiar, fell out. The article about the two missing sisters, the photo of them, some accompanying notes. He looked over them again; nothing new. But still – something ticked over in his mind.

Of the two photos in their file, there was one with the sisters smiling broadly into the camera, backpacks on and standing in front of a brick facade. Their home in Warnbeen, most likely. He studied the photo closely. Nothing came to mind, but still. He flicked to the second one, the image that accompanied the newspaper report he'd read. In this one, the girls leant against the side of a vehicle, arms folded and feet crossed. The younger of the two (or older?), in her blue outfit, peered slightly to the left of the camera, mouth half-open, as if she was in the middle of a conversation.

This case, he thought. It was about images and stills of videos and photos. He recalled Sander on the wall of the backpackers, Michael Denby's beaten wife, Ingrid and Joanne in the roadhouse donga, Michael Denby's twisted and burnt frame at the bottom of his vehicle.

But what was he looking at here exactly? He peered at the sisters, Raelene and Adele Cunningham, in the photo. Mark put the images down and read the article again; the descriptions of them being well liked, the townsfolk worried and so on. He turned to the photo once more, held it up to his eyes and, with a jolt of recognition, saw what it was. Tiny and half-hidden by Raelene, an image of a leaf-shaped flower on the vehicle's frame. The Sturt Desert Pea – he'd seen the sticker before on a vehicle just like this one. He'd seen it. The vehicle the sisters leant on was the same one he'd seen on the backpackers wall and on Foobie's phone: the

LandCruiser that belonged to John Baber, husband of the local doctor and the man who discovered the broken body of Michael Denby.

Mark reeled. Doubles, he remembered. John Baber was a man who enjoyed reading about duality, two sides of the same person. The thought made Mark uneasy. Unable to keep still, he stood and walked around the room. John Baber's reputation was impeccable around town – the barman from the Opal Inn had said so.

He checked the time. The pub would be open. Googling the number and then dialling, Mark watched the boys while he waited, unsure exactly of what he should ask.

'Hello there.' A woman's voice. Friendly and warm. The Dolly Parton lookalike. He tried to focus on that and not the image of her on the bed that Foobie had thrust in his face.

'Hi,' Mark said. 'Acting Inspector Ariti here. The policeman from Adelaide who ate at your—'

'Oh, I remember you,' she broke in, voice warm. 'When're you coming back to town, love?'

He chatted for a while and then asked her about John Baber.

'John,' she said. 'We couldn't do without him. Anything we need, he's on his way to Port York, he's coming around here fixing things, the sort that would do anything for you. Reliable as clockwork.'

Mark held the phone a little distance from his ear. *Gandhi wouldn't get a better recommendation*, he thought. 'Back in the day, John was the type to pick up hitchhikers? Give people lifts on his way back and forth to town?'

'Oh, always, love, he was always giving lifts to people. Anyone who needed one. He used to give them to me on occasion! Big heart, our John, big heart. And seriously, you can set your watch by him!'

Mark said his goodbyes, promised to visit once more, and yes, he'd bring his family, and yes, he'd make sure to make himself known.

He put the phone down. Thought about John in his house, the violence in the books he liked, the stillness of the room. The dark. He called Jagdeep, left a message for her on what he'd found.

CHAPTER 39

Days later, at his mother's house in Booralama, there for the thirty-two-year reunion, rose bushes leant in, their heavy, wet scent taking Mark back to his youth. This house, this old weatherboard with drooping verandahs, big windows and a luscious garden, brought him back. In the oak tree out the front he and his father had made a treehouse with a rope attached to it, dangling below for his mother to put food in baskets for him to haul up. Once, he lifted his baby cousin in the bassinet up, up all the way to the wooden structure in the leaves, and then lowered him back down, down, down. It made him smile to think of it now. No thought of consequences when you're young. He resolved to finish the treehouse he'd promised Charlie and Sam.

He called out hello and his mother hurried out from the side, pulling her gardening gloves off and holding her arms wide. 'Darling!' she said. 'You're home!'

In his mother's warm embrace, he felt the shyness of a man who knows he's loved despite all his failings. He hugged her back, lifting her off her feet, making her exclaim, because this is what mothers love about their boys – the strength, the vulnerability. He stepped back from her, looking into her face. Helen had aged in the few months since he'd seen her last. New wrinkles lined her face and her bones felt sharp on her small frame.

'You've put on a little weight, Markos,' she said to him, tapping his stomach, and he rolled his eyes. Always the weight! What happened to small talk about the weather?

'It's good to be back, Mum.'

'Come on in,' she said. 'I've made Anzacs.'

He reminded her of his weight gain – which *she'd* only just pointed out – and she waved her hand in the air. 'So, go for a run or do yoga or whatever it is you do nowadays. You're here with me, and I've been cooking.'

So she had. He went into the kitchen and saw a freshly made batch of Anzacs alongside a pile of vegetable cuttings and saucepans of water. Bunches of flowers perched on windowsills and tables and the tops of books, photographs and artwork from grandchildren adorned the walls beside botanical paintings of grevilleas and snow gums and kangaroo grass. The place was a mess, but a happy one.

'I'm making lasagne with home-grown pumpkin,' his mother said. 'And the sauce is all from my tomatoes.'

'Sounds good,' he said. 'But I'll be leaving around 7 pm for the reunion.'

'Plenty of time, we've got practically the whole day!' His mother ducked down to a cupboard and wriggled about looking for something. 'I've got a . . . here it is!' She resurfaced, brandishing a bottle of gin. 'I knew I had it somewhere. We'll have a drink together before you go out.'

'For sure,' he said, feeling slightly ashamed by how obviously pleased she was to see him. He should visit more often, he thought. Bring Kelly and the kids – they loved Mum.

'Oh, and Kelly called,' his mother was saying as she darted around the kitchen, scooping potato peel into a bowl. 'She's coming up with the boys, I'm so excited – she said she wasn't sure what she was doing this weekend and I said, come up here and we'll make it a real party! I said if she doesn't want to go to the reunion, she can stay home with me, or if she does want to go I can look after the boys – either way, isn't it wonderful, Mark!'

It was. It was also a surprise to him. Kelly hadn't seemed too fussed when he'd left for the weekend.

'And your sister should be calling soon on the Skype,' his mother said. 'I told her you were up here, so we can all have a talk.'

'That's great, Mum.' Mark hadn't spoken to Prue for at least three months. Again, that feeling of guilt. It rankled. He should be a better brother; he should be a better son.

His mother continued clanging away in the kitchen while he took his bag into his old room. The moon and stars doona was gone; but still there was the single bed, the rickety bookcase, the fading stickers of Freddy Krueger and U2 on the chest of drawers. He tried calling Kelly: no response.

During the week he'd had a few jokey texts from old schoolmates. *Looking forward to a few frothies, B good 2 catch up*; that type of thing. By all accounts, Ingrid and Joanne would be there. It was, Mark admitted, part of the reason he'd decided to attend the reunion. Having the two of them there together was an opportunity to ask a few pointed questions. His mother had told him a couple of days before that Joanne had flown down from Sydney, then hired a car to drive up to Booralama. Helen, usually so friendly, breathed dismissively down the phone – Joanne's parents, she said, were so religious. More so now than ever. Helen was so nervous she might say 'shit' in front of them that she went the long way around the block just to avoid them.

Mark had forgotten that part about Joanne – the religious upbringing. Perhaps it was the rituals, the restrictions, which made her seem so cool. Reminders of a burning apocalypse were surely one way to dampen high spirits.

His mother was calling him. Mark left his bedroom and entered the chaos of the kitchen, where Helen was shouting into the screen of a laptop. 'HERE'S MARK! LOOK, MARK, HERE'S PRUE AND THE KIDS, SAY HI, MARK!'

Mark said hi. Prue waved back through a shaky screen.

Helen continued, 'LOOK, MARK, PRUE AND THE KIDS ARE HAVING A PIZZA NIGHT!'

Mark sighed. He remembered Prue's pizza nights from when she lived in the Adelaide Hills. All fun and games till someone had to clean up. There was flour everywhere, by the look of it.

'THERE'S FLOUR EVERYWHERE! AND YOU LOOK SO PALE LIKE THAT FAMILY FROM *FLOWERS IN THE ATTIC*.' Helen was still shouting into the screen. 'HELLO, LITTLE EDDIE, BEN AND ALEX, NANNA LOVES YOU.'

Prue waved back, trying to talk over Helen. It really was exhausting. Mark rested on the bench, head on elbow.

'How are you, Mark?' Prue's face was suddenly clear on the screen. 'You home for the reunion?'

He said he was and gave a brief rundown of what the night promised: party at the Northo, a bonfire at Jason Crisward's afterwards for those who wanted to kick on. His sister nodded, interested. He remembered how much she liked people. Prue was a few years older than him, knew all the people he mentioned. Plus, she was much more sociable than him – kept in contact with people from the town, let them stay when they visited Vancouver.

Helen left the room, saying she'd call Prue in a few days. 'I'LL CALL YOU IN A FEW DAYS.'

In response, Prue held up Eddie's chubby little arm and together they waved floury hands.

'Who'll be there?' Prue asked after Helen left.

He told her; all the old friends – Ingrid and Joanne included. She listened in, asking questions, remembering funny little anecdotes about people they knew. He had a sudden thought: 'Did you know that Joanne had a baby while she was in America on exchange?'

Prue knotted her brow, shook her head. 'What? Who told you that?'

'Mum. She heard it from . . . I don't know.'

On the screen, little Eddie started bawling and Prue shoved something into his mouth. 'Listen,' she said, face close to the screen, 'that's bullshit. Probably invented by Joanne's Jesus-loving parents, the lesser shame and all that – who the fuck knows.'

Mark recoiled. What the hell was this? This had taken a turn. 'So, what happened?' he asked.

'Joanne didn't have a baby in America, she had an abortion. Worst thing ever for her parents and family, ridiculous!'

'I did not know that.'

''Course you didn't, the family kept it quiet – said that she'd had a "little holiday", which was the euphemism in those days for "having a baby out of wedlock".'

Mark thought about Joanne when he first saw her after her trip to America. Thinner, features sharper, cooler. 'I did not know.'

'Well, that's not the main thing,' his sister continued. 'Abortions are sad – but a lot of women have them.'

'The main thing?'

'Joanne was raped. During the last semester of her exchange, some arsehole raped her at a party. It went to court and everything. Didn't you know any of this?'

Mark shook his head. He'd heard none of it.

Prue brushed flour off her face. 'Don't feel bad you didn't know – I doubt many people did. It was all hush-hush, that's how they treated sexual assault in the good old days. That, or they still thought that if a woman stayed out of society for more than six months it must have been that "she got herself in trouble". I think Joanne's family pushed that line. Better than admitting to the town the abortion, the rape.'

'How did you know?'

'Dean Hooper, one of her cousins, told me. I used to go out with him, remember? He'd heard it from his father, who helped out with some legal stuff for Joanne.'

'Well, shit.'

'Yeah.'

The siblings chatted a little longer, easy with each other. They made vague promises to speak again soon and then hung up, after Mark watched his nephews give fat little waves. *It's funny*, he pondered, thinking about Prue, *how much we take siblings for granted. They're the most constant and longest relationship we have in our lives, yet we're so casual about it.*

Mark wandered out to the garden, where Helen was knee-deep in pruning, flinging rose branches behind her like a plough. He thought of telling her about Joanne and the assault but decided against it. Instead, he rolled up his sleeves and, taking a rake, began moving the prunings into a pile. He raked, remembered how much he liked pottering about in the soil and leaves. It was pleasant, there with his mother in the garden, the smell of dirt and roses, the sky falling into dark. They settled into an easy way of talking.

'You and Prue were funny kids,' Helen was saying. 'Like two peas in a pod – but the fighting! My word, your father and I had a hard time of it.'

Mark couldn't remember the fighting, or not much of it.

'For a little boy, you had a toughness about you.' His mother laughed into the roses. 'Not afraid to give anyone a whack if it meant getting your own way.'

The image jarred and was in opposition to the childhood photos of himself on various walls inside; the angelic hair and toothy smile, the little boy holding up a flower.

'I remember Dad telling me never to hit a girl,' Mark said. His father *had* told him that, stern, his direction not to be messed with.

'Maybe Prue didn't count as a girl then,' Helen said. 'You had a real temper on you when you were young.'

Mark watched as a wasp settled in the air beside him like a drone. He stood still. The wasp could attack or leave. It came closer, slowly, slowly, before flying backwards in a zigzag pattern. Up in the air and away from sight.

'Was I violent to anyone else?' he asked, and the garden seemed impossibly quiet.

Helen put down her secateurs, looked at the pile of pruning like it was a shrine, and stood up. 'Not to my knowledge,' she said, laying a gentle hand on his shoulder as she passed.

Before he left to go to the reunion, he and Helen had a gin together on the porch. As they drank, his mother shared photos of him when he was in high school. Football teams, class photos, him on his twelfth birthday, him holding up a Murray cod. There he was, a *Top Gun* hairdo and a bad suit at graduation; beside him, Joanne in a black dress and dark straight hair and Ingrid in a red dress, blonde hair done up in some sort of bun. Other people crowded into the shot, but it was the three of them the photo was aimed at. He and Ingrid were grinning into the camera, Joanne with a small smile – perhaps a smirk. He looked at it closely before passing it to Helen.

'Such children!' she said. 'You really are so young.'

'You'd call us children?' The word rang in his mind.

His mother nodded. 'Anyone under twenty-five is a child to me.' Looking at the image again, he could see why. On the cusp of adulthood perhaps, but juvenile nonetheless. Joanne seemed a little older, but he and Ingrid could well be described as kids.

Mark noted the time, finished the rest of his gin and went to get ready for the reunion, surprising himself by feeling a flicker of nerves. The invitation forwarded to him by Ingrid stated: 'Class of '89! A chance to catch up with old friends and share tales from the last 30 (or 32!!!) years.'

He put his shirt on, eyes averted from the bathroom mirror where his gut hung like a side of beef over the top of his jeans. 'Suck it in, old man,' he breathed to himself, turning away. What tales could he share? Police college, police work, Kelly, the kids, the occasional game of tennis and trip to Bali. What tales wouldn't he share? The tales that were, he recognised, the true parts of himself; not the actions themselves, but the reasons behind: the loneliness, the laziness, the yearning, the drinking, and the mourning for a life that promised much but delivered less.

He checked his phone; a text from Kelly: *Be there around 8.30 pm.*

He texted back: *Come to the Northo if keen.*

He regretted the text. Why ask his wife to come to a school reunion? Kelly would hate hearing all about his younger years and the schoolboy talk; he'd hate having to introduce her to people whose names he couldn't remember. Oh well, not much else he could do but get hammered.

But only after he talked to Joanne and Ingrid. Only then could he truly relax.

His phone beeped. Not Kelly. Jagdeep. She'd sent a photo, no accompanying message. He held it up close, studied it. Didn't know why she'd sent that – he'd seen it before. He looked at it. Still didn't know what Jag was getting at.

Looked again. Still didn't get it. And then.

And then, he did.

CHAPTER 40

The photo was of notes that both he and Jagdeep had read before. Old casenotes, recorded by some tired cop in a Port York station thirty years before. The writing looked hurried; no doubt the policeman or woman on duty was run off their feet with phone calls from the public and media. The humdrum of police life, so often filled with red herrings, but there it was and, fishy or not, it filled Mark with dread.

Person A saw a car being driven by a woman who looked like a killer.

Person B saw a driver in a Sahara LandCruiser who was most definitely on drugs, two kids beside him – we should definitely lock him up.

Person C had a feeling that he'd seen what happened in a dream and that the culprit is now in a hospital suffering heart pains.

Mark read it again and called Jagdeep. This time, she picked up the phone.

'The LandCruiser,' he said. 'Same vehicle as the one in the photo with the sisters who went missing. John Baber's.'

'I know.' Her voice cut in and out. 'Time to bring Baber in.'

He agreed.

'The children.' As before, Jagdeep's voice came through in uneven spurts. 'Baber doesn't have kids – most likely not him, of course.'

Of course. It wasn't enough for an arrest, not by a long shot. But the sighting and the article warranted a conversation of the hard kind.

Eighteen-year-olds look like children to older people. Mark thought of his mother referring to him as a child in the photos. *They call them kids.* It didn't seem like much; he didn't say it aloud. 'Worth checking out, though. You going to call Baber in tomorrow then?'

'What's that? Finding it hard to hear you.'

Mark repeated, 'Are you going to call Baber in to the station tomorrow?'

'Actually, I'll be in Cutters in just over two hours,' Jagdeep said. 'Could drop in tonight. I've . . . it's . . . been in Adelaide for a few days.' She said something about the roadhouse. 'Packed, doing a roaring trade – all the tourists at the Rock.' Her voice faded out.

'I'd wait till tomorrow to call Baber in.' Mark spoke loudly down the phone, heard a distant crackle. 'Get Darryl to meet you there. No need for you to go there tonight.'

'Yes . . . better. Hear . . . ? Good . . . John . . . you . . . tomorrow.'

Another crackle. It was no use; Jagdeep's phone was cactus.

After the call, Mark thought about John Baber, a good citizen, solid and reliable. No heroics in his past, but what was it that the couple from the Opal said about the man? *Could set your watch by him.* A punctual man. *Reliable as heartburn.*

John Baber was the sort of man you'd call if something went wrong. If, for example, your television wouldn't work or if your car broke down or if a generator wasn't working and you needed lights for your party. A thought was building in Mark, probing around the edge of his conscious, swelling: '*When he arrived everyone cheered like idiots,*' Mark repeated Darryl's earlier words aloud.

John was known to be reliable. Punctual. So, why was he late to the New Year's Eve party in 1989? Everyone was waiting for him to fix the generator.

Mark looked at his own watch. Time to be heading off to the party. There would probably be a disco ball. Strobe lights even. It was the 32nd reunion, after all.

On his way to the party and walking beneath a mild sky, Mark thought again of Baber, the things he could say about him: solid citizen, husband to the local doctor, dependable, always ready to help. Then he added: *John Baber is not* always *punctual. John Baber gives lifts to hitchhikers. John Baber found a dead man on the side of the road.*

At the front of the Northo, Mark was relieved to see a woman handing out name tags.

'Maria,' the woman said, pointing towards her own tag. 'Bet you wouldn't have recognised me.'

It was true, he wouldn't. The woman before him had sleek long blonde hair, wore white jeans and some sort of flimsy top. *Leo Sayer, eat your heart out.*

'You haven't changed a bit,' he said.

Maria gave him a look somewhere between a smile and a sneer and turned towards the other people now lined up. Mark cast around, trying to spot familiar faces. 'Ariti!' someone shouted out. 'Come and have a drink, you big prick.'

A face was smiling into his, sunburnt and large. 'Spadger!' he said, relieved to remember. 'How are you, mate?'

Spadger was good. Still lived in the old town, married with three kids, concreter, had a boat for waterskiing, bit of fishing. Got to Thailand last year with the family, saw some strange things, some really fucking strange things. 'You ever seen a ping-pong show, Mark?'

He hadn't. Was glad of it. But curious all the same.

Spadger continued: fucking weird shit that ping-pong show, and not the whole of it.

Someone interrupted them, Cheryl somebody. Mark remembered her too – got another beer, started to feel his joints loosen. Compared to Spadger, he thought, catching his reflection in the bar window, he didn't look too bad. Compared to Cheryl, he looked like Brad Pitt.

Cheryl was good. She still lived in the old town too, married with two kids, also got the stepdaughter. Didn't have a boat but a bit of land down the river, and kept a little shed there for when they went camping. Fishing and whatnot. 'Remember you caught that massive cod, Mark?' Never been to Thailand, but went to Surfers Paradise three years ago and did all the Worlds.

Mark drank his beer. Spadger, Cheryl and another who'd joined their group looked to him. His turn.

'I'm good. Live in the big smoke, married with two kids, no steps as yet. Don't have a boat or a bit of land, been to Bali a couple of times. Ubud and whatnot. Mum showed me a photo of that massive cod, Cheryl, I must've been about twelve. Yeah, I'm a cop. Don't hold it against me. Yeah, made it over that wall in training, not too bad but couldn't do it now.'

Their small group nodded, satisfied. Everyone had told their tale adequately. It was enough, and now to drink. Mark drank. Beer and a red wine. Checked his phone; no calls from Kelly. He went to the bathroom, had a chat to a bloke he played footy with who was now a doctor and who had been to Bali and Thailand and also Paris. While walking out of the bathroom towards the bar and hearing about the man's marital status, he saw Joanne enter the room.

Joanne, and Ingrid not far behind.

He started towards them but was interrupted by a woman whose name he thought might be Kristy or Kirsty.

'Mark Ariti!' The woman was very drunk. 'Remember you called me a fat slag in Year 11?'

Mark suddenly felt ill. 'Did I really call you that?'

Kristy or Kirsty gave him a hard slap on the back. 'Only joking, Ariti – got you a beauty though, didn't I?'

Mark breathed a sigh of relief and felt a wave of gratitude when Joanne and Ingrid joined them.

'Hello, Olivia!' Ingrid was saying, hugging the woman. Joanne stood beside her, a faint smile on her face.

The three of them listened as Olivia told them what she was doing with her life. Who she married, where she went on holidays and what she did for a living. Mark felt himself drifting when he heard Ingrid exclaim, 'Grave inscriber! That's amazing!'

Olivia smiled proudly and the others looked at her with admiration.

'What would you have written on your tombstone?' Mark asked the women.

'When your number's up, it's up,' Olivia said, and even Joanne laughed.

Ingrid thought for a second; she liked this sort of thing. 'I'd have "Succumbed to general wear and tear."'

'You, Joanne?'

His old friend rolled her eyes. 'Died of thirst.'

Their small group was overtaken by a larger one and Mark watched how easily Ingrid mingled, laughing and touching people on the arm as she spoke. Joanne was more reticent, smiling but detached, as she had been for all those years. He went to the bar, saw that she followed. 'How's the case going?' she asked, not looking at him but somewhere in the direction of Ingrid.

'I have to ask you a few questions,' Mark said, clearing his throat. 'I need you to shed some light on a few things.'

Joanne ordered a vodka, lime and soda, leant against the bar, shaking her head. 'Ingrid staying in that little room with me that night?' she said. 'Is that all you've got? Honestly, Mark. Just call the case closed. There's nothing there.'

'There's more,' he said, and wished he hadn't already drunk so much.

'There are so many other, more important things you should be looking into,' Joanne said, handing over money to the barwoman and taking her drink. 'Crimes that are happening right now, not a hundred years ago.'

'Not a hundred, Joanne, just thirty-two.'

Together they gazed out into the crowd, where now dancing had begun to some tune from their youth. Duran Duran maybe. In any case, there they were, the class of '89, dancing and having the time of their lives. Just thirty-odd years ago they were all eighteen or nineteen, on the cusp of life. Ingrid, dancing hard in the midst of a group, beckoned for them to join in. Joanne, looking half-amused, shook her head and Mark mouthed, 'No.'

The grave inscriber sashayed up to them. 'Come on!' she said. 'Just one dance, for Chrissake, don't be boring!'

Mark turned to Joanne. She was his old friend, no matter what was happening now. He took her by the arm. 'Come on,' he said. 'Let's not be the boring old farts by the bar, let's have a bit of a dance.' *Before it all goes to shit*, he wanted to add.

To his surprise, Joanne put down her glass and allowed herself to be led to the middle of the floor. And so they danced, to all the eighties music; to Madonna, to Prince, to AC/DC and Jimmy Barnes. The class of '89 danced with abandon, forgetting about their shitty jobs, the school fees, their failing marriages, their disappointing sex lives, and the stains on their new white shirts. The class of '89 danced knowing that at the next reunion some of them might not be there and that all of them were on their way there. Fifty years old most of them were, the class of '89. The doctors, the policemen, the childminders, the grave inscribers, the concreters – for just this one song they were young again, they were beautiful again, and they had their whole lives in front of them.

But always, the song must end, and when it did the class of '89 smiled at each other a little self-consciously, a little embarrassed and very red-faced. The party drifted off. People had to go and relieve babysitters, the grave inscriber had work in the morning, the hardcore drinkers and lecherous divorcees were off to the bonfire.

Mark searched around for Joanne and Ingrid. They were by the door, saying goodbye to people. He hurried after them, delayed a little by the doctor who insisted on swapping numbers. Numbers exchanged, dates to catch up half-agreed on, he walked out into the cool night and shoved his hands deep in his pockets.

At first he couldn't see them, but then he caught the dark figures of Ingrid and Joanne walking close together on the footpath a short distance away. The two of them were indistinguishable in the weak light of the streetlamp. They could have been the same person for all he knew. He jogged towards them and they both turned around at the sound of his approach, startled and pale in the night.

'Need to talk to you two tomorrow,' he said. 'Stick around for a bit, can you?'

Joanne continued walking, folded her arms. 'Just talk to us now, Mark, I'm leaving early in the morning.'

Ingrid shrugged, looking towards the river, the dark trees hugging it, hiding it.

'Either of you two heard the name John Baber?'

Joanne shook her head and Ingrid said no, exhaling loudly.

He pulled out his phone and the two women stopped, exchanging glances. Mark began searching in his phone for the photo of John beside his vehicle, the one that Foobie had taken. 'Here,' he said, finding it and holding the phone out, 'recognise this man?'

The women leant in close to the screen, narrowing their eyes. Then in one quick motion, Joanne stepped back, jaw clenched. Ingrid remained still, the two saying nothing.

'See?' Mark enlarged the photo, John's face taking up most of the screen. 'Seen this man before?'

In the streetlight, Ingrid's face appeared a deathly white. She slapped a hand to her mouth. 'God,' she half-whispered.

'You recognise him?'

Ingrid turned to Joanne, her voice a strangle. 'It's him.'

A moment of shocked silence.

Mark went in hard. 'There's evidence of another body at the site where Michael Denby was found. Probably one of two sisters who went missing, or—'

'Or a Dutchwoman,' Ingrid breathed. 'Isa Anne Modderman.'

'Ingrid,' Joanne warned. 'You need to—'

'How the hell do you know this?' Mark wasn't in the mood to be kind.

'I've known for a long time, suspected it for longer.'

With a jolt, Mark had a sudden thought. 'What's Sander's surname, Ingrid?'

'Modderman. What took you so long?'

Mark breathed hard. 'Isa was Sander's sister.'

Ingrid nodded. Joanne stood back, arms clenched over her chest.

Mark shook his head, trying to make sense of it. He moved in front of them both. 'Tell me everything. Now.'

Ingrid looked at Joanne, her voice a plea: 'We've got to tell him, Jo, please.'

Joanne's eyes were steely in the weak light. 'I want a lawyer,' she said.

CHAPTER 41

Mark looked at his old friends standing now like two halves, one broken, one brittle. He thought of Jagdeep, calling Baber in. Turned on his phone, dialled her number, watching the two women as he did so. Straight to message bank. He called again.

'Whatever this is, whatever happened, we can protect you,' he said, and far above a night bird gave a strangled cry. 'There's no need to be afraid.'

'Mark'—Joanne gave a half-laugh—'you really don't know much about the law, do you?'

'I . . .' He looked at his phone, noticed the glittering lights – a missed message: Jagdeep.

'The law doesn't protect victims.' Joanne's voice was hard. 'It doesn't protect them at all. We all have to protect ourselves, Mark, don't you see?'

He was ringing his messages, dialling the number, and all the while images raced across his eyes: the girls in the car,

John giving the sisters a lift, John being late to the New Year's Eve party, John Baber who was never late . . .

Jagdeep's voice broke out loud and clear in the still night: 'Get help!' she screamed over the phone. 'John, it's—No, please, no!' and then a crackling and then horrible silence.

The two women stared at him while he tried to call back, punching numbers into his phone.

Jagdeep, he thought. *Please be okay.*

And suddenly he wanted nothing more than for Jagdeep, his colleague, to be safe.

He rang the number and all three listened in vain as the warm night passed by and a single gum leaf fell from the sky and settled on the ground by their feet. They listened. But the phone was dead.

Five minutes before, Jagdeep pulled into the long driveway of John Baber's house. She was alone, saw no need to call up Darryl on a Saturday night and ask him to join her. She'd considered Mark's idea of meeting John the next day, but decided this would be easiest. The long drive up from Adelaide had made her weary; she wanted to get home and lie on the couch. Wedding plans and guest lists loomed; those made her weary too. It had been a busy couple of days. She'd put a few quick questions to Baber now, ring Mark with an update, and then fall asleep over a toasted sandwich.

John Baber's property was quiet. No vehicle out the front. No lights on in the house either, but as she walked up to the front door, she heard something crash. A distinct crash, something being broken. She called out, peering through the window. The single glow of a match or torch lit up the room for an instant, before falling into darkness again. Jagdeep thought vaguely of leaving, coming back in the morning, but now she was here it seemed stupid not to investigate.

'Hello!' she called, and from somewhere inside there was another crash. Her voice shook. 'John!' There was a sick taste in the back of her throat. She turned the door handle – 'Hello!' – and pushed. It was open and she stepped inside, started walking towards the faint glow at the end of the hall where she knew the lounge room to be.

Another thudding sound now, and she sped up to a slow trot, one hand tracing the wall, the other clasping her side, feeling the shape of the taser.

'John!' she cried again, as she flung open the door of the lounge room to reveal an empty space. She reached for her phone, rang the first number on her calls list: Mark. No response.

She reached for a light switch, her hands searching over the wall. Finding one, she flicked it on to darkness. Nothing; the electricity was gone.

'John?' she called more hesitantly, turning on her phone's torch and slowly shining it around the room. 'Hello?'

The beam of light lit up the room in long, narrow shards. A bang from the wall near the fireplace and the light trembled, then focused on the mirror above.

'No,' she breathed, her hands fumbling her phone and dialling the first number there. 'Get help!' And then, she screamed.

*

Mark called the station at Cutters End, left a message there, called the Port York cops too, even though they were at least five hours away. Told them what he'd learnt, what he'd heard. With assurances they'd be travelling up to see her, he paced around the quiet street, checking his phone, waiting for a response. *Jagdeep.*

'What happened?' he said to Ingrid and Joanne, his voice angry. 'Just tell me what happened. It's now or down at the station with some other cop, I'm done with you two.'

Joanne stood with her arms still folded, staring somewhere beyond the trees. Ingrid, looking at her for a moment, spoke. 'I'll tell you everything, Mark. I've wanted to for ages. In a way, I tried to tell you the truth. It was there all along.'

Mark rolled his hand for her to continue.

'Remember I said that the man who gave me a lift was Don or Ron? It was true – I didn't know his name, but now I know his name was John. I left stuff out, but I told you stuff too.'

A fog began to lift somewhere in the back of Mark's head. 'Well, you could have been clearer, Ingrid.'

'I know. But in a way, I suppose I wanted you to keep questioning me – get to the truth. I'm tired of all this. It's been so long.'

'Tell me.'

And she did.

CHAPTER 42

New Year's Eve, 1989

A lift! She'd be in Cutters End by tonight, maybe even get to that New Year's Eve party everyone in Adelaide had told her about. That would be good.

She buckled her seatbelt, turned to the man who was driving. 'I'm Ingrid,' she said, and he nodded before looking out the window and pulling onto the road.

Ingrid turned to see that the old creep from the road-house was staring at her through the window, the fading light on the glass giving him a ghostly air. She smiled back hard, giving him the finger as they drove off. *Stuff you, you old sleaze*, she thought. *I'll never have to see you and your shitty shop again.*

'Been travelling long?' the man asked, turning onto the highway.

'No,' Ingrid replied. 'Just a few weeks. Have a break after school and all that.'

There was a silence. Ingrid worked to fill it. 'Year 12 was so full on. We just needed to get out of town, have a holiday before uni starts up. Maybe get a bit of work . . .'

Another awkward pause.

'Skimpy, are you?'

The question startled Ingrid. 'What? No!' She felt a vague ache in the back of her head. She stretched her hands, placed them on her knees, rubbed them together.

The man's car had a faint whiff of hospital. It was very clean. Ingrid shifted on her seat, aware of how dusty and unkempt she must appear.

'You meeting up with anyone tonight?' he asked, and they gained speed on the long highway headed north.

She looked at him sideways. 'No,' she said. 'Well, hopefully my friend Joanne. There was a mix-up last night and we've missed each other today.'

'She get lucky, did she?' The man laughed and Ingrid gave a weak smile. Maybe he was kind of a creep, she thought. *Just my luck.*

'I said, did she get lucky?' The man's voice had an edge to it and, changing gears, he looked at her.

Ingrid stared straight ahead, the drumming in the back of her head growing louder. 'I don't know,' she said.

'You girls should be more careful. People think you're sluts, how you go around sleeping with anyone you meet. It's wrong.'

A thrumming now behind her eyes. She studied her knees.

'Anything could happen to you,' the man was saying. 'I mean, look at where we are! You lot must be really fucking stupid.'

Ingrid looked outside to the enormous empty landscape. Her brain raced and she heard her voice shake. 'We should be more careful,' she said in a weak voice.

'You're all the same.' He shook his head.

She sat still. Tried to control her breathing, tried to think. Couldn't.

'I've seen them all,' he continued. 'Aussies, Dutch or what the fuck, you never learn, do you?'

'I need to go to the toilet. Can we please stop?'

The man stared straight ahead, muttered something under his breath.

'I want to get out now. Please.' Ingrid's voice shook, her whole body trembled.

'Shut the fuck up, will you? You lot never stop squawking.'

Ingrid crept her left hand to the door handle.

Outside the world sped on by, thousands of kilometres of desert and no towns and no people. *We haven't passed one car*, she thought. *And not one car has passed us.*

The man sped up, his anger and her fear filling the space.

Fingers on the door, a sob in her throat, Ingrid felt that she was ready to open it, when she saw something out of the corner of her eye, a piece of colour underneath her shoe. She moved her foot slightly to the side and for a second was struck dumb. A silver and black velvet scrunchie. The one Joanne had borrowed.

And then, with a gaping realisation, she threw open the car door at the same time as the man veered suddenly to the side of the road and continued driving through the scrub. Frantically, she tried to unbuckle her seatbelt and the man grabbed at her arm. For a moment, she was half-suspended out the car, watching the earth speed below. Watching rocks, dirt, a blaze of red and brown.

With an aching jolt, he pulled her back into the car and turned the wheel suddenly. Her head hit the dashboard and then, all went black.

A text on Mark's phone from an unknown number: *John Baber.*

He texted back: *Jag?*

No reply.

'What next?' Mark asked. They'd crossed the road, following Ingrid.

Ingrid slumped on the riverbank while Joanne and Mark stood, the former leaning against a gum tree, still not speaking.

Bleary and bruised, Ingrid woke to a darkening sky and blood in her mouth. It took her a minute to remember all that had occurred and when she did, she tried to call, but there was something in her mouth – a cloth – and it made it hard to breathe or cry.

'Joanne!' she screamed from the back of her throat. 'Joanne!'

She was tied to a tree with cable wire, her arms in front of her around the skinny trunk. Half-kneeling, slumped, she rested her cheek on the trunk and cried for Joanne. In front of her, perhaps five metres, the vehicle was parked, still with the passenger-side door open.

'Joanne!' she cried and then, 'Help!'

Footsteps to the back of her and a rough hand reached down, grabbed her by the hair. 'Shut the fuck up,' he said, banging her forehead on the bark of the tree. She cringed from his hand, sank down lower, tried to make herself as small as possible, away from his sight.

He walked past her up to the vehicle and, reaching from the rear of the ute, peeled back the tarpaulin. With one movement, he pulled up a struggling, hunched figure and threw it on the ground. Joanne.

Ingrid watched as her friend lay there in a foetal position, hands tied behind her back, brown hair covering her face, and mouth bound with a gag the same as hers.

The girls watched each other. They'd known each other all their lives. Speech does not need words.

The man lit a cigarette, pondered them. 'Two Aussies.'

The girls kept their eyes on him, Ingrid's breath suspended. She felt the world constrict.

The man went to the front of the car, opened the passenger-side glove box and got out some pills, throwing them in his mouth. 'So fucking messy,' he said. 'Messing up my truck.' He put a knee up on the seat and began chucking things out; a coffee cup, a folded bit of paper, the scrunchie.

Ingrid felt a renewed panic and tried rubbing the cable against the tree trunk, wriggling her hands within the ties.

Joanne, seeing what she was doing, gave a small nod. While the man raged about his vehicle, now scrubbing the seats with a cloth, Ingrid rubbed and rubbed at the cable till bits of bark flaked off the tree and her wrists grated against the cord. It was no use, she saw that. The cable would never give. But still she tried, small patches of blood appearing on her skin.

The man was now in the rear seat, ranting.

Ingrid rested her forehead on the bark of the thin tree. In her line of vision, she could see Joanne raising herself on her elbow and attempting to sit up.

Ingrid felt then that she would die and Joanne would die too. Out here alone and with no one to know. She looked at the bark, felt its dry surface, felt her tears on it, and saw that they coloured it dark. She focused not on Joanne, now sitting up, or on the man, burrowed in the back of his ute, rearranging things and swearing.

She focused on the tree and saw that there were markings on it, three distinct markings, and now – when she blocked out the sight of Joanne and the man swearing and the pain in her wrists and knees and head – she could see that they were initials. I.A.M. Just like hers.

I AM.

It was a sign, she thought, as the sun made its final descent. She would always be here, no matter what happened.

I AM.

Her initials were here, she was here, she was here.

With great effort, she called, '*Jo!*' and though it came out as a strangled cry, she could see that Joanne raised her head – looked at her. Ingrid wanted to tell her friend what she'd seen, but now the man was coming towards her, not seeing Joanne and walking fast. Forgetting the initials, she tried to stand by hugging the tree and then inching upwards.

In the background, Joanne looked at her hard, trying to say something. But Ingrid didn't know what.

Night set in.

Another text on Mark's phone, same number as before: *Jag OK. Foobie D in station. Call us. Darryl.*

A moment of confusion. Foobie? He looked up at Ingrid, unable and unwilling for her to stop.

She stood, feet apart, hands wrapped around the tree like a lover. He came towards her, five steps away, four away, three steps away; she bent her knees a little, mind a whirlpool; tried to spit out the gag.

He put his face close to hers. 'You're a noisy bitch, aren't you? See how that goes for you. They usually stop after a night.' He stroked the side of her face and she turned away, straining. 'Aussies,' he said again, fumbling at her top, feeling under it and making her gag. 'Two more bloody slutty Aussies.'

Ingrid clenched her eyes shut. Stepped away from the tree, arms stretched out around it.

He moved closer to her, rubbing his body on her side, nuzzling into her face and neck. Moving her face from side to side, she felt bile rise up in her throat and she began to gag. And then, when she opened her eyes for a brief moment, she could see that Joanne had, in some incredible feat, brought her tied hands from behind her back underneath her, and they were now in front of her body. Her friend was trying to stand.

The man was feeling the front of her jeans now and she stood still, hating him, hating the world. But she must give Joanne time. Her mind went blank and she thought only of the initials on the bark, I.A.M.

Joanne was limping now, half-running around the front of the vehicle and slipping into it, her eyes always on Ingrid. Ingrid locked eyes with her friend, thought of nothing else but the initials on the tree.

From far above, a bird gave a cry and Ingrid thought that it was a sign; of hope or horror, she didn't know. But it had to mean something.

The man gave a groaning sound but still, Ingrid looked only at Joanne. Time stretched and lengthened, moment after terrible moment, but still, Ingrid looked only at her friend. The engine started and the man turned, giving a half-yell and trying to run, at the same time pulling up his jeans.

'Just move!' Ingrid tried to call out, and the engine stalled. 'No!'

The man was closer to the car now, a metre away, and the engine started up again.

Half a metre, and Joanne slammed her foot on the accelerator and put the engine into reverse.

Ingrid was shouting, shouting for her friend, wanting her to drive, drive away – but the man was getting closer to the vehicle and the wheels were spinning in the sand. Even so, the vehicle sped up and backed away fast.

Ingrid felt her heart leap. Joanne would be free! But then she saw Joanne hesitate, was slowing, had stopped with the engine still running.

'No!' Ingrid tried to yell, sobbing now, pulling, pulling, pulling at the wire on her wrists. She could see through the lights of the vehicle's interior that Joanne was looking directly at her in the beams.

Ingrid looked back, saw her oldest friend and willed her to turn the ute and drive off, when she heard the changing of gears again, heard the engine rev – and Joanne, rather than turning around to certain freedom, drove straight into the man who was running towards her. She ran straight into him and over him and he collapsed, screaming in the dirt. With the engine still running, Joanne leapt out of the car and ran to her.

Joanne had returned to save her. Love surged like a wave.

'Hurry, hurry, hurry,' either she or Joanne was saying. 'Hurry, hurry, hurry.'

The man's leg was trapped under a wheel and he roared, trying to pull himself out.

'Hurry, hurry, hurry.'

Now Joanne was running back to the tray of the vehicle, rummaging around.

'Hurry, hurry, hurry.'

Joanne found a knife and raced back, running the blade back and forth across the cable till it broke. Ingrid pulled the gag out of her mouth and let out a sob. The man was still trying to pull himself away, groaning and swearing. 'Hurry, hurry, hurry,' as Ingrid took the knife from Joanne and cut the cable ties from her too.

'Let's go,' Ingrid said. 'Let's just drive and leave him here. We'll go to the police, let's go, Joanne.'

But her friend walked over to where the man was squirming on the dirt.

'Get me out of here,' he said. 'I wasn't going to hurt you. Really, I'm sorry – get me out.'

Joanne kicked him hard in the head.

'Let's go, Joanne,' Ingrid said. 'Come on.'

Joanne knelt down by the man, away from his stretched-out, pleading arms. 'You fucking arsehole,' she said in a low voice. 'You piece of shit.'

'Let's move, Jo!' Ingrid was screaming now and the man seemed to gain some leverage, started trying to sit up, pulling away from the car. 'He's getting up!'

Joanne kicked him again, hard in the face. He tried to grab at her leg and she jerked away quick.

'You think you can get away with this?' Joanne was not listening to Ingrid.

The man said something.

'What was that?' Joanne said, holding her hand up for Ingrid to be quiet. 'What did you say?'

'Slut,' the man said. 'Stupid sluts always getting yourselves into trouble. What did you fucking expect? You put out raw meat and don't expect flies?'

Ingrid stood, pleading, crying, standing on one foot, then the other, urging her to go. But Joanne was at the tray of the ute again and then the front passenger seat. She came back with a jerry can and the man looked up at her with understanding.

'No,' he said. 'You wouldn't.'

Joanne began pouring the petrol over the man's head and upper body before throwing the can away.

'Say you're sorry,' she said.

'I'm sorry, I'm sorry,' the man said, trying to wipe the petrol out of his eyes.

'Say, "I'm a piece of shit."'

'I'm a piece of shit, I'm a piece of shit.'

'Now,' Joanne said. 'That's all you needed to do.'

'Come on, Jo,' Ingrid urged. 'We don't need to drive, we'll just get another lift – go to the police, or go back to the roadhouse, yes, come on, Joanne. He's not going anywhere with the car on top of him. Let's leave, leave . . .'

'Please,' the man said. 'I'll never do this again, I never meant to hurt you. Please, I've got a family.'

Joanne stood above him. Matches at her side.

'I've got a daughter,' he said.

And then Joanne threw the match.

CHAPTER 43

Mark slumped against the side of a tree. 'Jesus,' he said.

Joanne's voice came out of the dark. 'I'm glad I did it. I've never been more glad of something in my life.'

'Because of what happened in America.'

Joanne gave him a sharp glance, then shook her head. 'Not just that, but yes, that too. If we had let him go, no one would ever have taken our side. This was the end of the eighties, remember? Rapists were being let off left, right and centre.'

'He'd done it before,' Ingrid said. 'I.A.M. Isa Anne Modderman.'

'And probably the sisters, Raelene and Adele from Warnbeen,' Mark said. 'You were researching them too, weren't you?'

'Yes,' Ingrid admitted. 'For ages. I've told their older sister what we did too. It was harder this time – I'm friends with her.'

'She wanted to be close to them all, didn't you, Ingrid? The families, the friends.' Joanne sounded bitter rather than angry. 'All this time, despite my pleading, you just couldn't let it go.'

'I had to tell them what I knew. Imagine not knowing. And besides, it could have been . . .'

It could have been us.

'And did you think the families would be happy when they found out?' Mark asked.

'Of course they'd be fucking happy.' Joanne turned on him. 'Wouldn't you?'

Would he? If someone attacked or abused his boys, what sort of justice would he want? Where did all the anger and grief go?

Ingrid sat with her head between her hands and Joanne continued: 'The man was burnt up badly, just screaming and screaming. Ingrid kept shouting at us to leave, I was worried about the noise and we knew he wouldn't last long. The sound! You can't believe what it sounds like; a man like that screaming in pain.'

For a moment, Joanne looked as if she was almost smiling. 'Ingrid wanted to take the car, but we thought that someone might pick us up for it being stolen, or he might manage to scramble away somewhere, or – we weren't thinking straight. Really, we didn't know what the hell we were doing.'

'You didn't think to go to the police?'

'Ingrid wanted to. I was a firm no. We hadn't been raped, or not exactly.' Joanne gave a brief glance to Ingrid. 'What *we* had done was run over a man and burn him to death.

We were two young women, scared, panicked really – and we weren't thinking clearly at all. Besides,' Joanne's voice was hard, 'what would the cops do really?'

Joanne grew quiet, as if listening to something in the dark. Mark waited.

'The screams died down and we just ran. We ran to the highway, thinking we'd just get a lift somewhere or something, I don't know – and then almost straight away, a vehicle came towards us.'

'John Baber.'

'Well, whoever it is in the photo you showed us. Him. He pulled up and we got in, and we must have looked in a bad way, because he did a U-turn, saying he'd drive us back to the roadhouse and help us make a call. But the thing is, I started to feel calm. The man, he said his name but I thought it was Don or Ron. He seemed nice, not like the other one. I said that we'd had a scary experience hitch-hiking, but we'd got out of the car and we were now okay. I said that we'd probably end up staying in the roadhouse. I felt kind of numb. Ingrid was quiet. I even managed small talk. He said he was on his way to a party, with fuel for the generator to fix the lights. I remember that because I was concentrating on listening very carefully. For some reason, whatever that man said seemed to me to be the most important thing in the world. He was, I think, a kind man. He offered us ham sandwiches, but we said no. He said that he was always eating ham sandwiches and that it used to drive his wife mad. I think he was trying to put us at ease. It's strange that I remember all of this so clearly. He advised us not to hitchhike again, said there were buses up and down the highway all the time now. I said that that seemed very sensible. He dropped us off at the roadhouse and we went to the toilets outside to wash our faces. Ingrid had a bad cut or bruise on her forehead, she covered it with her hair. The man waited for us, to see if we were okay. I think he even offered us money for the bus the next day. I went inside and booked a room for one night. I didn't mention Ingrid, didn't think of it, just paid for a night.'

Ingrid spoke up, her voice listless. 'When we got to Cutters End the next day, via the bus, I wrote the wrong date on the backpackers' register, to make it look like I was there the night before. I just thought it would make things easier – I'd eradicate the whole night, erase it from my memory, and if we were questioned, I wouldn't have to explain the time lapse from when I was in the roadhouse to getting there the day after. It was Joanne who booked the night at the roadhouse, not me. No one saw me there. So, I wrote down the wrong date. Probably it was stupid.'

It wasn't stupid, Mark thought. It had cost the investigation time and money. It had given her space to move further from the crime.

Joanne continued, 'When I came out after booking the night, the man, John, was still there. He said if we needed anything, we could look him up in Cutters End. We said thank you, he left. I said hi to some weird guy in the next room and we tried to get to sleep. Ingrid was crying and crying, it was an awful night.'

The crying, Mark thought. It looked like laughing on the videotape.

'We never saw John again till you showed us that photo.' Joanne swept up her hair and tied it into a bun. Businesslike.

Mark breathed out. He was quiet for a moment. 'So, Denby didn't rape you. But he did kidnap you both against your will, he sexually assaulted Ingrid, he probably had intentions to rape and murder. You could have gone to the police.'

Joanne laughed. 'We got in the car willingly with him, remember? Two young girls – no doubt seen kissing boys the night before in some pub. Great witnesses we would have made, the media would have had a field day.'

'Still, the police would have made a report and—'

'I repeat,' said Joanne, 'we ran over and burnt him to death – you know the police wouldn't have been much help. This was *then* – great for high hair and lace, not so much for women on trial for murder. Especially when we'd been "picking up", they'd have brought up all sorts of shit about us. In America, want to know what the cops asked me when I reported the rape? They asked me how many men I'd slept with and what was the reason I wore red underpants that night. It's not even worth it.'

Mark suddenly felt immeasurably tired. 'I'll have to report all of this,' he said. 'You know I will.'

'Do it,' Ingrid said. 'I just want it over and done with.'

'There'll be a lot of sympathy for you both.'

'Of course there will!' Joanne said. 'You'll have people wanting to make martyrs out of us. It's the cops who'll look bad when all the stats on rape trials and assaults from thirty years ago come out. The law's a dog, Mark, waiting to be shot.'

He was quiet and Joanne moved closer to Ingrid. 'You know what, Ingrid?' she said softly. 'We could just push Mark into the river right now. He was drunk, he slipped and drowned.'

'Shut up,' Ingrid said, and Mark looked up to see Joanne sneer.

'I don't regret throwing a match on that arsehole,' Joanne said. 'From the moment he picked me up on my way to the bus stop, after hearing I was planning to meet Ingrid, and after he bound and gagged me and threw me in the back of his vehicle, I knew I'd kill him. He drove for hours, hours around Port York and God knows where else, getting petrol, getting snacks, talking to people so that I could hear, and all the time I thought, "You're going to die, motherfucker." And then when I saw what he was doing to Ingrid, I knew he would die in pain. I just knew it. Throwing that match was the best thing I've ever done. Put that in your report, Acting Inspector.'

CHAPTER 44

When Mark woke the next morning, Kelly was beside him, curled up like a little bird. He could barely remember stumbling in last night, wandering around like a blind man trying to find the bathroom, the bed. And here she was, Kelly. He thought about brushing the hair from the side of her face or giving her a kiss on the forehead, but decided against it. Her sleeping expression was grim. No doubt she was dreaming of her case, of violent men on the loose, of injustice all round.

He sat on the edge of the bed and looked out the window to his mother's garden. Ingrid, Joanne, John Baber, Michael Denby; he would have to write it all up in the report, due to be submitted to Angelo tomorrow. He wandered into the kitchen and made himself a cup of tea, took it to the table where he opened up his laptop. His head ached, his chest hurt. He needed to ring Darryl, to see what had happened in Cutters End, hear how Jagdeep was. He rubbed his neck. He needed to tell them about Ingrid and Joanne, he must.

Mark rang the station's phone at Cutters End and was put through to Jagdeep's home number. His colleague was okay; she was shaken (what a shock it was to see Foobie there, crouching in the darkness! Tell you all about it soon, work to be done) but glad the case was coming to an end. They would be talking to John in the arvo, cover all bases and whatnot.

'But really, what's the point?' Jagdeep said. 'So what if John gave lifts to the sisters? Darryl says he probably did too, for all he can remember. And I checked out that early report of the vehicle on New Year's Eve '89 which matches John's. It definitely states there were two kids in the car. Oh, and Darryl says hello. He's sorry he sent you that text with John's name on it. Thought he was replying to the Port York cops asking whose house we were at – we told them to turn around and go back. No point coming up to Cutters, it was just that I got a fright with Foobie being there, that's all.'

Jagdeep seemed hyped up, energised by the night. It felt like years ago that Mark was frantically punching numbers on his phone, desperate for someone to help. Her energy would fade, he knew. When the adrenaline died down, she'd recall her earlier fright – however trivialising she made it out to be. Once, Kelly told him how her clients, victims of family violence, relived their fears over and over, years after the event. Terror, she said, always returns.

Jagdeep asked for his Adelaide address, she said she had something to send him in the mail.

'Are you going to get any rest today, Jag?' he asked. 'You've had a big night.'

'Soon,' she said. 'Let's talk tomorrow.'

Mark didn't tell her what he'd learnt the previous night from Joanne and Ingrid. *Not just yet*, he thought. Jagdeep needed a rest after her shock at Baber's house. Yes, no need to tell anyone immediately. He'd talk to his colleagues later. He needed to write it all down first, get it straight in his head. The report would do the trick. Then he'd tell them everything. Then.

The report: where to begin with these last revelations? *Begin at the start,* he thought, *begin with what the girls told you and then work backwards, to the video of them in the same room on New Year's Eve, of the lying. Link the bones found by forensics at the scene to the possible disappearance of Isa, Raelene and Adele, and so on.* Up to this point, Angelo had received next to nothing. Only reports on the initial interviews and so forth. This one would blow Superintendent Conti's mind.

Mark began, titled it 'Final Report, Acting Inspector Ariti, Denby case', and was in the thick of writing what Joanne and Ingrid had told him about the night of New Year's Eve when his mother came singing into the room. She'd been to mass and would he like a cup of tea?

Mass, Mark thought – he hadn't been since he left home and never had the desire to. In films or books, it was always a cathedral or a church the cop went to for respite or to think. Usually, a kind and wise priest would turn up to offer gentle words of advice and wisdom. *Save that for the movies*, he thought. But he did feel envious of those movie cops – some gentle words, sage advice, he could do with that right now.

His mother asked him how Kelly was. 'Still asleep,' he said.

'Well, she's not,' his mother said. 'She's up now, gone out walking by the river.'

Mark shrugged.

'Do you want some advice?' his mother asked.

'Are you a priest, Mum?'

His mother gave him a blank look. 'Kelly's not happy, you're not happy. I don't know what's going on, but you two need to have a chat. Your father and I used to discuss everything.'

Yes, Mark thought. That was true, his parents did discuss everything; usually while one of them was throwing a plate against the wall or storming outside to rage in the garden.

'Okay, Mum. I'll have a chat to her, just got to continue this.'

'Go now,' she said. 'It's a shame she didn't bring the boys, I would have looked after them, given her a bit of a break.'

Mark felt a smack of self-reproach; he hadn't even thought of his sons. He saved the report, grabbed a hat, and gave a backward wave to his mother as he walked through the front gate. The roses leant in and he smelled once more their heady scent.

He didn't have to walk far to find his wife. She was in the nearby playground, trudging back towards him on a squiggly path, hands in her jeans pocket, hair loose and make-up free.

He saw at once that she was still beautiful, perhaps more so than when she was younger, and for some reason the fact filled him with misery.

'Hi,' he said.

'Hi.'

She gestured towards a bench and they sat down.

'How was last night?' she asked.

He told her what he'd learnt from his old friends.

'They'll be charged with murder,' she said.

He felt a heaviness in his chest. 'Yes.'

'It doesn't seem right,' Kelly said.

'No.'

'A few years ago, I would have said that the law will do the right thing and get them off. Now, I'm not so sure.'

'Out of my hands.'

'But is it?' Kelly turned to him, eyes bright. 'Do you have to report everything? Couldn't you just swing it somehow – water down the girls' involvement or—'

'Fake a report, you mean?'

His wife was silent for a moment. 'What actually *is* justice, Mark?'

'It's not withholding evidence, I know that much.'

Kelly's shoulders sagged and he went to put his arm around her, but she shifted away.

'Why are you here, Kel?'

'I had to come and see you.'

Mark asked why, but already he could feel the answer, could see it coming at him down a long corridor, howling up at him from the bottom of a cliff.

'I need a break. I don't think I can do this any longer.'

Mark spoke, hesitant. 'But things are getting better, aren't they?'

'I don't think so. Not really.'

There was a pause. Heavy.

'Is it the lawyer bloke?'

'No. At least, I don't think so.' She looked up at him. 'But even without him, I think we need some time apart. It's not working and you know it.'

'Was it something to do with him that time you were drunk and going on about "next Tuesday"?' Mark could hear his voice, petulant.

'Yes. I think it was.'

'I'll punch him in the face next time I see him.'

'No you won't.'

A pause.

'We've been trying, Kel.'

'We have, but still – it's not the same.' Kelly ran her fingers up and down the armrest of the old seat, paint flaking off with every stroke.

Back and forth they went, the old recriminations and the new. A tired tennis game with a flat ball and dodgy net.

'I'm moving into Mum's for a bit. It's closer to work and she can help with the boys. We can work out shared care for them and we'll see how we go, and . . .'

Her voice went on. On and on. Hurt as he was, Mark couldn't deny that even as he felt resentment and jealousy, a wave of relief was waiting to brush over him. It was just there, on the horizon.

They sat together, staring at a child's swing set, shoulders not quite touching, already wary of how to connect. Mark thought briefly of where he would live. Somewhere small, close to Kelly. Near a gym perhaps.

Now was not the time to discuss finances or more permanent living arrangements, but in a small crevice of his mind, Mark was already moving on.

After Kelly left, hugging Helen hard and giving him a pale goodbye, Mark went back to his report, door firmly shut to his mother's questions. The report was the thing.

He wrote, hardly noting the time. The document stretched to over ten pages, including the relevant articles and photos, and as the story began to emerge, he realised once more that he needed to call Angelo. Charges would be laid, but surely there was no risk of absconding. He could, if he really wanted to, arrange for Ingrid's and Joanne's passports to be confiscated.

Mark continued writing, but the early smooth flow he had been in began to falter. Something was wrong in the story. He read over his report again, went through all he had learnt in his head. He was missing something and it nagged, like a dull toothache. The story fitted, but it didn't. Locard's exchange principle.

He read the witness reports again, looked at where he'd written the women's account of the evening, looked at the photos of the crime scene; the ones taken when John Baber had alerted police on 4 January. Denby's burnt vehicle, the broken body. It fitted. The dust storm and poor weather had made any footprints obsolete. Aside from forensics, still waiting to confirm the other bone fragments, there was not much else he could see. But still. What was it?

What was it? Mark looked closer. Held the photo up to his nose. Sat back, closed his eyes and remembered an earlier conversation, a witness statement from the first investigation, early news reports. Thought about them in conjunction with the image before him.

He knew.

Without his eyes leaving the photo, he picked up the phone and dialled Angelo's number. His boss answered on the second ring, voice heavy from old wine.

'Ready to move on?' Angelo said. 'There's other cases we need men of your ilk working on.'

'You'll need to get me a flight from Adelaide to Port York, I'll hire a car from there. I'll only need two days.'

'This sounds interesting. Where's the report?'

'It's almost done. Just one more thing.'

'One more expensive bloody thing.'

'Just do it, Angelo, arrange it now. I can have this whole case tied up in a day.' Mark waited, willing his boss.

There was a pause and a clearing of the throat. 'This better be good, Mark.'

'It is.'

Another pause. 'Okay, I'll sort it.'

'Thanks.'

'I want this case wrapped up, Mark.'

Mark put the phone down. Packed his bag.

CHAPTER 45

That evening Acting Inspector Mark Ariti, warmed with the Best Coffee in the World, drove past the scorched golf course and the parched scrub outlining Cutters End.

Jagdeep was at the station, deep in reports and businesslike about the encounter with Foobie. Darryl hovered around her like a butler. Mark still hadn't told them about Joanne and Ingrid – had held back, just for a little longer.

Mark wound the window down and wondered at the warm air and the fierce last rays of a sun descending fast. To the north-west, hundreds of kilometres of red dirt and sand for as far as the eye could see. *A place where so much is hidden and yet it's so hard to remain unseen.*

Funny how it had all come to this, he thought, like the denouement of a novel; he would find out which twin prevailed. Or did there need to be a prevailing one? He'd been listening to *Dr Jekyll and Mr Hyde*, the beast within. It was with these thoughts that Mark pulled up at the front of John Baber's house.

The tall man met him at the door, sneaking a quick look at his watch as he did so.

'Sorry I'm a bit late,' Mark said. 'Got caught up at the station.'

John nodded and led him down the dark hallway to the little room that he and Jagdeep had sat in last time. As was the case then, the drapes were down, the room close.

'Is this where it happened?' Mark asked, looking around. 'This is where Jagdeep got the fright of her life?'

'Yes,' John said. 'I was out the back – electricity wasn't working and I was trying to fix the fuse. She called me apparently, but my hearing's not too good these days. Only got to her when I heard the crash.'

They both looked to the corner, where Foobie Dixon had raced to hide, knocking over a vase and a footstool as he did so.

'In the mirror, she saw the reflection of him crouching there. She caught him – ran after him and dragged him down. That's when I came in: Phillip shrieking and kicking, Jagdeep telling me to call the police, calling you and then you on the phone. It was the strangest night of my life.'

Foobie, or Phillip Dixon, Jagdeep told Mark, had been stalking the Baber home for years. Not doing anything in particular – taking photos, thinking of happier times, returning to where he used to go as a child, to places where he felt comfortable. He told the police that he liked to sit in the armchair where Gillian Baber used to sit. Sometimes he went there at night, he said – or during the day when John was out. To Mark it sounded sinister; to most of the townsfolk in Cutters End, however, it was the behaviour of a damaged yet harmless soul. Small towns and the law; who to protect and who to give up. He supposed it depended largely on reputation, on family. Briefly, he thought of Joanne and how she had fared in Booralama.

'Phillip was very fond of my wife,' John said. 'She treated him many times for all his illnesses and she was kind to him. He used to come around for little visits, they'd be having tea in the garden when I got home. He helped her in the vegetable patch, small jobs around the place. After she died, I knew he still came around here. Sometimes I'd find him looking in the window. That day you first came here, I thought I saw his face through the curtains.' John closed his eyes for a moment. 'Gillian liked him. She felt sorry for him too, and that's a powerful argument in forgiveness. Maybe that's why the whole town let him do what he did. He was always going to be an outsider, so we gave him titbits of our lives. What's an illicit photo here and there when you've got no one to go home to, no one who will call you a friend?'

John was quiet for a moment and Mark looked through the window, imagining faces there – innocent and not. He nodded for John to go on.

'When she asked him to take photos of Lynette – Michael's wife – I think she hoped he'd go around telling everyone, show everyone like he usually did and make them act. There wasn't mandatory reporting for doctors then, remember. She was bound to silence.'

'So, you did know your wife asked him to take the shots?'

'I did. To my shame, I did nothing about it either.'

The men were quiet for a moment.

'But,' Mark said, 'you did do something, didn't you, John?'

'I tipped off Phillip when he got in trouble with the police for taking photographs, if that's what you mean. I told him to make copies of the important ones, and I meant the ones of Lynette Denby of course, on a mobile phone. Even though I didn't do anything about them, I recognised that the photos might be important one day. She may have already died, but I hoped that in years to come, someone better than me would finally speak out for Lynette.'

'I thought it might have been you who warned Foobie,' Mark said. 'Either you or Darryl.'

'It was me.'

There was a short silence.

'But that's not all you did, was it, John?'

An old clock ticked above the mantelpiece. Outside, a bird shrieked in the evening sky. Mark could imagine purple streaks of sky like hands held up, waiting to be engulfed by the dark.

John Baber clasped his hands together.

'I know,' Mark said.

'How?'

'The bonnet of Denby's car was up. The girls wouldn't have done that – they didn't. They were panicked, traumatised really. It wasn't until the roadhouse that they began thinking straight.'

John listened.

'You put the bonnet of Denby's car up, didn't you, John? To make it look as if Denby had been checking the engine when it blew up in his face.'

John sat still.

'Why were you late to the New Year's Eve party at the Cutters End backpackers? They were waiting for you to help get the lights going. You're never late. Everyone in the town knows that.'

Still, the man didn't speak.

'You didn't find Michael Denby on the fourth of January, did you? You found him on the thirty-first of December – not long after the girls left him.'

Silence.

'What did you see, John? What did you cover up?'

Outside, it would be fully dark now. Night came fast in Cutters End. The lights of the three pubs would be turning on, Dolly Parton would be singing her sad songs, and Foobie Dixon would be yearning to stalk forgiving streets.

The clock ticked on.

John looked at the photos on the table beside him and brushed some dust off the surface.

'When I saw the girls on the side of the road, they were terrified. I mean, *I* was terrified looking at them in the headlights. The blonde, she was sobbing, and the other was as white as a ghost. I turned around, picked them up. That wasn't unprecedented – I often picked up hitchhikers, especially after those sisters went missing. I worried for young women on the side of the road after that. But these two,

I could see straight away that something was terribly wrong. Even after they quietened down, I was worried. But they were insistent – they said they were okay. The dark-haired one did the talking and I didn't push. In those days, you just didn't.'

'What did you think happened?'

'I thought that maybe they'd been in an accident or seen something they shouldn't have – but they said no to everything, save for some minor unsettling incident with the previous lift. Nothing out of the ordinary for then. They said they were okay.'

John rubbed the top of his hand, then stared at his palms as if they could tell him something. Mark waited.

'After I made sure that they'd got a room at the roadhouse, I turned around, started driving back to Cutters. I still could have got to the party on time, I was running a bit early before I picked up the girls. But I couldn't stop thinking about them. It just wasn't right. I decided that I'd have a chat to Darryl when I got to Cutters, see if he could write something up, maybe check out who they'd got a lift with. But then I noticed, in the headlights, the track marks leading off the road.'

John kneaded his thighs. 'I followed the tracks, thought maybe there'd been an accident – but I had this feeling, this feeling, and I knew it wasn't going to be good. Those girls . . . Straight up, five or six k's in from the road, I saw Mick's truck and a body under it. It was windy as all hell and I could smell petrol and something else burning, and when I ran over to Mick, I could tell it wasn't good. It wasn't good.'

John took a deep breath, shook his head. 'His face was burnt to buggery and his leg was half under the truck. For a few seconds I remember just standing there. Just, not thinking. In shock maybe.'

'You didn't think to move the body? Cover it?'

John looked at him strangely. 'No, I didn't.'

'Why not?'

'He was still alive.'

Mark felt a jolt run through his whole body. *Still alive?* He clenched the side of the chair and leant forward.

'Mick was moaning, just moaning, and when I leant down to try to hear him it was hard because his lips on one side were like bubbles. He was saying "Help", and I think he said "Water" but I couldn't be sure. He was in a bad way, barely conscious. His hands were completely burnt, probably from where he tried to stop the flames on his face. It was . . .' John looked at the darkened window. 'It was the most horrific thing I have ever seen in my life.'

'What did you do?'

'I went first of all to move the truck, get it off his leg, when I saw one of those spangly hair things on the ground, one of those big hair ties girls used to wear back then.'

The scrunchie, Mark thought. *They all wore them in their hair.*

'I saw that, and I thought of those two girls, and then I took a quick look around. There was cut-up cable wire, there was the tipped-over jerry can, the bits of material like a headband, and I knew. I knew what Michael had been up to. What he'd been up to all those years. And I thought about his wife Lynette and how Gillian worried about her, and how she said that no one ever did anything to help that poor woman, nothing! *I* did nothing to help her. I saw those photos that Foobie took all those years ago and I did nothing. "A private affair," we all thought. "Best not to interfere." I looked at Mick there on the ground, writhing and dying, and I knew what had happened. My first thought was, "Those girls will never get away with it." Mick could probably survive if I took him to hospital right then, and he'd spin some story and they'd all believe him. The police, the courts, the public. Now it might be different, but *then*. He'd say they robbed him or something, he'd accuse them of being fast.'

John paused and pressed the side of his forehead. 'Mick said "Help" to me and he kept saying it, or trying to say it, and I thought of his poor wife while I pushed the hair tie in his mouth and shoved it to the back of his throat. I thought of Gillian too, while he struggled and tried to scream. She'd been dead for less than twelve months and why did she have to die? A good person, someone who helped people. Why was she dead and not him? Michael kept moving, straining about in the dirt, but I held his burnt nose firm and kept my knee hard on his chest till he stopped.'

Mark felt a deep weariness seep over his body. His bones felt old and cold and he longed to be in bed, away from this place and the world.

'Then,' John said, 'I tidied up. It was windy, so I knew footprints wouldn't be a problem – I covered my hands with a hanky and picked up the bits of cable, gave the vehicle a wipe down, retrieved the hair tie, moved the cigarette butt on the ground closer to the front of the vehicle, and then I lifted the bonnet up, poured the rest of the petrol on the engine and lit it up.'

'I thought you might have covered up the scene,' Mark said. 'But as for the rest . . .'

'Yes. I did the rest,' John said. 'Then I drove to the backpackers in Cutters End and delivered the fuel for the generators. A little late, but I made it.'

Mark recognised a faint pride in the other man's voice. Even at this point, he was pleased with his punctuality.

'You must have been surprised when no one found the body in the following days.'

John looked at him. 'I was. I kept waiting for someone to notice the vehicle marks off the side of the road – even with the wind they were still visible – but no one came forward. And then I thought that with every day it was buying us time, the girls and me. People started talking of course, worrying where Mick was, and it would have seemed off if I, who travelled the road all the time, saw nothing odd. So, on my next trip up the highway I called it in.'

'You weren't worried about someone seeing you on the thirty-first? Seeing the smoke from the engine burning up?'

'I was past worrying about that. And remember, it was New Year's Eve. No one about, quietest day of the year on the roads.'

Mark stood up to go, then looked down at the other man. 'What sort of man did you think you were when you killed Michael Denby, I wonder?'

John gave a soft laugh. 'Have you been studying psychology?'

'Reading. *Jekyll and Hyde.*'

'I see.'

'"Man is not truly one, but truly two,"' Mark quoted from the book.

John looked amused. 'Ah yes, which part of myself did I display in those moments? Maybe my best side, or not. I don't know. What do you think?'

Mark thought, with immense sadness, *It doesn't matter what I think. You're about to be charged.*

CHAPTER 46

After leaving John Baber and heading back into Cutters, Mark called Jagdeep, telling her he'd catch up with her tomorrow. She pressed, wanted to know what was going on. He deflected, told her he'd see her the next morning. Exhaustion seeped into his bones.

Back in the dingy motel room, Mark collapsed on the bed. Strange dreams of people crying and burning and women in blue came to him. Someone singing, the scratching of animals in the scrub outside. In the middle of the night, he woke suddenly. A lone bird screeched, or perhaps it was a person coming out of the Desert Dawn, he didn't know.

Unable to go back to sleep, uneasy from John's testimony and that of the women, he fired up his computer and searched for his final case report. As reluctant as Mark felt, he needed to add John's part in the murder of suspected murderer and rapist Michael Denby. He clicked onto his work folder, scrolled down to the date where he'd saved the latest file, the final report. Nothing.

Mark frowned at the screen. He refreshed the page, searched again, wider this time, not just in the folder where he thought he'd saved it. A slight unease, a growing awareness. The file was not there. He'd saved it, knew he had. Even copied it and placed it in another folder – that was gone too. It was, he thought, as if someone had hacked his computer and deleted both copies.

Mark sat for a moment on his bed, stunned. It was late, but he looked at his phone. There was only one person in the world who knew his new password, who knew the extent of the report. He jabbed in a text message: *You wiped the report.*

Within seconds, despite the hour, his phone beeped loud in the night; a response from Kelly: *Justice. You're a good man Mark. Be just.*

What is justice? he thought. Perhaps in some ways, out there in the desert, it had already been served.

The next morning, later than usual, Mark opened up another cardboard breakfast of stale cornflakes and poured warm milk over them. He needed a coffee and knew where to find it.

In the early hours, a new report had been written up, dated and sent off to Angelo. Superintendent Conti was impressed, pleased to stamp a conclusive finding on the case. No need now for a lengthy investigation into earlier police procedures. The South Australian police force was vindicated. This was exactly why, Angelo said when he phoned him first thing, he'd asked Mark to join the reinvestigation of the case. He was underutilised in Fraud – was he looking for a more permanent role in this area?

Mark couldn't answer, not yet. 'Have confidence in yourself!' Angelo boomed to him over the phone. 'You're smarter than you think, Ariti!'

Perhaps he was, but not in the way Angelo thought.

Already, too, he'd met with Jagdeep and Darryl, handed them his final report. Both agreed, based on what they'd discovered and what they had not, that in the case of Michael Denby, the reinvestigation's finding was: accidental death. The burns on the palms of his hands and face, the motor explosion, the cigarette, the petrol, the sense-dulling effect of the drugs. An accident and nothing more. The original finding: correct.

Hugh from the *Port York Advertiser* called; no results from the 'Can you help us?' advertisement as yet. The older bone fragments found near the site of Denby's death. Any more news on that? And did they have anything else on Denby himself, the unpopular hero from Cutters End? Did they have anything, anything at all they wanted to share with him?

No, Hugh. They did not.

Jagdeep and Darryl did agree, however, that there was more work to be done on the forensic findings and on the files of missing persons dating back decades. The old copper's file with the missing people on it would be re-examined in painstaking detail. Police work. John Baber picking up hitchhikers – possibly even the sisters – was something they would continue to check out, although it didn't seem like much. Almost everyone they interviewed in Cutters End who regularly drove the Stuart picked up people from the side of the road; out of sympathy, for company, to keep them safe. They concurred, John Baber's vehicle and the sisters: no discernible lead.

A slight suspicion, perhaps, in his colleagues' eyes when Mark told them about his reason for travelling up and meeting so late with John Baber? The boss needed loose ends tidied up and confirmation that there were no further areas of interest in the Denby case. Angelo Conti was obsessed with details, Mark explained, needed this reinvestigation wrapped up officially and finally, in order to focus on police funding.

Jagdeep gave him side-eye from the corner of the room but said nothing.

After saying goodbye, Mark walked along the deserted main street, already hazy with heat, and on to the council offices, mean-looking in the sharp morning light. There it was, he'd been meaning to find it – the plaque on the side of the building. Bronze and dignified, a small square, head height, adjacent to a rose garden and one of the few patches of lawn in the town.

The Commendation for Brave Conduct Medal was awarded to Cutters End resident Michael Denby on 26 January 1986 for the rescue of a young mother and her child in dangerous floodwaters.

This plaque was unveiled by Cutters End Mayor Noreen Parnell OAM on Australia Day 1987.

Mark wondered how it must have felt to receive such an award. Did Michael wish his wife, too ill by then to attend, could be there? Is there love when there's been violence? Does bravery equal goodness? By most accounts, soldiers from the First World War commended themselves admirably, helped to shape the Australian myth. Some returned home to beat their wives and kill Aboriginal people. Can one man be two?

It had rained 240 mm in less than twenty-four hours on the day Denby rescued the Millers. It must have been difficult to see on that day – the rain, the swirling brown water with all its moving parts. It must have been noisy, the shouts, the people rushing to and fro, and all the time the little car circling slowly and tipping deeper into the fray.

And there was Denby, diving down there into the rushing floodwaters, the desperate efforts as he broke the back window, the screams, the flailing arms. He did it and no one else. If he hadn't done it, two females would not be alive today. A hero.

And yet. Not five years later, Michael Denby kidnapped two other women, tied one to a tree and went about preparing to murder them. Years before that he'd killed Isa, and the two Cunningham sisters in between. Can one man truly be two? Perhaps the face, our outward self, was a great actor, as Jason Dimler surmised. Maybe, when John Baber shoved that scrunchie far down Denby's burnt throat, it was a type of rescue; the image of the hero, intact for another thirty years, and who doesn't want to be remembered like that?

Mark walked back to his car, got in and drove out of Cutters End onto the highway, shimmering now in the mid-morning sun. He turned off the radio and wound down the window. Hot air rushed over him; fine red dust filled the car. Land, immense and powerful, rushed on by. Clouds gathered on the horizon, a promise, a tease. John said that after the floods, the land took on a new life, wildflowers sprung up all across the desert: poached egg daisies, native geranium, eremophila. The pinks, the greys, the yellows. All that beauty, vast and uncontrolled. It must have felt like a gift.

Just before the roadhouse, Mark slowed, parked on the side of the road and took out his phone. *Case closed. No more questions.* He sent the text and stared hard at the screen. The car heated up and he waited, sweating. He was sixteen again, waiting for a response from Ingrid Mathers. He tapped a second text, pushed send: *You okay?*

Mark undid his seatbelt and got out of the car, stood in the burning sun. It took a moment for him to realise that there was no sound. No crickets, no rustle of the wind through trees, no traffic, no evidence at all of human presence. Silence. Rare and unsettling. But wait, was that a bird? Mark strained to listen, wanting to hear the sound, a bird's call. Was that it, a high sound – somewhere around him, the shriek perhaps of a flock in the distance? He held his breath, focusing, focusing. But no. Nothing. He exhaled. The land and its creatures, impervious to his needs, gave him nothing.

He turned on his heel and got back into the vehicle. His phone beeped, a text: *I'm okay. We're okay. Flight booked 2 Amsterdam. Thank you.*

*

Already, he could see how it would go for the rest of the trip.

He'll drive, think about Ingrid and Joanne and Isa, the sisters and all those missing. He'll watch the harsh beauty of the place and think what it must be to die far away from home.

A thought will come to him of a blue high heel lying in the dirt, and he'll find it hard to let the image go. None of them will let it go.

Back at the station in Cutters End, Jagdeep will be examining old articles and Darryl will be pinning the photos of the sisters and at least two other girls on the board. People will be coming forward, there'll be more names to add. Missing persons, up and down the Stuart Highway. There are maps, photos, people to ID, old police files to go over. Locard's exchange principle.

So much always to do.

In his pocket, Mark could feel the creamy wedding invitation Jagdeep had passed him before he left the station, and already in his mind, he's left his lonely Adelaide home and he's travelling on this road up north again.

He'll drive and drive; up from Port York, past the roadhouse, past the place of Isa's death, past the spinifex and the low sandhills. He'll drive and drive underneath glorious skies and he'll make it, whether it be a few weeks' or months' time – he'll make the drive all the way up the Stuart Highway and return to Cutters End.

ACKNOWLEDGEMENTS

I am grateful to everyone who helped in the creation of *Cutters End*. This book was written mostly on dining tables in various houses, so for those family members who shoved their plates aside for my notes, who made me cups of tea, who yelled back when I yelled for quiet and who read aloud over my shoulder giving mostly good instruction, I say thank you. I also say, I need an office.

Thank you to early readers Bernie Dowsley, Marni Witts and Rosie Koop for their insightful comments and to Cath, Paul and Elizabeth for listening to my ideas. Thanks to Luke Read for his expertise on cars, Dan O'Sullivan for his advice on guns, Mark Staley for all things policework and Dr Corina Modderman for sharing her stories of Dutch and Friesland life.

A massive thank you to the wonderful Bev Cousins from Penguin Random House who first took on this book and to Kalhari Jayaweera for her sensitive and thorough editing. Thanks too, to Talie Gottlieb, Claire Gatzen and all the PRH team. I'm fortunate to be backed by such professionals.

Thank you to all the booksellers and librarians and readers. You make the world a rich and varied place.

To my cousin Josie, who sat with me by the side of the road on long, lonely highways listening to my stories while drinking Erin cream. We shared it all, the good, the bad and the creepy: really, it was the time of our lives.

Finally, and most of all, thank you to Bernie, Alexander, Eddie and Ben.

AUTHOR Q & A

What prompted you to write *Cutters End*?

I love crime fiction and always thought I'd like to write a crime novel. One day I was talking with my cousin, who I used to travel with all the time when we were in our twenties. We did a lot of hitchhiking, especially around Australia, and we started talking about some of our experiences. Mostly good memories, but there were creepy ones too – and these were often in lonely, isolated spots along the Stuart Highway. These conversations inspired me to begin writing *Cutters End*. Important to note, however, this book is most definitely fiction!

What is your writing process?

I'm a binge writer; I write when I can. And when I do, I write hard. I work full time and have a family, so I don't have the luxury of sitting down at a desk everyday – although it is something I aspire to. I usually write on weekends and holidays when I can find some peace. Other than a sense of place and some overriding themes, I don't plan. I just write and see where the plot takes me. I'm constantly culling thousands of words, but I don't get upset about it, I like the process.

The internal dialogue in your writing is very funny and natural. Do you find it easy to write?

My first published works were playscripts, so dialogue is obviously a key component. I enjoy writing dialogue and a lot of it is inspired by people I hear on the street, people I talk to, my family and friends. The idiosyncrasies of the Australian vernacular really are a gift to the writer.

There is a strong sense of landscape in your writing. The Stuart Highway and its surrounds become a character. Was this a conscious decision?

Yes. My PhD was on depictions of landscape in Australian literature and I find it so compelling and rich. I live in a rural setting; aside from a stint in London and for a few years during and after university, I always have. The bush near my home, the long walks I go on, the camping trips with my family; I'm always aware of the vivid surrounds. Sometimes when I'm walking by myself in the bush, I get the feeling that something is watching me – and perhaps it is, perhaps it's the bush itself. The whole complex notion of white belonging, it's something that is deeply interesting to me. Of course, the rural community and communities I have lived in provide terrific fodder for writing too. I'm very fortunate.

STONE TOWN

Margaret Hickey

The sequel to *Cutters End*

With its gold-rush history long in the past, Stone Town has definitely seen better days. And it's now in the headlines for all the wrong reasons . . .

When three teenagers stumble upon a body in dense bushland one rainy Friday night, Detective Sergeant Mark Ariti's hopes for a quiet posting in his old home town are shattered. The victim is Aidan Sleeth, a property developer, whose controversial plan to buy up local land means few are surprised he ended up dead.

However, his gruesome murder is overshadowed by the mystery consuming the entire nation: the disappearance of Detective Sergeant Natalie Whitsed.

Natalie had been investigating the celebrity wife of crime boss Tony 'The Hook' Scopelliti when she vanished. What did she uncover? Has it cost her her life? And why are the two Homicide detectives, sent from the city to run the Sleeth case, so obsessed with Natalie's fate?

Following a late-night call from his former boss, Mark is sure of one thing: he's now in the middle of a deadly game . . .

Read on for an extract

CHAPTER 1

Detective Senior Sergeant Mark Ariti stamped his feet hard on the front porch of Jacqueline Matteson's house. Outside was raven black, rain pelted hard. Inside, though it was barely 2 am, the living room was lit up like a showground and filled with people young and old. Mark recognised no one. Stone Town, barely twenty-five kilometres from where he lived in Booralama, may as well have been another universe. Consisting mainly of old farming families and an influx of tree-changers, the area was known for its mines, remnants of settler stone houses scattered about the bush, and significant wheat yield.

Riveting, Mark remembered thinking, in Year 10 local history. *Take that, Machu Picchu.*

But the gold from Stone Town was long gone and it had been years since farmers' sons returned from boarding schools to make a life on the land.

Stone Town now had a different footy team from Booralama, different netball team, different CFA, CWA. But not a different police station.

In the lounge, three girls sat huddled on a couch and a wiry older lady nursed a drink beside the fireplace.

Mark introduced himself to the tired-looking woman who opened the door to him.

'Morning. Detective Senior Sergeant Ariti, Booralama. I'm here to speak to the three kids who found the body.'

The woman's face was metal-grey in the bright light of the room. 'Can't it wait till the morning? We're exhausted.'

Mark made an apologetic noise and indicated the note-paper and pen in his hand. 'Procedures.'

The door from the kitchen swung open, and with a burst of energy an attractive woman in a wheelchair entered the room.

'Jacqueline Matteson,' she announced, holding out her hand.

He shook it. 'Detective Senior Sergeant Mark Ariti.'

'Well, Sergeant, do they need a lawyer?' She tipped her head towards the girls, who were now staring up at him with tired and tear-stained eyes.

'That's up to you,' Mark said. 'But I'm just here to ask a few questions.'

The old lady with the drink piped up. 'You're Helen's son, aren't you?' She didn't wait for a reply. 'I'm sorry for your loss, dear. Helen was a lovely lady.'

'She was.' Mark cleared his throat. 'Thank you.'

Jacqueline's face shifted, softened. 'You can talk to them

in the kitchen. Evan's just gone in there. Girls?' She nodded to her daughters, gave them an encouraging glance. 'The policeman here needs to speak to you about what you saw. I'll be just in here.'

Two of the girls untangled themselves from the couch and walked past Mark into the other room. He said his thanks to the women, and followed.

In the kitchen, a young boy sat at the table, head in hands. 'Evan?' Mark asked.

The boy looked up, red-faced and anguished. 'It *was* Aidan Sleeth, wasn't it?' he said.

'Yes, I'm afraid it was.'

'I thought it was, but – his head. It was . . .'

'Yes.'

The face remained Aidan Sleeth from the nose down, but the back of his head was an explosion of gore. Bits of brain, skin and bone matter on nearby shrubs and trees, blood soaking into the wet earth. The rest of the body appeared unharmed and strangely comfortable, huddled into the side of an acacia tree, knees up to the chest. Cream chinos, brown brogues, a light blue shirt and a navy Country Road jumper. Wallet in the jeans pocket. Aidan Sleeth, forty-one. Successful farmer and property investor. Ex-wife, on good terms. Beyond that, Mark knew little else. He'd safeguarded the crime scene, set up barriers, taken photos, arranged for the body to be taken away. Tomorrow, Forensics and Homicide would arrive from Adelaide.

The teenagers were frightened. Each had the look of a face not quite put together, features pained and uncertain.

'Names and ages?' he asked, pen held high. 'Just for the official stuff.'

The older of the girls answered. 'I'm Emma Matteson, fourteen. This is my sister, Sarah Matteson – she's twelve – and our neighbour, Evan Williams. He's fourteen too.'

'That's great. Now, can you tell me – and take your time – how you came to see the body?'

There was a slight pause, a shift in the air.

'We just saw it there, in the torchlight – all crumpled up on the side of the path near the creek,' Emma said.

'Did you touch the body at all?'

'No way! Why would we do that? No, we just came back here and woke Mum up. Then she called Sue – that's Evan's mum. My grandmother, Beth Matteson, lives in the house out the back, so she came in too.'

'Was it only you three out there tonight?'

'Yes, only us.' Emma was firm.

Mark thought for a moment. 'There was another girl in the lounge room. Was she not with you?'

Sarah gave a snort. 'That's Isabelle, our other sister. She only got out of bed when we came in.'

There was a silence and Mark wondered if their mothers had broached the subject yet.

'What were you doing out there in the bush after midnight?'

Emma looked hard at the table. Sarah, the youngest one, mimicked her sister's action, but not before she threw Evan a quick sideways glance.

'You were sneaking out, weren't you? I get that. But why?'

'Are we in trouble?' Sarah asked in a small voice, eyes still cast downward.

'Not by me you're not. I'm only interested in the body – but still, I'd like to know why you were out there and if you saw or heard anything.'

At 'heard' the boy flinched.

'Did you hear something, Evan?'

'We heard screaming.' Sarah spoke for him.

Mark straightened, tried to keep his voice casual. 'Screaming?'

'Yeah. I was so scared and we were running and running, and that's when I fell over and we saw the dead man.' Sarah's face crumpled.

'This screaming, was it like someone in pain, or someone frightened, or someone screaming, you know, for fun?'

'For *fun*?' Emma was scornful. 'Yeah, the screaming was like fun, fun, fun. That's why we were running in the opposite direction.'

The girl had a point. 'Was it a woman's scream?'

The three went quiet, then Evan muttered something.

'What was that, Evan?' Mark had to bend down towards him.

'I said, it was a bird.' Evan raised his head and looked blank-faced at Mark. 'A Barking Owl. Their cry, it sounds like a woman screaming.'

'It didn't sound much like a bird,' Emma said, doubtful.

'It was.'

Barking Owls. Mark had heard the tales; the screaming bird that wakes you in the night thinking a woman is being raped and murdered just outside your door. 'Those birds common round here?'

'Not really.' Evan's head was drooping. 'But it's breeding time and there are a few out there in the bush along the creek.'

'You know a bit about birds, do you, Evan?' Mark kept up his light, friendly tone. The one he used for kids and belligerent drunks. God, he was tired. And cold. He realised he hadn't yet taken off his coat after standing outside in the dark, in the rain, staring at Aidan Sleeth's shattered head.

The boy muttered in response.

'What's that?' Harsher than what he was aiming for, but couldn't the boy speak up? *Shoulders back, son!* he wanted to say. Mark repeated, 'Could you say that again, mate?'

'There's this person who sometimes stays near here, he knows a bit.'

'He's a twitcher,' Sarah said, and she mimicked a bird, her arms flapping, then cupping her hands to make binoculars. 'Not Evan, I don't mean him. I'm talking about the man from the co-op.'

Out of the three of them, she now appeared the brightest, eager to help, her little face aglow. She was probably over-tired, bordering on hysterical. His two sons got like that after a party or a movie about superheros. He should go. His doona called like a beautiful siren.

'Twitcher, okay.'

'They're people who watch birds, like *a lot*.'

'Shut up, Sarah,' Emma said, irritated. 'He's a twitcher, so what? There's weirdos everywhere.'

'Nothing wrong with birdwatching,' Mark said, and looked at Evan.

The boy shrugged, turning his face away.

'That why you were out there? Listening for birds?'

Emma laughed, a short bark. 'Evan said there was something cool in the bush and that we should go there with him to check it out. He made it sound really good and Sarah kept nagging me, so we met him at the bottom of the driveway and walked there, into the bush. It's not like there's anything else to do around here.'

'Okay.'

'Really cool, wasn't it, Evan?' Emma turned to the boy. 'Thanks for that, arsehole.'

Evan's face, anxious before, now sagged and his eyes welled up.

Mark reached out and patted the boy's hand. 'No need to blame anyone.'

Just then the door opened and Jacqueline Matteson entered, her eyes bright despite the hour.

'Time for bed, kids,' she said before turning her chair back into the lounge room. 'Sue, want Isabelle to drive you home?'

Mark pretended not to hear. He'd only seen her briefly, but Isabelle did not look old enough to own a licence. That said, she was a farming girl, probably been driving since she was ten, and it *was* just next door. He said nothing. Went to say something. Said nothing.

Jacqueline caught the look. 'She's fifteen. And it's just up the drive and across the paddocks. A track, not the road. I'd never let her drive on that. It's okay. Issy knows to drive slow, I'm very strict about it.'

Mark raised his eyebrows in a helpless gesture, then gave a sigh. It was an act: Frustrated Rural Cop.

'Yes, please,' Sue called back, listless. The woman had all the features of cardboard.

Evan stood up and Mark shook his hand, then watched his drooping shape leave the room. The two girls followed: Emma defiant and without glancing back, Sarah giving a small wave.

With the teenagers gone, the kitchen expanded and became lighter.

'Here.' Jacqueline was offering him a towel and a coat. 'You're still soaking.'

'Yup. Bit wet out there.' Mark took the towel and gave his hair a rough dry, rubbing it over the back of his neck and behind his ears. He wrestled off his wet coat and mimed where to put it – back of the chair? Or the table? Jacqueline nodded towards the chair. He put it there.

The new coat, much too big, was a great relief. Its dryness seeped into his bones. Comfort. He felt like curling up right then and there on the Mattesons' kitchen floor.

'What do you think happened?' Jacqueline picked up two empty cups from the table with one hand and wheeled them to the sink.

'Difficult to tell. City detectives will be arriving soon enough, they'll be able to give us a clearer picture.'

'Surely there's no clearer picture than the back of a man's head blown off.'

He couldn't argue with that. 'What about you? What do you think happened?'

'It sounds pretty obvious that the man has been shot. Maybe by accident, I don't know. Probably a hunter, there's deer out there.'

'We can't rule out suicide.'

'No, you can't.'

Mark caught the tone, recognised it in his own thoughts. Rural men suicided all the time, twice as often as their city counterparts. Depression, the fishbowl existence, divorce, loneliness and drought. Factors that didn't seem to fit with what he knew of Aidan Sleeth, but even so. Rural men weren't generally talkers. Counselling? Maybe in a blue moon. *Maybe.* Still, why go into the bush, far from your home, in the dead of night, in the pouring rain, and shoot yourself? Most rural men suicided on their properties, had planned for it, practised even.

There was nothing so far, in the little he'd learned about Sleeth, that suggested this scenario was likely. Sleeth's farm wasn't failing. His divorce, according to Brian, the paramedic from Booralama whom he'd met at the scene, was reputed to be amicable. This rain wouldn't dent Sleeth's bank balance – his farm could withstand the rough seasons – but still, suicide could not be ruled out. The stats were clear on that. Police in rural stations across the country told grim tales of cutting people down from ropes, unhooking gas pipes from cars, and prising the family gun from fingers grey with death.

'The kids mentioned screaming, a Barking Owl. You ever heard it round here?'

Jacqueline gave an exaggerated shudder. 'Yes. Horrible! First time I heard it, I made Rod get up with me and go out looking for some woman I was convinced was being strangled in the bush.'

'Can't have been fun.'

Jacqueline shook her head. 'Took me a while to get used to the call, but I did – sort of.'

'They rare, Barking Owls?'

'Endangered I think, but I'm no bird expert. I haven't heard it for at least a couple of years. Doesn't mean they're not out there, of course.'

'You think that's why the kids were in the bush tonight, to hear it?'

'They said that's why. With Emma, though, I'm never entirely sure. She can be a bit wild.'

Wild. What did that mean? Reckless, fast? Different connotations for males and females.

'They've had a rough night,' he said.

Jacqueline yawned, ran a hand through her hair. 'Word got out pretty quick, as you can imagine. Emma and social media . . . People are already messaging to let me know what type of casserole they'll be dropping around. I'll take a few days off, see how the girls go. It's actually Evan I'm more worried about.'

Mark thought of the boy, slouched over the table, a portrait of misery. And something else – fear?

'Better be off.' He felt in his jeans pocket for his keys. 'Thanks for the coat. And for letting me talk to the kids so late.'

'I hope Emma wasn't rude to you. She can be a nightmare.' A dark curl bobbed at the side of her cheek.

Fetching, Mark thought. He coughed. 'Fetching': a funny word to think of right now. 'Three teenage girls, don't know how you do it.'

'Three! I've got four. Georgia's at university.'

Mark gave a low whistle. 'Hats off. That's impressive.' He walked out the swing door into the lounge, Jacqueline following. He lingered a moment in the warm room. A photo on the living room wall showed a family of six: four girls, a younger Jacqueline, and a big man in a blue polo shirt and jeans. A happy shot. Mark pointed to the man. 'That your husband?'

Jacqueline looked up at the photo, head tilted in a fond expression. 'Yep, that's Rod. He died four years ago.'

'I'm sorry.'

'You weren't to know.' She fiddled at her hair, pushing the errant curl back into line behind her ear. No use, it sprang out again.

Mark stood awkwardly, studying the photo. He coughed into the crook of his elbow and thanked Jacqueline as she opened the door for him and said goodbye.

He gave a quick wave and stepped onto the dimly lit porch, clicking the button on his keys. The mention of the dead husband had made things awkward, though it needn't have. He knew, after all the stilted conversations about his mother, how difficult it was for people to talk naturally about what was the most natural of progressions.

Most natural, that is, unless you were shot in the back of the head.

The police HiLux lit up like an old friend as he hurried towards it, sludging through the puddles. Headlights on, he pulled out onto the dirt driveway, now a moving thing of potholes and running streams. It was another freak storm with flash flooding, crops lost, old gums falling. Dangerous for anyone caught out in it. Why choose such a night to impress the girls? Wouldn't Evan's bird be there tomorrow?

On his way home, in the darkness along Stone Town Road, then the lonely stretch to Booralama, Mark listened to radio updates about the missing woman, last seen eight days ago. No real news as yet, neighbours were shocked, leads were thin. He switched it off.

In the quiet of early morning, Mark thought about the Matteson family photo. Rod standing proud in the centre with a small girl on his shoulders, Jacqueline beside him holding another. No wheelchair. Two older girls were laughing into the camera. Four children. Oldest away at university, the youngest two in the kitchen, the ones to find the body.

So why, Mark asked himself, was it the second-born daughter, Isabelle, who was sobbing?

In the brief seconds his headlights had lit up her face as their vehicles passed each other on the Mattesons' driveway, Mark had seen the girl's distraught face; her expression anguished and full of woe.